D0058181

MARY B

Mary B

A NOVEL

KATHERINE J. CHEN

RANDOM HOUSE

NEW YORK

Published in the United States by Random House, an imprint and division of Penguin Random House LLC, New York.

RANDOM HOUSE and the HOUSE colophon are registered trademarks of Penguin Random House LLC.

LIBRARY OF CONGRESS CATALOGING-IN-PUBLICATION DATA
Names: Chen, Katherine, J., author. | Austen, Jane, 1775–1817. Pride and prejudice.
Title: Mary B: a novel / Katherine Chen.
Description: New York: Random House, [2018]
Identifiers: LCCN 2017033802 | ISBN 9780399592218 | ISBN 9780399592232 (ebook)
Subjects: LCSH: Austen, Jane, 1775–1817. Pride and prejudice—Adaptations. | Courtship—Fiction. | Sisters—Fiction. | GSAFD: Love stories.
Classification: LCC PS3603.H4485 M37 2018 | DDC 813/.6—dc23
LC record available at https://lccn.loc.gov/2017033802

Printed in the United States of America on acid-free paper

randomhousebooks.com

2 4 6 8 9 7 5 3 1

FIRST EDITION

Book design by Victoria Wong

To Einstein

2004–2017

She certainly took a kind of parental interest in the beings whom she had created, and did not dismiss them from her thoughts when she had finished her last chapter. We have seen, in one of her letters, her personal affection for Darcy and Elizabeth. . . . In this traditionary way we learned that . . . Kitty Bennet was satisfactorily married to a clergyman near Pemberley, while Mary obtained nothing higher than one of her uncle Philips's clerks, and was content to be considered a star in the society of Meriton.

—from *A Memoir of Jane Austen* by James Edward Austen-Leigh, chapter X, "Observations on the Novels"

I was quiet, but I was not blind.

—Jane Austen (*Mansfield Park*)

MARY B

PROLOGUE

A child does not grow up with the knowledge that she is plain or dull or a complete simpleton until the accident of some event should reveal these unfortunate truths. My eldest sister, Jane, did not know that she was Hertfordshire's answer to Helen of Troy until well into her adolescence. Walking out with the rest of her siblings in a new pink frock, she attracted the attention of two young men who had been wrestling and who suddenly stopped to gawp at her, like animals that have for the first time looked skyward and spotted the sun.

From a young age, Jane had been elevated by our mother to as high a rank of divinity among the common folk of Hertfordshire as false modesty would permit, while Papa never scrupled to show his preference for Lizzy, his second-born. In appearance, it is true Lizzy never possessed the natural elegance and mildness which blessed her sister. She preferred skipping to walking, dirt paths to paved roads, and the scent of wet earth to any fragrance that could be bottled. But what she lacked in conventional beauty was amply compensated for by an open and spirited temperament which rendered any conversation with her highly energetic and amusing.

It was therefore acknowledged, long before my younger sisters and I had any say in the matter, that beauty, goodness, and intelligence had disproportionately concentrated themselves in the two eldest and gone woefully amiss in the three following; namely, that I had been touched with a plainness in appearance unrivaled through-out the whole country and Kitty and Lydia with a willful propensity to ignorance that exposed them continuously to ridicule without their ever becoming aware of the fact.

I will tell you the story of how I knew myself to be plain and therefore devoid of the one virtue which it behooves every woman to have above all else, if she possibly can. A plain woman, unless she is titled and independently wealthy, will always find herself in a position of extreme disadvantage to her more attractive peers, and the deficiency will haunt her until she reaches an age by which the condition of being withered and crippled will excuse her from her plainness. I can attest to the numerous petty prejudices she will suffer at the hands of individuals she has never wronged or even met before, like the butcher who, for the same money, would choose to save a better cut of meat for a more attractive patron or the surly housemaid who'd accept abuse from a beautiful mistress while resenting the same treatment from a plain one.

I discovered my plainness before I was fully a decade on this earth. The incident occurred in a small wilderness that formerly bordered my family's modest estate and which concealed all sight of the house once you'd fully entered it. Someone—probably Lizzy—proposed a game of chase, and it wasn't long before the wilderness shook with the peals of our laughter. Out of all of us, Lizzy was by far the best runner, for she had long arms and legs that reached un-cannily far, and she could leap through a space no more than two feet wide without tearing any part of her dress. When she ran, her black boots clipped the earth as sharply as the cloven hooves of deer that spring, from birth, with unstudied elegance.

After the first few minutes of frenzied running, I began to tire of the noise and of the pain in my chest from being unable to catch my breath. Even as a child, I did not often avail myself of opportunities to study my reflection in the mirror, but I can well imagine what a sight I looked stumbling from tree to tree with my mouth hanging open, trailed by an orb of gnats that formed a sort of mock halo around my head. My tongue tasted dry and bitter, like old leather that had begun to flake. I thought of calling Mrs. Hill to fetch me a glass of water. But Mrs. Hill wouldn't have heard me, not even if she were at that moment hanging the washing out to dry or beating the bedsheets with her stick.

Those who have tended to children or remember being young themselves will know the far range of a child's imagination. A mother or governess may leave a room for only a few moments before a child will believe he has been forsaken by all who love him. In silence, he may think he hears ghoulish cries; in innocent furnishings, frightening apparitions transpire to haunt him. At the bottom of a tall shrub, I quietly considered my fate. Should I fail to find my way back to the house, I was sure I would transform into a raving feral child. I envisioned myself kneeling at the mouth of a stream, lapping water like a dog. Soon I would know every tree and bush in this wood by their name and speak fluently the language of the swallow, the house martin, and the nightingale. I would sleep on a bed of moss and dress my wild, unkempt hair with the wings of butterflies and their midnight brethren. I would make rings of beetle shells and swallow eggs whole. Over time, my nails would turn as black as the earth from foraging. I'd mash elderberries with my hands and drink their pulp and sustain myself on turnips, mushrooms, and spider legs, all of which I'd consume on a slab of stone. Then, one morning, I'd discover that I'd forgotten my own name and the names of my sisters and my parents.

While brooding on these thoughts, I suddenly heard the papery rustle of leaves and spotted a slight figure advancing towards me at an alarming pace. The white dress identified this person as Lizzy. I sat up and straightened but didn't make any attempt to stand, much less run away.

As the distance closed between us, I watched her face weave in and out of shadows cast by overhanging foliage. Drops of scattered sunlight glistened across her forehead, illuminating her eyes. I waited for her to look away or to laugh or to appear a little embarrassed at finding me, but her gaze was as concentrated and impassioned as that of the goddess Diana in the ecstasy of the hunt. With a single airy leap over a clump of dead leaves, Lizzy landed in front of me and placed a warm hand on the top of my head. Smiling now and seemingly restored to the cheerful disposition I'd always known, she said, "I've got you, Mary. You've lost."

If the game had ended then, that afternoon would have little to distinguish it in my memory beyond Kitty crying at the discovery of a torn sleeve. But when Lizzy helped me to my feet and we rejoined the others, we found that a sport of a different nature had begun in our absence.

After cornering Jane in a small hollow, our youngest sisters had commenced to celebrate their hard-won victory by throwing fistfuls of earth at her dress. As it had rained only that morning, the soil was wet and easy to shape, and they stamped and shouted and baited poor Jane, like two rosy-cheeked devils performing a ritualistic dance. Lydia, in particular, enjoyed the activity so much that all speech she uttered seemed an indecipherable jumble of giggles and screams.

In Lydia's defense, whatever scandals may now be associated with her name, she never possessed a deliberately malicious character. But years of indulgence from Mama and Aunt Philips, who both happened to find the senseless amiability with which Lydia approached all matters in life endearing, had emboldened her to say and to do whatever happened to take her fancy, with little concern for others' feelings and no thought to the consequences of her actions. Kitty, the elder by two years, witnessed our mother's affection for her younger sibling and, in seeking the same, imitated Lydia to the effacement of her own learning and otherwise colorless disposition.

I mention this because I've never doubted that the instigator of this rather savage game was Lydia, who, in all probability, would view this childhood incident and eloping with a well-known rake with the same equanimity. It was also clear that whatever pleasure Jane might originally have derived from the jest had long expired. I'd never seen her face so red. One section of her hair had become loosed from its pinnings and had fallen over her shoulder. Her eyes glistened with unfallen tears. She raised her hands in front of her dress and begged them to stop, but their attacks only escalated. We arrived in time to watch Lydia press a fistful of mud against Jane's back while screaming to Kitty, who taunted Jane as though she were a bear in an arena: "Look, I got her! I got her!"

"What on earth?" Lizzy cried. And channeling something of the goddess I'd witnessed earlier, she lunged forward and grabbed Lydia, who was still laughing, by the shoulders and slapped her.

I took the opportunity to rush over to Jane and ask if she was all right.

"Mary, it's only a bit of fun," Kitty whined before Jane had any chance to answer. "Jane knows it's only a bit of fun."

"Kitty," I said in my bravest voice, "put that down." I'd noticed that Kitty had bunched another ball in her hands and was rolling it between her palms. She shook her head, unable to stop chortling, and took a step back.

"No," she said.

"Kitty," I repeated. I endeavored to speak with some authority, which was difficult as I stood at most an inch or two taller than she did. "This isn't funny anymore, so I'll ask you to please put that down at once." To show my purpose, I advanced and reached for Kitty's wrist, but before I could stop her, she released the missive she had been holding full into my face. Stunned, I stumbled backwards. Where there should have been only dirt and grass, something hard and sharp cut into me. I heard Jane cry out, her voice turning strangely hollow and distant. Instinctively, I touched the soft pocket

of flesh under my right eye, then held my hand in front of myself.
The tips of my fingers shone a vibrant, dark red, and twin rivulets of
blood oozed down the length of my palm. The ground tilted, and I
might have fainted at that moment but for Jane calling my name
and squeezing my hand, still moist with blood. In distress, she wiped
her own forehead and left three marks above her eyebrow that made
it look as though she had been cut herself. "Mary's hurt!" she shouted
to Lizzy, pressing her handkerchief against my wound to stop the
blood. "We have to get back to the house and tell Mama to call for
the doctor!"

WHEN OUR MOTHER caught sight of Jane and me a few minutes
later, she screamed, which sufficed to weaken my knees, and Papa
was compelled to carry me into the sitting room. Once I'd been
placed on the settee and a cushion lodged behind my back to prop
me up, I was able to witness the movements of all the occupants of
Longbourn from a vantage point of relative comfort. Mrs. Hill was
sent to fetch a pitcher of water and left the room with as much urgency as her advanced age and persistent gout permitted. Lydia and
Kitty sulked in a corner they deemed distant enough from the rest
of the company to ensure their own security, while Lizzy reported to
Papa the whole of what had taken place in the woods.

It very soon occurred to me, however, that far from being the
sole object of pity and the recipient of such familial affection as I
considered my due for having braved injury on behalf of an innocent sister, I had been, for the better part, forgotten. As Lizzy captivated Papa with the account of Lydia and Kitty's unruly behavior,
Jane sat some few feet away from me at the table, though it was
difficult to see more than a fraction of her face at any time. There
were never less than three women around her: our mother; Aunt
Philips, who had fortuitously been visiting when we burst through
the door; Sarah, the housemaid; and Mrs. Hill, who though wholly

responsible for providing the pitcher of water, drank most of it herself in an excited state. I heard, from my seat, snippets of their conversation: Mama's insistence that we'd been attacked by an unknown assailant in the woods, Aunt Philips admonishing her sister for allowing us to go outdoors at all, Mrs. Hill entreating both women to calm themselves and take a cup of tea (which she wasn't, of course, prepared to make), and Sarah gently inquiring if Miss Jane's injuries were serious enough to warrant someone going to fetch the doctor. Jane's own protests remained unheard, and she was shushed for exerting herself unnecessarily. As for myself, I found the scene before me too diverting to interrupt and continued to press Jane's handkerchief to my face, both to quell the flow of blood and to stifle my laughter.

"Heaven help us if this should scar," Mama cried.

"But nothing's the matter with me," Jane replied. "I'm not hurt. It's Mary you should—"

"You have blood all over your forehead, my dear," Aunt Philips noted, clicking her tongue.

"And if it should scar, then we are all ruined," Mama said. "For who will want to take a wife whose face has been disfigured? Not even one as beautiful as yours, I daresay, though it pains me to confess it." Turning to Aunt Philips, she continued: "Am I not to be pitied, sister, for having children who live in such disregard for their mother's feelings, who would drive me to madness by cutting and scraping and burning themselves every time my back is turned, though my own health has always been exceptionally poor?"

"Your mother has certainly taken pains to raise you well, Jane. It is unkind to repay her efforts by running barbarically through the woods."

"Aunt Philips!" Jane could hardly keep herself from laughing, and, I confess, nor could I, though the pain beneath my eye worsened considerably when I smiled. "I promise you I am not hurt. It is all Kitty's fault. She threw something at Mary, and Mary started to bleed. I took her hand and must have touched my own face afterwards. That is all."

It was Mrs. Hill who, to her credit, finally settled the matter by dipping her own handkerchief in the pitcher of water and dabbing Jane's forehead with it. In a matter of seconds, Jane's face had been restored to its original radiance, with not the smallest blemish or scratch to be detected, not even under the hawklike scrutiny of Mama and Aunt Philips, who alternated in inspecting Jane's face, turning her head left and right, then up and down, with a care more appropriate to handling one's best china.

Though she'd never admit it herself, a childless marriage and the general tedium which accompanied a life that boasted neither particular tragedy nor happy distinction had caused my aunt Philips to devote the majority of her energies to originating and circulating as many miniature dramas as possible to disturb the normal course of a day. She enjoyed hosting frequent parties at her home, as doing so kept her informed of all goings-on in the county and provided ample opportunity for her, in turn, to share updates on the latest dissolution of marriages, the futility of acquiring good help, and such other misfortunes as have been mankind's lot to suffer since our ancestors' first fall from grace. She prided herself on being able to name a vast network of friends she possessed owing to her good sense, unshakable principles, and intelligence. I have, in fact, witnessed on many occasions, whether at balls or at private dinners, the generosity of my aunt's memory in naming individuals of less than half an hour's acquaintance her intimate companions and within the first few moments of introduction entrusting virtual strangers with her ever-increasing knowledge of the private affairs of other people's households.

Her features having been restored to as near a state of indifference as could be expected in so short a time, Aunt Philips happened to turn from the table where her favorite niece and sister remained sitting to where I lay, some few feet away. She started, as if seeing me for the first time. From an early age, I was aware that she noted little in me to entertain her and, therefore, felt entirely at liberty to ignore me whenever she wished. As she perceived the state I was in, however, a flicker of hope, even of gratitude, livened her expression. Her cheeks reddened. Her eyes gleamed, and she wetted her lips before opening her mouth and releasing a delighted and guttural moan.

"Oh, Mary," she shouted happily. "You're bleeding!"

The timbre of her exclamation was so shrill and so unexpectedly emitted that everyone was instantly roused to attention. Mama declared that if this continued for much longer, she would most certainly be dead before the day had ended. Lizzy urged Papa to call for the doctor, which the latter obeyed with more than usual alacrity, looking for, I suspect, any excuse to leave the noisy and crowded room. Mrs. Hill set down the pitcher she'd been holding, which was now empty and which, by the looks of it, she had no intention of refilling, lest an event of considerable import should occur in her absence. (She sent Sarah to refill it instead.) And Aunt Philips, continuing to gaze with enchanted horror at the cut under my right eye, insisted on holding my hand, which none of my weak protests could discourage, while Mama stood on the other side of the settee and proceeded to console me in her own way.

"Well," she said, "I never took you for a wild one, Mary. But if you have indeed protected Jane from being hurt, as she informs us is the case, then that is very well done, and you deserve to be commended for your act of bravery."

I might have failed to grasp the full meaning of Mama's words and taken them merely for the praise deserved had it not been for some comments exchanged shortly afterwards. We had been waiting some time for the arrival of the doctor, and I'd dropped off into a light and uneasy sleep. No one had thought to draw the curtains, and the sun remained full in my eyes, so that, tired as I was, I remained conscious of everyone's speech and movements—Lydia and

Kitty sulking watchfully in their corner; Mrs. Hill imbibing the water Sarah had brought, in large, noisy gulps. Over my recumbent body, Mama and Aunt Philips began to speak in hushed tones.

"Sister," Aunt Philips whispered, "it is lucky for you that Mary was hurt and not Jane."

Mama was quick to agree: "Of course I shall have a very strong word with Kitty later and tell her to have a care what she throws at her sisters, but it is very lucky. Very lucky indeed."

"Can you imagine if Jane were to suffer such an injury?" Aunt Philips's enthusiasm at the prospect was, I thought, poorly disguised, even by her standards.

"Though she is my child," Mama sighed, "it is just as well that this happened to Mary and not to the others. To be sure, they are none of them as beautiful as Jane, but the difference between Mary and her sisters is too marked for anyone to ignore."

"It pains me, too, sister, that all my nieces have not turned out as fine as the eldest, but perhaps Mary has other qualities which will make up for her outward deficiencies." Then she added, with considerably less conviction, "We must hope this is the case."

"It is unfortunate," my mother replied, "that these other qualities you mention are seldom admired by the opposite sex and, when appreciated, are taken note of only after a pleasantness of figure and complexion has already been ascertained. No, I wonder sometimes that Mary is so plain and what, in consequence, will become of her!"

The doctor arrived at this moment. He was a tall, thin man with gray whiskers and eyes of such pale blue they appeared almost white. Kneeling beside me, he removed his glasses with the delicacy of one accustomed to undertaking all tasks in an unhurried manner. I wish, among the jumble of insignificant details I have retained over the years, that I could remember his name, for I haven't forgotten the gentleness and civility with which he addressed me and which was, at the time, as alien to me as it was welcome. The room became very quiet and still. As he leaned over me, a part of his beard brushed my arm, and its softness reminded me of the gentle swish of a cat's tail touching the back of one's hand. He asked me if I was in pain and studied the wound.

"Looks worse than it is," he said slowly, considering the cut from all angles before unfolding a cloth from his bag. "You must be more careful when you play with your sisters, especially outside, where it is easy to have an accident." He asked for water, and Sarah was forced once again to leave the room. Upon her return, he commenced with cleaning and dressing the cut. As the injury did not, in his opinion, warrant any further attention, he was soon finished with his task and rose to leave. Fastening his bag, he turned to me and said, "I'm afraid, my dear, that it is very easy for cuts on one's face to scar, and this may leave a lasting impression. The skin, unfortunately, is very delicate there, which is why you must be more careful in future."

And raising his voice by the smallest discernible volume possible, he added, "Take care not to scratch the cut when it is healing, as doing so will increase the likelihood of a scar."

Recalling Mama and Aunt Philips's earlier conversation, I considered for a moment before answering. "But will it make any difference?" I asked. "I mean, will it make any difference whether it scars or not on my face, as opposed to . . . Jane's?" Mama reddened and opened her mouth to protest, but our guest spoke first.

He looked at me strangely. "Of course it will, my dear," he said. "Of course it will. What a shame it would be for a pretty face like yours to scar, so you must do all you can not to touch or pick at the wound when it itches, eh?"

He patted my hand and, nodding slightly to the whole room, departed. No sooner did he leave than Mama began to chide me for making such foolish comments in front of the doctor, which she was certain would be imparted to all the patients he visited before the day was out. Aunt Philips then announced that I was tired and should be sent directly to bed. My father, the only other individual in the room besides my mother and aunt who was permitted to express an opinion, considered this a very good idea, and Jane and Lizzy were tasked with escorting me upstairs, in case I should have a fainting spell on the steps.

AFTER I CHANGED into a clean nightgown, Lizzy called me over to the dressing table. "I'll brush your hair before you go to bed," she said. I thanked her and fixed my gaze on the chipped corner of a lacquer jewelry box while her fingers removed the pins in my hair.

Jane glided over and kissed the top of my head from behind. "You were very brave today, Mary," she said, smiling. Our eyes met in the glass, and I looked from her to Lizzy, then back again. They began discussing a pair of embroidered slippers belonging to Jane that had gone missing from her room. Lizzy suggested that Kitty had a habit of borrowing things without permission, which made Jane laugh and explain that even if Kitty had taken her slippers, they could be of no use to her, being too big for her feet. When Jane smiled, her large, round eyes became sparkling crescent moons, and her mouth an instrument perfectly formed for the cheerful, elegant mirth she released into the world. In taking her beauty for granted, I had never thought to admire it. Now I found myself enraptured by the elements which, together, created a face that many would willingly think of in the vague and absent moments before falling asleep.

"There," Lizzy said. "All done." She set the brush on the table.

I stared at myself in the mirror and registered all the parts of my face, which in functionality at least seemed to be in good order. There was nothing that could be considered misshapen, and yet the sum total was such that I, as the proprietor of my own nose and mouth and cheekbones, could not look with satisfaction upon any part of my countenance. There surfaced in me a sense of wonderment that one could arrive in this world so wholly unadorned by even the slightest advantage of beauty. I felt racked with emotion, yet my eyes betrayed nothing and returned my gaze like two dark stones, hard and unfeeling. Though still a child, I already saw, unfolding before me, a life lived ingratiatingly in the shadows, of sitting like an old gargoyle at dinner tables while, some few feet away, the living laughed and exchanged stories. I would have no stories to tell. No estates to run. No children to speak of. I would not be blessed with the holy rites of matrimony and would thus be compelled to live my years beholden to the loveliness of one or two older sisters, who would, by their charity, ensure that I always had food to eat and a roof over my head.

Thoughts can be as potent as wishes. That night, I dreamed I had returned alone to the woods outside Longbourn. Between the ghostly birches, there flickered a pale light, which moved towards me until it took the shape of a human figure. I saw at once who it was, having studied her likeness many times before, and dropped to my knees and bowed my head. She wore a blue cloak, the cloth of which was so fine it floated like a dewy mist over her white body. A ring of stars encircled her head, and when she moved, the stars quivered in their orb. Though her face was engulfed in light, I perceived that she smiled. She extended her hand to me, and, clasping it in my own, I pressed my mouth to her skin, which felt against my lips as cool and pure as the water of a fresh spring and which stilled the rapid beating of my heart. I felt I could never want for anything again, yet when she spoke, she asked what I desired most in the world. I raised my eyes to meet her gaze. But no sooner did I look upon her face than the light which she exuded overwhelmed me, and I was forced to turn away else I be struck blind.

"I wish," I said in a weak voice, "that I weren't so plain."

"Is that all, Mary?" she asked. "More than anything else, you desire to be beautiful?"

"Yes," I replied. "I wish I could be as beautiful as Jane, or even more beautiful. If I could, I would be the loveliest girl in Meryton."

"If that is what you really want, then you have only to wake up," she said, turning to leave, "and your wish will be granted." Trembling, I gathered the ends of her cloak and kissed them until the threads slipped out of my hands. Though she moved slowly, it wasn't long before I lost sight of her, and she became again a single point of light. As I pressed my hand to the place where she had stood, a welcome darkness enfolded me, and for many hours afterwards, I was lost to all sensation of pain or happiness in a dreamless sleep.

It was late morning when I awoke. At once, I remembered the Holy Virgin's promise and bolted to the dressing table. With the tips of my fingers, I traced the cut under my eye, which was still tender and red. I observed myself in the mirror for as long as it took to realize there had been no change; in its absence remained only the humiliation of having expected, in defiance of all logic and reason, that some miraculous transformation could have taken place during the night.

Just then, the door opened and Jane came bursting through with a spray of heather in her hands. Tossing aside her bouquet, she made immediately for the window and stood full in the sun with her arms outstretched, as if to embrace the very air she breathed. She cried, addressing the window, "Oh, Mary, it's a wonderful morning. The weather hasn't been like this for ages." When I didn't answer, she looked over her shoulder at me. Though she was then but thirteen, it would be only a short time before the full potential of her slender figure was realized. And as for her face . . . From my seat across the room, I observed the delicate lines of her nose, the soft blush that entered her cheeks, as unobtrusive as the first touch of color in spring buds, the pleasing shape of her mouth as she asked how I'd slept. With new eyes, I marveled at the head of wondrous, golden hair washed in morning light which seemed, in that moment, an extension of the sun itself and of all things touched by heaven and by God that are put on this earth to be worshipped.

"Mary," Jane said, taking my hand as my vision blurred. "What is it? Are you crying?"

I shrugged and covered my eyes. Then, turning away from the mirror, I hung my head and wept.

PART I

CHAPTER 1

Because I am plain, others have always assumed in me a disinterest to the opposite sex, to romance, and, accordingly, to marriage. But I will write here, as if with my own life's blood, that I have indeed loved. I have loved not once or twice but three times, which is three times more than anyone would believe of me.

In none of these episodes did I believe my love to be any the less true or good because my energies failed to attain that happy conclusion which has often blessed others. I loved in earnest all three men. I loved also with the kind of desperation that afflicts only the very plain and the very poor, who, in knowing they have nothing to give beyond the shirt off their backs and their own bodies, will do everything to compensate for the absence of wealth and beauty.

So to anyone who has ever doubted that the sour little creature sitting on the sidelines of the ball isn't capable of the same purity of love as her two esteemed sisters, I say you do not know her or her heart. Though she looks upon the lines of skipping couples with indifference, I can tell you she does not feel it. She, too, wonders what it would be like to stand up for every dance with a partner, to run wantonly through a red sea of regimentals shouting "Denny!" or "Andrew!" at the top of her lungs while laughing and spilling punch onto the front of her dress. She has often imagined this scene in the tired but happy hours after a ball has ended and the entire family has gathered in the drawing room to discuss the dances, the fashions, and how well or ill such and such of their acquaintance looked. While these conversations took place, it became common for her to lose herself in her imaginings and to rewrite, in her mind, the events of that evening, had she been singled out by the richest man in the room or had two officers come to blows for the privilege of dancing a cotillion with her.

I am no longer this lonely girl-child. But if I shut my eyes and concentrate, I can see her as vividly as though I am next to her. It is the ballroom at Netherfield Park when the owner of that estate, Mr. Bingley, threw a party to announce his settlement there. I see her hard eyes, her tight mouth. I hear the voice inside her head repeating how lucky she is that she won't have to risk spraining an ankle by dancing like other young ladies. Among the bobbing and weaving faces, she spots Kitty dancing the *Boulangère* with a breathless, corpulent officer who has two boils on his chin. Both talk excitedly, and she wonders what they could possibly have in common to discuss with so much animation. At the opposite end of the room, she perceives Lydia pressed up against the wall with a cup of wine in one hand and a fan in the other, encircled by half a dozen young officers. Their epaulettes shimmer from so much laughing and bowing. They are all too well trained to touch her, but they enclose her nonetheless like hungry wolves around a single, bleating lamb. Lydia throws her head back, and the feathers in her hair tremble. She is wearing white, and my former self sneers and rolls her eyes. Her hands shuffle the pages of Handel's *Water Music* she has brought, busying herself with nothing. In another world, another life, a lieutenant might have enfolded her in his black cloak and whispered saucy inanities into her ear. Above the violins, she listens attentively to his voice. *Look at how others stare, Mary. They are staring at you because you are the most beautiful woman in the room. A man could go mad just from gazing at you.* At this point, her father arrives, handing her a plate of fruit and encouraging her to enjoy herself a little more and not to look so miserable all the time. She accepts the plate in silence, her ears burning.

I'd realized early on in life that most people did not look at me for any longer than they needed to. This was especially true of the apprentice milliner in Meryton who, every time we engaged in conversation, would pay most deliberate and unwavering attention to my left ear, addressing his professional opinions regarding the latest fabrics and hosiery to that tender and useful organ, while I respectfully watched his averted gaze. I could not blame him or any of the countless others who preferred the view of a doornail to a face that held all the attraction of a dandelion in a garden of roses. It is human nature to recoil from or, at the very least, to ignore what is unpleasant and inconvenient in the world.

Over time, my plainness had become a second, unshakable religion. I have seen its effect on my family and acquaintances far too long for it to be disputed. To those who'd argue that I am no mind reader, I'd answer that as happy as I might have been to remain perfectly ignorant of my deficiencies, these patterns of behavior were simply too frequent and too familiar an occurrence for even the most willingly oblivious of persons to overlook.

Perhaps this is why I prefer reading to any other activity. When one reads, one is forced to look down at the words, and the imperfections of the face become less noticeable due to the angle of one's head. More so, the act of reading is a silent rebellion. To read in the presence of company is a most convenient excuse for not partaking in conversation. The book is a better tool than the piano in this regard. If you play and sing, then visitors are expected to listen, to applaud, and to compliment you on your so-called accomplishments. But if you are sitting behind your sisters and occupied with a book, it is as if to say to the guest, "I would rather spend time with the litigious husbands, gamblers, and spendthrifts of this novel than with you, dear sir, even if you had no interest in wooing me in the first place."

I remember these things and share them so others will know there lived a passionate spirit behind my oftentimes taciturn exterior. I, too, hoped quietly for romance and also for marriage as much as any of my sisters did. However, the discrepancies of nature, which would give blessings to some and none to others, had reduced me to the pitiable role of a living corpse. For my whole life, I had been adequately clothed and fed. I enjoyed my family's protection. But I remained largely ignored, even to the point of being forgotten.

MR. WILLIAM COLLINS arrived at Longbourn precisely a week after my nineteenth birthday. It was a fine afternoon in the middle of November, and his modest curricle was fortunately spotted from a distance by one of the household, providing us with ample time to prepare ourselves for the occasion of receiving him. By the time the horses reached Longbourn, we had been arranged for some minutes in a neat and elegant formation on the drive. The effect of this sight was not lost on our esteemed guest and, mindful of the honor paid to him, he returned our efforts with many delighted flourishes of his wide-brimmed hat as he traveled up the path to the house. With a boyish jump that belied his twenty-five years of age, he alighted from his seat and paid us the final obeisance of a very low bow, the formality of which would have been acceptable for the veneration of kings and princes but seemed wholly out of place to a country family of respectable, albeit modest, means. Papa's gracious welcome gave my cousin sufficient courage to greet the female members of the household with a bashful smile. And to Mama he expressed particular deference by showering her with so many compliments and inquiries after her health that she seemed to forget, however temporarily, that our visitor would inherit her husband's estate after his death, thus rendering us women homeless. As my father had no sons and as Longbourn could be passed only along the male line, Mr. Collins was, by law, heir presumptive of our childhood home.

Mr. Collins walked with a light step and, upon being escorted by my parents into the hall, praised the upkeep of the furnishings and the fine, though appropriately humble, taste we exhibited in the decoration of our rooms. As he proved profuse in his admiration and would brook no interruption to his stopping and making an observation of every small feature that seemed to evidence Mama's superior running of the household, nearly half an hour had passed before we finally gathered in the drawing room to take tea, which by then had to be brewed again for turning cold. On crossing the threshold of that room, he found his attention instantly arrested by a porcelain shepherdess on the mantelpiece. The sight of it appeared to move him deeply, and cradling the piece in his hands, he exclaimed what a happy coincidence it was that his own benefactress, the great lady responsible for his recent installment as the clergyman of Hunsford parsonage, possessed one very similar to it, though hers, if he remembered correctly, was larger and had been purchased at auction for nearly fifty pounds, numbering only one of many items of value that constituted her impressive estate. We listened with appropriate deference, and our guest, pleased at finding a willing audience, was quick to follow up this account with the number of times he'd already been invited to take refreshment in the company of Lady Catherine and her daughter at Rosings Park. Having by this time fully recovered from my cousin's initial charms, Mama replied that it was very well for some people to enjoy all the luck while others could be destitute of good fortune their whole lives, as she knew firsthand.

"But that cannot be so, madam," Mr. Collins said with feeling, pressing a hand to his heart. "You have not only this lovely and most comfortable house but also boast among your children the most graceful women as man has ever laid eyes on. I've heard much of their beauty, and I can tell you, as an impartial witness, that none of the rumors have been exaggerated." Whereupon he bowed in her direction with his hand still pressed to his chest.

"I would," Mama replied, fingering the lace on her collar, "open my arms to anyone who might show kindness to myself or my daughters. They are all sensible girls with talent and beauty enough between them to deserve good marriages, and let us hope this is the case. I would like nothing better than to see my daughters settled and happy with homes of their own, though if this should fail to occur before a certain event takes place . . ." Here, she turned and looked to Mr. Bennet, who had just finished pouring himself another cup of tea and was pointedly gazing out the window. Seeing there was no comfort to be had from those quarters, she blinked with watery eyes at our guest. "I don't know whose charity we could then rely upon, Mr. Collins. You witness my predicament and how it affects me. My daughters—bless them—find me in this state every day, but there is little they can do to help, being so miserably situated themselves and with no estimable wealth of their own."

Mr. Collins colored. His ears turned as pink as Mama's eyes, and it was fully a minute before he could bring himself to speak. Replacing his hand upon his heart, he cleared his throat and endeavored his most sympathetic expression. "My dear Mrs. Bennet," he began, "being a clergyman and having been blessed with the occupation of a post that requires me to set an example for the members of a small but prosperous community, I am by nature and by habit more sympathetic to the troubles of my fellow men than most." Taking a moment to sip his tea, he then continued: "Therefore, in seeing you grieved, I cannot help but be stirred to pity in light of your and your daughters' situation, of which I am bound by law to play a most awkward part. And while, madam, I have no doubt that *all* of your daughters will make suitable marriages and that, in their leaving this home to run their own, you will thereby have not one or two but *five* different homes in which to settle and live at your choosing in your old age, you may be assured that I will do everything in my power to safeguard the welfare of both you and my fair cousins upon the passing of your husband, the event of which I do not think will occur for many more years, as happily for all of us, Mr. Bennet looks to be the very picture of good health." And smiling pleasantly, he asked if Mrs. Bennet wouldn't be the first to agree with this, while bowing with practiced grace.

My mother, however, wasn't in the custom of listening to, much less answering, any parts of a conversation that did not interest her and replied accordingly to only the sections of Mr. Collins's speech that gave her the most reason for joy. "Sir, you are most kind," she answered gratefully and folded her handkerchief for the next time it should be used.

Mr. Collins resumed his seat, which, being opposite my own, permitted me to observe his appearance from a close distance. He was not handsome, but in his face there was something more interesting than mere attractiveness. As he gave lively attention to Mama's description of the neighborhood and the succession of dinner parties, balls, and other engagements that monthly filled our calendars, every aspect of his countenance played a distinct role in the expression of delight and amazement. His eyes sparkled obligingly. His cheeks, full and round when he smiled, gleamed like two wax apples. And upon hearing that we dined with no less than four and twenty families a year, he lifted his brow to such heights it seemed to contort the entire shape of his face. He conveyed wonder that we could spare the time and the energy to fulfill all the invitations we received, and Mama assured him that our lives, though by no means capable of matching the level of idleness which was the privilege of the truly wealthy, were certainly ones of active leisure. As the hour grew late, we were soon called to dinner, and over cups of wine and crowded platters of venison, pork, and pheasant, Mr. Collins shared select accounts of his interactions with Lady Catherine de Bourgh as evidenced the latter's beneficence. I noticed, in recounting these impressive stories, that he seemed particularly keen on attracting the attention of the eldest Miss Bennet.

"And what do you think was served at dinner the next evening?" he asked, pausing for dramatic effect and resting his eyes on Jane.

"Onion soup!" he answered himself. "Onion soup!" he repeated when none of us said anything. "All because the previous afternoon at tea I had happened to mention to her ladyship a preference for the dish, which she, too, professed to favor. Does not this small gesture indicate to you an unparalleled greatness of character?" But in finding no admiration in the gaze of his first choice, he turned in sequence to Lizzy. And finding even less to be had there, he turned at last to me. Our eyes met, and I blushed. Encouraged by this, he helped himself to another serving of potatoes, seemingly forgetting that not two minutes ago he had replenished his plate from the same dish and hadn't yet touched any of that portion. Seeing this filled me with pleasure, and I consumed the rest of my meal with more than usual relish.

"This is truly excellent," Mr. Collins said, working diligently with his fork at the mound of potatoes that overwhelmed every other food on his plate. "There is nothing, in my mind, quite like the potato. It is a vegetable, yet it fills the stomach as adequately as any meat and involves none of the aggravation of picking out bones, which the eating of fowl often requires. Besides, I do not think I have ever tasted a bad potato, though the same, alas, could not be said for the many dishes of meat I've sampled at various tables, which were indigestible for being too tough for my palate." Seeing Mama redden at this last comment, our guest lost no time in adding that there had only ever been, in his life, two tables at which he could partake of and enjoy *all* the dishes prepared, and these were at Rosings Park and at Longbourn, which must boast two of the very best cooks in England, despite the grandeur of the former and the modesty of the latter. As no one ventured to either agree or contradict Mr. Collins in his opinion of potatoes as a laudable vegetable, he continued on the same subject by relating the particulars of a discussion he had overheard while dining on one occasion at Rosings Park. "Lady Catherine," he began by way of explanation, "dedicates herself to all matters with equal energy and rigor, regardless of how large or small these problems may be and what level of person they may affect. Owing to her superior breeding, she also possesses unequaled taste in all things, not least of which is what and how food should be served. I will share her thoughts on the preparation of potatoes in case the knowledge she owns on the subject may also benefit this household, and this is that the peeling of potatoes should always occur before boiling and not after. I know that some would boil the potato first and, in softening the vegetable, peel the skin off afterwards with either their nails or a rough cloth, but I have it on the very best authority that this should not be done and that the potato should be pared of its skin before entering the water."

"Well, Mrs. Bennet," Papa replied, spearing the last chunk of potato on his plate with his fork, "you may impart this wisdom to our cook at your earliest convenience, though before you do, it may be wise to ask if, in the preparation of this dish, she had taken the trouble of paring the vegetables before boiling them or whether, in a desire to skirt her responsibilities, she had peeled them only afterwards. If the latter, you have my permission to reprimand her thoroughly."

Mr. Collins did not know what to make of Mr. Bennet's comment. In later conversations, he owned to me that prior to writing the letter in which he begged Papa for the privilege of visiting Longbourn, he'd heard his uncle was a well-read though eccentric character. And perhaps wary that Mr. Bennet was at present exhibiting the wit he was reputed for at his expense, Mr. Collins deemed it unsafe to instruct us any further on the subject. Still, in raising another piece of potato to his mouth, he couldn't help but search the table for any indication that the knowledge he'd divulged had been well received. Our eyes met again, and this time, I ventured a small smile. He hesitatingly returned it before resuming the hearty ingestion of the food and drink before him.

Dinner was soon over. After losing two consecutive games of backgammon to Lizzy and having to abort a highly unpopular reading, Mr. Collins indulged in a polite though audible yawn and professed himself tired from his journey. He wondered therefore if his host or one of the servants would be so kind as to show him to his room and apologized that he hadn't the stamina to entertain his fair cousins for a longer interval on this first night of his visit. He concluded with the promise of endeavoring to do better in the future, of his joy in being united with a family that in all respects worthy of commendation far exceeded his expectations, and of his hope that the nature of our relations would be considerably strengthened by the time he was called back to Hunsford the following Saturday. Papa volunteered to take Mr. Collins upstairs, and the latter parted from us with a bow that, in the extremity of its depth and duration, left no one in any doubt of his deeply felt gratitude.

No sooner had Mr. Collins left the room, however, than Lydia declared her opinion of our new acquaintance. "Lord," she said with some bitterness, "I thought he'd never leave. What a laugh Denny will have when I tell him about our guest and how he tried to read Fordyce's *Sermons* to us before going to bed." Jane shushed her, and for some minutes longer, we listened to the pleasant burble of praise that emanated from the direction of the staircase until, rising higher and higher, it could be heard no more.

"What an unfortunate choice of text," Lizzy exclaimed. "If all Papa's relations are like Mr. Collins, it's a wonder madness doesn't run in our family."

"Now, girls . . ." Mama chided.

"And though he must be a learned man to have attained his position," Lizzy continued, interrupting our mother, "he shows no trace of intellect in any of his thoughts. What can his sermons be like?"

"As rambling and dull as any other sermon, I suppose," Lydia snorted.

"I'm sure he means well," Jane offered.

Kitty stood up and began flouncing her dress at us. "Lady Catherine!" she cried. "Oh, Lady Catherine! How tall you are! How fine you are! How ugly you look this morning, Lady Catherine! May I give you a hand?" And she bowed until her head reached her ankles, which sent the whole room, even Jane, into fits of laughter.

"This is most unkind of all of you," I protested. "You seem to forget that Mr. Collins is our guest, and I, for one, think he is . . . he is . . ."

"Yes, Mary?" Jane asked kindly.

"I think he's very nice!" I declared, standing up myself.

In a whiny pitch Lydia and Kitty mocked in unison: *"I think he's very nice! I think he's very nice!"*

Then Lydia said, clasping her hands together and swooning, "Oh, Mr. Collins, how long I have waited for you in my ivory tower!"

And Kitty replied, "Shall we read together another passage from the Bible before going upstairs, Mr. Collins?"

And Lydia, making as if to kiss the air, added, "Won't you permit me to have your children, my dear clergyman?"

This proved too much for Mama's patience, and Lydia was rebuked and silenced accordingly, though no one could mistake the smile that played upon our parent's lips.

CHAPTER 2

T he next day, having risen earlier than any of my sisters, I went downstairs alone. I was a frequent visitor to my father's library, and in approaching it, I thought I heard a sneeze from within. That small, crowded, and dusty section of the house provided the altar at which my father worshipped daily, and his studies often engrossed him so that nothing, not even the gentle urgings of Lizzy, could persuade him to join us at the dinner table. I have seen him transfixed by texts of such marginal influence and limited readership as would bore the most learned scholars of this world to distraction. In the preferment of his books to his daughters, he was always unabashedly vocal. Given the opportunity, he could explain with conviction the manifold advantages of reading Andersen's exhaustive treatise on the migratory patterns of the common house sparrow to sitting with his family and inevitably embarking on one of three subjects which never lost popularity with his wife and children, these being first and foremost marriage; second, the entailment of Longbourn, which meant that our estate would pass directly to our cousin due to Papa's having no male heir; and third, his own death. Owing largely to Mama's indifference to reading and the aversion she showed to being in the company of books when they were being so engaged, the library remained the only room in the whole house upon which Papa could depend for quietude. In her mind, reading could lead to nothing of material value, and she did not, for her part, see much usefulness in knowing about things that fell outside the concerns of daily life.

I confess I sometimes visited my father's library, not because I'd already exhausted the books I had borrowed, but because I hoped to endear myself to him. I admired his monastic devotion to reading, his talent for reciting long quotations by heart, his eloquence at public gatherings. My own childlike logic determined that if I appeared enough times in front of him with my books, he would eventually bring me into his confidence, and then we could discourse for hours upon subjects which were quite beyond the understanding of my mother and sisters. But this never happened. What dialogue we might have exchanged on the early comedies of Shakespeare or the works of "Glorious John" were only ever the product of my overactive imagination. We rarely spoke, and my attempts to catch his eye while dawdling listlessly in front of his favorite historical tomes prompted at the very best a polite inquiry as to what title I was looking for and, at all other times, complete silence. He reserved his better self for Lizzy, and she remained the only one of the family whom he invited to his study in the evenings, though, in truth, she did not read nearly as much as I did and was often prone to skimming.

Pushing open the door, I found not my father but Mr. Collins in Papa's armchair, a copy of Fordyce's *Sermons* perched philosophically across a single hand. He balanced the volume so that it was level with his chin, and my initial impression was that he wasn't reading at all, but posturing for an invisible artist who was painting his likeness. Upon seeing me, he put down his book, stood, and articulated with one or two flowery turns of phrase his hope that I had slept well. Having by this time overcome my surprise at seeing him, I assured him that I had and shyly broached the matter of last night's reading.

"I'm sorry my sister didn't appreciate your selection, Mr. Collins," I said. "You must excuse Lydia for interrupting you. These days, her mind is very differently engaged, what with the militia being quartered so near Longbourn."

To this, Mr. Collins sighed and waved a dismissive hand over his brow. "It is true I took some offense when the incident occurred," he began stiffly, "and couldn't bring myself to read any further. But the whole matter has since been forgotten and, I promise, will not cross my lips again. I forgive my young cousin wholeheartedly for displaying the impetuosity characteristic of her age. My wish, even now, is entirely benevolent, which is that she may yet show some interest in the improvement of her mind by the instruction contained within sound and honest books, such as this. Though her fascination with the militia is, I suppose, natural for her youth and unmarried condition, in circumstances as these, the application of moral and virtuous teachings is rendered even more vital by the presence of so much temptation."

"You seem to comprehend a good deal on the subject," I said.

"I admit I do," he replied, smiling. "In the last year, I've made it a particular study of mine to investigate and approve such texts as, in my judgment, show great promise in outlining the manner of behavior which is most befitting to ladies. There is, at present, a wealth of publications in circulation that I would eagerly recommend to the youngest Miss Bennet should she welcome my suggestions and which I have been honored to endorse by way of recommended reading to both my benefactress and her daughter, however little either may be in need of the instruction offered."

"I am an avid reader myself, Mr. Collins," I said, "though my younger sisters tease me because I do not share their interest in fashions or parties."

"It is both delightful and rare indeed to meet a young woman who chooses to live her life unburdened by such un-Christian vanities, as you have! How liberating it must be to conduct one's daily schedule without frittering whole hours away in front of a looking glass."

Touching my chin, I grazed a pimple at the height of its swelling and cringed. His comment surprised me, and I didn't know whether to smile or to appear offended. "I cannot claim to possess no vanity, sir. I believe that would be impossible for any person, man or woman," I said, hoping the hardness I felt didn't show in my voice. "I only meant that I share your love for books and would be happy to pass a whole month in my father's library with enough food and water to sustain me, if it meant I could decline every invitation to a ball."

"I understand your feelings, Mary, but we must take care not to fall victim to extremities," Mr. Collins replied, "for that is a vanity itself, no better than the unneedful purchase of ribbons!"

"But there is a pleasure, is there not, Mr. Collins, unrivaled by any other feeling in the world, to reach the last page of a book and know that you have lived in it, that you have stood witness to the performance of momentous deeds at the hands of extraordinary personalities? I have only just turned nineteen, but I feel I have already known great romance and tragedy. Do you not sometimes marvel at how the construction of a beautiful line can leave you either shaking with laughter or bawling like an untended infant? Is that not a miracle which deserves as much scrutiny as the wonders of science and nature?"

My little exposition met with silence, which is perhaps what I deserved. I had been saving these same lines for Papa, had rehearsed them over and over in my head, sometimes delivering them with fanatical zeal, other times imploringly. I had so many other beautiful speeches in reserve, scribbled in the margins of books, that might never be spoken for lack of an audience, a kindred spirit, a friend. And as the silence between us lengthened, my humiliation increased. I pretended to remove a piece of lint from my sleeve, even as my skin felt too hot to live in. If only I could shed it and slink unnoticed out of the room . . . or if we could change the course of the conversation. I frowned from the effort of thinking. *Favorite foods? What species of flowers did the gardeners cultivate at Rosings Park? The proper paring of potatoes?*

"You must forgive my silence," Mr. Collins said, at last, smiling a little. "I was only thinking how very different you are from your sisters. To an outsider such as myself, you could not be more unlike them if you were a stranger, though you were born of the same parents."

Not seeking to discuss the subject any further, I admitted that he was probably right, and after an interval, he took up the volume at his side and inquired if I'd be opposed to his continuing the reading he had begun last night. As I wished to humor him and make amends for the previous evening's discourtesy, I encouraged him to proceed, and without delay, he turned to the fourth sermon, on female virtue. I'd read Fordyce's *Sermons* before, so I was familiar with the excerpt he'd selected, which enumerated the various evils of the novel—its lascivious descriptions of love between the sexes, the many indulgences taken in scenes of pleasure, and the proliferation of immoral behavior among its principal characters as would be certain to influence the highly impressionable minds of female readers. The sermon offered, by way of a safe alternative, the reading of chivalric romances, which, though as much filled with passionate declarations of love as their dissolute counterparts, were always tempered by the censorious whip of honor and chastity, rendering them significantly less treacherous to members of the fair sex. To myself, I conceded that the author's description of novels was quite flawless, but that the elements which he considered offensive were exactly what made them so delightful. I did not mind that Mr. Collins was opposed to novels. It was the "proper" thing to pooh-pooh the likes of Mrs. Ann Radcliffe in public, even if one did read *The Romance of the Forest* under the covers, and a differing of intellectual opinion would, in the long term, make for far more interesting conversation than if two people simply agreed with each other on everything.

" 'The parents of the present generation, what with selling their sons and daughters in marriage, and what with teaching them by every possible means the glorious principles of Avarice . . . ' " He stopped. Above us, in one of the bedrooms, the beginnings of a heated argument had erupted, followed by a rash of hurried footsteps in the hall and the flinging open of doors.

Mr. Collins wisely set aside his book. "It appears your younger sisters have awakened," he said with more grimness than he perhaps intended.

I smiled. The surprising pleasantness of his voice hadn't yet released me to the full awareness of the tantrums occurring upstairs. Mr. Collins stood and, running his hand over the cover, held the book for me to take. I accepted it with a questioning look. "For you to read," Mr. Collins explained, "as I hear I'm to accompany my cousins on a walk to Meryton this morning, and Mrs. Bennet told me that you are usually the only one among your sisters who can't be prevailed upon to go. The shops of Meryton, the sighting of a redcoated officer in the street, the thriftless spending of one's pocket change on attractive bonnets hold no pleasures for our dear cousin Mary." And with that, he bowed and excused himself from the room.

CHAPTER 3

Kitty was in a foul mood all through breakfast. She would not touch her food and sipped her hot chocolate only when Mama bid her to take some refreshment. At unexpected intervals during the meal, she kicked the table leg closest to her, once with so much violence that the teapot lid rattled and a few buns stacked high on a platter rolled off their perch and onto the ground before anyone could catch them. Her behavior drew the notice of our guest, who gently inquired if his young cousin had taken ill.

"She isn't ill," Lydia replied energetically. "She's just angry that I took one of her bonnets apart and made something better out of it."

Kitty gaped at her sister. "Without asking me!" she shouted across the table. "You're always taking my things without asking me, and Mama always lets you have your way!" The last part of her charge was uttered with especial bitterness through clenched teeth and fresh tears.

"Surely," I said, endeavoring to bring peace to the breakfast table and look well in front of Mr. Collins at the same time, "we should take care never to let our vanity threaten the bonds of sisterhood which bring us together." Glancing in my cousin's direction, I hoped for an encouraging nod or some other acknowledgment of my virtuous character, but Mr. Collins was then engaged with scraping the last of the apricot marmalade onto his bread roll. I returned with disappointment to my dry toast but not before Kitty piped up and with exaggerated civility asked if I wouldn't mind kindly holding my tongue for the rest of the meal.

"No one wants your 'thou shalt not' teachings here, Mary," she added vehemently.

Lydia giggled. "And anyway, the only reason you would want to share with the rest of us, Mary," she said, looking at me with twinkling, malicious eyes, "is because you don't wear anything even remotely attractive. Not that it would make you look any the better for doing so."

"Then it's just as well I have no care for my appearance," I replied hotly.

"A thoughtless remark," Jane chided, radiating beauty this morning as on all others.

"Beauty is indeed a virtue unappre—" Mr. Collins began.

Lydia snorted, interrupting our guest. "There's no need to declare the obvious to us, Mary," she said, wet crumbs of plum cake dropping from her mouth. Considering her late rejoinder a very witty one, she burst into a self-congratulatory fit of laughter, joined soon after by her Kitty, while Lizzy and Jane exchanged looks across the table. The laughter would have continued for some time more if Papa hadn't cleared his throat and made his usual complaint about having fathered three of the silliest girls in England.

"I wouldn't consider myself silly, Papa," I said petulantly, near tears myself.

"No, I daresay you wouldn't, my dear," he answered and, catching the eye of his favorite, gave her a small, appreciative smile.

KITTY WAS STILL in a sour mood after breakfast. Doubtless she would have recovered sooner had Lydia decided to wear to Meryton any other bonnet than the one that rested at the very heart of their dispute. But discretion had never been Lydia's strength, and she pranced prettily up and down the vestibule, waiting for her sisters and Mr. Collins.

"Have a good walk," I called out from the pianoforte, where I was practicing my scales.

"We'll say hi to the officers for you, Mary," Lydia snickered, popping her head in, "and ask Denny, your dashing lieutenant friend, if he thought about you at all while he was in London."

"I wish you wouldn't," I replied. "I'm sure Mr. Denny forgot about me as soon as you introduced us. It was over a fortnight ago."

Kitty crossed the room and observed my fingerwork from over my shoulder. "I really don't know why you bother, Mary," she sulked as I continued to play. "You're such an awful musician. Everyone hates it when you stand up with your music at parties."

My fingers punched the keys. I imagined they were Kitty's teeth and smiled to myself.

"Why are you smiling?" Kitty said, her voice and temper rising. "I hope you don't think it's funny. It's not funny, you know. It's embarrassing the way you always parade yourself in public with your quotes and your sheet music, as if you play any better than the rest of us."

I stopped. These were not new insults, and over time, I'd grown accustomed to them. Almost as soon as I'd learned my first scale, I'd known that I would never become a great proficient at any instrument, bereft, as I was, of both natural talent and formal instruction. But it would have been a poor excuse to give up an exercise which I enjoyed solely because I was not gifted at it. How, too, could I abandon one of the only devices, within my power, of causing headache and strife among my younger sisters?

Turning towards Kitty, I observed that Mr. Collins had joined Lydia in the hall and that the two were watching us like spectators at a gladiator pit. But I wouldn't be the tiger.

"Kitty," I said, shutting my eyes and exhaling. "I know you're upset about your bonnet, but it won't help to be angry at me. You had much better go with your sisters and Mr. Collins to Meryton and meet some officers and leave me to my practicing."

"Don't tell me what to do," Kitty snapped. "You're always taking Lydia's side. All that talk at breakfast about sisterhood, which is just nonsense. That bonnet was mine. I'd bought it with my pocket money, and Lydia ruined it. She had no right."

"Fine, Kitty. Whatever you say."

"And I meant what I said about your disastrous playing. No one will say it to your face, of course, but everyone thinks the same thing." Leaning forward, she removed the sheet music I'd placed on the rack earlier that morning. It was a new Irish air I hoped to learn by the next ball.

"What's this?" she asked.

"One of Thomas Moore's *Irish Melodies*. I copied it from Aunt Philips."

The pages crinkled in her hands. She frowned as she scanned the lines of inky notes and unevenly drawn bars, listening for the song that wouldn't materialize in her head.

"Careful, Kitty," I said. "You'll smear the—" But it was too late. In her rage, her fingers worked faster than scissors. I could only watch as pieces of "The Last Rose of Summer" scattered like a shower of black-and-white petals over the piano bench and carpet, taking with it hours spent meticulously copying every musical notation by hand. I bent to gather the fragments while Kitty stalked away, rejoining Lydia and Mr. Collins in the hall. Mr. Collins, standing a little apart from Kitty, lest she should turn on him as well, asked how far they would have to walk to reach Meryton, and Lydia, having made the journey over a dozen times since the militia's arrival, answered that the distance was no more than a mile. This seemed the extent to which any civil dialogue could pass between them, so it was to everyone's relief when Jane and Lizzy made their entrance from upstairs, a few moments later, with many breathless apologies.

The whole party being assembled, they departed from Longbourn without any further delay, and I promptly resumed my practicing. As I breezed through a few Scottish ditties I knew by heart, my eye caught sight of the ravaged song, which, having no better place to put the pieces before throwing them out, I'd uselessly restored to the music rack in a small pile.

A restlessness came over me, and I no longer heard the melody my hands mechanically constructed. In its place, I recalled a voice— a male voice—that some weeks ago had addressed itself to me out-side the milliner's shop in Meryton on one of the rare occasions when I'd agreed to accompany Lydia and Kitty on their walk. "De-lighted to make your acquaintance," Mr. Denny had said as I curt-sied, and our eyes met briefly, disinterestedly, before turning to objects of more amusement: for me, a pile of excrement left in the middle of the road by some passing horse; for him, the youngest Miss Bennet, all smiles and good humor where officers were con-cerned. He had a handsome face framed by thick sideburns and a full head of rich, chestnut-colored hair, which I imagined many women would have liked to comb their fingers through, if modesty permitted. Our group walked for some time together, Lydia whis-pering in Mr. Denny's ear, Kitty shooting jealous looks that the other ignored or failed to register. I recalled Lydia's introduction, spoken in the pleasing, coquettish tones she'd already mastered at her young age. "And here is Mary," she had said, giggling, "who Kitty and I practically had to drag from Longbourn just to meet you and who, you'll remember, I told you all about before now." *And pray, what did you tell him all about?* I wondered. *What could you pos-sibly know about me that would be true?*

I imagined how very different I might have felt that afternoon had he not looked away, had I held his gaze for a few moments lon-ger than might have been considered proper between a man and a woman who had just met. In my mind, I composed the beautiful words he'd say. *You're unlike anyone I've ever known,* he'd stammer, holding me at arm's length with the gaze of a madman. *You have enchanted me, enslaved my spirit, and I am no longer the free man I once was. I am now your servant, your plaything to do as you like with my body and my soul, which is no longer God's or the Devil's to have but yours. I love you, Mary Bennet. I love you, so help me God.*

The discord of a wrong key being pressed startled me from my reverie. Fingering a piece of the torn music, I sat for some moments commiserating with myself before turning towards the empty doorway where Lydia's head had earlier protruded. *I'm sure Mr. Denny forgot about me as soon as you introduced us.* Yes, I thought, a familiar numbness taking hold. There would be no love affairs here.

My restless hands soon found their way back to the piano, and the room swelled with the plaintive longing of "Robin Adair." A voice sweeter than my own sang to me from a distant memory some years old when, wandering through the house, I happened upon Sarah standing alone at a window in our drawing room, her small body encased in the pale yellow light of a newly risen sun. *"What's this dull town to me? Robin's not near,"* she had sung, unraveling the old rags she always carried with her for cleaning. *"What was't I wish'd to see? What wish'd to hear? Where's all the joy and mirth, made this town a heaven on earth? Oh! They're all fled with thee, Robin Adair."*

When I opened my mouth to sing now, the words came out dry and uninspired, and try as I might, I couldn't reproduce the unstudied emotion that had filled the voice of our lovelorn housemaid. I finished the rest of the song in silence, recalling how the year of my memory, Papa had dismissed a young footman for reasons I'd never learned. For a whole week afterwards, I hadn't seen or heard anything of Sarah, until the morning she surfaced in the drawing room with her song. *Yet him I lov'd so well, still in my heart shall dwell. Oh! I can ne'er forget Robin Adair.*

But I had had enough of playing songs I did not in my heart feel. Out of the corner of my eye, I spotted the ornately bound volume which enclosed the Reverend James Fordyce's *Sermons to Young*

Women. I admit I possessed a low opinion of the work. Intellectual welfare was a concept quite beyond our mother's understanding, and none of us had been brought up under the watchful instruction of a governess, our father being both too poor and too involved in his own studies to be anything but the most liberal-minded of parents. The effect of his and Mama's apathy was that I owed my education largely to reading whatever books I wanted to. Over the course of nineteen years, their diffidence had given me ample opportunity to consume all the plays by our revered Bard, the great poems and epics of antiquity, manuscripts of human anatomy and natural science, and much more scandalous fare in the form of novels borrowed from the circulating library, which, luckily for me, Papa enjoyed with as much relish as I. But budding admiration will do strange things to one's taste, and I found myself spending the rest of the afternoon in the company of Mr. Fordyce, committing what I could to memory in the event that an excerpt might prove useful the next time Mr. Collins and I spoke.

CHAPTER 4

$\mathcal{TOG}$

$\mathbf{M}$r. Collins and my sisters returned to Longbourn in time for dinner. Judging from the animated chatter, the day had not been without its share of thrills. Every member of the merry party had his or her own opinion of the people they had met and the events that had taken place, and each was quite determined to share a complete narrative of their adventures with those who hadn't been fortunate enough to go. Over the space of the next half hour, there wasn't a moment of peace or quiet to be had in the dining room. Kitty and Lydia enthusiastically apprised Mama of the new acquaintance they had made in Meryton, one Mr. George Wickham, who had a lieutenant's commission in the militia and who was the most handsome man either had ever laid eyes on and not even in his regimentals, if it could be believed! Even Lizzy conceded he was handsome, though when Jane was asked what she thought of their new friend, she added that she still preferred Mr. Bingley.

It was impossible to pass a whole day without being reminded of that gentleman, who had only a month ago entered the neighborhood. Indeed, I could not sit down to breakfast even once without Mama inquiring if Jane had received any new letters from Mr. Charles Bingley or his sisters. And Mr. Bingley's name could not be mentioned without also bringing into the conversation that of his friend Mr. Fitzwilliam Darcy. Mr. Bingley had hired Netherfield Park, a very grand estate not far from Longbourn. He was twenty-two, unmarried, and his late father, though he'd made his fortune in trade, had left him close to a hundred thousand pounds to be distributed in his lifetime. His annual income was five thousand pounds a year, a sum amply sufficient for the keeping of a large staff and other necessities which it behooved every wealthy gentleman of leisure to maintain, and it was a sum, too, infinitely more promising than my own father's meager income of two thousand pounds a year. Mr. Bingley was universally considered handsome, with the bright, rosy complexion acquired from excessive horse riding and dancing, and an even more attractive personality that instantly commended him to all the families of the neighborhood. His unexpected entry into country society had stirred matrimonial hopes in more than one maternal breast, and in consequence, Mr. Bingley received no shortage of dinner invitations; even personal deliveries of mince pies and rum cakes were considered fair game among those who vied more vigorously for his attention and favor. What a disappointment it had been to those overzealous mothers when, within the first hour of his arrival at the Meryton assembly, he had singled Jane out as his equal in good looks and charm, dancing no less than two times with her and doing very little to conceal his preferment of my sister's company.

Myself, I thought Mr. Bingley resembled the cherubs of Italian paintings who nestled in clouds and tumbled over rainbows. He was always in good humor, and though he was very thin, with a figure that had not yet matured out of the awkwardness of adolescence, the muscles in his face must have been exceptionally well developed. I say this because he could never stop smiling, not even while he ate or talked or sang, which he sometimes did at parties, in fits of happiness. I much preferred his friend Mr. Darcy, who resembled the melancholy princes I envisioned every night before falling asleep, and indeed, it became my custom after I had made his acquaintance to replace the blurry faces of my Hamlet-inspired heroes with his own.

But Mr. Darcy, though he had twice Bingley's annual income and lived in the grandest house in Derbyshire, was hated by nearly everyone, particularly our Lizzy, for he was overheard at the Meryton assembly remarking that my sister was not handsome enough to dance with. It was unfortunate for Mr. Darcy that he had not been gifted with the practical talent, exceptionally useful in society, of being able to conceal from his face what he felt in his heart. He frowned often and had the repellent habit of grinding his teeth whenever a courageous mother with a single daughter attempted to endear herself to him. His other crimes, no less remarkable, were that he fraternized exclusively among members of his own party at balls and, unlike his more winsome friend, refused to dance every dance.

But I did not find him disagreeable, even if he had injured poor Lizzy's pride. The air in that awful hall had been too warm that night, and there was no square of ground on which to stand without running the risk of being trampled upon by a dancing couple. When the fourth dance of the evening was underway, I stepped out to catch my breath and fan my face with a pair of gloves.

Behind me, someone coughed, and I turned.

"Excuse me," Mr. Darcy muttered, addressing his speech to his finely polished shoes. He had gone a funny color and was wiping his face with a handkerchief. "It's very hot in there."

"Yes, it is," I replied. At the sight of him, the warmth returned to my cheeks. When he didn't say anything, I added, "But your friend doesn't seem to mind. He hasn't yet sat through a single dance."

"Oh, Bingley—he would still be dancing if the entire hall collapsed this very moment. Nothing will deter *him* from having a good time." Then, taking a closer look at me, he added, narrowing his eyes, "You're one of the Bennet girls, aren't you? We were introduced earlier. Kitty, I think it was."

"Mary," I corrected. "Kitty's my younger sister."

"I'm sorry. I've been introduced to so many women in the last half hour, and all their faces are beginning to look very much alike."

"And you're Mr. Darcy," I pronounced, "for whom half the population of Meryton has come in the hopes of attaining an introduction."

"I am not fond of balls," he said, and in his voice there was true exhaustion.

"Neither am I."

"All that skipping . . ." he complained, shaking his head.

"And turning . . ." I offered.

"And jumping."

"More like hopping, really," I said with a sigh.

"As if dancing were not unpleasant enough, sometimes one's partner expects to be engaged in conversation."

"I've personally never understood that custom—to pass the time of day while changing hands or clapping a beat. It is not practical and, I would venture to say, even inconsiderate, if your partner is already out of breath."

"In my experience," Mr. Darcy puffed, smoothing the front of his waistcoat, "I've found that the manner of people who attend such occasions can make a great difference in the enjoyment of the event."

The insult of his comment did not escape me, and feeling the need to defend the rural charms of my little town, I said, "To be sure, in London, the women may wear finer gowns, and the rooms may be much grander in scale. But I have yet to hear of any ball which did not feature dancing, whether in the country or otherwise. And if one is displeased with the general theme of balls, then it would follow that no variation could render them favorable."

Perhaps it was my own wishful thinking, but I thought I discerned the faintest glint of a smile pulling at the corners of that distinguished gentleman's mouth before the features restored them-selves to their former solemnity. When neither of us spoke again, he kicked a loose pebble at his foot, and we listened to the *clack-clack-clack* of the stone as it skidded away into the dark.

"I sometimes think of sneaking off during a party and going to play a game of billiards on my own," he suddenly said. Then, with-out any prompting, he added, "Something has been weighing on my conscience, Miss Bennet. I'm afraid I've offended your sister. Not Kitty, I don't think—I mean the tall one wearing yellow with large eyes. It was a thoughtless remark and meant only for Bingley to hear, though I know that is no excuse. But he would keep pestering me to dance and to socialize among complete strangers, and it was the only thing I could come up with to convince him to leave me alone."

Now it was my turn to smile. "Yes, I think your comment will provide enough fodder to last all the women of Meryton through both this evening and the next. Lizzy is well liked by everyone, and I fear public opinion will be against you."

"Do you think I should ask her to dance with me—just in order to make amends?" he inquired.

"I would advise against it, Mr. Darcy," I replied, "at least for this assembly. The insult has been paid; let her revel, for the time being, in the sympathy and kind attentions of her friends, and you may ask her at the next gathering. There is nothing a woman likes so much as a change of heart."

Again, he smiled briefly. I felt him turn towards me and glance over my simple dress, a pale blue muslin whose sleeves had become frayed from excessive wear and washing.

"Though we are agreed that dancing is the most unpleasant of pastimes," he began to say, hesitating, "if the elder Miss Bennet will not dance with me this evening, then may I propose—"

Whatever he intended to propose, he had no time to finish his thought, for emerging from the doorway at that moment was his friend's unmarried and extremely eligible sister, Miss Caroline Bingley, whose feet itched to dance a Scotch reel.

"Thank you for a most enjoyable conversation, Miss Bennet," he said, bowing to me before taking his leave, and I stared after him until he and the elegant specimen disappeared from view.

For the rest of the evening, though I did not stand up once to dance, I couldn't resist smiling whenever I considered my brief exchange with that most illustrious of personages, Mr. Fitzwilliam Darcy. And none of my sisters' needling, not even Jane's or Lizzy's, could wrest the truth of my good humor from me, which I claimed was entirely owing to the large spread of excellent fruit and cheese provided at the assembly.

These cheerful reminiscences, however, were soon interrupted by the high, singsong pitch of my younger sister's effusions on Lieutenant George Wickham, the Adonis of Great Britain's indomitable military, and I returned my attention to the Longbourn dinner table.

"Did you notice, Lizzy, the way he knotted his cravat?" Kitty questioned from my elbow.

"Or how admirably tall he was?" Lydia pressed, nearly upsetting her glass of wine.

"And the fashionable cut of his coat?" Kitty squealed.

"Well, no," Lizzy said, and the corners of her mouth twitched, a giveaway to those who knew her well that she was fibbing. "But I did find admirable the way in which he excused himself when our aunt invited him to tea. That was very well done, I thought."

Upon the mention of Mrs. Philips, Mr. Collins became excitable once more and was eager to name in front of his host the many merits of that lady's character, foremost of which had been her exceptionally gracious treatment of himself. "She is all ease and good humor," Mr. Collins said, sighing at the remembrance, "with an elegance of speech and movement so unstudied and natural. And though she did not know me before today, she at once entreated that

I should be in attendance at the gathering she is hosting tomorrow night and which she confessed would be woefully incomplete without my presence. 'Mr. Collins,' she said to me, 'our little affair would hardly be worth having if you did not grace it with your own person, and it would make such a difference to me if you deigned to join us for some cards and dinner.' I left her at once in no doubt of my answer and replied, I hope, with equal civility of address, that not only would I be present at what promised to be a very enjoyable party but also that I would happily satisfy her request of making up the fourth person at whist, though I myself am unfamiliar with the game."

Knowing firsthand how wearing my aunt's personality could be, I thought this exceptionally generous of Mr. Collins and was about to tell him so when Mama pronounced her agreement that her sister was the most genteel and well-liked of women. She considered it her duty, however, to warn him that the provisions of *their* dinner table were not anything like what her guest may have become used to at Longbourn, owing largely to the stinginess in housekeeping which Aunt Philips had inherited from their mother, God rest her soul, and to which failing she herself had thankfully never been disposed. (Papa coughed gently at this remark.)

The meal concluded with a return to the topic that had aroused and livened the hearts of nearly all the women sitting to dinner.

"I'm sure he looked quite directly at me no less than three times," Lydia murmured thoughtfully, cutting her beef without eating it.

"Well, well! Three times!" I cried. "Let the wedding bells ring, Lydia! Do!"

"They'd sooner ring for Lydia than for you, Mary," Kitty said, her mouth full of food.

"I should like to see Mr. Wickham fall for our Mary," Papa added, winking at Lizzy. "I daresay it would put out all the women of Hertfordshire to witness such a sight. Mary, how should you like to be a model to other young women by marrying a handsome lieutenant?"

"No one would dance at balls," Lizzy teased.

"And they'd dress very plain and ruin their eyes with reading," Kitty joined in.

"What a strange formula you propose for finding a husband," Jane commented abstractly.

"But it is Mary's way of finding a husband," Lizzy said, smiling.

"Which means, of course, that she will never have one," Mama sighed, whereupon I cried aloud to God and asked Him to deliver me from this clucking, ridiculous brood of hens.

"Amen," Mr. Collins mouthed across the table to me, and we exchanged a brief smile before returning to our food.

In transitioning to the drawing room after dinner, our guest seemed to have something on his mind and could not be prevailed upon to read to us, to avenge his losses at backgammon with Lizzy, or to make any kind of answer when Lydia facetiously asked whether he thought a red coat or a blue one would suit Mr. Wickham best. Begging his hosts' pardon, he suddenly stood, said he had one or two letters to write that had hitherto slipped his mind, and asked if he could be pardoned from the evening's revelry to return to his room. Papa made the usual, polite show of protesting before finally relenting to his guest's wishes, and Mr. Collins departed from the drawing room, issuing many more variations of apology as he left.

"Well!" Mama cried as soon as she deemed it safe. "What do you make of that, Mr. Bennet?"

"That he is a cleverer man than I thought," Mr. Bennet replied. "I, too, have often wished to stand up and leave the room when you and the girls have got your heads into something silly."

"Oh, but Mr. Wickham isn't silly," Lydia said on behalf of her new favorite. "Ask Lizzy or Jane. I daresay they would sing his praises, too. Lizzy nearly fainted every time Mr. Wickham so much as glanced in her direction."

Lizzy reddened. "I'm sure I did nothing of the kind," she said, shooting a hard look at Lydia, "and I'll thank you not to let your imagination run away with you where I'm concerned."

Lydia only laughed. "You see? I told you it was so," she answered cheerfully and turned to me. "Mary might have fallen in love with Mr. Wickham, too, if she had come with us today," she continued, swinging her feet up on a nearby stool. "The sight of him in regimentals may suffice to pull even your eyes out of a book for five whole minutes, Mary."

"Or away from the piano," Kitty added.

I wrinkled my nose and put down the copy of Fordyce's *Sermons* I'd endeavored to continue reading in their company. I could not reasonably entertain that there was anything truly singular in this Mr. Wickham to set him apart from all the other officers Lydia and Kitty had been in the habit of falling in and out of love with. "Colonel Forster's regiment isn't quartered here just to provide amusement for all the unmarried women in the neighborhood. You and Kitty seem to forget, there's been a war going on with France for several years now."

"It's just like you, Mary, to cast a shadow over everything that is delightful," Lydia said, pouting. With a sigh, she stretched her arms, then balanced a cushion on her head for some seconds before tossing it over the back of the settee. "Lord, I'm so bored—how dull all of you are. Since Mr. Collins has skipped off to bed, why don't you read something to entertain us, Mary? What book was that you were pretending to read before? If you wouldn't mind taking it up again and reading a passage to us, which you do so well in your schoolmarm sort of way . . ."

I propped an elbow over the book. "It's not a title you would have any interest in, I'm sure. I would have picked up something else, except there was nothing better to read—"

"Don't make me come over there and get it from you," Lydia said, sitting up, intrigued.

"Oh?" I replied nonchalantly, reopening the volume that just minutes ago I'd determined to give up for the evening; I'd forgotten what a Herculean effort had been required to get through it the first time. "I didn't think you or Kitty would want to listen to any more excerpts from Fordyce's *Sermons* after how well it was received last night."

Lydia scowled. "Fordyce's *Sermons*?" she repeated, and Kitty echoed her sister's indignation from her seat at the card table. "Why on earth would you want to pick up *that* awful book again, unless . . ."

"Unless what?" I asked, my face and neck burning.

"Unless you are in love with Mr. Collins, of course!" Lydia barely managed to get the words out before her whole body convulsed with violent laughter, as though she were in the grips of a seizure. She rolled off the settee, kicked her legs gleefully in the air, and would have likely performed more acrobatics to express her pleasure had Papa not raised his voice and demanded that she at once restore herself to a proper and upright position.

"You know, I was wondering why anyone would look at an unattractive man so much, unless she were in love with him," Lydia remarked thoughtfully from the carpet. She cocked her head at me the way birds do when they have spotted something unfamiliar that may yet be edible.

"I don't know what you're talking about, you stupid girl," I retorted.

"No name-calling, Mary," Mama chided.

"Goodness knows you're welcome to him," Lydia said, installing herself in a chair. "Certainly no one else will have him, even if he does take his meals with that pompous Lady Something-or-other, as we are reminded of daily."

"Mr. Collins's connection with Lady Catherine may not mean anything to you, Lydia," Lizzy said, "but many others would consider it a great advantage and proof of his respectability."

"It's very well that *you* should say so, Lizzy," Lydia replied, practically glowing with smugness, "as I have it on good authority that Mr. Collins likes you best of everyone."

Lizzy's face turned the peculiar shade of unripe tomatoes. The idea of being distinguished among her family for the poor reward of Mr. Collins's affections was evidently repellent to her, and so long as the expression of her emotion was not abusive to others, my sister had never seen reason to conceal her true feelings from the world. She professed she had done nothing to encourage Mr. Collins's regard for her, had, moreover, neither received nor detected any special attention from those quarters, and begged Lydia to learn the difference between the wild conceptions of her fantasies and the banal realities that encompassed everyday life. Lydia, however, would not be so easily put off. She continued to smile at the priceless dramas she had unearthed, while Kitty watched her in awe.

"You can deny it all you like, Lizzy," Lydia continued. "I heard it myself. I was listening at the door of the breakfast room—"

"Lydia, what did I tell you about listening in on other people's conversations?" Jane said.

"I was listening at the door of the breakfast room," Lydia repeated, ignoring Jane, "and I heard Mr. Collins tell Mama, though not in such simple language, that he wanted to marry one of us. That's the errand, if you like, that Lady Catherine has sent him on in coming here. At first, he liked Jane, but Mama told him Jane was as good as married, what with Mr. Bingley being in love with her, and then Mr. Collins said he wouldn't mind settling for Lizzy, who, he said, was almost as pleasant to look at as Jane, even if she wasn't as pretty or elegant."

"Lydia!" Jane and Lizzy cried together from their corner.

"Lydia, dear, do be quiet," Mrs. Bennet said, stepping in at last. Making as if to busy herself with the primping of an old cushion, she added, "But since Lydia has put us on the subject, I do hope that whatever attentions Mr. Collins condescends to show any of you will be accepted and reciprocated with the utmost civility and gratitude. I have welcomed his advances on this front on behalf of everyone in the family except Jane. The reason for this should be self-evident." Setting down the pillow, she smiled at Jane, though her meaning had already been well comprehended by all of us. She alluded, of course, to the expectation that Jane would soon be married to our distinguished neighbor of five thousand pounds per annum. If it were not for Mr. Bingley and his recent attentions to the eldest Miss Bennet, I fear Jane would have been offered as the choicest of sacrificial lambs for the preservation of our entailed estate; the task of saving her mother and four sisters from destitution would have fallen squarely on her delicate and well-shaped shoulders.

"There, Mary," Lydia said, twisting a lock of hair around her finger. "You will have your chance with Mr. Collins after all. Doesn't that make you happy?"

I said nothing. Taking my silence for submission, she soon moved on to the equally inane diversion of asking Lizzy and Jane whether they thought she or Kitty would look better on George Wickham's arm once he was dressed in regimentals. This subject being exhausted after a quarter of an hour's heated discussion, everyone professed their desire to go to bed, and it was not long before I entered the welcome seclusion of my room and undressed in the cool and unseeing dark.

That night, I recalled various instances of praise from respectable gentlemen who, in viewing all five of us sitting carefully arranged across settees and chairs, would exclaim that we were the handsomest women they had ever seen and that they felt quite overwhelmed by the concentration of so much beauty in a space as small as our drawing room. Decorum demanded that they address their compliments to all of us, but I have always known better. To pretend otherwise would be laughable—the beggar playing the part of the king. I have, as a result of the episodes already mentioned, refrained from showing much emotion in public. I prefer that those who do not know me should consider me aloof rather than believe I am invested in concerns which will always be the birthright of the attractive, the titled, or the wealthy. It is a small consolation for a stranger to think that I don't dance because I do not wish to, not because no man in the room will ask me. And there is, of course, a reason that people will not generally discuss the marriage prospects of an ugly woman. This reason, I imagine, is not so very different from why we do not ask a fat man how many helpings he must eat before his stomach feels full or why we take pains to avoid the subject of age to a woman who has spots on her hands and whiskers on her chin.

In truth, not all five of us combined could have equaled the worth produced by a single son, had he ever been born, and the daily reminder of my father's mortality and of Longbourn's entailment had often compelled me to revisit the poor contribution I made to my family in my birth and subsequent survival.

For several hours that night, I could not sleep. As soon as I shut my eyes, I felt the fresh cut of Lydia's teasing, sharp as the first, ravenous bite into an apple. *You will have your chance with Mr. Collins after all. Doesn't that make you happy?* I saw Jane's face, a ghostly apparition taunting me with its loveliness. I saw Papa, the little smiles he had exchanged with Lizzy and Lizzy alone over dinner. The sheets were damp by the time my body gave in to its exhaustion. Outside, the first light of dawn glowed like pale fire behind threadbare clouds. I dreamed I had curled my body into Mr. Collins's black cloak and that his delicate chin rested on the very top of my skull. I'd whispered, "Save me" into the cavity of his ear, which in my dreams was as smooth and luminescent as the inside of a seashell, and from the opaque hollow his voice had answered in dulcet tones: "I will."

The arrival of Mr. Collins, though initially dreaded by Mama, who'd determined to thoroughly dislike the man on behalf of us poor and unfortunate females, had conversely been anticipated to some small degree by our father, who, in having every expectation of finding his nephew an individual of weak understanding and meager scholarship, had hoped to derive some amusement from his stay at Longbourn. Soon after Mr. Collins's arrival, however, Papa began to despair of his original assurance of pleasure, and Mama, who'd always been inclined to think things settled at the very first indication of victory, joyously admitted to herself the probable hope that Longbourn would, after all, remain the property of at least one of her daughters, even after our father's passing, by the happy means of marriage. And what with Mr. Bingley's continuing attentions towards Jane, Mama was in extraordinarily bright spirits on the third day of Mr. Collins's stay, for she had every reason to be confident in the prospect of marrying off at least one of her children before the conclusion of the year and, with any luck, a second by the beginning of the next.

As for Papa, I'm sure that Mr. Collins hadn't intended any offense in following his host to the library after both breakfast and lunch and enthralling my father with firsthand accounts of the grandeur of Rosings. He could not have known the insult he paid Mr.

Bennet in overtaking his second-best armchair and clumsily handling the largest and heaviest tome that Longbourn's small library offered. According to my father, our cousin made a truly convincing pretense of studying this thousand-page historical treatise and even recited out loud passages that, he claimed, resonated with the sensitive chords of his literary soul. Upon Mr. Collins's insistence that he would complete the entire history of the rise and fall of the Roman Empire before his departure from Longbourn next Saturday, Papa had no recourse left but to remain in his bedroom with enough books to last out most of his waking hours.

For me, Mr. Collins remained a diverting and welcome curiosity. I was able to extract some comfort in the discovery of a character who seemed relegated, like myself, to living as an outsider.

It was in a scholarly attitude that I found Mr. Collins in Papa's library a second time, with the aforementioned title draped like an unwieldy blanket across his lap. Hunched over the yellowing pages, he appeared to be studying for some duration a single sentence and, on closer inspection, a single word, for his index finger remained motionless, until his head fell so much forward that he tumbled out of his seat, and I realized from his dazed expression that he must have been asleep for some time. Determined to keep from laughing, I committed myself at once to helping Mr. Collins up from the carpet, and with a grateful if not somewhat abashed acknowledgment of my assistance, he asked if I wouldn't take a seat and hear the impressive progress he'd been making with the book.

"I was just reflecting," Mr. Collins began, and the tip of his index finger alighted gently across the rounded point of his chin, "on the number of military highways which stemmed from Rome at its peak—no less than twenty-nine, if it can be believed, and tens of thousands of miles of these roads were said to be stone-paved, some of which to this day remain intact."

I remarked that this was indeed incredible, and Mr. Collins continued with renewed confidence: "Yes, I flatter myself in being a great student of history, and in this, Lady Catherine and I are once more perfectly aligned in our interests, for she is a firm believer that one should be able to extract from the historical annals lessons both moral and political to be applied to the rigors of daily life. Observe, for instance, the decadence of the French philosophers, and the unthinkable chaos which the indulgence of those persons ultimately led to."

I supposed what he said was true, and seeing that I comprehended his meaning, he began to stare at me with a certain thoughtfulness. I returned his look with curiosity, and in observing that I had become aware of him, he promptly turned away and made as if to continue reading his book, his eyes flitting from one corner of the page to another like a pair of unsettled flies. "I find it fascinating," he continued in a measured voice, "that where Caesar and Caligula had both failed in their conquest of Britain, a half-deaf man with a limp should succeed instead . . . and riding on an elephant, too! How extraordinary, wouldn't you agree?"

"Claudius," I said.

"Yes," Mr. Collins replied, his cheeks flushing. He gripped the edges of his book and, raising his head to peer at me again, said suddenly, "I'm afraid my young cousins don't think very much of me, do they? You may be honest with me."

I could barely keep from rolling my eyes. "Lydia and Kitty see, hear, and know nothing except the comings and goings of the officers," I said. "For my part and for my family's, I am certainly sorry for their behavior, but rest assured it is no poor reflection of you. They would not see a perfectly sensible man standing in front of them, if he were not also dressed in regimentals with his sword drawn."

"I don't mean just your two younger sisters," Mr. Collins said, hesitating. "I'm certain I have caught my cousin Elizabeth laughing at me on at least two separate occasions at the dinner table."

I sensed here a fine opportunity to put Mr. Collins off the idea of marriage to my sister, if indeed he had entertained such a notion in the first place. "Lizzy can be a little facetious at times," I began carefully, not wishing to bungle my chance, "but I'm sure she did not mean to laugh at you. I feel obliged to tell you, however, that she takes a great deal after my father, whose continued indulgence has encouraged a bit of a stubborn streak. This may also explain her penchant for being less inclined to listen to the advice of others, since she has always possessed a confident assurance of her own mind." I hastily added, feeling a flash of guilt, "Though Lizzy is wonderfully adept in all manner of debate, being wittier and quicker on her feet than the rest of us."

"Well!" Mr. Collins cried. To my satisfaction, he appeared somewhat shocked at this revelation. "Though I am grieved to hear this, I cannot but feel sorry, too, for I may tell you in all sincerity that Lady Catherine's suggestions on a wide range of affairs, both in the running of domestic households and in the dealings of entire countries, have been sought after on numerous occasions by her friends and that she, depending on the season, is sometimes so much in demand that I have had to remind her ladyship not to be too overwrought by the need society has of her. I feel sorry for anyone who cannot think fit to benefit from her wisdom."

"Lady Catherine seems an extraordinary person by your description," I commented, grateful for any opening to steer the conversation away from Lizzy and further endear myself to him. "One point, which I've always been curious to learn, Mr. Collins, is how you made her acquaintance."

I had assumed that even the smallest mention of his benefactress would have rendered any further incentive for conversation wholly unnecessary, so I was surprised when Mr. Collins did not immediately answer. Instead, he leaned his diminutive body deeper against the back of his chair and seemed to consider how to reply. The several seconds of silence generated enough discomfort that I felt compelled to apologize for creating any offense by my question, however involuntarily. In hearing my voice, he started a little in his seat and waved my concerns away with one hand while the other gripped the arm of the chair. He then shrugged and said he had not recalled the instance of their first and most fortuitous meeting for some time now and that though it was a pleasant memory, the events preceding it remained considerably less agreeable for him to remember.

"I'd like to tell you the story," he began, and in his voice, there was an uncharacteristically solemn tone, "though I'd consider it a great favor if you didn't share what I am about to say with anyone else, not even with your own sisters."

I quickly assured him of my discretion, and staring into the flames of the library's hearth, he continued: "My father, who you may have heard tell of from your own father, was an illiterate and miserly man given to drink, and if I'd been so unlucky as to remain under his guidance, I shudder to think where I'd be now. By luck, a relation of mine on my mother's side who visited on the unhappy occasion of her passing took pity on my situation and, observing quickly that should I stay forever with my father I would suffer greatly, decided to bestow upon me some money and secured, through a connection of his, entrance for me into one of the universities. Having no few children of his own, he could not give me as much money as he wished, but he was convinced by what he had seen of me that I would profit by a good education. Shortly after our first few meetings, my relation died—he'd been ill for some time with a poor heart, and I am unashamed to say that I grieved his death with more sincerity and more tears than ever I did for my own father when he died, God rest his soul. Though what he had parted with in his lifetime was already mine and could not be withdrawn from my possession, I was informed by the remaining members of his family, in no uncertain terms, that I should expect no more gifts from *them* and that I'd gained too much already by his kindness and charity. The money he'd given me—amounting to some two hundred pounds—as great a sum as others might consider it, given our brief acquaintance, was by no means sufficient to pay my way through university, but in writing a letter to the connection of my relation's at the college, I was happily informed that my admission still stood. I would enter that most revered institution as a student of, as it was described to me in the letter, 'comparatively modest ranking,' that is, as a servitor, who would receive, I was told, as rigorous and comprehensive an education as any of his classmates but must work some light tasks in addition to his studies to pay for his room and board and instruction."

I knew that my uncle, Mr. Collins's father, had died only the previous year. Owing to the rift which existed between them, Papa never spoke of his younger brother, though I'd heard from Mama that he was a brutal man and had beaten his wife so terribly on one occasion as to induce a miscarriage. Two of my uncle's children had died in their infancy; I remember it clearly because Mama had said it was a blessing, and in my innocence at the time, I couldn't understand how the death of babes could be termed anything but a tragedy. From my seat, I observed Mr. Collins's hands, the way they alighted upon his forehead to massage the corners at right angles. They were as fine as a musician's hands, his fingers like delicate white reeds tinged at the ends with soft dashes of pink.

He wetted his lips before continuing. "The prospect of light labor didn't concern me, as I'd been accustomed for most of my life to working hard and learning with few resources at my disposal. Soon after my arrival, I was assigned to wait upon a group of four students of higher ranking, known as noblemen commoners, to shine their shoes and make their beds, to sweep their rooms, to run menial errands for them, and to serve them as though they were my lords and masters and I'd entered not an institution of higher learning as a student but a private estate as a housekeeper or butler. I received no wages for my services and slept with the other servitors in a dirty room that was too hot in the summer and too cold in the winter. Two of the four men I looked after, one the second son of an earl and the other the eldest son of a baroness, gave me their assignments to complete while they whored and drank and gambled with their families' money. And it was in this way, not by attending lectures, that I received the vast part of my education. These men also entrusted me with their secrets and various tales of indiscretions and, provided no one of any importance or rank was near enough to see, would often enter into conversation with me so that I naïvely came to believe they considered me less a servant than a true friend."

I listened to his every word, enthralled. It was as though the narrator of one of my novels had materialized in flesh and blood from the pages and was speaking exclusively to me—his sole reader and confidante. Before my eyes, a physical transformation seemed to occur. His figure, previously small and prancing, became enlarged by the glow of the fire. The gravity of his voice, coupled with his eloquence, rendered him nearly handsome. His brow darkened, as the complexions of all heroes were wont to do before the hour of their greatest trials, and my heart quickened.

"I learned otherwise one evening approaching the conclusion of my second year," Mr. Collins continued. "The two men I mentioned—Master Spencer and Master Randolph, I called them— came to me very late in the night and told me that in return for the services and loyalty I'd paid them, they would invite me to a private costume ball to be hosted in one of the college's dining rooms. I felt bound to tell them, of course, that I did not possess a costume, nor did I have money to commission one, and, smiling, they said they would purchase one expressly for me, along with shoes and a wig, so that I did not have to worry about my clothes. They said that as my face would be heavily made up, no one would know a servitor had entered their ranks and that they would vouch for me by telling everyone I was a visiting relation."

"And do you mean to say you believed them?" I asked, incredulous.

"Not entirely," he replied, and he shielded one half of his face, as though an invisible hand had struck him. "My friends, for that is what I considered them, brought me my costume a few days later. As soon as I saw the nature of the garment and the accessories they'd obtained, I confess I would have gladly forgone the honor of their invitation, though by then it was too late. I was to dress as a French nobleman, and a more exaggerated interpretation of that character could not be found in the best satirical cartoons of the day. They had prepared for me a long white wig and silk stockings and buckled shoes and helped me to draw several large moles on my powdered face, which, they said, would prevent anyone from recognizing me and add some humorous authenticity to my appearance. Observing me fully dressed, they left me with many compliments and went to go prepare themselves. Neither of them would reveal what their own costumes were, but they assured me that they would appear just as foolish as I did and that I wouldn't be able to keep from laughing when I saw them. Shortly before the party, a letter appeared under my door, instructing me to meet Master Spencer and Master Randolph at the entrance of a certain dining room—you see, previously, we'd agreed to go together. As I'd no wish to keep them waiting, and thinking that something must have happened to prompt them to leave without me, I proceeded at once to the location they'd specified in their letter, with my wig on and my makeup in place, only to discover upon my hurried arrival that everyone had already been seated at the table and that, far from being a costume ball, the affair appeared no more than a typical dinner of several noblemen commoners and a few gentlemen commoners who were lucky enough to be counted among their acquaintance. Neither of my so-called friends were in fancy dress, and on spotting me in the doorway, they clapped their hands, roared as loud as twin lions with laughter, and bid everyone in the room to look at who had come."

"How horrible! How you must have felt!" I cried out, unable to suppress my indignation any longer. Indeed, my pity for him was so great in this moment that if he had asked me then and there to marry him, I might have been prevailed upon to accept his hand.

Turning away from the fire to meet my gaze, Mr. Collins continued: "I wish I could describe to you, dear cousin, how deep and terrible was my mortification, but there are no words. I had no time to consider my friends' betrayal, and being too humiliated to summon even the most primitive faculty of speech, I scarcely heard the sarcastic compliments of the young man who sat at the head of the table and who, when I didn't immediately answer his address to me, bid me sharply to speak up. I later found out that he was the eldest son of a marquis and very soon expected to inherit both his father's estate and title. All my better feelings implored me to run, to leave these dreadful people behind and salvage what little remained of my pride and honor—but something, a small voice barely discernible between the raucous pounding of the table and the wild beating of my heart, froze me to the spot of ground I stood on. Hardly conscious of my own actions, I found myself bowing to this young man and smiling behind a film of tears. I replied in a voice half-breaking that it was very kind of him to admire my costume, which induced, of course, more laughter and applause from the table and pleased both Master Spencer and Master Randolph, who were glad to find me a willing player in their cruel game. As there were eight of them and only one of me, I hadn't the luxury to consider my situation until all four courses were served, the plates and leftovers cleared, and wine poured and poured again for all members of the party. It was well past one in the morning when I returned my wig and costume to their procurers. Finding them alone, I took care not to bring up what had just taken place at dinner and offered no accusations or indications of my disappointment. In a few short words, I expressed my gratitude for their having invited me—nothing overflowing, mind you, for I didn't want to give the impression that I was mocking them—and left.

"Though I could never forget, much less forgive, the trick they played on me, I remained in their good graces for the next two years and was, in this time, appointed by the provost to become a Bible clerk, for which service I received a small annual stipend. My other duties, of cleaning and looking after the rooms of the four men, remained largely unchanged, and it was in this way that I stumbled one evening across an opened letter. The note was from an acquaintance of Master Randolph's who'd set his sights on entering the church, and in it, he mentioned a vacancy at the Hunsford parsonage, near Rosings Park, where a noblewoman and her daughter resided, a Lady Catherine de Bourgh and Miss Anne de Bourgh of extensive property and even greater fortune. As Lady Catherine and her late husband were well acquainted with Master Randolph's family, this acquaintance now begged his friend to put in a good word for him in the attainment of this vacancy. I saw my opportunity and at once acted on it. Losing no time, I spoke with Master Randolph in confidence, and though he was at first enraged by my confession that I'd read his private correspondence, I had only to remind him of one or two indiscretions which he'd divulged to me in the past, before he quickly changed his mind. Taking up his pen, he wrote by my dictation a letter to Lady Catherine on my behalf, which I watched him sign and seal with his signet ring and which I took immediately from him to post. Not long afterwards, he received a short but encouraging reply from that great person, who thanked him for the introduction, and I was promptly summoned to visit Lady Catherine at Rosings Park, where she could ascertain my worthiness for herself. Satisfied by what she saw, she discussed the appointment with her daughter, who echoed her feelings, and I assumed my position as the rector of Hunsford parsonage no less than two months later."

Mr. Collins released a sigh whose heaviness filled the room, and for some moments, both of us sat staring at our feet. I wished desperately for something to say—and, indeed, he seemed to wait for me to make a reply—but my thoughts ran wild, and nothing cohesive emerged. Had my sense of propriety not been so strong, I might have given vent to my admiration and confounded both him and myself in doing so, but, fortunately, I said nothing and offered only the inviting silence of a captivated audience. Turning back to the fire, he closed his book and swept his fingers over the dusty cover, leaving a clean black trail on the leather. He seemed to me a new man; I could look upon him now with full comprehension of his speech and feelings and motivations. Where there'd been from the first a dramatic and exaggerated obsequiousness, even a laughable servility, at any mention of those persons whose private fortunes entitled them to conduct their affairs many levels above the rest of us, I perceived that this flattery, this mood that was always obliging, humble, and grateful, was merely the means with which he had secured his aims. Mr. Collins knew better than any of us that neither pride nor honor could feed or clothe him; a good word from the eldest son of a baroness . . . *that,* of course, was an entirely different matter.

"To be sure, it was a painful time, but I've no regrets," Mr. Collins said, shrugging. "It is only through the trials of life that one attains a kind of wisdom. Because I was poor, others believed I should remain as poor as my father had been before me, but I did not think this should be my lot in life. And because I smiled and simpered while sweeping the floors of my superiors' rooms, they probably thought I was unable to differentiate between cleaning for them and attending class or being permitted to access the library, which none of the servitors, including myself, were ever allowed to do. Perhaps they believed that when they sent me into town to run errands for them, I considered the exercise as educational for my soul as the recitation of Homer or Virgil, but it is good they believed this, for they let down their guard and then . . ." Mr. Collins smiled. "And then there might not be any going back for them, if there was something very important that they could one day do for me. So you see, dear cousin, the lesson to be learned from this is that one should never settle in life for what others may think is best and right for you. There is always the larger and more delicious fruit hanging from a higher branch, just out of your grasp, and which might easily be yours, if someone would only lend you the ladder to reach it. And the ladder is what will make all the difference."

The determination which had entered his face as he'd concluded his story emboldened me to speak. I, too, had been humiliated, and in our shared experience, we were kindred spirits. I wished him to know this, and I'd already leaned forward in my chair, prepared to launch into the unhappy memory which had risen to the forefront of my thoughts, when something stopped me. I opened my mouth, but the words would not come. It was different for him—he had proven himself, turned his circumstances to his advantage, but I'd remained exactly where I was, despite my hardships. I remained unchanged. Perhaps it was best to say nothing, I thought, and I looked bashfully away from him, even as my mind traveled back to that fine-weathered afternoon in May, many months ago, which had ended so miserably.

Earlier this year, the youngest child and only son of Sir William Lucas had accompanied his two sisters, Charlotte and Maria, on their walk to Longbourn. Charlotte, who was twenty-seven and still unmarried, had been in the habit of visiting us often and was considered the particular friend of Lizzy, whom she admired greatly for much the same reasons everyone else did.

In Hertfordshire, she was thought by her general acquaintance to be a practical young woman of sound intelligence—in other words, the "good sort of girl" a mother can count on to sit obediently for as long as she is told and to never get into any kind of trouble.

In spite of her respectability and the fair prospect she had of making a good marriage, owing to the comfortable fortune her knighted father had acquired in trade, she remained an unexceptional human being with an appearance so forgetful that her frequent attendance of balls and dinners had never succeeded in generating any stories of which she had played a larger role than the report that "the eldest Miss Lucas was also in attendance." Except for Mama, no one considered Charlotte to be especially plain, but the consensus was, among the females of the neighborhood, that her face was too long, the space between her eyes too wide, and her mouth too big for her face. By way of consolation, the same females added that there was a fleeting kind of prettiness to be detected whenever she smiled while tipping her head at a certain angle, like a piece of glass that will at rare moments catch the light of the sun. Her sister, Maria, was an even less noteworthy person than herself, and there is little to be said about her other than that she was fond of dancing, sported many lavender and pink frocks at balls (these being her favorite colors), and was as well pleased with her father's knighthood as, no doubt, he was himself. As for their young brother, Thomas, who plays a central role in this story, he had always been of a romantic disposition and entertained very grand designs of one day making something of his life, though he hadn't yet determined at seventeen years old what this would be. For as long as anyone could remember, he'd also been in love with Jane.

This itself was not surprising, as Jane had always had her share of admirers. But I imagine the chivalric strength of his affections, when mingled with the fevered and self-tormenting behaviors symptomatic of first love, must have caused him no shortage of private suffering. No subject could be too trivial, no observation too irrelevant, if it afforded young Thomas Lucas an opportunity to exchange a few words with his beloved. The rare and joyous occasions in which Thomas could share with Jane his thoughts on a week-long succession of rain or his preferment of ragout to a plain dish were sufficient to elevate him to the very heights of paradise.

On this visit, Thomas was in particularly lively spirits, and as the afternoon boasted sunlight and warm breezes, our group walked together along the gravel path to the copse where Papa had conveniently installed a few stone benches. Mrs. Hill brought us raspberry shrubs, and as we sipped our cool drinks, Thomas, who had been shyly glancing at Jane, suddenly declared that he had an idea. He guzzled the remainder of his drink and ran off in the direction of the garden before any of us could delay him with questions. Nearly a quarter of an hour later, he returned with his arms full of flowers and his boots coated in dust. He was out of breath, but this did not deter him from speaking—primarily to Jane—of the diversion he had in store for us.

"I have here collected seven samples of flowers from Mrs. Bennet's garden, which I think best represent each of you," Thomas said, briefly exhibiting the bouquet to all of us. A few of his audience seemed very pleased by this entertainment and accordingly voiced their approval with the delighted coos which females are especially prone to in the company of men. "And I will now distribute the flowers that I have matched to each of you with some words of commentary as I do so," he continued. Some fool among us began to clap her hands and laugh, which compelled the rest of us to follow suit.

"I'm not sure Mama would approve of having her garden ransacked for the sake of an idle game," I said, frowning in the direction of the flowers he clutched.

"Oh, do shut up, Mary," Lydia replied. "Will you never tire of ruining other people's fun? I want to know what flower I am, and the rest of us do, too."

As no one ventured to disagree with this sentiment, our performer felt confident enough to proceed. He stopped in front of Jane, his face and neck flushing a brilliant shade of scarlet, and tentatively passed her three peonies in full bloom. "The most beautiful flower in the garden," he said, his voice wavering, "for the most beautiful girl in the country." Jane, too, reddened and, in a voice barely audible to the rest of us, whispered her thanks. To my right, I heard Maria utter a small "Oh Lord" in the ear of her sister.

Next, Thomas presented a large cluster of lilacs to Lizzy and said the flower had reminded him of how her many virtues succeeded in making up the loveliness of her entire person, just as the lilac's tiny blossoms composed the splendor of the whole. Lizzy was visibly gratified by this and smiled more conceitedly than was her custom, which is not surprising, given that most females who have just been told by a man that they are perfection feel very pleased with themselves, even if they don't think anything special of the man himself. Lydia and Kitty both received small bouquets of sweetbriar, accompanied by a few pretty words extolling their youth and levity, which at first perfectly charmed and contented them. But then Lydia asked why she hadn't received a different flower than Kitty and Thomas was forced to admit to the difficulty he always had with telling them apart. This, of course, diminished Lydia's original enthusiasm for the game. Tossing her sweetbriar roses aside, she protested that this could not be so, as she was the tallest of any of her sisters even if she was the youngest, and said anyone who should mistake her for Kitty must be a "dumb and disagreeable simpleton with glass eyes and a hollow skull."

Thomas, who had never shown interest in either girl and undoubtedly thought the two as silly and empty-headed as the rest of us did, ignored Lydia's comment and moved on to his own sisters. For Charlotte, he gifted two long strands of mignonettes and, unable to keep from laughing, said he had selected this particular flower for his eldest sister because she smelled much better than she looked. Charlotte, who fortunately was good-humored, laughed with the rest of us and only chided her brother in a teasing sort of way for being unkind to his own flesh and blood. Towards Maria, he was comparatively more gracious and had picked for her as many shades of sweet William as our garden offered. "Because you are your father's daughter," he said, "and would sooner forget your own name than Sir William's knighthood." This account was followed by more appreciative laughter. Maria, turning as pink as her flowers, confessed that she did occasionally talk too much about her father's title but, as she had no wish to appear ridiculous in front of others, wouldn't mention the subject in the future.

"How shall I serve thee, Mary?" Thomas asked, finally turning to where I sat at the end of the bench. "What flower could I present to Miss Mary Bennet that would not pale and shrivel in the glory of her visage, that would in its properties encompass the breadth of her blinding beauty?" Receiving no reply but the suppressed giggles of his amused audience, he revealed the final flower in his hands, which I accepted and studied for some moments before crumpling in my fist.

"This is not a flower," I said. "This is a weed. I dug out several like it just this morning."

"You missed that one," Thomas replied, bouncing on his heels.

"That may be so," I said, "but aren't you going to recite a poem to me now? 'Ode to Bindweed' or something equally ridiculous?"

"Nothing so grand," he said. "Just that if the world is a garden, then the less weeds there are, the better. They choke the beauty of the flowers and thrive at the expense of others."

"I'm afraid I don't quite grasp the comparison," I replied, goading him. "Come on, quickly now. Tell me how I'm like a weed, Thomas, and choke the beauty of the flowers."

He looked and sounded a little bored as he answered: "The fewer Mary Bennets there are in the world, the better. They add no beauty to their surroundings and will all grow up to be ugly old maids, living on the charity of their families."

Everyone reacted quite as I'd predicted they would. Jane gasped. Lizzy and Charlotte appeared too stunned to speak. Maria squirmed in her seat and looked yearningly towards the hedgerow, and Lydia and Kitty turned so red from noiseless laughing, I wondered they didn't rise and applaud him.

I stood. Being quite tall for his age, Thomas loomed over me, but I was too angry to care. "What have I ever done to you, Thomas

Lucas, to deserve this?" I asked, nearly choking on the rage that rose like smoke from the pit of my stomach.

"A joke, Mary," he said, turning pale but endeavoring to laugh all the same, and raised his hands in mock surrender. "It was only meant to be a joke. I was quite mean to Charlotte just now as well, wasn't I? And to Maria, too."

"Then I'll also make a joke and see if you are able to laugh at it," I replied, staring hard into his eyes. "I will treat you as fairly as you chose to treat me. This, Thomas," I said, gesturing at the land around me, "is *my* garden, and *you* are the weed that will be cast out. You will look no more upon any of the flowers here. Now get out. I never want to see you again. GET OUT!"

Charlotte announced they should leave, and Thomas—with one last forlorn look at Jane that, under any other circumstance, would have sufficiently moved me to welcome him back into the fold—straggled after his sisters. Just before he disappeared from view, he suddenly stopped, his shoulders began to shudder, and we watched in uncomfortable silence as Charlotte and Maria were forced to guide their brother, one on each side of him, for the remainder of the walk to Lucas Lodge.

Charlotte visited the next day and found me squatting in Mama's garden with a trowel and a basketful of weeds.

"Oh, Mary" were the first words she exhaled.

"You've come to tell me that Thomas is very sorry for how he behaved to me, haven't you," I said, tossing another weed over my shoulder and not looking at her.

"You know Thomas will say and do anything to impress Jane," Charlotte pleaded. "He's at such an awkward age."

"Which, I suppose, makes everything he says and does excusable," I replied.

"Now, you know that isn't true. Maria and I are thoroughly ashamed of him, and being unmarried myself, Mary, I feel the insult of his words deeply."

"I've been thinking, Charlotte. . . ." I threw down my trowel and stood. "I've been thinking it is unfair that there should be no recourse for a woman to take in this world should she find herself singularly unsuited to marriage. It doesn't matter for Thomas that he bears an uncanny resemblance to a monkey, because he is a man. And thanks to your father's connections, Thomas will attend university and take up either law or a position in the church. One day, he might even become a famous barrister or a bishop, and neither of these occupations will ever discriminate against him because he resembles a hooting chimpanzee. Do you comprehend how unjust that is? If I could only seek some useful employment . . . but to be employed in any capacity is considered an insult to our sex."

Though I didn't think I'd said anything funny, Charlotte began to laugh. "I daren't ask what kind of employment you have in mind."

"I sometimes envision myself working in a little bookshop, collecting money from customers and wrapping beautiful books in large sheets of brown paper. . . ."

"You'd grow tired of it after the first day."

"I wouldn't, Charlotte. I wouldn't, because it was my choice. Not something that was foisted upon me, but a situation I entered into of my own free will. It angers me that Thomas will eventually be able to make something of himself, and I can't!"

"But you can, dear Mary," she entreated, squeezing my hand. "You can, and you will. Through marriage."

I did not reply, and my expression must have indicated to Charlotte that further discussion on the matter was useless, for she soon sought the company of Lizzy, while I returned to the house. A view from a window caught my attention, and I looked out towards the lonely fields and the thin, uneven line of the horizon. I listened to the heaving lamentations of the cows, the unsettled cries of sheep, the scuttling of plump, edible birds being ushered from one confinement to the next, never knowing in the short span of their lives much more of the world than the few square feet of muddy earth they were born into. I felt their stupidity and the fog that effectively dimmed their minds to everything but the bottomless emptiness of their own stomachs. My own existence did not seem so very different from theirs.

Though I treated Thomas with civility on every one of the occasions in which he visited Longbourn thereafter, a divide persisted between us that prevented either party from feeling totally at ease in the other's company. In laying bare to my sisters and friends the most vulnerable part of my soul, he had bestowed upon my private fears a certain inescapable reality. To run from it would be akin to covering one's eyes like a child, and to face it would be an acknowledgment of everything I had ever despaired of—my plainness, my unformed education and so-called accomplishments, and my predestined dependence on the good fortunes of my sisters. I couldn't witness his happy manners in front of others without also remembering the many hours I'd spent after the incident crying noisily into a book, unable to read a single page. The racket of my tears had eventually summoned Jane and Lizzy upstairs to my room, and they'd embraced me with consolations uttered softly into the top of my head.

"Our poor Mary," Jane had sighed.

"What an unfeeling ass Thomas Lucas is," Lizzy had said, squeezing my shoulder. "In fact, what asses all men can be when the mood takes them!"

A FAINT KNOCKING at the door interrupted my reverie, and Mrs. Hill entered without waiting to be summoned. She looked with some wonder from Mr. Collins to myself, then back again. Her eyes glittered with poorly disguised pleasure at the discovery of her young mistress sitting alone with a male houseguest. With less decorum than was her custom, Mrs. Hill managed to utter the following few short words without entirely abandoning herself to baser feelings.

"Mary," she said, having turned by now quite pink, "you're wanted upstairs."

"Thank you, Mrs. Hill," I replied stiffly. "Please tell Mama I'll be up directly." No sooner had Mrs. Hill departed from the room than we heard a peal of gleeful chortling from the far end of the hall. I turned to Mr. Collins, who, having no concern for Longbourn's housekeeper, had resumed his study of stone-paved Roman highways and handicapped emperors straddling the backs of elephants.

Looking discreetly at him, I thought again of his story. It is an unfortunate aspect of our society that the people whose conditions in life are the most enviable, and whose wealth and power we would most willingly emulate, should also be some of the most disagreeable, arrogant, and unsympathetic characters whom the good Lord ever determined to create in His own likeness; that while there is much to admire in their possessions and various titles and the exorbitant amounts they pay each year in taxes and death duties to the Crown, they are rendered no less reprehensible by the comfort and opulence of their upbringings. This nation's peerage had been cruel to Mr. Collins, had belittled him and toyed with him, as though he were a plaything installed within their lives solely for their amusement. Yet a great paradox remains, which is that while Mr. Collins may have secretly hated his tormentors, he would undoubtedly have relinquished his own identity and principles at the very first opportunity in exchange for a life lived in hedonistic albeit respectable idleness as one of England's esteemed nobility. I think he would have savored, too, with no little pleasure, the chance to turn his nose up at a beggar and her family of starving children in an alleyway or to thoroughly whip a servant who did not brush his hat and coat with appropriate deference.

Mr. Collins had faults—glaring ones that, in the eyes of other females, might have rendered him so ridiculous that the prospect of being married to such a man would have driven many to pledge their virtues to the nearest nunnery. But something in his unabashed eagerness to impress his betters, in his capacity to serenely anguish behind a mask of solicitude while others laughed at him—I confess that something in these peculiar qualities stirred in me a small but fervent admiration I couldn't quite ignore, and I considered to myself whether I might have a reasonable chance of happiness in being married to the rector of Hunsford parsonage and entrusting my respectability and future well-being to a man who, though not as handsome as Mr. Bingley, not as rich as Mr. Darcy, and not as well-read as Papa, was also not entirely without his own hidden depths and the various miniature tragedies which lend to all our lives a little more color than otherwise would be the case. In him, I identified the same yearning to prove one's detractors wrong. If the dream of gainful employment were to be denied me, perhaps I could content myself with helping another realize his ambitions. Perhaps, if there really existed no other means for a woman to attain success and purpose in the world, I could settle for marriage. Perhaps it wouldn't be settling.

I rose to leave; however, feeling a small flutter in my chest upon seeing him crook his left eyebrow at an item of note in his book, I could no longer subdue the emotion which rose to the top of my throat and filled my mouth. I spat out his name with more violence than I'd intended, and like a pupil unexpectedly called upon by his instructor, he snapped to attention and stared at me. Embarrassed, I pretended to cough and, after dislodging the nonexistent irritant from my throat, spoke with as much belated dignity as I could muster. "Mr. Collins," I said. "I'm afraid Mama has asked me to attend her upstairs."

"Yes," he answered. "Yes, I heard Mrs. Hill tell you so just now."

"I just wanted to say," I went on, faltering like an idiot. "I just wanted to say that you mustn't take too much to heart what my sisters think of you because I think . . ." Again I hesitated and, like the apprentice milliner in Meryton, I focused with passionate intensity on the bottom half of his left earlobe before proceeding. "I think . . . that is, I *don't* think you're silly at all. I think you're actually the most respectable and good sort of man to come into our neighborhood for a very long time. And I wanted to tell you, too, how grateful I am that you have entrusted me with the history of your acquaintance with Lady Catherine. You may be assured of my secrecy and that I will tell none of my sisters—"

"Dear cousin," Mr. Collins cried, fortunately interrupting me just as I was in danger of dithering, "while I don't doubt for a moment your sincerity, I wish you wouldn't trouble yourself with these trifling concerns. Almost as soon as I entered the house, I singled you out as the one among all your family nearest in sensibility and thinking to myself. We are, I think, fated to be extraordinarily good friends, and my heart exalts at the joy of finding any true companion in this sometimes dark and confusing world with whom I may share the private thoughts and concerns of my soul." He then stood and, removing an object from his inner breast pocket, gently took my wrist and folded my fingers around the flat parcel. "I'd meant to give this to you sooner," he said, patting my hand in an avuncular manner, "but there was never any opportunity. These were, as it happens, the so-called letters I was working on when I excused myself from you and your family's company early yesterday evening."

I hadn't sense enough to ask what the package contained. Murmuring my thanks with my eyes still pinned to the fleshy pink of his earlobe, I left the room, unsure whether my legs would take me as far as the door without giving way. I thought of looking back and smiling at him, but at the last moment, my courage failed me. As soon as I was out of sight of the library, I ran up the stairs, giggling to myself like a lunatic, his present tucked away in a pocket of my dress. On the landing, I heard the familiar, tinny laughter of not one but two voices, which, despite being of slightly different pitch, managed to complement each other in raucous harmony. They belonged, of course, to Mama and Aunt Philips, who must have come to the house while I was in the library with Mr. Collins. My feet skipped a little as I proceeded in the direction of the noise. The sensation of his thumb gliding gently across my wrist had stunned me into the most blissful of stupors.

CHAPTER 6

I shouldn't like the reader to think that I am in the custom of listening at other people's doors or that my doing so in this singular instance is indicative of my taking after the bad habits of my two younger sisters. However, the substance of Mama and Aunt Philips's conversations never failed to please as a source of frivolous entertainment, and if one had just been reading an academic tome filled with many vague and heavy philosophies with words of several syllables each and origins in ancient tongues, then it would do well for that same person to sit and sip a cup of hot tea while listening to my mother and aunt opine on subjects which, despite the pair's extremely limited purview and the unlikelihood of any of their theories being actually true, made them no less scandalously thrilling. Standing just outside the frame of the door, I caught the rattling of cups being brusquely returned to their saucers amid passionate chatter, and I entered into their conversation a silent and unseen audience.

". . . and I am told they were witnessed by the housemaid, holding hands—" Aunt Philips said.

"Holding hands? No!"

"And . . ."

"And?" Mama asked expectantly.

"And leaning into each other!" my aunt declared.

"No! I won't believe it," Mama cried in jubilation. "I refuse to believe it! It can't be! Oh!"

"Yes, sister," Aunt Philips continued with relish. "It is just as I say. I knew this would happen. I predicted it as soon as I set eyes on that girl. I said to myself, 'This is a bad one. This one will be up to no good.' And look what has happened now! Naturally, poor Mrs. Horbury has had to let her go and without a letter of reference, too, but it really is for the best, you know."

"Of course it is! Just think of the shame!" I heard the grinding of jaws working away at hard biscuits.

"One can always tell," Aunt Philips said with her mouth full. "You've never met her, I know, but you could just tell from the artful little way she'd take your hat and coat from you in the hall that she'd get mixed up one day with, well . . ."

"A man!" Mama practically shouted.

"Yes, dear," Aunt Philips said. Again, I heard the clattering of china. "And so it has come to pass, just as I said it would. How awful that one can't trust one's servants anymore. They're so emotional now, so needful of companionship and such passionate creatures." She clicked her tongue and sighed.

"This is true," Mama replied sadly. "We had, you'll remember, that small incident with Sarah, the housemaid, a few years ago. If I'd known that was how she intended to make use of her room . . . well! I'd have had the door removed from its hinges."

"I've never heard of anything so vulgar," Aunt Philips exclaimed cheerfully. "On a pleasanter subject, how is Mr. Collins? What a charming man! So wonderful in his little, elegant manners. I wonder where he picked those up."

"I'm sure he'd be very happy to hear you say so. He could talk of nothing and nobody else for a whole hour! I thought he'd never stop going on about how wonderful you were."

"And do you think he means to make good on his word to choose a wife among one of your daughters?"

"Oh yes, sister. I have every confidence he will make a proposal before he leaves for Hunsford on Saturday."

"This is an excellent development," Aunt Philips assented. No doubt she had plans to circulate this piece of news to every member of her intimate acquaintance before the actual proposal had taken place. My aunt preferred to live several steps ahead of everyone else. In hearing rumor of a marriage proposal, she would consider it her duty to express at least a few thoughts on the arrangement of the flowers in the church, the best material and fabric for the bride's gown, the likelihood of the marriage's success, and how many surviving offspring it would produce. She was prevented from making any of her usual prophesies in this instance, since she did not know the identity of the intended bride, and after a momentary pause, she asked (as I'd predicted she would), "And who, Mrs. Bennet, do you think Mr. Collins will ask to marry him? Has he shown any special preference for one of them?"

"Lizzy seems the obvious choice," Mama said, "although she hasn't exchanged more than three words with him since he arrived."

"That is of little consequence," my aunt said consolingly, "but I would have thought Mr. Collins was more Mary's type. In temperament, Mary seems well suited to be a clergyman's wife. She looks the part and is capable of expelling great quotations."

"We'd be lucky to get her married at all," Mama huffed. "No, I think Mr. Collins will settle on Lizzy. He as much as said so when I hinted that Jane might very soon be engaged, and he agreed that in such circumstances, it would be best to honor sequentially the seniority of the sisters, which he would have done with Jane had Mr. Bingley not fallen in love with her first. Besides, sister, you'd do well to remember that Mr. Collins is still a man after all, and an unattractive man is just as inclined to choose a pretty girl as a handsome one is."

"Then it's settled," Aunt Philips announced, as though the decision were hers to make. "Lizzy will be Mr. Collins's wife. But if you don't mind my saying so, Mrs. Bennet, I don't think my niece stands much chance of being happy with him."

My mother answered magnanimously: "As far as I am aware, happiness doesn't enter into it. She'll be saving Longbourn for myself and her sisters; on top of which, I recall Mr. Collins mentioning that Lady Catherine would wait upon him and his wife when they were returned to Hunsford, so she has that to look forward to, if nothing else."

"There are many marriages with far less to credit them," the other agreed. "Well, where is Mary? I believe you called for her nearly twenty minutes ago, and we've already finished all our tea and biscuits. I hope she hasn't taken to locking herself in her room."

I opened the door—perhaps too suddenly, for my aunt and mother jumped in their seats, and, like birds that have been disturbed from their roosts, neither could settle in their chairs again for some minutes.

My countenance must have given away the distress I felt at overhearing their conversation, for Mama at once asked me what the matter was.

"Nothing," I replied simply. "I'm sorry for keeping you waiting."

"Well, where have you been? I asked Hill to fetch you some time ago," Mama complained.

"I've been out . . . walking."

"Well! Have you ever heard of such a thing?" Mama cried. "And why should your face be so red from walking, Mary?"

"Some color would do her good, sister," Aunt Philips murmured. Looking me over, she clicked her tongue accusingly. "Color, Mary," she scolded, as my cheeks throbbed with warmth. "You might take some advice from your sisters and wear more than just these ugly browns and grays all the time. They do you and your figure no favors, you know."

"She has no figure," Mama replied on my behalf before I could speak. "And we've given up trying to do anything with Mary. First, she won't accept any interference, and second, nothing seems to improve on her anyway." She told me she'd forgotten what it was she'd called me up for in the first place and said she'd send Mrs. Hill to fetch me again once she remembered it. I then left the room, making directly for my own, and Mama and Aunt Philips resumed their animated conversation as though nothing had ever interrupted it.

My sister's acuity had not failed her. What asses men were.

So! Mr. Collins had determined to settle on Lizzy, and with Mama's approval, too. Hateful man. How boring and expected! How ridiculous and stupid! Well, if she accepted him, the wedding would be a merry one indeed, for all the laughter in the church when the time came to kiss the bride and the groom found he had to stand on his toes for being too short to reach her mouth.

I executed a little twirl in my room as I thought of his bumbling, greedy fingers undoing the back of her dress and the multitude of depressed-looking children they'd bring into the world soon afterwards—at least eleven, I decided, with one set of twins, and all stampeding after their mother in the small rooms of the parsonage house, while downstairs, their father expounded to Lady Catherine and her daughter some obscure passage from the Bible. Yes, a fine scene of domestic bliss!

I pictured myself purple-faced and drunk at their wedding, executing a flawless cartwheel across the lawn of the church in a hideous saffron dress. "Color, Mary," Aunt Philips had said. "Yes, Aunt," I'd reply, before emptying a glass of wine over her head. I smiled to myself, shoving my hands into the pockets of my dress, and my fingers grazed the parcel which Mr. Collins had given me earlier. With some difficulty, I wrenched out the package and tore it open. A half-sheet of paper detached from the other pages and slipped through my fingers, onto the floor. It contained only the following short lines in an elegant hand, which I might easily have mistaken for a woman's had I not known its author to be Mr. Collins:

To my dear cousin Mary—

Being a cultured man, I am able to appreciate in kindred
spirits (such as yourself) a refinement of taste, which souls
untouched by the divine balm of our Lord's sweet music will
sometimes consider repellent to their uncouth sensibilities.
Though lesser and ungifted minds will attempt to dissuade
you from your endeavors, you must never give up your instrument and continue just as you have always done. My
condensed thoughts on the matter being thus dispatched
and hopefully of some helpful instruction to my young audience, I've thereby taken it upon myself to restore to you
that which you have lost in the expectation you will find it
useful, and I hope my gesture—the motivations of which
are entirely steeped in kindness and concern for the happiness of my musically inclined cousin—will not be discred-
ited for its boldness and presumption.

Respectfully,
Mr. William Collins

P.S. I will undertake to return the original to your estimable
aunt at the first opportunity, so kindly have no worries on
this account.

Tentatively, I unfolded the remaining pages. It is a strange and, I
think, peculiar behavioral trait that wrath and discontent should be
so easily dispelled by the receipt of a bouquet of flowers, a silver
locket enclosing a tuft of hair, or, in my own case, a few pages of
meticulously copied sheet music containing "The Last Rose of Summer" by Thomas Moore. I'd already determined not to be put off by
Kitty's violence and to beg my aunt, in my next walk to Meryton,
for the opportunity of borrowing the same music again in order to
recopy it, but this . . . this I hadn't expected and wouldn't have ex-

pected for another hundred years should I have lived so long, as strange and wonderful a surprise as it was.

Smoothing the pages against the wall, I marveled at the cleanness of the lines, the mechanically even spacing between the notes, the remarkable absence of ink blots, and the neat annotations written with an especially fine point over and under every bar to denote where one should play louder or softer or repeat a refrain. I pictured him stooped over the small table in his room, crafting, then coloring in each rounded note and drawing with a steady, disciplined hand measured rows of black lines in the moving, inconstant flame of a single candle. I felt happy. Looking up and around my empty room, I wished he were here now, so I could thank him better than I had done downstairs. But I wanted selfishly to savor, too, the feeling of being singled out and respected and admired. Was it possible that Mr. Collins loved me? Even if it were true that he'd come to Longbourn intent on choosing a wife and had at first admired Lizzy or Jane, his affections could change, as feelings often do, and alter from their original course. He could come to realize, upon steady and gradual interaction with myself, that the third and plainest Bennet sister possessed qualities which might prove more valuable than mere physical attractiveness and feminine charm.

This was not, I think, impossible to believe. Perhaps Mr. Collins had discovered a virtue which others before him had been unable to discern, and if he had, there could be no reason why I shouldn't reward him accordingly with the greatest love and esteem in my power to give. It was impossible—everyone knew it to be impossible—that either Lizzy should be in love with Mr. Collins or that Mr. Collins should be in love with Lizzy. By his own admission, she had laughed at him at the dinner table, though perhaps she mightn't have been so much in danger of falling in his estimation had the subject which she found amusing been anything other than the Right and Honorable Lady Catherine de Bourgh. Surely this was a breach of decorum too near all that Mr. Collins held sacred and dear to be forgiven. And Lizzy, who was candid to a fault, had confessed that she'd perceived no special preference from the man most unsuited to her in personality, opinion, and, I daresay, physique. No, Mr. Collins would be sensible. *He,* unlike the multitudes of unknown others, would not abandon all reason for the trophy of a hollow partnership with a pretty face, not even one as bright-eyed and agreeable as Lizzy's. *He* would know which among Papa's daughters would be least likely to dishonor him in the partaking of tea and cake at Rosings Park and, therefore, best able to secure his own success and future happiness. I sighed, and hugging the pages of sheet music to the flat expanse of my chest, I tried and failed to recall a time when I'd felt so enamored of myself.

CHAPTER 7

"Good Lord, Mary, what *is* that you're wearing on your head?" Mama cried, gawping as I descended from my room that evening to join my sisters and Mr. Collins in the hall. "And your dress . . . where did you get a dress like that, Mary?"

"Jane lent it to me, Mama," I replied, smoothing the folds of cream-white muslin.

"And Lizzy lent the feather in your hair," Jane added from below.

"And Lizzy lent the feather in my hair," I pronounced exuberantly, beaming at everyone from the landing and ignoring Lydia and Kitty, who looked quite ready to explode from unvented laughter.

"But . . ." Mama protested. "But you're just going with Mr. Collins and your sisters to your aunt Philips's for supper and cards. It's hardly a special occasion."

"I know," I said and descended the final stair with a light hop and a skip. Love filled my heart, and my awakened spirit would not be thwarted. I turned to Mr. Collins, who I hadn't seen since leaving him several hours ago in the library, and to my pleasure, he seemed to look at me, too, with visible wonder at my transformation. "Mr. Collins," I said with more garrulousness than was my custom, "I'm so glad we'll be going to Aunt Philips's tonight. I have every expectation that this evening will be a most engaging one, and I'll be treating you all to a new rondo by Steibelt I've recently learned and committed to memory."

At this, Lydia and Kitty could restrain their laughter no more and, standing huddled together in front of the mirror above the hall table, started howling at their own reflections. Mr. Collins, glancing in their direction and then at me, answered politely that he looked forward to hearing my well-known proficiency at the piano, a sentiment unquestionably shared by the rest of my family. I thanked him with a bold smile, at which he turned a little red, which made me blush as well. We then spent a few moments wordlessly regarding the well-worn tassels of the carpet and the faded calico of the window curtains. But Mama hadn't quite finished with me and, continuing to gaze with confused horror from the white feather perched at the top of my head to the embroidered front of my dress, said, "Mary, my dear, does this . . . erm . . . arrangement you've put on have anything to do with what your aunt said to you earlier today about your usual clothes?"

"No, Mama," I replied simply.

"Well, Mary," she continued. "I can't be sure what's inspired this sudden change, but I feel, as your mother, that I must take advantage of every opportunity to share the wisdom I've accrued in my old age, which is that while in *some* cases effort certainly can make a difference, sometimes *something* . . . or rather *someone* . . . will look much better undecorated than—"

"Ah, look, Lizzy's here," Jane exclaimed, and Mama had no chance to say any more, as the next ten minutes were spent arranging all our persons into the carriage that would take us to the elegantly furnished parlor room of my aunt Philips's home, which, despite its crowded dimensions, had never quite abandoned its pretensions of resembling Blenheim or Chatsworth.

For most of the evening, I occupied myself with entertaining Aunt Philips's guests at the piano. But when I felt least in danger of committing a mistake, I'd venture to look around the room and search for Mr. Collins among the crowd. In doing so, I was happy to find him on almost all occasions talking excitedly to his hostess with many histrionic gestures while the latter listened and nodded and beckoned one or two others over to show off her new and well-connected friend. Lizzy, who'd quickly established herself as the reigning favorite of the most handsome man in the room (Mr. George Wickham), was too engrossed with the latter's tall figure and coaxing smiles to pay any attention to the plain black garb of our clergyman cousin. As for the rest of my sisters, Lydia and Kitty were perched in the part of the room where the population of officers was thickest and ladies, excepting their own selves, of course, were scarcely to be found. And Jane—dear Jane; in the absence of her light-footed Mr. Bingley, she entertained herself by sometimes sitting with me and helping me turn the pages of my music and sometimes chattering with female acquaintances she without fail proclaimed to miss very much.

Even if her emotions are not outwardly displayed, owing to exceptional self-control, a woman will remain as obsessive about the object of her affections as a cat that has smelled the odor of fish and will continue to think about the fish, though the cat cannot see the fish or taste it. And rain may pour on the cat and people may unkindly strike it for no other reason than that it is a cat, but the beast will still be contemplating the gray-finned delicacy it hopes one day to hold between its black-and-white paws, though by then, the fish may already have been eaten by the humans who purchased it at market. I use this comparison simply to illustrate the behavior of women in love.

So we might conclude that Jane's claims to have missed her female friends since Mr. Bingley's arrival may be considered mere polite formality, spoken with moderate conviction on one side and received with even less conviction on the other. But this was civilized society, and everyone smiled and laughed most cheerfully to one another's faces, even if they hated each other. On behalf of Jane, I was pleased to find that these same women showed themselves eager to overlook the fact that no less than a month ago, they, in partnership with their fanatical mothers, had also contended vigorously for a certain newcomer's affections and miserably failed.

Otherwise, the evening progressed with little to distinguish it. On two occasions, Mr. Collins came over to the piano to listen to me play, but as Jane was in my company both times, neither of us ventured more than the wordless exchange of a few friendly though, I think, meaningful and admiring smiles. And when Jane finally left my side to join her friends in a game of lottery tickets, I wished Mr. Collins would again return to the piano so that we could talk and make a spectacle of sitting together on the same bench, but by then, he had resumed his conversation with Aunt Philips and three other guests. I entertained no hope of his being able to excuse himself anytime soon from this discussion, as I heard uttered several times from that group's general direction the name of his noble patroness and that of the lady's daughter, as well as the phrases "chimneypiece at Rosings Park" and "eight hundred pounds."

Some point after Aunt Philips and Mr. Collins had together lost more rounds of whist than was acceptable to the sensibility of the former in so short a time, my hostess visited me in the middle of a doleful sonata to ask if I could play anything more appropriate to the mood of the occasion.

"For goodness' sake, Mary, this isn't a funeral," she whispered, leaning over the keyboard.

"Not even though you've lost every game so far?" I asked.

"Please don't be disagreeable now, or I'll have a word with your mother in the morning."

"No, Aunt, I don't mean to be," I replied.

"You look . . . well, you look different tonight," Aunt Philips said.

"Do I?"

"A bit much, don't you think? The feather in your hair?"

"Jane said it lends a certain dignity to my appearance. She said I look as fine as a queen, *especially* with the feather in my hair."

"She did, did she?" Aunt Philips said. "And may I ask to what we owe this charming alteration?"

"I don't know, Aunt. I think I may have become quite vain overnight," I lazily replied. From his seat at the whist table, Mr. Collins unexpectedly caught my eye, and my aunt, who had the instinct of a hawk in circumstances as these, noted at once my flushed cheeks and spun her head in the direction of my gaze. She raised her eyebrows to nearly the edge of her forehead and, turning back to me, grinned in the manner of one whose world has received sudden and most revealing illumination.

"I see," she said, drawing out her syllables and tapping her fingers on the edge of the piano. "I see very clearly now, my dear—no need to explain any further." Smiling, she waved to an unseen person at the other end of the room and left my side in considerably better spirits than when she'd first arrived.

All concluded happily, however, and the carriage returned to Longbourn that night amid the overlapping chatter of Lydia and Kitty. When we reached the house, our parents greeted us at the door, and Mr. Collins instantly plied them with tales of the evening's revelry.

"I lost all games at whist and put Mrs. Philips very out for the whole evening," he admitted bashfully to everyone's laughter. "And Colonel Forster brought many of his officers to dine, which pleased the youngest Miss Bennets exceedingly."

"I lost and won a fish at lottery tickets, Mama!" Lydia exclaimed.

"But it was Mary who made the evening worthwhile. . . ." Mr. Collins continued.

The whole company went quiet.

"Mary?" Papa inquired doubtfully of his nephew.

"A delight which surpasses all other delights to hear her play!" our houseguest gushed. "A true songbird! An angel at the piano!"

"A songbird?" Mama questioned, chuckling weakly.

"An angel," Jane repeated softly. "That is high praise indeed."

My family's disbelief was quite lost on me, for in that moment I could not have been surer of Mr. Collins's intentions towards myself and of the great odds I would defy in being the very first among all my sisters to enter into that most holy of institutions: marriage.

CHAPTER 8

The next day, Mr. Bingley and his sisters paid us a visit, the purpose of which was to invite our whole family to a ball at Netherfield Park. Having heard a great deal already about our distinguished neighbors (and all to their credit), Mr. Collins did not disappoint in his effusion. To Mr. Bingley, he performed an exceptionally handsome bow, which took even that amiable gentleman by surprise, and poured so many compliments on the heads of Miss Caroline Bingley and Mrs. Louisa Hurst that their initial twitters of pleasure eventually gave way to an uncomfortable silence. Even my affections could not spare me from the embarrassment I felt at witnessing the toadying behavior he so naturally adopted before his social superiors, and I might have visibly cringed when he likened Mrs. Hurst, who was ten years Bingley's senior, to Egypt's legendary ruler by reciting those immortal lines, "Age cannot wither her, nor custom stale her infinite variety."

But my sympathy was once again roused when I spotted Lydia and Kitty pulling mocking faces behind Mr. Collins's back, and this, in turn, reminded me of the men who had taunted him and how he had risen, in those critical years at university, above his numerous and powerful adversaries to receive the good fortune of Lady Catherine's patronage. The recollection of his long-suffering heroism, which I considered our intimate secret, instantly restored my finer emotions, and for the remainder of Mr. Bingley's visit, I envisioned all the stories we would share of our respective upbringings once we were married.

Notwithstanding my dislike of balls, I could not help feeling excited at the prospect of another chance to sing and play for Mr. Collins, and the rest of my family seemed to share my enthusiasm— all except for Lizzy. Complaining of a headache, she excused herself and went upstairs, perhaps hoping that one or two of her family would trail after her. But none did, not even Jane, who had still to digest the personal honor of Mr. Bingley's calling on her, and it was only in passing Lizzy's room later and finding the door open that I discovered her splayed across the bed with her head rooted facedown in a pillow.

"Lizzy," I said. "Are you ill?"

In hearing her name, the corpse raised a limp arm, which hovered a few moments in the air before collapsing with a dull thump across the mattress and becoming motionless again.

"Have it your way then," I said, "but I'll close the door for you."

"No, Mary," the body replied, rolling slowly onto its back. "Yes, close the door, but don't leave. Stay awhile, won't you?"

Shutting the door, I proceeded to navigate the cluttered floor of my sister's room, which, excepting a narrow trail she had cleared from the entrance to the foot of the bed, was covered entirely with coils of stray ribbon, dirty slippers, the odd button, and several books I'd given up for lost from Papa's library downstairs. Skipping over the final hurdle of a mud-soaked petticoat that smelled oddly of horse manure, I gratefully accepted the drooping hand extended to me. She asked me to sit down, though in looking about the room, I perceived that the only chair was swathed in many layers of stockings and shawls, with a few tattered-looking bonnets flung carelessly across its arms and back.

"You really should let Sarah or Mrs. Hill clean your room, Lizzy," I said, and with my right foot I slid out what appeared to be a single grass-stained glove from underneath her nightstand before sitting down on the bed.

"I know, I know, but I can never find anything afterwards," Lizzy groaned. She released my hand and, draping her wrist dramatically across her forehead, wearily exhaled. "Mr. Collins has asked me to dance the first two dances with him," she blurted out.

"That's just politeness," I replied, as much to console my sister as myself. "He has to ask you because you are second oldest, and it would be rude for him not to. He has an exceptionally strong sense of decorum."

"I can't think of anything, at the moment, more horrifying or unpleasant that any innocent female should be forced to undergo than to have to dance with a man who shames her by association alone," Lizzy continued. "Just think—I must stand up not once but *twice* with Mr. Collins and in front of all those people, too—people like Mr. Wickham, Mr. Bingley, his two awful sisters, and probably Mr. Darcy as well! It is more than anyone should reasonably have to suffer."

"But why should standing up with Mr. Collins be shameful?" I asked. "He is just as respectable as any other gentleman, if not more so, for having made his own fortune in life instead of simply inheriting it."

"What fortune?" Lizzy sneered, and I felt the injury of her words. "What do you think the living at Hunsford is worth?"

"More than sufficient to live on."

"Well, I will not be married off for *that*!" my sister cried, sitting up. "And to the most ridiculous man in England besides! No, I refuse to accept such a fate. Do you really think that my vanity would be satisfied by receiving a profession of love, much less a proposal of marriage, from the likes of Mr. Collins? This isn't to say that my vanity doesn't exist—of course it does—or that it wouldn't receive a very great boon to its self-importance, should a man possessing even half Mr. Bingley's wealth and a fraction of Mr. Wickham's good looks dedicate bad poetry in my name. I can assure you, Mary, that when *that* should happen, you'll find me as silly and conceited as any other woman who is loved by a man she has no intention of accepting."

"But Mr. Collins has no intention of marrying you," I said bluntly.

"Then you have not noticed the signs?" Lizzy asked, crooking an eyebrow. "Why else should a man compliment the way a woman chews her food every time she sits down to a meal? Or worship the shape of her fingers when she works on netting a reticule? Or ask her what she is reading when she has just turned the first page of a book?"

"Mr. Collins does that with everyone, Lizzy. Don't you remember how he complimented Jane on the admirable smallness of her feet the other day? And even Kitty for her cleverness with cutting paper flowers? No, personally, I'm convinced our cousin's affections lie elsewhere," I added, hoping Lizzy would take my hint.

But it had no discernible effect on my sister, absorbed as she was by matters concerning herself. "Well, I would never settle for a man like him," Lizzy pronounced. Then her expression grew thoughtful. "No, I shall find myself a husband worth at least a thousand times our blockhead cousin, for if a man is nothing else, he can at least be rich. And though Jane is the most beautiful of us all, I daresay it would still be a pity for me to rise to no greater station in life than a clergyman's wife."

I found I couldn't laugh at my sister's vanity, but making as if to tease her, I said, "Well, I can think of only one man in our neighborhood, aside from Mr. Bingley, who is worth as much as *that*. And I'm afraid you despise him as much as he dislikes you."

"Mr. Darcy?" Lizzy said, and her eyes glittered much as they had all those years ago when she had caught me in the forest. "Perhaps not, Mary. Perhaps not."

CHAPTER 9

As the day of the Netherfield ball drew near, the discovery that we had not a single intact shoe-rose in the whole of Longbourn threw Mama and my sisters into a state of panic. The shoe-roses could be procured only from the milliner's shop in Meryton, and to make this journey, one had to walk a dirt road which extended from the periphery of our estate to the end of a stone bridge, an exceptionally wretched venture on a wet day.

I knew it would rain even before I set out on my task, for which I had volunteered in order to demonstrate my courage and selflessness to Mr. Collins. Normally, Sarah would have gone, but as Mama reminded us at every meal in a voice certain to reach the servants' quarters downstairs, Sarah had been in the throes of a high fever for two whole days, and Mrs. Hill was too preoccupied with looking after her ailing charge and tending to the blisters and corns on the toes of her own person to walk as far as Meryton and back herself. Except for Lydia and Mama, who considered the threat of my being caught in the rain a small price to pay for the retrieval of an object which would bring happiness to so many, the rest of my sisters attempted at first to dissuade me from going. I wouldn't return in time without getting drenched and risking a cold, they said. But in the end, vanity prevailed. Reminded that the Netherfield ball was only three days away, they soon became inclined to encourage my quest of salvaging from the milliner's limited stock as many of the prettiest shoe-roses as hadn't already been purchased by the shop's other greedy patrons. Jane, who was naturally the most invested of us all in ensuring that her appearance at this ball would be as near immaculate as possible, embraced me at the door and blessed the righteousness of my endeavor with a tender kiss on both cheeks and a sweet entreaty for me to hurry . . . but to have a care not to drop the shoe-roses, of course.

It was late morning when I waved to my sisters from Longbourn's rusted gate, and the sky was already swollen with low-hanging clouds that drifted ominously into the bodies of their neighbors. The air was cold, and the ground packed hard beneath the heels of my boots. Upon reaching a long-abandoned parasol, the sight of which indicated that one-quarter of my journey was over, I heard a hollow cry from a short distance behind me, and thinking it a bird, I continued to walk and toss my drawstring purse in the air until the same cry gathered strength and uttered words in a human tongue and, finally, my own name. I turned and witnessed, running breathlessly towards me, a familiar figure in a wide-brimmed hat and large, black shoes that clopped wearily against the earth like the iron-shod hooves of horses.

"Mr. Collins!" I cried out, and waved. He, too, flapped a limp hand in the air and subsequently bent forward to clutch his shaking knees. I retraced my steps to his side and laughed at the sight of his face, which shimmered with a moist sheen of sweat and the reddish-pink of one unaccustomed to taking brisk exercise in cold weather. He wheezed several times, releasing small puffs of warm air as he did so, and, steadying himself at last, turned cheerfully towards me.

"I thought I'd never catch up with you," he said, still panting. "I must have been calling your name for ages, and you never seemed to hear."

"But why have you come?" I asked.

"It's a cold morning," he replied. "And I noticed that you left the house wearing only a spencer of thin linen over your dress. I thought . . ." He unfolded a long piece of thick, black cloth that had hung from his arm and draped this lightly across my shoulders. "It's a small blanket I keep with me when I travel," he continued, "for the knees, you see. When the weather turns cold, they ache terribly, and Lady Catherine tells me . . ."

He stopped, for while he'd been talking, I'd covertly extended my arm and looped it through an opening in his own. He looked down, and his mouth twitched for the briefest moment into a crooked smile before restoring itself to a thin, solemn line. Turning towards the hedgerows, he remarked in a faint voice that it was a fine day for walking, even as the first spare droplets of rain touched our faces and the backs of our hands. From this, we quickly moved on to pleasanter subjects and, reaching at last the foot of the stone bridge, we continued to chatter in mild tones on a variety of intimate topics, such as the volatility of country weather, the number and variety of animals on the Longbourn estate, and the impressive acreage of the paddock at Rosings Park, which Mr. Collins was able to describe to the minutest detail so as to leave nothing, not even a single bush or daisy, to the autonomy of the imagination.

The streets of Meryton were predominantly empty, and we entered the milliner's shop the only customers. Losing no time, I selected the dozen shoe-roses according to what I knew of their wearers. For Mama, Lydia, and Kitty, only the largest and brightest colored of rosettes would do, and for Jane, Lizzy, and myself, I chose the very ones which I suspected would most displease my younger sisters, these being comparatively modest in both design and size. Once the shoe-roses were purchased, Mr. Collins had the honor of ensuring the safety of the treasured parcel for the return trip to Longbourn. As soon as we had put some distance between ourselves and the shop, I restored my hand to the crook of my cousin's arm, and in so doing was glad to receive no objection from the gentleman. This small accomplishment encouraged me to break the silence that had settled comfortably between us.

"Ever since you shared the account of your past with me, Mr. Collins, I haven't been able to put it out of my mind," I said. "If I'd been in the same situation, I do not know that I would have acted as rationally as you did." Indeed, I was fairly confident that I would have either run sobbing out of the room or launched the first meat pie at my disposal into the faces of my so-called superiors.

"I hope you will take some lessons from it, Mary," Mr. Collins replied. "There are many things in life that only seem impossible, and it is part of the challenge to decide when we should take action and when we should hold back. If you aim for the best, you might achieve second best, but if you aim for what society thinks you deserve, you'll be a pauper for life."

It was then that thick droplets began to fall. One-two. One-two, hitting the side of my nose and staining the leather of my gloves. We were still a fair distance from Longbourn when the rain started to come down in sheets. The landscape before us changed instantly, and the mud stuck to our shoes, so that the effort to take one step might have been the equivalent of taking five or six when the ground was dry. We were soon drenched, and the blanket that Mr. Collins had kindly delivered to shield me from the cold was now a heavy, water-logged burden which I was forced to drag through dirty puddles. Beside me, Mr. Collins used his small body to shield the package containing the precious bundles of shoelace and ribbon that would separate, in Mr. Bingley's eyes, Jane's delicate, dancing feet from the delicate, dancing feet of her peers. Of course, it was inevitable that one of us should fall.

"Woo-ahh!" Mr. Collins screamed in a cry more feminine than I'd imagined possible and flailed his arms like a goose attempting flight before gravity won the upper hand.

"Oh, Mr. Collins! The box!" I shouted and watched as the parcel landed upside down a few feet away from us.

"Save the shoe-roses, Mary!" Mr. Collins spluttered, spitting out rainwater and dirt. "I'll be all right in just a moment!"

"Oh, Mr. Collins," I uselessly repeated, and reached down to help him up.

He had just taken hold of both my hands when I, too, lost my footing in the mud and crashed on top of him with a scream. Beneath me, I heard a yelp of pain and managed to extract my elbow from the middle of his waistcoat before crawling off his body and kneeling miserably at his side. For some moments, he lay flat on his back, wriggling like an overturned turtle struggling to right itself. When he was finally able to sit up, he extracted a soggy handkerchief from his pocket and began to apply this to his mud-speckled face, though doing so only served to smear dirt across a wider expanse of his cheeks. Stuffing his handkerchief inside his coat, he straightened his hat and stared at me through the rain. I looked wordlessly back at him.

That was when his expression changed. I didn't notice it at first—the shift was barely discernible if one hadn't been paying attention to the small alterations that began at the ends of his eyes and in the corners of his mouth. Then one of his eyebrows twitched, and gradually the transformation spread over the whole of his face in an animated wave. His lips parted. His cheeks bulged. His shoulders rose up and down, as though a faint tremor had entered unseen into his body, and balancing the back of his dripping hat with one hand, he started to laugh. He laughed and laughed, his whole torso shaking violently in the grip of his merriment, until my own mouth convulsed, a strange blubbering released itself from the bottom of my throat, and I began to laugh, too. The branches cracked and swung above us; the wind swept and tangled my hair. But we remained sitting for some duration in the middle of the dirt road, shivering without minding the cold, both our sides spasming with extraordinary pain, and my lungs so out of air I'd already begun to cough between bouts of my chortling, which instead of prompting my cousin's concern, provoked him to laugh even more. Eventually, he paused to wipe his eyes of tears and raindrops, and the laughter between us faded until it could no longer be distinguished from all the sounds of water trickling, falling, and gushing around where we sat.

"What shall we do about the shoe-roses?" I asked at last, and in answer, he swept his palm across my forehead, removing a thick clump of hair that had fallen, limp and wet, along the length of my nose. His hand lingered awhile on my cold, practically numbed skin before sliding down the sharp angle of my face to the end of my chin. I felt his thumb arch up and over my mouth to graze the fleshy center of my bottom lip. He leaned closer and closer to me until his face rested nearly on top of mine. But just when our mouths would touch, he wavered and seemed to pull back. I couldn't suffer the moment to escape and bent immediately forward. The kiss was brief. Our lips slid off of each other in the rain, and mine landed in the hollow above his chin. In backing away, I couldn't look at him again, though I knew he was then gazing steadfastly at me, studying my expression. He rested a hand on my shoulder, and I felt both thrilled and tired at its weight. I wanted to say something but remained too light-headed to form any coherent words or ideas.

"Mary," he finally said, addressing my profile. "I'm sorry . . ." He flinched when I looked up at him, and I shook my head to show him I didn't understand. "I'm sorry . . ." he began again, stammering as he removed his hand from my shoulder. When I made as if to reach for him, he visibly recoiled. "I'm sorry . . . about the state of the shoe-roses. Do you think all of them are ruined?" he asked weakly.

I didn't offer an answer, and he didn't wait for one. We picked ourselves up cautiously, and recovering the box from where Mr. Collins had dropped it, we slipped and stumbled down the narrow, puddle-filled lane until, at last, the familiar rectangle of Longbourn appeared to us behind the screen of falling rain. I pushed open the gate, and we walked side by side though not arm in arm slowly towards the house.

When I look back on the incident that followed, I can only de-scribe what happened next as an instant of hysteria. As we neared the front entrance, I suddenly lunged sideways and briefly, politely, respectfully pecked his cheek with my puckered mouth before run-ning away from him at full speed and tearing down the drive with the soggy box of shoe-roses in my hands. Laughing, I banged on the door with my left fist.

"Let me in!" I cried. "I come bearing gifts! A dozen pretty orna-ments to adorn all your misshapen, foul-smelling feet!"

The door opened, and I collapsed into the maternal breasts of Mama and Mrs. Hill, as the shoe-roses settled with a pathetic squish on the floor. "There," I said dramatically. "There are your shoe-roses, Mama. For my life and soul, your shoe-roses."

Mr. Collins skipped in from out of the rain a few moments after me and again extracted the wet handkerchief from his pocket to dab his brow.

I heard Mama ask what kept me so long, while Mrs. Hill de-plored the state of my dress and stockings, which had been washed by Sarah not five days ago. "Well?" Mama repeated. "What have you to say for yourself, Mary, for staying out more than two hours in this weather and making Mr. Collins suffer along with you?"

The wave of concerned siblings arrived as Mama and Mrs. Hill were still wrestling off my coat, and the hall was soon noisy with complaints and anxious inquiries after the state of the shoe-roses. But I could entertain in my mind none of these things. As the heads and bodies of my mother and sisters divided me from the gentleman wringing his hat of rainwater at the door, I could think only of Mr. Collins's face after I'd kissed him, how he'd touched the spot on his cheek as though he'd felt the prick of a needle; how, as I'd sprinted away and looked back at him, his face had flushed, even in the cold of the rain, and he had smiled tenderly at me through the storm.

CHAPTER 10

For the next four days, Longbourn was a hive of activity. I hadn't a single moment to myself without one or another of my family asking my opinion of a pair of gloves or the suitability of a coral necklace. And though my judgment was never heeded, I was still expected to sit with the rest of my sisters while they deplored the wretched state of their wardrobes, which, despite containing a profusion of dresses, featured not a single garment suitable for the upcoming ball. The immediate consequence of this was that I saw little of Mr. Collins, except at meals, and even then, there proved no opportunity to speak with him, for Lydia and Kitty dominated the conversation with squabbles over the outfits they planned to wear. But nothing, not even the rain that persisted until the very day of the Netherfield ball, could dampen my sisters' enthusiasm, and we arrived a little early in order to marvel at the exquisite rooms before they overflowed with people. For the first quarter of an hour, I had all four sisters at my side. Then the music started, and Mr. Bingley whisked Jane away to dance. Lizzy went in search of Mr. Wickham, as much to seek out his company as to avoid standing up with our cousin, and Lydia and Kitty proceeded directly towards the thickest clusters of red.

The ball at Netherfield Park was a much grander occasion than any of us were accustomed to, and the fortunes of our family were considered to depend a great deal on the evening's success. "If all goes well tonight," Mama had said, fussing with Jane's cloak, "I shouldn't be surprised if we received a visit from Bingley tomorrow morning, and then we shall have the banns published by Christmastime."

Netherfield was without a doubt one of the most impressive houses in the county, and its usual finery was enhanced tenfold by the guests our host had invited, many of whom had traveled expressly from London. Like birds of paradise, the women embellished the gilded rooms with their splendid gowns and sparkling jewelry. The men strutted as conceitedly as peacocks, posturing in their tailored waistcoats and artfully knotted cravats. Though I had worn my best dress and added to it a few embellishments in order to conceal its unfashionable simplicity, my inadequate efforts could not escape the critical eye of my hostess. And I confess I felt more ashamed of myself than angry when Miss Caroline Bingley openly sneered at my ensemble, her own, of course, exhibiting every advantage of her handsome and imposingly tall figure. There is nothing as effective as the view of so much wealth, culture, and beauty to serve as a reminder of the social and financial inadequacy of one's own family.

Being left alone permitted me to observe in practice several truisms, the first of which is that women who find themselves without a partner will instinctively gravitate towards other women similarly deprived. One will often see these small groups huddled discreetly in corners of large rooms, observing the fashions of the latest arrivals while picking grapes off their plates of fruit and moderately sipping wine. It is quite easy to spot them, but if you have any trouble doing so, here is another pointer from one who would know. These women will normally appear extraordinarily pleased with themselves and their company, for it is in their best interest that they look as happy in talking with members of their own sex as the women who are engaged in dancing or, worse, the women who are not engaged in dancing but are surrounded by more men than should justly be allotted to them, which, of course, is any number more than one.

Speaking as an intrepid survivor of every awkward and belittling circumstance that may possibly arise in the course of these joyous evenings, I will now share two advantages of existing as an outsider at an elegant ball. The first is that I have become an expert in several aspects of human behavior and can tell at a glance when a woman is jealous and displeased, even when she smiles. From several feet away, I can spot the critical moment when strife has arisen between husband and wife, and so long as I pay close attention, I can discern, too, the turning point in a conversation when a man begins to regret the company he has joined and commences to search the room for any excuse to leave it behind. These number only a few of a multitude of delicious and entertaining scenarios I've picked up over the years, which arise anytime a large group of respectable people have congregated to socialize in a shared space. But even more remarkable, I believe, is the second advantage I've gained from being generally ignored at these events, which is the ability to employ myself for hours with the undertaking of exceptionally meaningless tasks. These range from counting the number of women wearing the same color (blue appears particularly in fashion this season), the ratio of dresses featuring long sleeves to dresses featuring short ones, and the number of times Kitty and Lydia can publicly disgrace our family in an evening (the results vary but fall between three times on a good day to a standing record of thirteen separate instances on a night when both proved especially excitable and uninhibited).

Standing in the great ballroom of Netherfield Park, I had just finished counting the number of crystal chandeliers that spanned the length of the gilded ceiling (eight, four layers each, a dozen lighted candles in the two middle layers, six at the ends) and had embarked on the harder but more amusing task of noting the number of instances in which Mr. Darcy looked indifferently away from the worshipful gaze of Miss Caroline Bingley, when Charlotte Lucas, trailed by a starry-eyed Maria, arrived at my side. Like hostages who have been delivered into safety, we instantly embraced. I'd never been happier or more grateful for the sight of Charlotte and Maria, and they seemed equally pleased at seeing me, so much that both sisters squeezed my hands as they remarked how pretty I looked and that the large white feather in my hair was quite the inspired touch. Having eagerly received their compliments, I was now duty-bound to return the praise, and running a quick eye over both their persons, I soon settled on Charlotte's heart-shaped gold locket ("Really brings out the length and elegance of your neck, my dear") and Maria's dragonfly brooch with the sapphire eyes ("How positively lifelike it looks! Do you think it'll start flying about the room, if you don't watch it carefully?," which made both sisters laugh and gave our coterie the appearance of being the most cheerful and fashionable little group in the whole of Netherfield Park).

"Mary, how we've missed you," Maria exclaimed. Despite the fact that we'd walked the grounds of Longbourn together not five days ago, this was a perfectly natural thing to say, since all three of us numbered among the less interesting category of women at balls and, therefore, found strength in displaying to one another an unwavering allegiance and affection that, under any other circumstance, would have been considered quite excessive. I replied with no less enthusiasm that I felt the same and that it had been far too long.

"And look, none of us have anything to eat or drink," Charlotte pointed out.

The act of eating and drinking is critical, as I've explained, to the partnerless woman and her friends appearing at leisure on a stage in which they've been assigned the role of living scenery. She must also never draw excessive attention to herself by forgetting that her attendance at a ball is merely a polite formality, and that the host may not even know who she is without being first reminded of the names of her sisters and parents. The fruit plate and wineglass are both vital props in sustaining a quiet and unassuming dignity, and Charlotte, being a more tested veteran of these events than even myself, showed great intelligence in promptly leading us along the edges of the large room to an adjoining one where there were four long tables set with enormous pyramids of fruit, tray upon tray of cheeses and cold meats, and pitchers of wine. I shall also let my readers in on a little secret I've discovered over the years, which is that an empty wineglass should never be surrendered to a server without being immediately replaced by a full one. It is far better to hold onto an empty wineglass, if it cannot promptly be substituted for something else from which one can either eat or drink, should conversation reach an awkward lull.

We subsequently busied ourselves with selecting the choicest fruits and cheeses for our plates and, this being soon done, winding our way through all the rooms open to the ball in search of an unoccupied divan, should we be so lucky, or an empty corner that provided a good view of the dancing. With Maria and Charlotte flanking either side of my person, I could comfortably observe Mr. Bingley's most sumptuous gathering. Roses, columbines, and lilacs spilled thick from gold-plated vases. The servants wore clean, dignified frocks and impassive expressions on their faces (smiles and laughter being the prerogative of guests, not the staff). All around us, there was tasteful, pleasing music, and my feet glided across the polished marble floor to the perfectly unified lamentations of the violins.

I'd begun to wobble my head to the light and winsome entry of a flute when a partial family portrait opened up before me. At one end of the room, I witnessed Kitty and Lydia chasing two laughing officers. Between shrieks of delight, they grabbed for the ends of the red sashes secured around the officers' waists until Lydia, impatient to bring the game to a victorious conclusion, finally caught one of her victims and began, to my horror, to tug vigorously on the poor man's sash in an attempt to remove it. This was a ghastly enough picture in and of itself, but it was quickly supplanted by an even more mortifying one. Watching Kitty and Lydia from the other end of the room were my parents, Jane, and Mr. Bingley. Jane had turned as scarlet as the officers' regimentals; having never been a partnerless woman in her life, she could not know the indispensable purpose a plate of fruit and a glass of wine will serve in humiliating situations such as this. Empty-handed and voiceless, she looked imploringly to our mother, who undoubtedly saw something of her former self in her two youngest girls' enjoyment, for she wore a most satisfied and approving smile on her face. As for Papa, it is impossible for me to describe his inaction without feeling a deep sense of disgrace; he shook his head and, turning back to his plate of fruit, greedily munched on a large and succulent pear before murmuring something flippant about girls of a certain age to the elderly couple nearest him. His reaction encouraged others to do the same—that is, to glance knowingly at their neighbors and shake their heads at my sisters' collective shamelessness—while Mr. Bingley had taken to swirling his index finger around in his champagne glass and bouncing awkwardly on his heels.

Charlotte kindly guided me away, and I followed her and Maria wordlessly out of the room.

"You've run out of grapes, Mary," Charlotte said. "Let us go and replenish them."

To do so obligated us to pass the dancing, and it was here that Maria suddenly grabbed my arm.

"Look!" Maria cried. "What a sight to behold, for who do you think is dancing with Mr. Collins?"

I'd seen little of Mr. Collins for most of the evening. Though I'd sat next to him in the carriage to Netherfield, we had said nothing to each other, and my glancing at him often to check if any of my looks might be reciprocated had repeatedly ended in disappointment. Upon arriving at the ball, he'd disappeared from my view, and subsequent attempts to recover his company had proved unsuccessful, for no sooner would I glimpse him in a crowd and endeavor to make my way to his side, uttering several pardons to the guests I inconvenienced as I did so, than he would seem to see me and move swiftly away, adeptly dodging the many broad and delicate shoulders that obstructed his path. The first time I'd given up for bad luck, but in the third instance, I had called out to him. Upon hearing his name, he'd spun his head about the room and, spotting me waving at him several feet away, had briskly turned back around. After this, I'd followed him no more.

It was some moments before I'd recovered myself. Upon reaching the great ballroom, I had fortunately happened upon a quiet corner and had turned to the magnificent set of crystal chandeliers hanging from the ceiling. These I'd begun to count in my head, mouthing the numbers and starting afresh if I thought I'd miscalculated, even as a familiar heaviness gathered in my throat and in my eyes. I was glad Charlotte and Maria had discovered me soon after I'd finished, and it was a lucky thing that neither of my dear friends had noticed a few discreet tears in embracing me and kissing my cheeks.

But we presently looked upon a queer sight, and I confess that the picture in real life of Mr. Collins and Lizzy dancing showed itself much stranger than anything my imagination would have been able to conjure, even at the height of its powers. Whatever tasteful compliments he may have issued to my sister during the course of light-footed hopping almost certainly fell on deaf ears, so visibly disinterested did she appear to anything he addressed in her direction. She looked frequently over his head, and when they were obligated by the nature of the dance to hold hands, she turned away from him and flashed a charming smile at whoever happened to catch her eye, so long as it wasn't Mr. Collins himself. But he wouldn't give up his task so easily. His mouth continued to shape a thousand pleasing words, and his twinkling eyes betrayed the hope burning fervently in his optimistic breast of securing her attention. Though this is all speculation on my part, I do not think I stray too far from the truth in my interpretation, for both Mr. Collins and Lizzy took no pains to conceal their emotions, which were made much easier to distinguish by being the exact opposite of whatever the other was feeling. The dance, however, soon concluded, and I had just time to see Mr. Collins bowing so low to Lizzy that his forehead seemed in danger of touching the floor before Charlotte steered me away once again, back into the room of towering fruit and brilliantly polished silver.

For the better part of two whole minutes, I stared without moving at a pineapple, until, from a hollow distance, I heard Charlotte's voice. She seemed to be speaking to me, but I couldn't be sure.

"Mary," she said. Ah, now I was certain, for that was my name, and I slowly turned to meet her gaze. "Mary," she repeated. "I see you haven't refilled your plate. Oh, goodness, you do look pale all of a sudden. Are you all right?"

"I feel fine," I replied, just as more guests entered the room—Mr. Collins and Lizzy included. Walking swiftly in front of him, she seemed eager to acknowledge everyone in her vicinity except the one person most starved for her notice. He persisted, however, in trailing behind her as if he were her own shadow. In fact, the room might have been empty for the way he bungled past other guests in order to close the distance between himself and my sister, and when Lizzy swerved suddenly to her left, he nearly tripped over the train of a stranger's gown to keep his place by her side. At last they came close enough that I could hear some of their—or, rather, his—conversation, divided, as we were, by a small cluster of guests which conveniently obscured Mr. Collins and Lizzy's view of me.

"My dearest cousin Elizabeth," he said, "I do wish you would permit me to pick some fruit for you. I am certain you are needful of sustenance, as I have just consulted a clock and it will be at least another hour before supper begins. If only you would tell me which are best suited to your palate—for I would not risk selecting fruits that aren't completely agreeable to you—I would return immediately with a plate of your favorites. I know you mean not to put me to any trouble by refusing, for you place, like I do, the well-being of others before your own, but I can assure you that any difficulty I might meet with in completing this challenge would be well rewarded by the sight of watching you eat from the plate I have procured and your telling me, truthfully, that the morsels I have chosen are sweet and delightful to your discriminating taste."

To which Lizzy replied, "You are all kindness, Mr. Collins, but you do try my patience by asking me the same question over and over again. I have already told you that I have no desire to eat any fruit and that my constitution is not so weak that I am in danger of fainting after only two dances."

Mr. Collins uttered a cry before promptly throwing himself at my sister's mercy. "Dearest cousin Elizabeth," he exclaimed, "I feel certain I've offended you by the persistence of my concern for your well-being, but you might bring yourself to understand my own precarious position should anything happen to you while in my care."

"Yes, and I am certainly grateful for your concern, though you may find it hard to believe that I have survived many similar evenings of revelry without being so assiduously chaperoned," Lizzy answered. "Oh! Here are Charlotte and Maria! And Mary! How lucky that we have finally come across each other."

Mr. Collins bowed courteously to us, taking care to replicate Lizzy's cheerfulness towards her friends. His eye touched briefly a few points of interest on my person—the white feather, the thin band of pink ribbon I'd tied around my waist, the shoe-roses that wilted like dead poppies on my slippers—before wandering indifferently away.

The moment one becomes certain of defeat engenders a strange feeling. Possibly it is different for every person, but for me, it is a quiet, penitent moment, wrapped furtively within the confines of my body until it may be reopened and studied at a more convenient time. I swallowed my defeat the same way one hesitates to ingest something distasteful—the bitter skin of a grape, an underdone cut of meat that tastes a little too soft and bloody on one's tongue—but it must go down. One must swallow, though I can tell you that defeat is patient. It will wait quietly and without fuss until its host is at last ready to unravel the lifeless thing that was formerly a marvelous and miraculous vision. What had seemed possible, if not downright probable, less than a day or two ago was now cause for intense embarrassment. Garden walks in the twilight. Midnight carousing so loud it would wake up the servants. Shoulder rubs to help with sermon writing. And a year later, a brown-eyed, brown-haired child with a head as large and round as an apple dumpling. There was more, much more in the way of daydreams and fantasies conjured nightly in the warm and hazy minutes before one finally drifts off to sleep. But Fate wags a finger at me and says, "No, I don't think so, Mary Bennet. That is not for you." The parcel carrying one's wishes flies out of one's hands and into another's. Done, dead, and gone.

"Careful, Mary, you'll drop the plate if you hold it like that!" Lizzy cried out.

Eventually, Charlotte, Lizzy, and Mr. Collins moved off together, and only Maria was left standing by my side. As soon as they were out of our sight, Maria turned to me and emitted a piglike squeal. Every aspect of her face radiated what I can only describe as perverse hilarity, that variant of laughing expression which derives the majority of its amusement from another's pain.

"Mary!" she cried. "Did you not notice how Mr. Collins fretted and fussed over Lizzy? 'Oh, let me hold your wineglass, dearest Elizabeth.' 'Oh, be careful you don't trip over your dress, my dear.' 'Oh, cousin, are you sure you wouldn't like to sit down for a moment to rest your feet?' How she can stand it, I'll never understand! I would have gone half-mad by now."

"I wouldn't worry about Lizzy, if I were you," I replied, pretending nothing was the matter. "She has a high tolerance for madness, living with Mama and Lydia."

"But I am convinced this behavior is as suggestive as it is laughable," Maria said, "particularly if Mr. Collins has received permission from Mr. and Mrs. Bennet to stay close to Lizzy for the entire evening. Do you think he means to propose to her? I'm sure he does." After pausing to consider the matter, Maria added, "But the real puzzle is not whether Mr. Collins will propose to Lizzy, which is likely unavoidable, but whether Lizzy will have him. Do you think there's a very good chance she'll accept? She probably has to, poor soul."

"The way you're prattling on about it," I said, replenishing my wine and guzzling it down, "a stranger would think you wanted Mr. Collins for yourself."

"Goodness, no! You wouldn't catch me dead as the wife of a clergyman," Maria said with great emotion. "I wouldn't make it past two Sundays before collapsing from sheer boredom in one of the pews. But I will tell you something amusing, and this might put some color back into your cheeks. When Charlotte and I learned from our mother that Mr. Collins meant to take a wife among the Bennet girls, who do you think we first thought of as the most fitting match for him? I'm sure you'll never guess!"

"Lydia, I should think. She is the most sensible and would be more persuasive than any of us in assisting Mr. Collins with the collection of tithes."

"I wish you wouldn't joke, Mary. But since I see you're quite determined to be a bad sport, I will just tell you: Charlotte and I were both convinced it would be you. Wouldn't that be something, if you were to marry before any of your sisters did? Even before Jane or Lizzy?"

"Yes, Maria," I answered. "That would be something indeed, and about as likely as Mr. Bingley's friend Mr. Darcy falling head over heels in love with me and making me mistress of Pemberley. Some jokes are certainly less funny than others."

CHAPTER 11

B y the conclusion of supper, I was in a much better mood. I was, in fact, in so much of a better mood that if someone in that moment were to have pinched my nose and pulled my hair, I would have likely laughed in the perpetrator's face and pinched his nose and pulled his hair back. At the far end of the table, I noticed Jane and Mr. Bingley sitting very close together. Jane was engaged with daintily flipping a piece of chicken with the end of her fork, and this piece of chicken went round and round and round and round the inside of her plate until it bounced out onto the tablecloth. When this happened, she looked coyly at Mr. Bingley, who grinned back at her, and the two burst into laughter. Though they did not see me, I felt sufficiently moved by the scene to raise my glass to them.

"What a fine couple," I said and met the stare of an elderly woman with a sour face who I didn't know and who looked understandably nonplussed at being seated in the middle of a family she wasn't acquainted with, this family having as little interest in her presence at the table as she had in theirs. Mama was then deep in conversation with Lady Lucas, Mr. Collins was diverting Charlotte and Lizzy with tales of the Battle of Philippi and the Second Triumvirate, and Maria was anxiously eavesdropping on anything she could pick up between the two parties. Papa and Sir William were seated next to me, and true to the behavior of serious and learned men in public, they confined their conversation to only the most respectable of topics—that is, to the ongoing war with France, meetings of Parliament, and what either was occupied with reading at the time (military histories and articles of science; absolutely no mention of novels was ever made).

All around me, the air was golden and tinkling with musical sounds: laughter, silverware glancing off fine china, molars grinding against slabs of cold tongue and gobs of sweetbread. I caught snatches of interesting phrases from the other tables—"hard little bump," "two o'clock by the marble fountain," "no fool like an old fool," "baby's knees," "the dog would have made a better child," "bring the money," and "I'm still hungry." No one bothered to talk to me, which was just fine, as the wine proved more interesting company than any of my tablemates, and soon I was able to discover secret humor in places I had never bothered to look before, such as the drooping corners of Charlotte's mouth, the oily streaks of gray in Papa's hair, and Lizzy's lines of bad teeth. But at last, a voice from far, far away floated, as a leaf from a tree, to where I sat tilting back on the legs of my chair, and what this voice said was really the most sensible thing I'd heard all evening.

"Is there to be no singing tonight?" the voice shouted. "Come, we must have some singing! It has been far too quiet!"

I stood, very nearly toppling my chair, and bustled to the front of the room, sheet music flapping in my arms. As I plopped triumphantly onto the piano bench, I heard Mr. Bingley introduce me to my audience as the "reputed songbird of Longbourn," and the unexpected kindness of his words rendered me a little tearful between my hiccups as I waited to begin my first song.

"I shall not displease you, Mr. Bingley, nor any of you," I cried with feeling from my seat at the piano and, wiggling my fingers theatrically, launched into "The Last Rose of Summer," which I'd practiced for many hours over the last three days with this display expressly in mind. I recall that I sang with intense emotion, and this passion must have plucked at the heartstrings of at least a few members of my audience, for I heard a woman sitting at the table nearest the instrument comment to her husband.

"Good Lord," she said in a voice certain to carry to more than one table, "how agonizing to listen to."

Which was the truth, because anyone familiar with Thomas Moore's poem will know that this is a tragic song about living alone in the world, bereft of all hope of companionship and affection. As I sang, I envisioned myself a flower drooping from its stem and gazing sadly over the petals of my dead friends as they lay strewn in the grassy bed of the garden at Longbourn. It was all terribly poignant, and I howled the final few lines of the song with greater passion—indeed, passion that seemed to rise from the deepest pit of my being. "Oh!" I shouted to the rooftop of Netherfield Park and then paused for dramatic effect. *"Who would inhabit . . ."* I bawled, *"this bleak world alooooone?"* After finishing with a few inspired flourishes, I bowed my head in imitation of the dying rose, until the tip of my nose rested over my wrists on the keyboard. The applause, in my opinion, was a bit sparse for such a soul-rending performance, but more gratifying were the murmurs from the audience, particularly, as expected, from the women.

Lifting my head from the keyboard, I peered about the room in time to view two ladies fanning themselves and another clasping a gloved hand over her mouth. Some young men among the officers seemed at a glance to be laughing, but I expected no better from them, as they were sitting at the same table as Lydia and Kitty.

"Thank you," I said, flashing a smile at the expanse of blurred faces that watched me. "Thank you so very much."

"Won't you play another?" a mustached officer called out from the table of barbarians.

"What's that?" I slurred. "Who said that? Yes, I think that's a wonderful idea. I need to cheer us all up. We all need some cheering up tonight."

As no one ventured to disagree with me, I began the opening of "The Soldier's Adieu" by Charles Dibdin.

"Adieu! Adieu! My only life!" I sang in short, feverish bursts, the curls around my ears shaking violently to the bobbing of my head. *"My honor calls me from thee. Remember thou art a soldier's wife.* Come, everyone together now! Let us fill this hall with angelic music!"

A few scattered voices charitably joined in, but the result was weak. The majority of the guests still preferred to stare, and I had all but abandoned the idea of transforming the dining room of Netherfield Park into a patriotic theater of boisterous, impassioned singing when the mustached officer suddenly shot up from his seat and opened his mouth. The uniformed boor turned out to be a baritone, and a baritone with a voice so rich, heaven-sent, and miraculous that I quite forgot, for all of three seconds, to keep playing. Moving confidently in the direction of the piano, he reached my side a short while later, and I watched him beckon to the rest of his friends, who had remained sitting and nudging one another with amused looks. These men begrudgingly rose and filed one after the other to stand shoulder to shoulder around the instrument and supply their voices. Then additional members of the audience joined in, and every one of us remembered, for the better part of two verses, that we were a nation at war, until there were no more lines to sing, and the singing became thunderous applause contributed by the whole room.

"Thank you, Netherfield Park!" I shouted at the top of my lungs and executed a dazzling glissando before springing to my feet.

I spotted my sisters, Mama, and the Lucas family matriarch all gazing at me in a condition of bewilderment, as if I'd grown two horns and a tail. In fact, Sir William, who had always been unabashedly patriotic, appeared the only one at my table genuinely pleased by the performance. He stood up to shout "Bravo!" and "Encore!" and encouraged others sitting around him to do the same. The officers returned cheerfully to their seats, and I was considering what to play next when a lean, black silhouette appeared at the end of the piano and said to me in a voice I recalled from my infancy, "That will do extremely well, child. You have delighted us long enough. Let the other young ladies have time to exhibit." Looking up, I saw my father peering at me, an outstretched hand prepared to guide me back to my chair. I wanted to tell him I wasn't quite ready to leave the piano yet—I still had some excerpts from Handel's *Water Music* to perform. But the wine was finally taking a turn. My belly lurched, and I stared strangely at Papa before sprinting with my sheet music out of the room, into the hall, through the front entrance, and down the thirty or so steps to ground level, where I finally spewed a puddle of yellow froth at the foot of someone's carriage.

"Who's garn ter clean that oop?" a liveried servant snarled at me from the top of the carriage.

My stomach twisted again, and I was forced to lean forward and regurgitate another few glasses of the excellent wine I'd enjoyed at Mr. Bingley's expense. In a brilliant spray of translucent gold, the vomit splattered across the coat of arms emblazoned on the door, running in shining channels down to the spokes of the wheel. Breathless and feeling much better, I stumbled a few steps backwards to get a better view of the servant, who was still staring furiously at me.

He looked my cotton dress up and down, dwelling longer than I liked on the white feather that crowned the top of my head. Then he licked his lips and hissed, "Lemme guess. The ovver women made fan of your gahn and 'air. Ya got oopset and drank too much. Is that it? Did me mistress make fan of ya? Ya 'ave nah business vomitin' on 'er carriage, though. Remember, it's us poor folk that 'ave ter clean up after aw the bleedin' fan is o'er."

"No," I replied, as the ground tipped dangerously. Everything, even the vomit I'd expelled, had taken on a warm glow. "I don't know who your mistress is," I said, squinting up at the driver's face, which was also encircled by a wide-ringed halo. "Who is she?" I asked in a tone of disbelief.

At the sound of footsteps approaching, the servant straightened and averted his gaze. Thinking it my father, I spun around and came face-to-face with Mr. Darcy.

The sight of him succeeded at once in sobering me, and with that sobriety, I felt the first wave of shame which was my due. I'd rather it had been any member of my family come to rebuke me for my behavior, for I would have gladly received their censure to this gentleman's. It is one thing to be lectured on proper conduct in public by your own flesh and blood, quite another to receive the same chastisement from a prominent member of the landed gentry. I was aware I had done badly. So much of Jane's happiness was riding on this ball, and what had I accomplished with my antics, except to play the wine-soaked clown to Lydia and Kitty's usual impropriety.

"You look a mess" was the first thing he said. Then he caught sight of the carriage wheels and wrinkled his nose.

"Yes, yes, all right," I mumbled.

"Your behavior tonight surprises me, Miss Bennet," he began. "The first time we spoke, I confess you struck me as a very rational young woman. But I must say something on behalf of my friend, whose kindness you imposed upon greatly with what I can only call your inspired performance at the piano, to say nothing of the amount of alcohol you have consumed unchecked this evening."

Though the insult struck home, I continued to gaze impassively at him.

"Bingley thinks too highly of your eldest sister to reproach you or your family," Mr. Darcy continued, "but as no ties of affection can claim my heart, I won't deign to withhold my opinions. Haven't you any shame in your conduct? Did you not pause, even for a moment, to consider the consequences of your actions on the reputations of your sisters, particularly Miss Jane and Miss Elizabeth, before you committed to carrying them through?"

At the mention of Lizzy, I thought of Mr. Collins. At the thought of Mr. Collins, the memory of his diminutive body moving away from me in the crowd brought renewed pain, and I nearly lost my footing.

"I . . . I have been wronged. . . ." I managed to say at last, my voice fluctuating wildly. Or had I meant instead to say that I *was* wrong? Wrong for believing I could be loved by any man who was not obliged, as my father and uncles were, to love me? Wrong for thinking I could be the first among my sisters to marry? What a fool I was for mistaking a man's willingness to converse with affection! How could I, little weed, be a favorite of anyone? No, for all the books I consumed, I was still a dupe to my own vanity.

Even the most disciplined of souls will bend when there is enough wretchedness before them, and in this, Mr. Darcy proved no exception. His expression grew stilted and embarrassed. Fresh tears that had grown too heavy for my eyes wetted my face, and he silently passed me his own handkerchief.

"Perhaps I was too harsh. . . ." he suggested politely.

"No, Mr. Darcy," I replied. "The fault is my own, and I must acknowledge it. I have behaved . . ." I could not finish the sentence. "Will you please convey my apologies to Mr. Bingley and his sisters. . . . I admit I haven't the courage for such an endeavor. . . ."

"Unless my friend should broach the matter first, you have my assurance I won't bring up the incident again," he said quietly, folding the handkerchief I'd returned to him.

I thanked him, expecting that he would take his leave. Instead, he paused, and I thought he even smiled a little at what he was about to tell me.

"I thought you'd like to know, Miss Bennet, that I took your advice. To make amends for the offense I'd caused, I asked Miss Elizabeth to dance with me."

I had just strength enough to venture a light chuckle. "Oh, did you, Mr. Darcy? I am glad of it."

With more restraint than the comment warranted, he added, "Your sister is a fine dancer."

"She is," I conceded, and nodding to me, with the handkerchief still in his hands, he left.

How charming my sister is, I thought, my tears renewing their supply. Excepting Mr. Bingley, who was assuredly Jane's, how all the men of the world seemed to throw themselves at Lizzy's feet.

As soon as he had gone, I heard someone clear his throat above me, and I turned to regard the servant.

Rubbing his hand over his red nose, he said, "Ya goo ahn a'ead, miss. Daan't worry neemore abaht the carriage. I'll clean oop the mess."

"You're very kind," I said, wiping away the last of my tears. The servant nodded, and I went back up the thirty or so steps to the front entrance, through to the hall, and into the drawing room, where I resumed my seat at my family's table in time to catch the last minute of Caroline Bingley's tarantella before the audience exploded with cheers and applause.

Sometime during the carriage ride back to Longbourn, I must have fallen asleep, as I had a dream, and this dream was more vivid and lifelike than anything I could recall in recent memory. In it, I'm sitting alone beside Mr. Collins, and the carriage lurches and sways even more awfully than my wine-filled stomach. He's just finished covering his legs with a blanket, and he says, without looking at me, "Tomorrow, Mary, I'm going to do it. I'm sorry, but I have to." And I know at once what he's talking about. I feel my whole face shrivel into a tight, concentrated circle as I struggle not to cry. I begin to plead with him. "You have a choice," I say. "You can choose, Mr. Collins, to be happy. You can choose *me*." But the horses have stopped, and the carriage has rolled to a halt in front of the door. He pulls the blanket off his legs and turns away. "I'm afraid you don't understand," he says in a voice that grows increasingly distant from where I'm sitting, "and I certainly wouldn't expect you to. I've thought a lot about it, and I have to go through with it tomorrow. I'm sorry, Mary."

Lizzy later told me that when Papa lifted my sleeping body from the carriage, my face was streaked with tears. "You were crying, Mary," she said to me a few days later, after a great many other things had occurred. "You were probably asleep, if you can't remember. But you were crying all the same, as though something terrible were happening to you. And for all the shaking we did, none of us could get you to wake up, until Papa told us to leave you be. You couldn't stop."

CHAPTER 12

I awoke late the next morning with a headache the likes of which I'd never encountered before and discovered myself still dressed in the gown I'd worn the previous evening, complete with the feather stuck lopsided in my hair. This I plucked out wearily before changing into a clean frock and stumbling uneasily downstairs, gripping the banister with white knuckles. On the landing, I ran into Sarah, who was on her way up to our rooms with a large pile of clean laundry. I expected to receive from her a summons to attend Papa at once in his study, but she only informed me I'd missed breakfast and that if I went to the kitchen, there were some cold rolls and dry toast to be had, as well as leftover coffee and chocolate, which Mrs. Hill could heat up for me. I was grateful to Sarah for telling me this, though I couldn't make out why she did so in a voice that would have easily filled up an amphitheater.

"Mind you go straight to the kitchen and not into the breakfast room, Miss Mary," she said, and I thought I detected the beginnings of a smile tugging the upturned ends of her mouth. Another quarter of an inch, and she'd be in danger of laughing.

"Why shouldn't I go into the breakfast room?" I asked.

The smile stretched but did not break. "You might go and see for yourself," she answered cryptically. "But stay outside the door, mind, or Mrs. Bennet will have a fit."

We parted on the landing, and I continued downstairs. The door of the breakfast room was shut, and I drifted towards it until my right ear settled comfortably over the wood. The speaker was Mr. Collins.

"My reasons for marrying are, first, that I think it a right thing for every clergyman in easy circumstances—like myself—to set the example of matrimony in his parish. . . ."

For one crazed moment, I considered breaking into the room and stopping the proceedings. "No, sir," I might say, pointing an accusatory finger at our houseguest. "You love me, and I have the tokens with which to prove your affection!" Yes, it was true: I still possessed his letter and the sheets of music he had copied, though these alone evidenced nothing. He had admitted to feeling a kinship with me, but goodwill is a species very different from love. And how much more of a fool could I really suffer myself to appear?

As his overtures to Lizzy continued, I crept away. I wanted to get out of the house, to leave Longbourn behind and run eternally towards that horizon I'd always envisioned. But even this proved difficult; thoughts materialized like ghosts and lashed my brain. *You kissed him. He didn't kiss you; you kissed him. You pursued him. Shameless. Disgraceful. Degrading. No better than your younger sisters.*

On my way, I passed Mama strolling up and down the length of the vestibule. She was in brilliant spirits and stopped me in order to divulge the pleasant and excited state of her nerves.

"Mary, my dear, come and sit by me," she said distractedly, guiding me towards a pair of chairs. "These are undoubtedly happy times for our family but no less trying for someone whose health is as frail as mine. I hope you didn't venture into the breakfast room on your way down? You must still be exhausted from all your singing and playing last night."

I shook my head, and Mama covered my folded hands with her own. She released a short, rather unconvincing sigh and added, "It is always an unhappy thing for a mother to be separated from her daughters when the time comes for them to be married, but we mustn't allow such gloomy thoughts to overtake an otherwise most fortunate event. We must all of us be grateful for this stroke of good luck, so that the Lord may see fit to bestow our family with additional blessings, for there are still the rest of you to be dealt with after Lizzy goes away."

Feigning ignorance, I turned to Mama and asked, "Where is Lizzy going?"

"Why, don't you know," Mama cried, "at this very moment, Mr. Collins is in the breakfast room making an offer of marriage to your sister! And she'll accept him, of course."

"You seem very confident of that, Mama."

"I would never speak to Lizzy again if she didn't," Mama said with passionate intensity, squeezing my hands. "And that goes for you, too, Mary, if you were ever to refuse a perfectly respectable offer of marriage that was in your best interest to accept."

As I couldn't think how to reply, I leaned in to peck my mother's cheek, generating a surprised but satisfied "Oh!" Her skin was warm and a little moist with sweat from all the fretting she'd done while waiting for the young lovers to emerge. The natural light which filled the hall caught the ends of the tiny hairs that had materialized, seemingly overnight, over Mama's upper lip and around her chin. She looked older when she was quiet. Each of her eyes cast the shadow of a half-moon, and I told her she must try to sleep more now that the excitement leading up to the Netherfield ball was finally over.

"There won't be any rest for me," Mama sighed wearily, "not until every one of my girls is married, which I daresay includes even you, Mary. Something to keep in mind the next time we go to a ball and I've arranged an introduction. . . ."

"Poor Mama," I replied in earnest and stroked the back of her hand as she absentmindedly murmured her assent.

Somewhere in the house, a door was flung open, and Mama jumped to her feet.

"That may be Lizzy or Mr. Collins," she shrieked, running off in the direction of the breakfast room, and I quickly left the house before all descended into chaos, as I knew it would.

CHAPTER 13

When I returned to Longbourn an hour later, the house was eerily quiet. While the servants remained discreetly belowstairs, the members of my family had folded themselves behind closed doors, like black-feathered birds that sleep in the hidden depths of barns and attics. Lilting sobs haunted their way down the hall from Mama's room, where my younger sisters took turns comforting our inconsolable mother. I looked in on Jane as I passed and spotted her and Lizzy sitting together on the bed, making, between their drooping brows and folded hands, a very pretty picture of impoverished maidenhood. *Will no one pick these elegant flowers, though they grow in coarse and untidy fields?*

All was still, as the house and its occupants considered the tiny drama which had unfolded that morning; the high-spirited comedy with its many strange and diverting characters had turned decidedly tragic, and not tragic in the way which is glorious and cathartic, with poisoned goblets, stilettos, and heroes lying soaked in their own blood. No, the tragedy that had visited Longbourn this morning was quiet and inglorious. My own embarrassing display at the Netherfield ball might never have occurred, for how trivial it now seemed. A decision had been made, and our childhood home, our estate of several generations, our crumbling but endearing little shelter with its peeling wallpaper and soiled carpets and furniture ruined by undrawn curtains and excessive sunshine—all of these things felt suddenly lost to us, as though we'd realized for the first time that the world we had always lived in was perched on a bank of sand, its erosion concurrent with the remaining years of my father's life.

"Mary, if you will stand outside the door like that, you may as well come in," Jane called out.

The first thing I did when I went in was touch Lizzy's shoulder. "I'm sorry I didn't believe you," I said. I might have added, "I don't blame you, Lizzy. Nobody could ever blame you for refusing Mr. Collins," with appropriate sisterly ferocity, or "We kissed, you know, that day I went to go fetch the shoe-roses. In the rain, while kneeling together in the mud." How might I have summoned the courage to divulge the latter? But I remained silent, and Lizzy, her own eyes puffy and waterlogged, only patted my wrist to show she appreciated my gesture.

"It's fine, Mary," she said. "I did dread it happening, but one just doesn't take it seriously until it does. And even now, it seems a very big joke—laughable really, though I know it's unkind to say so, especially to you. I know *you* liked him. He was your friend, and you seemed rather devoted to him in your funny way."

"No, not really," I said, and the reply, which had been uttered hastily, rang hollow to all our ears. Flushing, I looked out Jane's window. The sky was bright enough to blind one's eyes, and I stared and stared until my vision penetrated the clouds and all the colors mixed and thawed into a brilliant white that stretched before me like a passage between this world and the next. My face burned. I couldn't remember a time when I had felt more ashamed.

I have heard Papa say that unrequited love, far from being a necessary evil, can actually do a man good. In recounting his youthful pursuits, he'd remarked that occasional rejection could work wonders in building out a man's character. "I thought of it as medicine," he cheerfully told us one evening after dinner. "To a gentleman who wishes to marry, it takes little more than a pretty face saying 'No' for

him to conjure all the strength and means within his power in order
to win her." But a woman could not do the same. For a woman to
chase a man was considered an insult to her character. A woman
must be silent until she is approached. She can never be too guarded
with her feelings. No wonder unrequited love is so hard on our sex,
I thought, for it cannot empower or embolden us, and she who is
rejected must alone suffer the humiliation for having indulged in
dreams which were never her right to entertain.

Two uncomfortable days later, on Mr. Collins's last evening at
Longbourn, I discovered a letter propped up by a stack of books on
my writing table. Recognizing the effeminate hand as belonging to
my cousin, I tore it open and read the following note:

Dearest Cousin Mary,

As the time draws near for my departure (on this visit at
least), I found that I could not leave for Hunsford without
thanking you personally for your friendship and hospitality
during my stay. (We will say nothing of why my visit has
only been generally pleasant and not exhaustively so.) I have
faithfully promised your mother that the subject of the unhappy and disappointing events which occurred on Wednes-
day will never broach my lips again so long as I live, though
I allude to them now only to tell you, knowing your charitable nature will share in my triumph, that things are far from
being as hopeless as they seem. My trials, in fact, have borne
fruit, and this fruit, as I shall momentarily reveal to you, is
sweeter for having been realized by a circuitous route. You
will pardon me for being unusually candid in this matter,
but it is a serious one—on top of which, I do not believe in
bestowing gratitude and credit where none are due. Therefore, I will refrain from expressing any thanks to your sister
for my present condition of felicity, as I am confident that
she deserves none and may yet regret the decision she has

made. But we shall say no more on this awkward subject out of respect for your good parents and yourself. Suffice it to say that I am a happier man for the acceptance I have received from quite another—and, I daresay, equally deserving and elegant—hand.

I must entreat you to keep both the news of my engagement and the identity of the lady to yourself for the present time, though it won't be long that you shall have to bear the burden of this secrecy. I've been told in no uncertain terms that Sir William Lucas will pay a visit to Longbourn tomorrow to deliver the news—yes, Sir William Lucas, and your intelligence will not, I hope, fail you now in determining by this vital clue the name of my bride-to-be. I am, by her parents' enthusiastic consent, engaged to Miss Charlotte Lucas, and I have every faith that Lady Catherine and Miss Anne de Bourgh will welcome her with open arms into our small but distinguished community at Hunsford. Even now, I am astonished by the blessing of finding so much beauty and grace in a single woman; I cannot think it fair that I am the sole recipient of all the joy to be had in the world. And as a close friend to my dear Charlotte, you would undoubtedly be the first to agree that she is in every way possible perfectly suited for the role which awaits her and will run my modest household admirably well, making, as Lady Catherine tastefully put it to me in the days before I set off for Longbourn, "a small income go a good way."

Destiny would prevent us being brother and sister by marriage, though you can be certain in your heart that you are no less dear to me as a friend than if you were my younger sister by blood. I hope therefore that you may be as happy for me in my choice of marriage as I am for myself. Trust that I shall always remember the many kindnesses you paid me during my visit to Longbourn—these are memories that Time itself is powerless to efface—and that I speak in earnest when I wish you equal joy in finding a partner as worthy of your innumerable virtues and talents as I have done.

Respectfully yours,
Mr. William Collins

Sometimes the pattern of life is circular, and one ends up exactly where one has started. The sky was still dark when Mr. Collins set off in a noisy curricle for Hunsford. In the drawing room, a great fire blazed in the hearth and melted the last fragments of "The Last Rose of Summer" in its many rippling tongues. Soon the sound of the horses gave way to the sound of my thoughts. I thought of shoe-roses and mud. I remembered two bodies drenched in rain, water tingling down their necks like the wandering trace of a lover's finger. I remembered a kiss impetuously stolen, and I promised the ghostly reflection which stared solemnly at me from the other side of the window that I would never fall in love again.

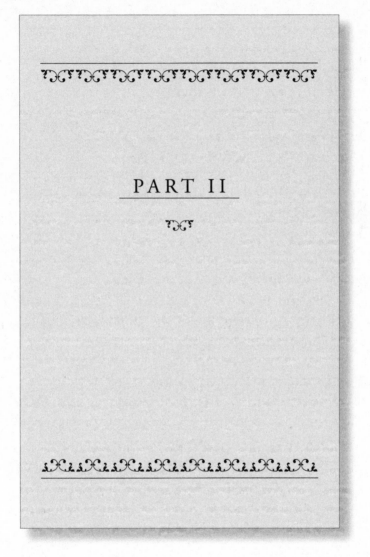

PART II

CHAPTER 14

Within the space of a year, three of my sisters married. First, Lydia eloped with Mr. George Wickham. They'd been living for some time in London, in cramped and not very hygienic conditions, when my uncle Gardiner at last discovered them. Lydia insisted that she did not mind the squalor of their lodgings, for even hardships became the sweetest comforts in the presence of her beloved, and the bed was fortunately of prodigious dimensions.

Jane, also, I'm happy to say, won her prize in the end. Under the influence of his pernicious sisters, Mr. Bingley had cowardly absconded to London, leaving poor Jane to assume, for a torturous period of time, his disinterest. But finding no reward in the city greater than her love, he eventually returned to Netherfield Park and proposed to Jane during a nondescript evening of supper and cards at Longbourn. His offer of marriage, comprising in equal parts steadfast affection and five thousand pounds per annum, was speedily accepted amid cries directed heavenward that we'd been saved—thank you, O sweet and merciful Lord.

This was only the first, however, of two major victories for our family, for never let it be said that Lizzy will suffer to be outdone by her older sister. Not content with marrying the equivalent of one Mr. Bingley, she married two—that is, she married Mr. Own-Half-of-Derbyshire Darcy of sprawling estate (Pemberley), ten thousand pounds per annum, noble and historic stock, and Hamletesque brow.

As for myself, I spent the year learning to keep my own company. I read voraciously. One week: Elizabeth Hamilton's *Memoirs of Modern Philosophers.* Another week: Mary Wollstonecraft's *The Wrongs of Woman* and Charles Brockden Brown's *Clara Howard.* I read with such monastic zeal that even Papa came up to me one day and, observing my furrowed brow absorbing a page of Jane Porter's four-volume novel *Thaddeus of Warsaw,* commented whether I meant to overtake him in the speed of my consumption. I created, too, a daily schedule, which regulated my waking hours. My mornings began with rising at least an hour before any of my sisters did in order to take exercise on the estate's grounds or, if the weather did not permit a brisk walk, to read what I hadn't finished the evening before. This was always followed by a light breakfast and at least three hours of uninterrupted study, then one hour of musical practice preceding lunchtime.

How grateful I was for my books. In the first throes of my pain, their pages had caught my tears when no comforting hand would. And when I grew stronger, what an anchor they were in my life, a constant dearer to me than any friend, which guarded my spirit against morbidity and despair. It was by their distraction alone that I was able to witness my sisters' betrothals with equanimity and avoid falling prey, as Kitty did, to infantile fits of jealousy at the good fortune which visited Jane and Lizzy in rapid succession.

When Mr. Collins married Charlotte Lucas, I expected my disappointment to last for a much longer period of time than it did. I admit I surprised myself with my own strength. Awaking one morning soon after, I felt an unprecedented freedom. I realized I could do as I pleased. I could sing and play without having to wonder if my voice and fingering met with that gentleman's approval. I could read without my mind conjuring even once the image of his face. If no one would speak to me, then I had no cause to speak to them, and

my time remained my own. I discovered, too, that because my opinion was valued so little by my family, I could say almost whatever I
liked without fear of reprobation. So I practiced this and told Kitty
that her bonnets looked just as facile as she was, that the pork at dinner was too tough, and when Mr. Wickham returned to Longbourn
with Lydia as his wife, I said to my brother-in-law in a voice audible
to everyone, "This isn't really the outcome you were hoping for, was
it?" Fortunately, I received little reproof for my sharp tongue. What
with Jane's and Lizzy's impending nuptials, Papa saw less reason than
ever to involve himself in the concerns of his daughters, and my
mother and sisters were far too busy with the writing of invitations
in florid script and the choosing of gowns to seriously acknowledge
any change in my behavior.

It was around this time that I also began to keep a journal. At
first, I used it just for rambling musings of how I had passed each
day, but growing bored with this exercise, I began putting to paper
observations of my sisters. I offer a few examples below:

*Rosy Cheeks is visiting the shops this afternoon to purchase lace
for her wedding dress, and Squalling Baby looked very petulant
and unhappy indeed that no one among her acquaintances will
yet propose to her. We have even less to say to each other these days
than we used to.*

*Queenie has become like Father Christmas and continues to
sweep about granting favors to everyone. She has already promised two new dresses to Squalling Baby and a visit to Versailles to
Mrs. Church's younger sister, the Virgin Mary. How good fortune
will change some people—and seemingly overnight! I cannot be
too harsh on Queenie, though—the fault, I concede, is not entirely hers, for she has been puffed up by so many congratulations
and good wishes as would turn anyone's head. I will admit she
looks excessively pretty these days; whether that is the effect of love*

or the expectation of becoming rich, however, I cannot in all
honesty discern.

In the weeks leading up to their wedding, Mr. Darcy visited
Longbourn frequently, and on every occasion, brought gifts intended to endear him to a family that had previously thought ill of
him. It was during such a visit that he and I found ourselves alone,
and though I was occupied with writing in my journal, he came over
to engage me in conversation. The awkwardness which characterized
our meeting at Netherfield Park had since been forgotten, and I'd
succeeded in restoring myself to his original impression of me, as "a
very rational young woman."

"There are some books waiting for you in the other room," he
began. "I thought you might enjoy them."

Brightening, I asked what titles he had brought for me this time.

"An epistolary novel called *The Wild Irish Girl,* a work by Plu-
tarch, and one I know you'll relish as much as I did—*Memoirs of
Carwin the Biloquist,* which is about a boy who creates all kinds of
mischief by impersonating the voices of others."

I admitted this sounded delightful and thanked him for his trouble. Then I returned to my journal writing, but it wasn't long before
he asked me what I was working on.

"Oh, I'm keeping a diary," I admitted.

"Georgiana has kept a journal for the last three years," Mr. Darcy
said, brotherly pride getting the better of him.

When I didn't offer an opinion, not being acquainted with his
sister, he continued: "I'm very curious what you have to write, Miss
Bennet. Will you not read aloud even a small glimpse of your daily
reflections while your sisters happen to be out of the room?"

Handsomeness in a man can certainly be as persuasive as beauty
in a woman. I found myself turning the pages of my journal, looking for the most innocuous entry I could find. But before I was able

to locate one, Lizzy returned, and when she saw Mr. Darcy sitting with me, her generous nature bubbled to the surface.

"Mary, I think I shall hold you to the obligation of visiting me at least two times each year at Pemberley," she said, beaming. "Mr. Darcy wouldn't mind. Would you, Mr. Darcy?"

The gentleman insisted that it would be a pleasure. "Then it is settled!" Lizzy shouted, for she did everything in the days leading up to the wedding with exuberance. "You shall come and stay with us at Pemberley, Mary. I promise I will write to you and send a carriage when we are ready."

Mr. Darcy's visit that day prompted the following entry in my journal, which I wrote outdoors in the company of Papa's ancient and drooling sheepdog:

Louis XIV has brought me more books. I have counted his gifts since his engagement to Queenie and calculated that he is responsible for at least a third of the new titles I've read since ghastly Mr. Church went off with his new bride.

Rosy Cheeks called Queenie away on some errand, and I was left alone again with le Roi Soleil. He repeated his earlier request, which was to hear an excerpt from my journal, and I chose a selection I'd written on Squalling Baby and how I'd discovered her one night in her room embracing her looking glass and kissing it. It did not take Louis XIV long to figure out who Squalling Baby was, and once he did, we laughed so much that Mother Hen, Rosy Cheeks, and Queenie all came downstairs to see what the matter was. Neither of us would give anything away, however, and I confess it a rather delicious feeling to share an inside joke with one as respectable as the Sun King.

He has promised to bring me Eliza Parsons's The Castle of Wolfenbach *on his next visit, and we are to make an intellectual exercise of counting how many times the words "faint" and "weep" appear over the course of two volumes. We are both agreed that the surfeit of sentimentality found in Gothic novels is deserving of the cruelest ridicule possible, though they remain the most amusing of books to digest.*

THE DAY OF the wedding did not disappoint. Jane and Lizzy had decided to get married together, and all was as it should be on such a happy occasion. The weather was fine; the guests were splendidly attired; the grooms looked as handsome as they ever did, if not a little smug. In our small and placid community, the air felt rife with miracle. Perhaps it was my imagination which endowed the brides with an almost unearthly loveliness, but they seemed less human than nymphs. The sight of them rendered me a bit tearful, and I had to borrow Kitty's handkerchief. I confess I surprised myself with my weeping, which was as much inspired by the triumph of seeing my two sisters in their fine marriages as it was by the desire which filled my own heart upon witnessing their great happiness. Their audience may well have been invisible; for the rest of the day's revelry, the young lovers noticed only themselves, and when the hour came to leave, they had hardly time for waving goodbye to us, bound already in each other's arms.

Lizzy and Mr. Darcy were not married half a year before her promised invitation arrived, and I embarked on a journey to that estate, which had come to occupy in my mind a near legendary status: Pemberley.

CHAPTER 15

It is hard, I think, not to envy the life which is lived in an attitude of leisure. Just as pigs will cover themselves in mud and the rooster will herald the first light of day with his cry, the idle rich will loll instinctively. In the library at Pemberley, on a wrinkly velvet green sofa, I lolled with my copy of Walter Scott's *The Lady of the Lake* under a ceiling constellation of griffins and cherubs and fruit-bearing vines. One had only to walk a few feet before a divan offered its supine comforts or a window seat begged to be sat on. Desks featured every instrument requisite to the composition and sending of letters except the writer himself, and ornate ottomans settled here and there like bright, exotic birds with tasseled wings.

In the whole of the library, there was, however, only one place ideal for lolling, and that was the wrinkly velvet green sofa with its infinite, swaddling depths and mossy expanse of softness. While lolling, the mind is prone to wander, and my own began to drift further and further away from the pages in front of me, as I dreamily contemplated all that had occurred since I'd arrived at my sister's new home two months ago.

It was at Pemberley that I began my first novel in earnest. The choice was not entirely voluntary. Georgiana, Darcy's younger sister by nearly ten years, had a reputation for sweetness but proved selective in who should benefit by it. She was a tall, slender girl of nineteen with hair so fine and fair that in the sunlight, it looked like ten thousand threads of uncultivated silk. Her wide forehead suggested innocence. Her dainty nose, purity. She expelled beautiful music from her lungs as well as from her fingers, painted serene watercolors of wildernesses she would never enter, and embroidered birds of paradise with a leisurely masterliness that would put even the most proficient seamstress to shame.

Every goddess must have a temple, and Georgiana had two. The first was the "large," or "main," music room of Pemberley; the second, endearingly named the "small" music room, existed in a remote corner of another wing and contained only a card table, a few chairs, and a square Clementi piano. On the third day of my arrival, I had entered the "large" music room alone and, finding no one in it, uncovered that magnificent instrument, a birthday gift from her doting brother. It was during the second movement of a lively sonatina that I sensed someone watching me, and looking up, I came face-to-face with the goddess herself. She glanced with contempt at my hands, which were still postured on the keyboard as if to play, and said, in a superior voice of thinly veiled anger, "Thank you, Miss Bennet. I am familiar with the piece you just performed, having learned it when I was seven or eight years old. But I will take it from here." Then she brought the piano cover down so swiftly that I'd barely time to snatch my wrists away. Even after Georgiana left Pemberley to spend her summer months in Bath, I never set foot in either the "large" or "small" music rooms again, though I cannot deny the relief I felt upon witnessing her departure.

Fortunately, I had other loves besides music. The idea that I might start a novel came to me one lazy afternoon not long after my unfortunate encounter with Georgiana. I'd been lolling on the sofa with another of Frances Burney's sentimental creations—*Cecilia* or *Camilla* or *Evelina,* I can't remember. But by dinnertime that day, the characters had assembled like obedient schoolchildren into a tidy compartment of my brain. I had named them, visualized them, and determined their fates with, I confess, callously little regard for their personal happiness or physical well-being. It was just as well, I thought, that I possessed neither fortune nor influence in real life.

A single page soon grew into two, and these seeds mushroomed into a prolific vine of fifteen-odd chapters within the course of days. Buoyed by an inexhaustible supply of fine-quality paper, quill pens, and ink, my story grew long and rich in its telling. Deaths proliferated, as did romances, forming the account of a rather remarkable queen who emerges from the rubble of a kingdom perpetually at war with powerful enemies and traitorous allies.

Despite being unfinished, the novel already boasted one illustrious reader, the last person I would have expected to take an interest in my work, and this was the master of Pemberley himself, Mr. Own-Half-of-Derbyshire Darcy. As I lolled undisturbed across the wrinkly velvet green sofa, I recalled one of my first meetings with that gentleman. Sitting at my usual desk in the library, I'd been working on an early chapter of my book when a door had burst open.

"No, no, please don't get up on my account," Darcy had mumbled, making swiftly for a small bureau and checking the contents of all the drawers. I pretended to busy myself; my pen made a few meaningless scratches in the margins, and I drew a wavy flower with curling leaves over the heading of an empty page that would mark the beginning of the second chapter of *Leonora*. I became so engrossed with my flower-making that I didn't notice until too late the figure standing in front of me, staring curiously at the two piles of paper at either side of my arms. When I did notice, my reaction was to jump in my seat and cry, "Mr. Darcy!" in the alarmed way of females who believe themselves to have been taken disadvantageously by surprise. He gestured with a courteous flourish at the pile to my left and inquired if they were unused. I shyly nodded.

"I've run out of paper in my study," he explained. "Could I . . ." His hand hovered expectantly over the pile.

"Oh, of course. I'm sorry." Though I didn't know what I was apologizing for.

"A few sheets will suffice. Thank you." He counted them, one-two-three-four. There, all done. Now he could go, and I waited for him to leave the room as briskly as he had entered. But instead he lingered and spread a large hand over the pile on my right. My face instantly warmed. I hadn't intended to tell anyone I was working on a novel, much less have its contents read by a third party. He lifted a page, turned it over, read the matter on the other side, and smiled, though I'd rather he didn't, for I thought he smiled in a condescending way. To a man who owned an entire library of ancient and spectacular beauty, my creation would surely seem among the paltriest of offerings to the eternal Muses. But he kept reading, and my shame increased with every page he exposed. After a while, he asked if this was how I'd been occupying myself during my visit. Prior to this, we had been in each other's company only at meals, and on such occasions, his mind had always been engaged by matters of business. A troublesome tenant had taken him away from Pemberley for several days, and he'd returned earlier that morning. Glancing at him, I noticed how tired he looked, while guiltily acknowledging to myself that his exhaustion did nothing to diminish his handsomeness.

"It would probably do me greater service to deny any authorship of the work," I said, trying to appear less mortified, "but I'm afraid I cannot. It is mine."

" 'By the time she turned sixteen, Princess Leonora's beauty had already devastated a sizable fraction of her male admirers, driving five to suicide, at least ten to madness, and dozens more to perpetual and incurable heartache,' " he read. " 'She was so beautiful that when other women saw her, they instantly began to despair of their own reflections and would rather cover their mirrors than ever look upon themselves again.'" Darcy raised the page and inspected it. "Can beauty really have such a terrifying effect, Mary?"

"I couldn't make her unattractive, sir," I replied. "That would never do."

"You may call me just Darcy, if you like." He turned another page. "This novel takes place in Denmark."

"Yes."

"Have you ever been to Denmark?" he teased.

"No."

"Or lived in a castle?"

"No."

"Or worn a 'dazzling gown encrusted with precious stones of a hundred brilliant facets each'?"

"I think you know I have not, Mr. Darcy."

"Then how can you presume, as you do on this page here, to describe the Danish kingdom during a 'fine spring morning in early May'?"

"I have had much time for thinking and for imagining since I've come to Pemberley."

"*Queen Leonora: A Tale of Love and Woe* by Mary Bennet," he read, returning to the title page. "Now, I knew before I married Lizzy that you loved books, but I didn't have you marked for a writer."

"I would not call myself a writer," I replied. "I have no ambitions in that regard."

"Then why have you started a novel?" he asked.

"Because I got sick of reading the novels of others, which, owing to my level of consumption, have all become wearily predictable."

My answer seemed to amuse him, for as his hands restored order to the pages he'd disturbed, he chuckled. Then he said, "What would you say if I told you that Lizzy had warned me that you were the odd one of the family?"

I rolled my pen between my forefinger and thumb. "Whatever my sister determines about other people, even if it is unflattering, cannot be far from the truth," I said.

"That's a very diplomatic and gracious answer."

"One has to be diplomatic and gracious in my situation. It is by her kindness that I'm here at all, as you well know."

"Then I shall leave you to continue your thinking and your imagining, Miss Bennet," Darcy said, taking the blank sheets of paper he had come for, "while I embark on the considerably less enjoyable task of composing a letter to my solicitors."

For the rest of the day, I could write nothing, distracted as I was with replaying the horrifying instant in which he'd lifted the first page of *Leonora*. I am convinced now that I'd merely imagined his censure, but in that moment, I had yet to recover from the humiliation of having my composition known to anyone other than myself. The next morning, as I worked on completing the third chapter, who but Darcy should come charging into the library again. I watched him collect three books from a nearby shelf before proceeding to stand in front of my desk.

"What do you write today?" he'd asked by way of greeting.

"Albert the Good King is dead," I said without emotion. "Princess Leonora is now Queen of the Danes."

"Will you tell me what's happened since yesterday? Then you may take the break to rest your hand, which has turned red from so much writing."

It was in this way that our meetings began—first, hesitating little accounts of what I'd written, timidly, even suspiciously dispatched while my fingers awkwardly shuffled the pages, and when I was done, he'd raise a few thoughtful questions, which he wondered if I could try to answer for him: What kind of poison killed the king? Other than Leonora, who stood to benefit from her father's death? Where is Leonora's mother, and why is she never mentioned? "But I don't understand," he'd sometimes say, crossing his legs, or "Could you repeat the end of that passage, please? I was still thinking about that other bit when you kept going." In a moment of silliness or humor, his face could melt into almost childlike laughter, forsaking every trace of its former solemnity, and I would become pleased beyond all proportion with my meager talents. Chapters soon multiplied in number, as did revisions, and Darcy, perhaps accustomed to occupying a position of authority, oversaw the progress of my novel, now titled *Leonora's Adventures: Chronicles of a Tragic and Deeply Unhappy Queen,* as a kind of personal editor.

LOST IN MY reminiscences, I didn't hear Lizzy come in, or I would have straightened myself to assume a "studious" attitude. But by the time I was discovered, one slipper had already fallen over the back of the sofa with the guilty bang of a judge's gavel, and the other, wobbling precariously from the end of my big toe, dangled over the dignified roses of the carpet. *The mistress of the mansion came, mature of age, a graceful dame, whose easy step and stately port had well become a princely court,* I recited from Walter Scott's *The Lady of the Lake.*

"Oh, there you are, Mary," Lizzy sighed. I sighed, too. Lolling was an indulgence akin to the first outbreak of birdsong in the ambivalent few weeks that mark the beginning of spring or the end of winter. Touch it, and the magic is instantly gone. From the sofa, I peered into Lizzy's face and imagined myself a mewling, upside-down kitten. Pemberley had turned me soft and nonsensical.

Lizzy stared disapprovingly at my slipperless right foot. She did not look well. Overnight, her face had swelled, flattening the contours of her beautiful features, which at their prime had been almost mischievous in their loveliness. She who had walked miles in damp mud, who had famously trailed a petticoat crusted with horse dung and long grass into the breakfast parlor of Netherfield Park and appeared more gorgeous for the exercise, now moved with painstaking caution. She waved a hand over her distended stomach as if to calm it and puffed out her cheeks. Some unexplainable impulse made me wriggle my own slender, unoccupied body deeper into the sofa. Her transformation, which had begun nearly seven months ago, fascinated me, though I hated it all the same for what it had done and was doing to poor Lizzy. Her face showed no trace of the glow which is said to descend upon those who will soon become mothers. What was pregnancy except an illness which day by day obliterated a woman's youth and beauty and good humor, all in the name of duty and honor? But Lizzy must have noticed my discomfort, for she looked from Walter Scott to my face and then smiled. Straightening to the extent she could, she gently reproved me for reading "like a worm left out to dry in the sun" and reminded me that I wasn't a baby anymore, so could I please keep my shoes on properly without being told?

"I wish you would eat more," I said, sitting up. "And rest. This can't be good for you."

At this, Lizzy's eyes darkened, and a terrible expression came over her. "The other day I heard the servants talking about Lady Winthrop. She died, you know, in childbirth. They saved the child, a son, but she'd lost too much blood. Darcy knew her family. I heard she was a beautiful woman in the prime of health. . . ."

"You mustn't become morbid, Lizzy," I urged.

"Oh, but, Mary, I feel so selfish." And she covered her face with one hand, while I gripped the other. "I didn't want it to happen this quickly, not so early in the marriage. I wanted to enjoy myself awhile longer. Is that selfish?"

"No, of course not, Lizzy."

"Jane doesn't feel as I do," she complained, flashing into another mood. "Jane eats and sleeps very well, and her appetite has even increased. Just last week, she wrote me a letter, admitting she'd finished half a tray of trifles on her own. Can you imagine our sister doing such a thing! Then Bingley discovered her, and they had such a laugh at . . . I don't know . . . how silly things looked that they finished the rest of the tray between them." She lifted up her eyes, which were filled with tears, and as they fell and partitioned her face, some of the old beauty returned in fleeting traces. I gazed dumbly at her. "Mary . . ." she murmured, and I clung harder to her hand. She turned to me. A tender blue vein, a slender estuary in a sea of white, pulsed over her left temple.

"Mary," she repeated, gasping. "I'm in so much pain, and I don't want to die! I don't want to *die* like Lady Winthrop!"

For all my sympathy, I was powerless to help her. It is easy to contemplate Death when he is only a small god that frequents the pages of literature and materializes in the sermons of religion. But when illness takes us, when the pall of darker and nebulous worlds threatens to vanquish the one in which we have lived since our birth, we shrink from it, and even the promise of heaven proves insufficient comfort.

I held Lizzy and told her she would not die. She would get better. A few months from now, a little Darcy would keep all of us too tired and happy in its bawling company for us to think any more sad thoughts, and I would be delighted to save the family the expense of a governess by offering my own humble services, if she would honor me with the post, and teach the child poor penmanship and even worse fingering at the piano. And so I went on, without stopping, until one or two things I said seemed to comfort and amuse her long enough to keep her from further crying. At last recovering, she rebuked herself for acting the hysterical fool, while laughing and dabbing her face with both of our handkerchiefs. She then revealed the real reason she had come to look for me in the library.

"Tomorrow we're expecting a guest," she said, becoming at once less Lizzy and more Pemberley in her attitude. "He may arrive very early in the morning; certainly, I am told, before midday."

"Who?"

"You may remember him from the wedding—Colonel Fitzwilliam?" She paused to give me time to consider the name, which registered nothing. "Very gentlemanlike and tall," she added, as if that would help! Yet another amazing attribute of the landed gentry is that its members tend to physically resemble each other, which is what will happen when a relatively small and confined population of lords and ladies resolve to marry among themselves. Nearly all Darcy's acquaintances (and now Lizzy's) were either "very gentlemanlike and tall" or "very ladylike and tall." What short persons they did host at Pemberley were commonly old, and as it is a well-known fact that elderly people shrink, there is the considerable possibility that they, too, had boasted at one time or another a superiority of height in addition to the many other inheritances of the idle rich.

"I'm sorry, Lizzy," I said, trying not to smile. "There were a great number of people at your and Jane's wedding, and I can't remember everyone."

"The middle son of an earl? Single? Around thirty?" Lizzy offered, growing increasingly desperate. I shook my head. "Cousin to Darcy? Nephew to Lady Catherine de Bourgh? Joint guardian of Darcy's sister?" Like a dumb pupil, I seemed to advance no further in my lesson.

"He trod on Kitty's dress and tore it when we were walking out to the carriages." Spoken with an air of tired finality.

"Ah, yes, thank you. I know exactly who you're talking about now."

"Well, that's Colonel Fitzwilliam," Lizzy said wearily. "As you've been staying with us for some time now, I wish you'd make more of an effort to familiarize yourself with Darcy's relations."

"There would be no point to that, as you well know," I replied, and hoped my saying so would be the end of it. "I've been blatantly ignored at every social gathering you've assembled since my arrival here. I can still never sustain conversation beyond the first course with the person seated next to me, and on the very worst occasions, it isn't a quarter of an hour before he—yes, it's no use to protest your innocence in this case, Lizzy, don't think I haven't noticed that it is always a *he,* and a single *he* at that, who occupies the chair next to mine—begins to look helplessly towards the other guests for some way out."

"That's as much your fault as it is his," Lizzy snapped, sounding more like our mother than she perhaps intended. "A little more effort on your part would make a world of difference."

"No amount of effort can convince a man to take an interest in a woman he has already determined to find uninteresting, unless she miraculously grows beautiful, which is unlikely, or is left ten thousand pounds by some deceased relative, which is more likely but not by very much," I argued. It was a subject on which I held several impassioned opinions, a few of them controversial. "It would be easier to carve Pemberley out of a mountain with a fish knife. Men see with their eyes, not with their souls."

"I only wish for you, Mary, the same happiness in marriage which has blessed me," Lizzy said. "You dedicate yourself so fully to whatever you do that I know if you spent a little more effort in certain areas—"

"Hello, Aunt Philips. I could have sworn it was Lizzy who sat here just a minute ago."

"Ha-ha," Lizzy said, and I couldn't tell whether she was annoyed with me or amused. "You've certainly missed a fine career as a fool in a king's court."

"I thought I was going to be governess to your hundred children, Mrs. Darcy," I replied.

We argued and teased until neither of us had anything clever left to say, and conversation degenerated to idle speculation about how long Colonel Fitzwilliam would remain at Pemberley. We had just settled on a month when Mrs. Reynolds, Pemberley's ancient and most estimable housekeeper, crowed from the doors of the library that Mrs. Russell and her daughter were come to visit Mrs. Darcy.

"Oh, not *those* two again," I lamented. "How could they have anything new to say in just two days?"

"I wouldn't underestimate Mrs. Russell, if I were you, Mary. She is a virtual sage when it comes to keeping her finger on the pulse of society."

"Well, on pain of death, I shall not go," I said, "unless I may bring my book and read quietly in front of them."

Lizzy laughed. "They might reasonably take some offense if you did, dear Mary."

My sister was led away on her swollen feet, a heaven-ordained vessel, though not even Mrs. Reynolds's expert and fretful maneuvering of her patient around the library's cluttered furniture could prevent Lizzy from launching some three to four battles between the sofa and the door. On a diminutive walnut table, a pair of obsidian Turkish dancers rattled their festive vengeance with smiling faces and outstretched arms. And beyond, an ornamental egg beset with sapphires and lapis lazuli rolled off its flimsy perch and into a carpet-bed of woolen chrysanthemums. A miniature warhorse handed down from Darcy's paternal grandfather proved unequal to the earth-shattering force of Lizzy's pregnant girth and toppled, defeated, onto its side. But the horse was soon righted, the egg restored unharmed to its jeweled pedestal, and the Turkish dancers' tasseled fezzes cheerfully patted to assure them that peace was at hand before I was able to return to my sofa for another episode of aimless and leisurely lolling with, as Mrs. Reynolds put it so well, my "ladies in the lake and other medieval tomfoolery."

꙰

CHAPTER 16

Dinner at Pemberley was a very different affair from dinner at Longbourn. With Georgiana in Bath, that left only three to occupy Pemberley's expansive dining parlor, and when conversation was lacking, the sound of a fork being laid to rest against one's plate resonated like a bell in all corners of the room.

Since her marriage, Lizzy had unexpectedly acquired a taste for the finer things of life. The mud-splattered petticoat, along with other articles of clothing deemed perfectly charming while she was at Longbourn, had since been parceled out among the younger servants and replaced with lush frocks of intricate pattern and exotic dye. Even her slippers proved too delicate to tread any ground which was not either carpeted or a finely cultivated lawn.

The majority of her monthly allowance now went towards the purchase of items she most certainly would have ridiculed in the days when they had still been unaffordable to her. In the first week of my stay, we'd passed much of our time marveling at the various treasures she'd procured since her installment as mistress of one of England's finest houses. In her richly furnished rooms, she had permitted me to finger the beadwork of her crepe dresses and the thousand colored threads which made up a single flower on the bodice of her gowns. Ornaments of pure gold proliferated in her several jewelry boxes, and strands of pearls, varying in luminescence and size, seemed as ordinary to Lizzy as cheap ribbons. As untidy as ever, she required two housemaids to clean her room each morning, and it was a common enough occurrence for one or the other to discover in the rug some dazzling brooch of rubies or a sapphire earring that had mislaid its partner.

Lizzy's expanding figure, far from subduing her extravagance, seemed only to increase it, and this evening, she entered the dining parlor swathed in layers of crimson taffeta. At her throat hung a stone which matched her dress, and silver bangles made light music whenever she moved.

Darcy sat at the head of the table, looking much as he always did—tall, his cravat a sculptural marvel, face fixed in an attitude of thoughtful gravity.

This night, we were served brown soup, salad, and roast fowl. Mrs. Russell's visit earlier in the day had excited Lizzy, and over a slippery chicken thigh, she expounded all that she had learned from the most feared gossip of Derbyshire.

"Mrs. Russell tells me that Lady Munroe has redone her gardens and is throwing a party to celebrate the occasion," Lizzy said. "She was very surprised to hear that we hadn't received an invitation. Don't you think it peculiar, Darcy, that Mrs. Russell should be invited but not us? You've known the Munroe family much longer than she has."

Darcy waited until he had swallowed his meat. "Oh, but we have, my dear. I meant to tell you but forgot. I have already declined on behalf of us both."

Lizzy looked down at her plate. "I would have liked to go," she said, pushing a fragmented joint with her knife.

"The party is in two weeks," Darcy replied calmly. "You'll hardly be in a fit state to attend by then." Venturing a small smile in his wife's direction, he added, "There are some pleasures you'll simply have to forgo during this period. After all, it can't be too grievous to miss an ordinary garden party hosted by a garrulous crone."

Lizzy continued to prod her chicken. "I'm sure you're right, Darcy, as you always are. You see how fortunate I am, Mary," she said, turning to me and grinning. "I have become the most delicate flower. I cannot take one step, even indoors, without Mrs. Reynolds supplying her hand, though I doubt she could bear my weight if I did fall. I cannot stick my head out of doors to feel the sun or the wind without one of my maids fetching a shawl to throw over my shoulders in the event I should faint dead away from a slight chill."

"Now, now, Lizzy . . ." Darcy said, laughing, though his expression betrayed his discomfort.

"But you are right, Darcy," Lizzy sighed. "Even if I did go, I don't think I would be able to enjoy Lady Munroe's party at all. No sooner would some elderly gentleman cough into his handkerchief than our poor servants would have to lift my person and transport me to a place of safety at least a hundred feet away. And, of course, my love, you would have to ascertain the freshness and cleanliness of every bit of cake, fruit, and pudding that passed my lips, and that would be a trial for you as well, which I think I shall spare you from enduring."

I couldn't withhold my laughter anymore. Whatever her physical condition, my sister had lost none of her wit, and it was hard not to be in awe of her during such moments.

"I am like the fabled princess in the tower," Lizzy said dramatically, curling a lock of hair around her finger. She was really playing it up now, probably encouraged by my giggling. "But no prince shall rescue me, Mary, for as soon as I look out my window, they will see that I am large with child and give up their cause, riding their white stallions away."

"What nonsense," Darcy said, shaking his head.

"And what's more, the evil sorcerer who keeps me confined is none other than my husband," Lizzy added, pouting.

"Yes, your husband, who would keep you safe and in good health," Darcy muttered.

I did not wish to take sides, so I volunteered no opinion on the matter, knowing all too well that defending one against the other would only create more bad feeling while resolving nothing. Despite the generous number of comforts I'd enjoyed at Pemberley, I was still little more than a guest and, as a guest, subject to the whims of my generally even-tempered hosts. My indebtedness to Lizzy and Darcy's charity dictated my every speech and action, and in such delicate circumstances, it was not only wisest but also safest to remain silent.

"Mrs. Russell thinks we should entertain more," Lizzy said, changing the subject.

"Now, why doesn't that surprise me?" Darcy replied, and I caught him rolling his eyes.

"You are predisposed to think it a silly idea for the sole reason that the thought originates from Mrs. Russell," my sister said in rebuttal. "But is it really untrue just because it is Mrs. Russell who expresses that opinion and not your uncle or Mr. Bingley? The Thorpes and the Palmers host no less than six or seven balls a year, and their estate is not half as large as Pemberley."

"Well, to make you happy, Lizzy," Darcy said, eating heartily away at the meat before him, "I think we shall take some of Mrs. Russell's advice and host a ball just as soon as a certain event comes to pass." Then he smiled not at Lizzy but at her midsection. "I will even go so far as to offer that in honor of the occasion, we may throw three balls for three consecutive nights, and if that does not silence Mrs. Russell and teach her to keep her pert opinions to herself, then I'm sure nothing else will."

Lizzy set down her knife, looking across the table at Darcy. "There was a time when I felt I could have asked for anything, and you would have fulfilled it without any conditions," she said softly.

Darcy frowned. He kept his eyes fixed on the table. "Nothing has changed in that regard."

"My love," Lizzy replied, and I thought I heard a small catch in her voice, "everything has changed in that regard."

"Nonsense," Darcy repeated.

Lizzy did not reply, and Darcy seemed to take her silence for a concession. When I'd first arrived, my expectation had been, of course, that their relationship should be an extension of the connubial joy I'd witnessed on their wedding day. But an unease had arisen between them, which, at first subtle, became more pointed as they'd grown accustomed to my company. In particular, it proved impossible to ignore the change that had come over Lizzy and that, in my bafflement, I could attribute only to the effect of her being exposed to more wealth than she had ever known in her life. To myself, I hoped this was a phase from which she would emerge once she came to realize that one trinket was, in fact, very much like another, whatever the final cost or the rarity of the stones in question.

The subject of the conversation fortunately shifted, and some attention was at last paid to me.

"How many chapters have you written today, Mary?" Darcy asked.

"Nearly three," I replied, slicing a turnip in two with the edge of my fork.

"That is a productive outcome," Darcy said, nodding.

"This is the story of the queen?" Lizzy inquired. "The sword-wielding one who kills and poisons?"

"When other people are not trying to kill and poison her," I answered practically, "yes."

"What a fine woman! My idea of a heroine," Lizzy said, beaming. "Highly preferable, I think, to the princess locked in her ivory tower awaiting rescue."

At this, Darcy grunted in assent, and for the next quarter of an hour, we devoted all our attention and energy to the food before us. Then Lizzy piped up to remind Darcy and me of Colonel Fitzwilliam's impending arrival.

"I have told Mary that your cousin is coming tomorrow," Lizzy continued. "He will bring some much-needed liveliness to this house."

"Or he may find Pemberley tiresome and move on after a week," Darcy countered.

"How can anyone find Pemberley tiresome?" Lizzy argued. "Look at Mary. She has been here over two months and shows no inclination of leaving us."

"It's true: Pemberley is a wonderful place," I offered shyly, thinking this sentiment wouldn't affront either one of my hosts.

"Ha! You see?" Lizzy said.

"Well, we shall see for ourselves." Darcy shrugged. "I give him a week. You know his character—a good man but flightier than a restless butterfly when it comes to staying in any one place."

"The colonel has always been excessively fond of me," Lizzy added. "I believe he even fancied me once. I say he will stay at least a month."

"As he fancies every woman—married and unmarried," Darcy rejoined. "A week."

"I daresay you are right in most things, Darcy," Lizzy replied, her voice dripping sweetness, "but in this, you are wrong. A month!"

"Is it very important how long the colonel stays?" I asked innocently from my seat.

"Of course it is," Lizzy said at the very same time that Darcy shook his head.

Dinner concluded not long after this exchange, and all three of us eagerly went our respective ways: Lizzy to her private sitting room, Darcy to his study, and I to the library, where new tragedies would soon transpire from the blank pages of my novel.

CHAPTER 17

⟡

A tall and very gentlemanlike man was struggling at the bottom of the main staircase with several parcels. It was perhaps two in the morning; being unable to sleep, I had just emerged from my room to retrieve another book from the library when I'd heard a noise downstairs, followed by a few halting footsteps, a crash, and then what sounded like a curse uttered with impeccable elocution. When I appeared at the top of the stairs with my candle, the intruder looked up. He was soaked through, and the ends of his black cloak had already contributed to a midsized puddle at his feet. Boxes, both round and square, encircled the pillar of his drenched person like disorderly ruins.

"You!" he shouted upon seeing me, which struck me as a decidedly ungentlemanlike way to address a woman. "Yes, you!" he repeated when I gestured at myself in confusion.

He pointed with a gloved hand at the boxes around him. "Pick these up, will you? And bring them to my usual room. Also, find Turner. He left me at the gate, and I haven't seen him since! I'm convinced the man is a drunkard. Well, you look new."

"I'm sorry," I said, unresolved between fear of his hostility and anger at being mistaken for a servant. The candle trembled precariously in my hand. I thought of making a run for it but steadied myself. "I don't know who Turner is. . . ." To my shame, my voice shook.

"I'm sorry, *sir,* and I don't know, *sir,*" he corrected, in the manner of a tutor repeating Latin verb conjugations to his pupils. "Yes, you must be new. You probably don't even know where my room is, do you? Be quick now, and answer me. I am in no mood to be kept waiting after the journey I've had."

"I'm sorry," I said again but deliberately, now despising him. "Yes," I added, for hatred fed my courage, and I decided that I would be as obstructive as possible. "I daresay I am quite new and do not know where your usual room is, so I cannot be of much help."

"Amazing, isn't it!" he shouted, spreading his arms, and his cloak flew out from him like a sinister black kite. "This enormous estate, which is as famous throughout England as any one of the great houses, and there is not a single competent servant to be found to help me take my bags to my room or to prepare my bath or even to remove my wet coat. What hospitality! I shall have a word with Darcy about you and Turner in the morning, though if I could guess, I'd say you aren't one of the regular staff. You must either be temporary or visiting some relative. And very likely hoping to be taken on at the end of it, too, if I know servants!"

"You might say that," I sniffed.

"I thought so!" he said, doubtless feeling very clever. "And who, may I ask, might you be visiting?"

"My sister," I replied simply.

"And what part of the house does she work in? What is her post?"

I strained my face, pretending to think.

"You could say she covers the whole house," I answered slowly. "That is, in a way."

He sneezed, and I admit my finer feelings got the better of me, seeing him in so wretched a state. That and a lingering curiosity as to Pemberley's latest arrival inspired me, against my better judgment, to venture downstairs and pass him my candle. Taking up three of the boxes, which were, fortunately, much lighter than they appeared, I begrudgingly asked if he wouldn't mind leading the way to his room and carrying the last parcel himself.

"That's much better," he conceded gruffly, and accepting the candle, he raised the flame and brought it dangerously close to my face. I thought he intended to burn me as punishment for my insolence and nearly screamed, but he only peered curiously at me, as though I had some unusual part that demanded examination. "An ugly little thing, aren't you?" he whispered, and the intimacy of his tone struck me more than his insult. "No wonder you sound so bitter," he concluded with something like triumph, and balancing the candle in his hand, he bent to pick up the last box before proceeding to the staircase.

We walked in silence for what felt a long interval, down narrow, carpeted corridors obscured in total darkness. He turned back once to bid me keep up with him, and I followed like an obedient moth, his candle guiding me past haunting portraits and furniture whose monstrous shapes seemed ready to spring from the shadows. At times, I imagined I was on the cusp of a daring adventure, the persecuted heroine of a Gothic romance being led by her villainous keeper to the dungeons. Other times, my arms began to ache, and I cursed myself for ever leaving the comfort of my own room. But at last, he stopped and, with what I considered unnecessary force, flung open a pair of double doors at the end of a hall. For the briefest moment, the novelty of standing alone in my nightclothes in the bedroom of a strange man took hold of me. My heart quickened, and I heard its erratic beating in my ears. If this were a scene from a novel, the man would surely take the lady in his arms and begin ravishing her. Fearful—and a bit excited—by this prospect, I didn't dare look at him.

"This is my room, and you'd do well to remember where it is, in the event you're asked to work here later on," he announced, bringing me back to my senses. "You may leave the boxes on that table there." He motioned to a round table positioned ritualistically at the center of an elaborate Persian rug. "Then you may go and find Turner, who is to bring up the rest of my luggage and unpack it for me. I will also require a hot bath prepared before I go to bed, as I'm convinced that I've already caught cold."

"I don't know who Turner . . ." I began to say before I tripped over a bump in the carpet and the room collapsed around me. The boxes tumbled out of my arms, and I had just time to cling uselessly to the edge of the table and then topple that fine piece of furniture before I sank quite harmlessly to the floor. Rubbing my arm, I looked up to find my tormentor staring incredulously at me from the doorway. He had, after regaining his composure, the decency to ask if I was all right, but being neither a servant nor a Gothic heroine, I finally decided that I'd had enough of this game of pretend. I stood. Perhaps it was the disillusionment of returning to a mundane reality which emboldened me. For some seconds, I stared with imperious disdain at him, and he returned my gaze with the superior sneer which the idle rich employ towards their dumb menials. I clenched my fists. The threat of violence suggested by my fists seemed to unnerve him, and he retreated cautiously out of the room and a few steps into the hall, knowing from experience, I suppose, what hysterics the lower servants could pull when adequately provoked.

"Pick up those boxes," he said uncertainly.

"No," I replied, remembering he had called me an "ugly little thing." My voice issued from my angry, exhausted body like a command: "I will not pick up those boxes, and I will not restore the table. I am tired, *sir,* and going to bed." As I passed him, an idea occurred to me, and I lifted my chin and coughed with my mouth uncovered a few times in his direction. This had an effect even more satisfying than that of my clenched fists, for he jumped back and spilled hot wax onto his hands. While he cursed in pain, I repossessed the candle, which had been mine, leaving him in total darkness.

"Good night," I called out, content with playing the mischievous imp, if the role of romantic heroine would be denied me.

"And what, may I ask, is your name for when I make my report to your master?" he roared.

Pausing, I turned, having reached the end of the hall. "Oh, I'm sure you'll find out soon enough, *sir!*"

Then I ran to my room as fast as my legs would take me and locked the door before bursting into a fit of giggles.

CHAPTER 18

Mr. Darcy sat serenely at the head of the table with a small silver spoon in one hand and a cup of steaming black tea in the other, as he inquired politely after the health of my heroine. We were alone at breakfast. Lizzy was still too ill to come down. As for our guest, I'd been informed by Darcy that Colonel Fitzwilliam had arrived in the early hours of the morning and would, understandably, take his breakfast in bed, having suffered both a tedious journey in last night's rain and some serious neglect at the hands of two surly servants. Plans had been made to dismiss Turner before luncheon, with three weeks' pay and no reference; he'd fallen asleep on top of the colonel's luggage cradling a depleted bottle of gin. As for the other and more sensational person, who had dared embody superiority where none could be permissible, that lady's identity had yet to be discovered, but Darcy believed it only a matter of time. Servants often betrayed one another for the sake of appearing well in front of their masters, and in this way were the low kept even lower. Hearing of the drama, I'd offered a few generic opinions on the unreliability of servants and feigned disinterest, knowing, of course, that all would be revealed in good time.

"Tell me, Mary, how is Queen Leonora these days? And where is she now?" Darcy inquired, looking up from his large cut of ham.

I struggled to recall the latest chapter and bought some time pretending to dab the corners of my mouth, though I'd eaten nothing. "She's been abducted by the grand duke, her father's cousin, whose loyalty has been purchased by the French," I reported, as though this were an everyday affair—which, for unlucky and stunningly beautiful Leonora, it was. "The grand duke is keeping her prisoner in a secret underground cell that no one knows anything about and blaming the abduction on their allies, the Swedes, with whom the French desire to go to war. Originally, he promised Leonora that he'd betray the French, too, but only on the condition that she marry him and make him king. She, of course, refuses and, at the suggestion, spits in his face. For this insult, he slaps her and reveals, in his anger, that he was also responsible for the poisoning of her father, the good and noble former king. When I last left her, she had just finished eating the entrails of a rat in order to survive."

"Good God!" Darcy cried, with genuine enthusiasm. His knife rolled off the side of his plate. "What is to be done?"

Growing smug, I broke off a piece of cake. "You forget that Wilhelm, the German prince, departed two chapters ago from the shores of his motherland to sail to Denmark. The unfortunate affair with the Spanish princess thankfully forgotten, he realizes he still loves Leonora, and I may have Leonora fall in love with him following a prolonged and tormented struggle with herself. As for her current, unhappy situation . . ." I paused to wet my mouth with lukewarm coffee.

"Yes, what of her current, unhappy situation?" Darcy echoed, smiling and chewing his ham.

"The grand duke still visits her every evening," I said, "but I'm currently undecided between two scenarios, both of which I'll gladly present for your consideration. Either a loyal handmaiden of Leonora's will discreetly follow the grand duke into the prison cell and bring help later on *or* Leonora will pretend to accede to the villain's request, entice him into the cell with promises of pleasure, then strangle him or bash his head in with a rock. The rest is easy enough.

All she must do then is find her way back to the castle and emerge malnourished but unharmed to her adoring subjects before revealing the truth."

Darcy considered the options for a long time before speaking. "I think I prefer the second scenario, and I'll explain why. This is, if I'm not mistaken, her fourth abduction since her ascendance to the throne, not counting the two kidnappings from her days as a princess. The reader might reasonably hope that our heroine has learned something from her previous abductions. I'd even suggest—"

Darcy broke off as a tall and not very gentlemanlike man entered the breakfast room and sat down. He did not speak. His mouth was a straight and bitter line, which underscored the three wavy ridges that creased his forehead. Two deep furrows running diagonally from either end of his nostrils triangulated the bottom half of his face into an expression of fixed and stubborn misery, while a pair of red-rimmed eyes gazed with prophesies of untold doom at the three beverage pots set in a neat arrangement in front of him. As the man splashed inky liquid into his cup, Darcy cleared his throat. His guest looked up, and thereafter a few minor events occurred in rapid succession. First, I crooked my eyebrow, because the intruder to an otherwise extremely pleasant and intimate breakfast had spotted and recognized me. And while that man's face was busy contorting into an expression which would eventually encompass both mortified amazement and embarrassed disgust, Darcy proceeded to perform a perfunctory introduction ("sister to my wife, Lizzy," "my cousin Colonel Fitzwilliam, nephew of Lady Catherine de Bourgh, who I mentioned arrived earlier today," etc.) that included, I'm happy to report, a few compliments paid to myself and mention of the "marvelous and highly imaginative book" I was working on. A blustering hand upset the cup of aromatic coffee, and a brown stream eddied beneath the jars of black butter jam and peach preserves, ending its journey at the edge of the platter of hot rolls.

"You!" he cried out in a tone reminiscent of our unfortunate earlier encounter. "You!" he repeated, aghast, as though I were an apparition that refused to disappear.

I coughed and tore off a piece of dry crust. "Yes, me," I said dispassionately. "I told you I was visiting my sister."

"But you didn't say who your sister was. I asked you what post she had in the house, and you didn't give me a straight answer. . . ." he peevishly added.

"Excuse me," Darcy interjected. "Am I missing something here? Don't tell me you two are already acquainted."

"Yes, the colonel and I met almost as soon as he arrived," I said. "He behaved like any gentleman would."

"Fitzwilliam?" Darcy asked, turning to his cousin.

"How was I supposed to know she was your wife's sister?" the colonel grumbled, looking more and more like a bloodhound that had just been kicked in the teeth.

Darcy's eyes lit up. A boyish grin spread over his face. "Oh, I see now!" Then, turning to me, he cried, "*You* were the surly servant."

"I'm sure I wasn't made to feel like one," I replied magnanimously. "The colonel paid me many fine compliments upon our introduction. He said, and I quote, 'An ugly little thing, aren't you?'"

At this, the colonel banged his fist on the table. The cups rattled fanatically in their saucers. "That's not fair," he barked. He seemed prone to boorish shouting. "You were purposely elusive in your answers!"

"Fitzwilliam!" Darcy cried out, appalled at the savagery which threatened to ruin his morning repast.

"How can I be expected to know . . ." The colonel trailed off. "Why didn't she say something, I ask you? There was ample time for her to have said something when we went upstairs. . . ."

"I'm sitting right here. You may ask me now, if you like," I retorted.

"Fitzwilliam, do apologize to Mary," Darcy declared from his throne.

"What?" the colonel gasped.

"Apologize to Mary, please," Darcy repeated.

The colonel grabbed a bread roll, tore a piece off, and offered a desultory "sorry" through his full mouth.

"I suppose that's the best he can do," Darcy said, shrugging at me.

"Did you say you're writing a book?" the colonel suddenly asked, perhaps desperate to change the subject.

Darcy jumped in before I could: "A brilliant work tentatively titled *Leonora's Adventures: Chronicles of a Tragic and Deeply Unhappy Queen.* I may send a speculative letter to a publisher I know in London when she's finished with it."

"Not another woman's novel!" he grunted. Then, in a halfhearted attempt at friendliness, he added, "What is it about?"

"Oh, you know, just another woman's novel," I spat, twisting the knife deep into the jar of strawberry preserves and slathering blood-red gobs onto my bread with more than usual delight. "One can't expect a mere servant to write well, you see."

"Fitzwilliam's apologized, Mary," Darcy reminded me with a nervous laugh.

"Which isn't to say I've accepted his apology," I mumbled.

"But since you pretend to take an interest," I continued, speaking up, "it's about the Queen of the Danes, Leonora, daughter of Albert the Good King, and all the awful things that happen to her at the hands of *uncouth* and *vicious* men who, despite their titles, have *little* learning and *little* breeding and absolutely *no* manners at all."

"Mary," Darcy jumped in. "I must insist that you refrain—"

"No such person as Leonora, Queen of the Danes," Colonel Fitzwilliam said calmly, sliding the jar of preserves over to himself. "I've never heard of Albert the Good King, either. It must be fiction you're writing."

"Yes, it must be, mustn't it?" I mocked and watched as that gentleman coarsely ate his meat and several bread rolls, washing down everything with cup after cup of black coffee. His appetite was enormous.

An ugly little thing, aren't you? he had said, holding the candle so close to my face I could feel the danger of its heat. And what if he had grazed my cheek with its flame and burned me? Would it have mattered?

I mean, will it make any difference whether it scars or not on my face, as opposed to . . . Jane's?

"Mary?"

I looked from the coffee stains on the tablecloth absently into Darcy's face.

"Mary?" he repeated. There was genuine concern in his voice. "You seem depressed."

"I'm fine," I just managed to say, tossing my napkin onto the table. "But I'm not very hungry anymore. Will you please excuse me?" Rising quickly, I headed straight for the library, for my desk and chair, and the stack of blank paper I knew would be waiting for me. By the time I sat down, I'd decided that Leonora would escape the grand duke's prison of her own accord. She'd bash his skull in with her own fists, if she needed to.

CHAPTER 19

For hours, I had written furiously, and it was dark by the time I emerged from the house to walk the grounds. The colonel had been frequently on my mind, and it had happened quite naturally that as I'd related the harrowing details of Leonora's escape from the dungeon, the villainous grand duke had begun to bear an increasing resemblance to that boorish man. I would, however, exact what little revenge I could by executing the scoundrel, if not in the next chapter, then in the following one.

The night air afforded no sanctuary from the cruelty of my thoughts. Did I really look like a servant? And, for that matter, what do servants look like? Wouldn't a duchess pass just as well for a scullery maid if she were stripped of her gowns, her furs, and her resplendent jewelry? Or was there some physical feature which distinguished a butler from a baronet, a cook from a countess? The scorn with which he had looked upon me, both in our first meeting and at breakfast, was not an intangible thing; it was as real and as solid as my own limbs, and I knew the impression of our unhappy encounter would last for days before time gradually dulled its sting.

My feet had grown tired from circling the gardens, and I finally settled on a stone bench beside a urinating Eros. There was so much I wanted—books I hadn't yet read, dishes I'd heard tell of but never sampled. I wanted, for once, to indulge my vanity and purchase a whole wardrobe of new dresses, stockings, and shawls, all of the latest fashion. Or if I could learn something surprising and useful—how differently others would perceive me upon finding that I could speak German or draw a nightingale so that it appeared it might sing from the page at any moment. Perhaps my weak learning showed, if not in my face, then in my manner of walking or even in my speech. Perhaps this was why the colonel had mistaken me for a servant. Mention of my novel had made no discernible impression on him. He had shrugged it aside, even belittled it.

I must have sat for a long time lost in my thoughts, so much so that I mistook my visitor's polite cough for the rustle of trees being disturbed by a gentle wind. But then a human voice addressed me, and I met the eye of Mr. Darcy. Endeavoring to smile, my mouth only flinched.

"How are you, Mary?" he asked.

The novelty of the question startled me. I hadn't ever considered how infrequently this query had been directed towards my own person. I assured him I was well, grateful, at least, that he did not despise me in the manner of his cousin.

"I used to come here as a child," he began.

Perhaps it was the night which enabled him to talk as he did. We could barely see each other, though we were then sitting practically shoulder to shoulder. The dark gave us a comforting anonymity, and he continued to speak in a nostalgic whisper.

"I loved my parents. But after my mother died, my father discovered greater solace in his work than in my company, and so I was often alone. It's strange, isn't it, the memories children take with them into adulthood. I remember coming to this bench and crying because I could not bear the solitude of this house. And even when I ran out of tears, I still howled with all the strength I had, because I hoped—no, I believed, I truly believed—my cries could make the heavens pity me and that they would then deliver a companion to my side, as Pegasus was delivered to Bellerophon in his hour of need." He paused to laugh at himself, and despite my mood, I managed to chuckle a bit as well.

"Mrs. Reynolds attempted to fill the void by engaging me frequently in conversation, not as an adult would communicate with a child, mind, but as if I were one of her peers come to commiserate after a long day's work. How that woman could talk! And on any subject you could possibly think of—blisters, the best poultices for burns, the general mischief of the underservants. I absorbed everything like a pupil shown for the first time the inner workings of the world, and it was wonderful. For as long as I live, I'll never forget those conversations. Do you know—she found me many times in this place, pitying myself and rubbing my eyes, and she would take me up by the shoulders and say, 'Sir, what's this? What's this? Well, we can't have this. We can't have this at all.'"

The sound of Mr. Darcy imitating his ornery housekeeper got the better of me, and I began to laugh in earnest. When I'd recovered, I said, "I can guess why you're telling me this. You think I am sitting here, as you once did, pitying myself because I am alone."

"I admit it crossed my mind," he replied.

"To that I can only say you are fortunate you have never lived in a household with four sisters, an abominably loud mother, a sheepdog who rejoices at the sound of his own bark, and several noisy livestock living practically outside one's bedroom window. Only listen! Listen very hard, and tell me what you hear!"

In the dark, he tipped his head and craned his neck. "Nothing," he responded eventually. "I hear nothing."

"Yes, it is silence, Mr. Darcy, and for the better part of my life I have been deprived of it. Only consider how many glorious dreams I have had to surrender to the constant bickering of Kitty and Lydia . . . or the countless erudite thoughts that have been unjustly ended before the hour of their flowering . . . only think of how much in our day-to-day lives is lost in noise and what can be gained in its opposite—in the depths of silence, which, thus far, only Pemberley has been able to afford me. It is a luxury, and I am so grateful for it."

I sensed that he was smiling, and I wondered if I had inadvertently said something foolish. A fragrant, cool wind had begun to blow the scent of turned soil and composted leaves, and I had the fleeting, irrational sensation that in that moment, I could have wished for anything and it would have come true, that the hollow of God's ear was angled perfectly to listen to my thoughts and my thoughts alone in this whole vast world. I would have been happy for the silence to linger between us a few moments longer, but Darcy spoke, and when he did, it was on a subject most unpleasant to my ears.

"When I met my cousin for the first time, I was five years old, and he had just turned seven. Our parents left Fitzwilliam and me in the garden to play, and I remember he said, in the most innocent voice, 'Let's go look at the ducks, Darcy!' I followed him to the pond, and he promptly pushed me in."

"Sounds like something he would do," I said bitterly.

"He bullied me for years. Every time we met, it was like reliving the same nightmare over and over again. He would wrestle me to the ground and pin my hands behind my back so I couldn't move."

"Well, I hope you told his father and that he gave the young colonel a sound whipping."

"That's not what boys do, Mary," he said, "at least not the honorable ones. We have an unspoken pact never to tell on each other."

"So what did you do?"

Darcy shrugged. "I put up with it, though I admit I hated him, and I assumed he hated me. Then I grew up, and he grew up. And one evening, when we were at a party and had gotten pretty legless from drinking, one arrogant fool—I can't even remember who it was—made a remark about Georgiana and how motherless daughters, particularly rich ones, were ripe for picking, something crude like that. And before I knew what was what, Fitzwilliam had pinned that laughing idiot against the wall. His feet were clean off the ground, and he was kicking the air like a strangled rabbit. That's when I knew." He paused. "I knew then he would be a great friend to me, which is why I made him my sister's guardian."

"And all those years of unrelenting torture at his hands?" I inquired. "Did those just fly out the window?"

"Funny you should ask. I did mention to him later that he was one of many contributing factors which made my childhood a living hell, and do you know what he said to me? After he'd gotten over the initial shock, he said, 'But I thought we had such fun together as children! You were the only friend I had!'"

Darcy fell quiet again.

"Were you really a lonely child, or were you saying all of that for my benefit?" I finally asked.

"I promise you I was the most miserable child I knew—highly introverted, couldn't even stomach mounting a horse until I was nearly ten or eleven, for fear of heights. My old tutor will tell you I wasn't naturally inclined in any subject—'a mediocre reader with a mild talent for mental arithmetic,' I think he once reported to my father."

"But you grew out of it. No one could accuse you of being any of these things now."

"Lizzy will tell you I'm still awkward around people."

"Never as awkward as I am around people," I said, feeling competitive about it.

"You'll appreciate that I had no friends when I was much younger. The colonel didn't count."

"Well, neither do I really, and I'm already twenty."

"And I hated balls with a vengeance. I still do, if I'm to be completely honest."

The night air, I think, rendered me garrulous, and I began to enumerate all the miserable times I had ever had at balls since "coming out" in society. I told him about the time I'd hid in my room, already dressed, while the rest of my family went downstairs. And when at last I emerged from the interior of my wardrobe, I found that the carriage had left without me. What a fright I'd given poor Sarah and Mrs. Hill! They'd heard footsteps upstairs in an empty house, and when I came out of the sitting room, they nearly leapt at me with a frying pan and a copper pot, shouting, "Thief!" But it all ended very amiably, and that evening, I had a delicious supper of leftover pheasant and cold pie in my best dress and white leather gloves belowstairs.

"Was your mother angry with you when she discovered you hadn't gone?" Mr. Darcy asked.

"Oh no, not at all. That was the best bit, you see, for when my family came home, my mother was so busy exclaiming Jane's virtues that she paid no heed to me. And even Lydia said later, 'Mary, I don't recall seeing you stand up even once to dance!' And Kitty immediately replied, 'Of course not, silly! Didn't you see her sulking the whole time by the piano, waiting her turn?'"

The telling of the story rendered the account more humorous than I had remembered it, and we laughed until the contagion of our laughter shook the tops of the hedges. But this moment couldn't last, and when our merriment finally subsided, Darcy rose from his seat and offered me his arm.

"I hope you won't stay angry at the colonel, Mary," he said.

"Ah, so that is why you brought him up tonight," I replied, scoffing, though I still smiled. "Well, it has all been for naught. Your cousin thinks I'm a fool."

"No one who knows you could think that . . . unless, of course, he is a fool himself," he said.

"Well, I shall always be open to flattery, receiving it so little," I answered, feeling much better about myself.

Restored to good humor, we went back the way I had come, along the invisible lane so dark one didn't dare look down at one's feet for fear the ground beneath would give way. When we reached the house, we bid each other good night and parted ways.

CHAPTER 20

For several days following Colonel Fitzwilliam's arrival at Pemberley, Lizzy felt well enough to leave her bed, sit on a cushioned seat at her table, and read some letters. On a low stool positioned some few feet away, I provided friendly but unobtrusive company, occupied as I was with the instruments of my writing. Alas, at a feast celebrating her safe return, Leonora had drunk a poisoned goblet of wine and was now teetering on the cusp of death, shaking in her fevered sleep with "lips the bluish tint of incurable venom." But if the grand duke had been arrested and indicted for treason, and if Leonora herself had presided over his execution by rack and fire and forced him to consume several live rats in order to better avenge her own tortured imprisonment, then who should replace him as chief villain of my most splendid novel? Her younger and hitherto faithful half sister, Agnes? Wilhelm the German prince, whom I'd originally intended as her one true love? Or would it be the grand duke himself, who had, after all, evaded death by substituting a look-alike slave for his own person and swapping his tailored robes for dirty rags? What possibilities! What control I exerted over these pitiful characters' fates! A love that had professed itself pure not ten paragraphs past could crumble into a traitorous scheme for power at a single stroke of my pen. Waving my quill in the air, I proceeded to raise Leonora's temperature a few degrees higher, and she descended into blissful unconsciousness.

"I've received a letter from Lydia," Lizzy called out. My pen ceased its scratching.

"What does she want? Been kicked out of her rooms again?" I wrinkled my nose.

Even from a writer's point of view, Lydia's was a repellent form of misery. Illness, if done right, could be ennobling; poisoning, heart-rendingly tragic; death by sword, medieval but heroic. Yet poverty can have no salvation; its hundred daily humiliations offer no possible redemption.

"She writes that they are currently renting a room with rotting floorboards in a section of London which is 'barely respectable'—her words. She hasn't set foot outside the building for fear the family of ruffians living belowstairs will steal the dress off her back. Can such atrocities be believed?"

As sole creator of the grand duke and other heinous villains both high-bred and low-bred, both cunningly clever and abominably stupid, but always startlingly, irrefutably, and most unpardonably evil, I assured my sister that yes, such people did exist and worse, too, than she could ever imagine.

"That awful Wickham," I spat out. "While I own that rakes sometimes make most attractive characters in novels, in real life, they are unbearable!"

"Dismiss Wickham from your thoughts, Mary. Lydia says she is ill."

"At Longbourn, she was hardly sick a day of her life, and now every letter tells of life-threatening fevers and colds. Possibly it is the shame of being married to such a man, and if this is the case, then I cannot blame her."

"That is a most unkind thing to say," Lizzy chastised, though she smiled. "Writing has made you cynical."

"What other news does she share?"

Lizzy reopened the pages. "Wickham has recently been dismissed as an ensign from the Northern regulars and is sometimes several days from her side, though he claims to be visiting friends who've promised to secure him a position in another regiment. How he managed to be dismissed she does not reveal, but they are very poor. She writes in a postscript that she has received no communication from Wickham for five days, except a short letter begging that she settle some gambling debts with a man named Wilkinson. That sounds rather worrying, doesn't it? She asks for forty pounds! Oh dear . . ."

"If you send her money, Lizzy, I wish you would stipulate in your letter that the funds should be spent towards her recovery and not on her husband's gambling debts. It may be a good thing for Wickham to remain forever in hiding or with these so-called friends, if it means he cannot lose another game of cards."

"Forty pounds . . ." Lizzy repeated. "Well, I shall have to send her some more. . . ."

"I wonder sometimes if she is happy with her decision. . . ."

"She still calls him her 'beloved Wickham' in her letters."

"For practically her whole life," I said, "she was oblivious to all her faults, and now she must live every day with the reminder of them."

"We must all face the consequences of our actions sometime, Mary," Lizzy replied in practical tones, frowning and folding up the letter. "Speaking of injustices, it doesn't seem quite fair for you to remain indoors just because I must keep to my room. Go and take a walk. The grounds of Pemberley are absolutely thrilling this time of year. I wouldn't wish to deprive you of them on my account."

So I took my cue and left.

THRILLING THE GROUNDS were not, but *beautiful* they were indeed. It was a morning to end all mornings. The sky glimmered with luminescent turquoise and the foliage of trees shuddered their pleasure at the touch of the wind and the stroke of the sun. A chorus of rooks screamed and sprang like black chains from the inside of one tree into the shelter of another. I could have collapsed onto my knees and kissed the ground and the worms that lived in it. I loved Pemberley this much.

I had walked a long way from the house, and the beauty grew wilder as the distance lengthened. Eventually, I discovered a shallow spot of grass, and I sat there, staring and blinking at a negligible view of the house and the lake. I say "negligible" because from this distance, the house became no more than a chip of white stone and the lake a glinting blue marble rolled beside it. For some moments I'd been admiring the view when I heard a sudden flurry of hooves beating the earth.

By the time I rose and turned, a horse had nearly reached me. It was darker than any beast I'd ever seen and, startled by my movement, reared up on its hind legs, its head thrashing wildly about. A man rolled off its back and tumbled with a yelp into the long grass.

My own knees nearly gave way from fright, but before I could form any coherent speech, a familiar voice called out: "You have no business sitting in the grass like that! What were you doing?"

It had been over a week since I'd last seen the colonel. No sooner had he arrived at Pemberley than, according to Darcy, an old school friend had called him away on a matter of some urgency.

"I will sit where I like," I finally said, my voice shaking despite myself. "And have a care where you lead that beast."

"Marmalade, pay no attention to the lady," Colonel Fitzwilliam sharply bid his accomplice, and Marmalade tossed her mane and snorted in reply.

I noticed only then that he cradled his left arm close to his chest and leaned heavily on one leg.

"Are you hurt?" I asked.

"No," he answered, grimacing in pain.

"You are hurt," I said and ventured a few guarded steps towards him.

"Nothing escapes you, does it?" he snapped. "Well, I won't be able to ride Marmalade back in this state. You may as well get on her, if you like, and return her to the stables."

I looked sheepishly towards the saddle. "I don't know how to ride."

"That is a tragedy," he said, still gripping his left elbow. "Riding is a requisite experience for living, in my opinion."

As I didn't answer, we both stood gazing at the horse, who stared back, blustering and shaking her head. With his good hand, the colonel patted her rump—a vulgar thing, I thought, to do in front of a lady.

I considered making my excuses and leaving him, but he drew his horse silently towards me as if to follow my lead. And we began to walk in the direction of the house, a strange procession of woman, man, and beast.

"How was your visit to your friend?" I inquired politely.

"Exhausting," he replied. "There's nothing so draining as having to console a lovelorn young man every hour of the day."

"Oh, I'm sorry."

"Don't be," he said. "It all ended happily enough. When I first met him, he was all tears and lugubrious looks. He couldn't mention the woman's name without bursting into either sobs or morbid poetry. He wanted to end his life, if you can believe it."

"And you were able to talk him out of it?" I asked.

"I didn't have to," he answered. "I introduced him to one of my cousins, the youngest daughter of a baronet. They were engaged when I left them, and I'm fairly confident they'll be happy."

I scoffed. "What a fickle thing is the human heart."

He laughed. "I see you would have preferred that he throw himself from a cliff, his remains lost forever in the foam of an unforgiving sea." Though I stared straight in front of myself, I could tell he was observing my face, perhaps searching it for any trace of humor, and I was careful to give none away. "While I wouldn't go as far as to claim it is a virtue," he continued, "I am grateful that the heart is able to change its course, if it should mean sparing a dear friend un-necessary pain. But enough of such morbid subjects. . . . Miss Ben-net, after you stormed off from breakfast the other day, Darcy and I had the chance to talk a little about you, and from our conversation, it occurred to me that we are more alike—you and I—than might initially be evident."

"I don't think we're alike at all," I said honestly. His sudden ami-ability took me by surprise, though I endeavored not to show it.

"No?" The colonel smiled. "We are both middle children, thus rendering us by nature awkward, unloved, and starved for attention. I have not only an older brother and sister but also three younger brothers. You have, I know, four sisters, two older and two younger. We are prevented by our circumstances from marrying for love, un-less the object of our love should also come with a fortune and, in my case, preferably a title as well. And though I cannot claim to know this, beyond what facts your brother-in-law has imparted as to your character, I would suspect that you find better company with your books than with people, just as I prefer the company of my horses to, well, quite frankly any member of my family."

"Sir, if you don't mind my saying, I consider it most presumptu-ous of you to draw such conclusions, knowing, as you do, nothing about me," I huffed, though inwardly, I acknowledged he had been right on all fronts.

"I don't mind your saying," he replied generously.

We had, by now, reached the stables, and I suggested that I should go up to the house and call for the doctor to look at his arm. He stopped me just before I went on my way.

"Wait, Miss Bennet."

I shot him a questioning glance.

But he seemed to change his mind, for he said it was nothing important. And I parted from his company a little more inclined to think well of him than before.

CHAPTER 21

I had a terrible time the next day with writing. The words would not come, though I paced the length of the library until my legs grew sore. I opened windows, then closed them again. At the height of desperation, I climbed one of the rolling ladders and, sitting precariously on the uppermost step, looked out across the expanse of the room to marvel idly at the forest of books on the opposite wall. From my perch, I was able to formulate a few weak sentences, but these I scratched out with vehemence almost as soon as I climbed down again.

I had just added another crumpled ball to the growing mound at my feet when the library doors clicked open. Grateful for any distraction, I looked up, expecting to see Lizzy or Darcy, but my visitor turned out to be none other than the colonel.

"Sprained" was the first thing he said. When I didn't immediately comprehend his meaning, he showed me his wrist, which had been bound in many thick bandages.

"Oh, I see," I answered, for there didn't seem anything more interesting to say at the sight of his injury. The persistence of silence between us eventually compelled him to make a cursory examination of a few books. But Herodotus and Homer held little between them to sustain his attention, and he soon returned his gaze to me.

"So this is where you keep yourself, Miss Bennet," the colonel said placidly, and I did not know whether he intended to mock me.

A childish impertinence seemed to dwell in his bright eyes, which betrayed both the mischief of his thoughts and the natural arrogance of his class. Though his features were not as refined as Darcy's (for whose could be), he had a well-chiseled face that boasted a deceptively scholarly forehead and a small, determined mouth. From my seat, I noticed the protrusion of a scar on his chin, where the flesh had healed but poorly. As he continued to study me, I grew self-conscious and blushed against my will.

"I am writing," I explained, as he moved closer to my desk.

"So I see." His attention turned to the sheet of paper in front of me, and I casually draped an arm over the one meager paragraph I'd been able to compose that whole morning.

"Oh, Miss Bennet," he said, starting a little, "I think . . . I cannot be sure . . . but I believe I observe a spider crawling over your shoulder just there!"

I was unafraid of insects and did not scream, as other females might have done. But I did warily lift my hand from the page I guarded. At once, I realized my folly. Too late. He'd already snatched the sheet away from me and was parading it about like a boy with a prize.

"What, I wonder, does the author write?" he chanted teasingly.

"Please give it back."

"Not until I've had the privilege of reading what you have written, Miss Bennet. If Darcy will go on about something, I have the right to be curious." Then he settled himself in a nearby chair and proceeded to read aloud:

"Prince Wilhelm, who had disguised himself upon his arrival in
Denmark with the wearing of a servant's livery, made his way
unrecognized through the castle. Discovering no one in Leono-

ra's private chambers, he quickly changed into his own clothes and waited for her. The fire warmed his body, and drawing nearer to it, he soon fell asleep. It was many hours before consciousness returned to him, and when it did, he awoke to company, for sitting opposite him was the Queen of the Danes, dressed in most resplendent robes of sapphire blue. At once, he threw himself at her feet and kissed her slippers. Then he embraced her, and they sustained a kiss half an hour long, until they were interrupted by an urgent knocking at the door. . . ."

I'd turned by now quite red in the face. "It isn't my best writing," I admitted.

"No, I don't think it can be," he rejoined.

My embarrassment fast turned to annoyance. "Doubtless *you* can do much better, of course."

"Well, with such a low standard as this . . ." he muttered, just loud enough for me to hear. At the challenge, he sat up in his chair, boyish anticipation flooding his countenance. "First," he began, "it doesn't make sense that he should throw himself at her feet. He is a prince, and men, contrary to what women might believe or desire, don't do that kind of thing. Second, it is irrational, not to say unhygienic, for him to kiss her shoes before he kisses her face. What if she had been walking outdoors and prior to returning stepped in a pile of sheep manure? And third, you obviously have no practical knowledge of these matters, or you wouldn't have written that they 'sustained a kiss half an hour long.' That is highly impractical. Their mouths would be parched by the time they separated."

"I see, sir, that you suffer, as many of your sex do, from a dearth of imagination," I said hotly, standing.

"And I see, Miss Bennet, that you are content to display your ignorance by writing of things you know nothing about. Now, if I were Prince Wilhelm," he said, standing up and pensively circling his chair. "If I were Prince Wilhelm . . ." he repeated.

"Yes?" I goaded. "If you were Prince Wilhelm . . ."

"Just a minute, please. I have only two questions. First, is Wilhelm in love with Leonora? Second, how long has it been since they've last seen each other?"

"He is, and over half a year."

The colonel smiled. I felt my danger and looked instantly away.

"The key to such a moment is that it must be approached slowly. . . . He might, upon waking, say something like 'Ah, there you are' or 'How long have you been sitting there?' Then they would sit observing each other for a good while. . . ."

I yawned.

"No, no, don't be unhelpful, please. As I said, they might sit looking at each other for a while, in the way I'm looking at you now. Why do you not look at me, Miss Bennet?"

I raised my eyes. The calm with which he returned my stare surprised me. How direct his gaze was, I thought. How different he looked now than when I'd first met him, dripping and cursing at the bottom of the staircase. Did he even remember his own cruelty, or had he already forgotten the poison which had so unthinkingly issued from his lips? *An ugly little thing, aren't you?* he had said, his face sneering demonically behind the flame of the candle. "No wonder you sound so bitter." I'd laughed afterwards at my own boldness. But once the giggles had subsided, his words had returned, taking shape in the dark like monsters, and they'd brought with them other monsters—Thomas Lucas's flowers, Lydia and Kitty's gibes, the solitude I'd suffered for years at every ball and public assembly my family had attended.

Yet it is difficult to dwell in the past, in a man's earlier contempt and insults, when he is standing less than a foot away and addressing you in soft, most gentlemanlike tones. I could feel myself wavering, though my body remained stiff. More than anything, I hoped my face betrayed none of its inner bewilderment . . . or my newfound awareness of his fine cheekbones and shapely mouth.

"Are we quite done with this performance?" I asked once I had strength enough to speak.

"What you don't comprehend in your rendition of this moment is that he is meeting the woman he loves after a lengthy separation," the colonel continued, ignoring me. "Unless he is extremely confident in himself, he would approach her uncertainly, carefully. . . ." He ventured over to my chair and offered me his hand, which I accepted, after a pause, with reluctance. I refused, however, to look at him again and settled my gaze at the bottom of an inkwell.

"Yes, good," he commented, thinking I was acting out my part as Leonora. "He would hold her hand tenderly, as if it were the most precious jewel to him. He would draw her body closer to his. . . ."

Surely he could hear. He could hear the beating of my heart, which resonated in my ears as loud and threatening as thunder. And if he couldn't hear, he would surely be able to feel. He would know how his touch transformed my hand from smooth, cold alabaster to hot and sticky flesh, as though I'd drowned it in a vat of syrup.

"Please . . ." I protested. "This is . . ."

We were standing so close to each other that I could smell his coat's warm fragrance. It was not an unpleasant smell, and against my better judgment, I inhaled the scent of grass, animal, and open air.

"At the right moment," he said, speaking into my face, "he would begin to guide her lips to his. His hand would touch her cheek and erase the tears of joy he found there. And then . . ." A queer shiver swept through my body. I closed my eyes and waited—but the remembrance of another man, a smaller, paler man with weak shoulders and a simpering smile, returned as vividly as an apparition materialized from thin air—and I retreated.

He released my hand, and it dropped back to my side like a stone. The performance had ended.

"Well, there you are," he said. "Have I done better than you thought I would, Miss Bennet?"

I had no chance to answer. A knock sounded at the door, and Mrs. Reynolds emerged from it to bid the colonel come immediately. In a fit of temper, Marmalade had bit one of the stable boys, and nothing would appease the beast except the soothing whispers of her master.

Prince Wilhelm, who had disguised himself upon his arrival in Denmark with the wearing of a servant's livery, made his way unrecognized through the castle. Having expected to find Leonora in her rooms, he was surprised to discover that her chambers were empty and took advantage of the time offered to change into his own clothes and wait for her. Several months had passed since he'd last laid eyes on the Queen of the Danes, and he could not predict how she would receive him. The journey to her kingdom had proved difficult, marred and delayed by a succession of violent storms, which had prevented him from resting more than two to three hours each taxing night. His whole body ached, but the discomfort of his limbs was nothing to the soreness and unease of his heart. As he waited, he warmed himself by the fire and, unable to fight the heaviness of his eyes, soon fell asleep. Whole hours elapsed before consciousness finally returned to him, and when it did, he realized he had company, for sitting opposite him in an imposing, velvet-draped chair was Leonora herself. By then, the blaze of the fire had died to a few lit embers. One half of her face was hidden in darkness, the other weakly illuminated by the faint glow of the hearth.

"How many hours have you been sitting there?" he asked when he found courage to speak.

"I've lost count," she replied, and the sound of her voice, the reminder of what he had missed for so long, temporarily stunned him.

In the near dark, he stood. The distance between them might well have been another ocean, but in time, he crossed it and of-

fered her his hand, which, after a pause, she accepted. For several moments, they stood facing each other. Then he touched
her cheek and found there tears, which he dried with a light
caress of his thumb. In her heart, she felt uncertain of him. An
inner voice told her she should not trust him, as she should not
trust anyone. And who could blame her for the suspicions she
still harbored? More than once she had been hurt by others, and
the long intervals of solitude which served as medicine for her
pain had since annihilated any trace of those memories that
might formerly have brought her happiness. Yet she was still a
woman—a queen, yes, but a woman also—and these feelings
which stirred to life at the end of a caress were not, could not be
a sign of weakness. Rather, she knew them to be no more than
a reminder of her own human nature. So at last she relented to
them, and she and Wilhelm kissed.

The page balanced thoughtfully in Darcy's hand, and I waited for
him to make some comment. But when he finally spoke, it had
nothing to do with the progression of events in my novel.

"You don't look quite yourself tonight," he said.

To this, I shrugged, as I was loathe to speak of my earlier encounter. "It is nothing," I replied. "I think I have sat indoors too long
today."

"That may be the cause," he said. "Or it might be something else.
The colonel, perhaps."

I felt the blood drain from my face. "What cause would you have
to think such a thing?"

"Mrs. Reynolds," Darcy answered, leaning paternally back in his
chair. "She claims to have caught the two of you standing, as she put
it, 'unnaturally close together' in this library."

"There was nothing to catch, I assure you. Mrs. Reynolds mis-
construed what she saw."

"There is also the matter of your performance at dinner today. . . ."

You made no conversation, played with your food, and did not laugh at any of the colonel's jokes."

"That is because I did not find them funny."

Darcy stood up. He began to walk restively around the perimeter of two footstools, glancing briefly at me every now and again, as though to ascertain that I was still there.

"Out of a sense of duty, I am obliged to caution you against developing any familiarity with my cousin. My intention is not to blemish his character, which has been, in all our interactions, irreproachable. To be sure, he is a gentleman. His breeding and education are both excellent, his career laudable. But he is one who has always laughed at life and deprecated the idea of marriage, both in my company and in the company of others. For a man, he may be the best and most amiable of friends; there is not a soul among my acquaintance who can claim to dislike him. But for a woman, particularly to one such as yourself . . ." Here Darcy's expression grew stiff, and he could not finish his thought.

"One such as myself?" I repeated.

Darcy exhaled. "Eloquence has never been among my greater gifts."

I picked up a pen and twisted it between my fingers.

"I think I understand your meaning," I said, staring at an ink-stained nib. "I am, I suppose, the daughter of a gentleman, but what relations I possess are nothing to the de Bourghs and Darcys of this world. My fortune, too, is so negligible that any man who chooses of his own free will to pursue me would be instantly cleared of wanting to marry me for my money. As to schooling and the cultivation of fine ladies' accomplishments, I confess I have never benefited under the tutelage of a governess. By these standards, my deficiencies would seem to speak for themselves. I possess no breeding, I am woefully uneducated, and I am poor. Yet for these faults I feel I might still hope to be forgiven had I been blessed with a little charm and beauty. Even if I were a dull woman with a pretty face, I doubt that my being the favorite of any man would be the cause of so much alarm and suspicion."

My words had flustered Darcy. As his disquiet increased, so did the boundary of his walks, and he made an outline of a settee, a lounge chair, and a divan before circling back to me.

"You are a woman of substance and intelligence," he said. "I did not warn you against the attentions of my cousin because I believed you to be inadequate but because anyone who is familiar with his situation will know that he is entirely dependent on the benevolence and generosity of his family, having no fortune of his own."

"And so must marry a woman of wealth."

Darcy's face brightened. "Yes, exactly. I'm glad you understand."

"And because he must marry a woman who is rich," I repeated, "it naturally follows that I am the most unwelcome of distractions, being, as I am, both unaccomplished and poor."

"He would never be able to marry you. Therefore, any communication outside of what is agreeable and polite would not only be pointless but also discouraged," Darcy said with finality, and I half-expected him to emphasize his declaration by pounding the table between us.

"Has it occurred to you, sir," I rejoined, "that the basis for this conversation rests entirely on two things, neither of which carry any weight: one, the highly imaginative report of a self-important housekeeper who must be seventy if she is a day, and two, the fact that I did not eat my sprouts at dinner?"

Darcy colored and immediately proceeded to make another round of the furniture. He emerged from his thoughts just as I reached the door to take my leave.

"Before you go, Mary," he said, "I feel I must extract two guarantees from you. The first: Will you promise to keep your distance from the colonel at all times? And the second: Will you also assure me, in your own words, that you'll do nothing to encourage his attentions? It is both for your sake and for my peace of mind that I ask this of you."

I noticed then that his hand still clutched the page from which he had read earlier and that it shook a little.

"No," I replied, and the danger, the excitement of my defiance was enough to make the hairs on my arm stand on end.

"No?" he repeated, almost in disbelief. "Then you acknowledge by your refusal that there is something between you . . . or that there could be something between you."

"Oh, but how could there be, Mr. Darcy?" I asked, even as my voice quavered. I had never stood up to him this way before. "As you put so well, it is impossible that anything of the kind should happen to *one such as myself.*"

"Mary, please . . ."

But it was too late. As I left, my hand acted faster than my intent and shut the door between us. I heard it close with accusing finality behind me before running to my room.

CHAPTER 22

Darcy's lecture had quite the opposite effect of what he'd intended. After the initial wave of insult had passed, it dawned on me that the prospect of such an unlikely romance ever visiting my life was, in actuality, rather flattering. I was determined to think no more of it, however. The colonel made a convincing German prince, but his performance, masterful as it was, revealed little more to me than a penchant for the dramatic.

Yet in the days following, I saw him everywhere. Entering the library to begin my work, I'd discover he was already there, sprawled luxuriantly across a divan, napping, or swinging his legs from a desk, reading a letter. But even in such proximity, he never went out of his way to make conversation, and we might have spent whole afternoons occupied with our own diversions had he not yawned in a manner to fill up the room or dropped a book so loudly as to make me blotch my writing. Only then would we happen to look at each other, and he'd feel inclined to launch into some subject, such as his sister's engagement to a marquis or how ghastly he found the food at Pemberley ever since a neighboring estate had poached Darcy's cook. When I made my rounds of the gardens, it was not uncommon for me to find him seated on a bench which it was my habit to pass, and he'd offer an excuse to accompany me for the remainder of my walk. He would then tell me of the grounds of his ancestral home, how there was once a tree from which, in their youth, he and his brothers would swing and fall into a lake, laughing and naked. He diverted me with tales of his three favorite dogs, no less dear to him than his thoroughbreds, and the abundance of pheasant shooting to be had at the end of the year. He claimed a weakness for buttered prawns and salmagundi, for cheesecakes and lobster. As a child, he had stumbled upon a pool in the wilderness, and for years afterwards, believed it to be sacred, until an extended drought depleted its crystal waters.

I neither sought the attentions of the colonel nor refused them. They were a novelty and a distraction from the lonely pastimes of reading and writing. I told him about Longbourn, about the squeaking stair my sisters claimed was haunted and the superstition we had concocted that whoever stepped on it after dark would be visited by a ghost. As a young girl, I had watched my father put down an old workhorse. It had kicked out its legs and stiffened, like someone playing dead, and I could not sleep for days afterwards without Mama or Jane holding me. My descriptions of Kitty and Lydia made him laugh, and, in turn, he entrusted me with the secret knowledge that Lady Catherine de Bourgh's breath smelled perpetually of onions. I learned the names of his siblings and those of his horses and terriers, both living and dead. I familiarized myself with the easy pace of his walk. Blue was his favorite color. He hated mushrooms because he couldn't stomach the idea of eating fungi. And the scar on his chin was the result of a boyish scuffle turned unexpectedly violent when his opponent pulled a penknife. Suddenly, not a day passed that we didn't spend some portion of it in each other's company. Even the solitude of writing no longer felt complete if he was not draped over a lounge chair and watching me over the top of a book.

Had I been more attentive to concerns outside my own pleasure, I might have noticed the silences which lengthened and proliferated between Darcy and my sister. I would not have then neglected Lizzy, as I did, the duration of my visits growing shorter and shorter, as my appetite for the colonel's stories increased. Indeed, he could spin tales better than anyone I knew. A cloud with curling edges put him instantly in mind of his mother's wigs; a gust of wind inspired him to recount a tale of twelve horned women and a cake baked with blood. At meals, we made up the only lively conversation, and Darcy observed our bantering cheerfulness with an expression of brooding solemnity.

When I reflect now on the tragedies that followed, and the series of unexpected losses which resolved to afflict a family considered by many to have been blessed for a time with unusual good fortune, I am able to mark, as if with a thin line of chalk, the exact moment that heralded the beginning of the end.

Lizzy kept largely to her bed. Though she recovered her appetite, she seemed to grow disproportionately thinner to the bulge that jutted like an unnatural hill from the narrow dimensions of her body. The morning of calamity, I'd read to Lizzy from William Godwin's *St. Leon* until she grew tired, and afterwards, I'd met the colonel at the stables. I found him brushing Marmalade's silky mane, while the mare snorted and tossed her head with pleasure.

Seeing me, he stopped, approached, and said in a grave voice, "Well, Miss Bennet, today is the day."

It occurred to me that he meant to leave Pemberley sooner than expected, and I nearly fell down.

"Today is the day," he repeated in a lower voice, out of the range of the groom, "that you will experience one of the greatest delights life can afford. Come." He guided me towards his horse. "Don't be afraid."

My arms felt as though they'd turned to wood. "I'm not," I muttered.

"Then get on."

"I told you before, sir. I cannot ride."

"How old are you?"

"Twenty, thank you," I said shortly.

He laughed. "By the time I turned ten, I'd already fallen twice off a grown horse, and the second incident would surely have crippled me had I not been delivered into the hands of an unusually competent physician. But that did not stop me. No, I've decided that I will not permit myself to be dissuaded by your protests, Miss Bennet. You will realize how wonderful it is just as soon as you've mounted."

I hesitated until even Marmalade grew restless, and the colonel settled the matter as barbarians have done for centuries by lifting me, kicking and screaming, onto the back of his oversized pet.

"There!" he declared and commenced to guide us out of the enclosure of the stables.

"Oh no, please, let's go back," I implored, once we'd entered the paddock. "You may lead me about in a few circles, if you wish, and I shall be more than contented by the experience."

The colonel paused, looking up at my wobbly perch. "Are you sure?"

"Quite sure."

"Well," he said, seeming to give in, "I have no intention of frightening a woman, particularly one as fainthearted as yourself. If you have no objection, I will just get on as well and lead Marmalade back the way we came. How does that sound?"

"Just fine, thank you, Colonel," I said, exhaling with relief.

Smiling, he mounted Marmalade, who neighed in complaint at the additional weight. As I felt his shape settle behind me, my whole body stiffened.

"Now," I said firmly. "Will you kindly escort me back to the stables and let me down from this animal?"

He never responded. His hands took the reins and lashed the horse's neck before I could scream, and the landscape melted away, dissolving the wilderness ahead into mere color. I closed my eyes against the thrusting wind, then opened them, when I'd mustered the courage, to a world of brighter green and blue and gold than I remembered. I leaned into the colonel, and the back of my head grazed his shoulder. He said, "Steady on, old girl," and I didn't know whether he meant the animal or me. Behind us, Pemberley became a smidgeon of yellow-white paint in an emerald canvas, a mirage in a desert that disappeared in the space of a single breath. I felt my hair loosen and tumble in curly waves over my shoulders, and my spirit transformed into something as light as the hollow bones of birds.

Perhaps it was the wind that sent my head spinning, or the height at which I sat—I don't know. I suppose I could blame the hills, whose rounded shapes suggested fertility, or the warmth of the summer day, which covered my body in a fine sheen of moisture after the first half hour of riding. The colonel sensed that Marmalade was growing tired, and we soon circled back. When we reached the stables, he lifted me down, and in the dark of the enclosure, I behaved like a woman who wanted to be kissed. So he obliged, guiding my mouth gently to his lips. Our faces did not slide off each other. He did not pull away so that my mouth landed on his chin. No mishap occurred, and the kiss was held long enough to mature and flower. Marmalade whinnied and beat the ground with her hoof, so he kissed her, too, and fed her some fresh hay. "I'll return tomorrow with a bright, shiny apple," I promised, tracing, with the tip of my finger, an immense nostril that flared at my touch. *I'll believe it when you bring it,* her placid stare said to me, and the colonel and I waved goodbye to her before commencing to walk back to the house. He kissed me again when we were out of Marmalade's sight.

"What was that for?" I panted, annoyed but only because I'd been taken by surprise.

"Nothing, my ugly little thing," he said. "I just wanted to kiss you."

I'd previously kept in step with him, but at his words, I stopped.

"Must you call me that?" I asked. I didn't want to grow angry. I'd just been kissed, after all, and successfully, too. When I spoke, I could still feel the impression of his mouth, solid and warm, as it had settled over my own.

"I was teasing," he said by way of apology, which didn't help, for I thought immediately of that idiot Thomas Lucas. *A joke, Mary. It was only meant to be a joke.* "Don't be such a stick-in-the-mud," the colonel added.

"I'm not," I retorted. "Just I'd prefer you didn't call me that again. You were a complete ass to me when we first met."

"Are you still not over that?" he said. "My God, woman, you do hold on to things. Well, what would you prefer I call you? 'Most beauteous maiden'? 'Brightest light of this sceptered isle'? Would that please you?"

"No, because you would be mocking me, sir."

For a moment, he gazed thoughtfully at me, offering no reply. "Well, do you think you're an 'ugly little thing,' Miss Bennet? Answer me."

My temper would not keep. I lashed out at him. "I wonder how you can ask something so impertinent!" I cried.

"Which means you do. Well, Miss Bennet, I cannot say honestly that you are either a beauteous maiden or the brightest light of this sceptered isle."

Any more of this, I thought, and I'd be in danger of bursting into tears.

"But I can tell you," he continued, "that I've never kissed an ugly woman in my life, nor do I intend to start now. I have quite a reputation, you know. I may only be the younger son of an earl, but most ladies, even those in the very best circles, consider me a catch. And because they flatter me with their fragranced letters and meaningful smiles, I have always been exceedingly discriminatory with my kisses and loving embraces, which is why I shall deign to kiss you again."

And he did, though I struggled my utmost not to kiss him back, as he was clearly a self-conceited, womanizing imbecile. I thought of all the other women he had kissed—the preening, rich daughters of the landed gentry, with their delicate, rose-petal mouths—and something prompted me to kiss him harder and more recklessly than before. When he released me, I looked shyly away, a little ashamed at my own passion. How ridiculous, I thought, rebuking myself, that I should consider his kisses the equivalent of compliments—and yet I did and craved many more such "compliments" besides.

"Now then," the colonel said. "May I call you my 'ugly little thing' or not?"

"What a truly awful term of endearment. If you can call me that, then it's only fair that I should call you something equally monstrous in return."

"Oh, feel free. I am quite open to anything insulting."

"'Uncouth barbarian'?"

"That's much too forgiving, I think. Can't your writer's brain conjure anything worse?"

I scrunched up my face in thought. "How about 'idiot drunkard'?"

"All real men drink, Mary."

"'Handsome rake'?"

"I thought we were doing insults, not compliments."

"I've got it," I announced. "'Womanizing, caper-witted coxcomb'! Or would you prefer 'blackguard'?"

"Now, *that* is excellent. I shall be your 'womanizing, caper-witted coxcomb or blackguard,' and you shall be my 'ugly little thing,'" he concluded.

"That's rather long, though, isn't it?" I counted the syllables on my fingers. "That's thirteen syllables total for you, whereas I have only five."

"Then what would you call me, if not Fitzwilliam?"

"I will call you Marmalade and content myself with three."

We entered the house laughing and charitably insulting each other. It was then that I saw them—the two housemaids crouched at the bottom of the stairs crying into their sooty handkerchiefs. Grief had not dulled their sense of propriety or weakened the servant's nose for scandal. The girls peered from my unkempt hair to my rumpled skirts, and considered that both my face and the colonel's appeared flushed with the radiance which is unique to men and women who have just finished doing what perhaps they should not have begun in the first place. They neatly totaled up these things in their heads, as though it were all a case of simple arithmetic and the resulting sum either that of marriage, for which they'd benefit by a cup of punch and a slice of wedding cake, or non-marriage, for which there'd be many evenings' worth of discussion around the kitchen table in the treasured minutes before bedtime.

"What's the matter, Bess?" I addressed the one servant whose name I knew.

"It's your sister, miss," she sobbed. "Mrs. Darcy, I mean. The baby . . . the baby's just died."

How can a mountain spring from a tree without also killing it? On my way to Lizzy's room, the child passed me, a formless mass of bright red which stained the cloth that covered it. Looking down, I beheld the speckled trail of blood which oozed like dark spots of ink on the carpet. No one had changed the bedding, and Lizzy had soiled herself, causing the air to smell putrid. Her opalescent face, damp where Mrs. Reynolds had wiped her skin, shone like a cold moon over the scene of massacre that ravaged the rest of her body. Between her legs, fresh blood saturated the mattress, the last remnants of a life expelled into sheets that would an hour or two from now be taken from my sister's bed and burned. I lifted Lizzy's skeletal white hand and kissed it. Her fingers quivered awake over my lips, but she didn't open her eyes. Then the doctor entered, a middle-aged man with an enormous head and pillowy cheeks.

"Where is Darcy?" I asked him harshly, as though the fault were his. "Darcy should be here."

"He's in the next room, resting," he explained patiently. A handkerchief fluttered out from inside a bulging pocket and dusted his egg-shaped forehead. I resisted the urge to strike him—how dare he tend to his own disgusting body, when my sister lay so weak a few feet away. "I've given him a sedative," he added in whispered, sympathetic tones that only came across as affected and impersonal. "If it's worked, he should be asleep by now."

"And my sister?"

"She's been given a sedative, too." More pretense to compassion.

I asked him to tell me what had happened, and he shrugged. Oh, that he could! "A terrible, most unfortunate affair," he said in the same tones, which I suppose he had learned somewhere was a pitch suitable for the communication of tragedy. "The child was stillborn. A boy. She initially thought he was alive, but it was clear to the rest of us. . . ." He shook his head and wiped his spectacles. *A very worthy performance,* I thought to myself. *And he might be able to spare a few tears as well, if we paid him another consultation fee for the trouble.*

At the suggestion that he should take some nourishment in the kitchen, the doctor relented and agreed to leave me alone with my sister. Then my tears flowed free and unreserved, and when Lizzy awoke, several hours later, and asked me where I'd been, I found I could not answer her.

"Oh, Mary," she muttered vaguely, as her own body began to shake with sobs. "I'm afraid I've let everyone down."

CHAPTER 23

In the days since the *incident,* for that is how *it* had been named, people moved quietly in and out of rooms, doing what they had to do before the grateful hour in which they could once more enfold their warm bodies within the safety of their beds. Mrs. Reynolds continued to fuss over the untidiness of the housemaids and bemoan the carelessness of the laundry maids, but her rancor gave way to pity much quicker than was her custom. In fact, pity, which materializes ghostlike in the wake of tragedy, prevailed at Pemberley. A heavily pregnant Jane left the side of her Bingley to console Lizzy. Her presence rendered mine excessive; they preferred each other's company and spent all their waking hours behind closed doors, speaking a language of intimacy I'd never learned.

And so, in the days following the *incident,* people worked silently but diligently, with the vague sense that a great *something* had been lost. This something was what we had all taken turns imagining at one time or another, the scullery maid and Lizzy alike envisaging the shape and features of the unborn child who would tumble like a comet into this dusty world, tripping the footmen and eating sweeties from the sticky fingers of the maids. Everyone had devised his or her own little story of the boy who would one day inherit Pemberley or the girl who would have her pick of a hundred eligible suitors, and each story had grown more substantial, more palpable, with the steady expansion of Lizzy's girth. Henderson, the butler, only hoped the child wouldn't be cruel to animals, according to Bess, who kept me apprised of goings-on belowstairs while she dusted the library. "He who is cruel to animals when he is young," Henderson had postulated to his underlings around the servants' dinner table, "will be cruel to humans when he's grown, mark my words." The game-keeper, however, wished for exactly the opposite and planned to teach the boy (it had never been imagined among the male staff of Pemberley that Lizzy could give birth to anything other than a boy) many subjects more interesting than the "stuff and nonsense" of phi-losophizing books. Bess herself had hoped for a girl who would be "as bonny as a dolly." Together, these hopes seemed more real to me than the corpse of the child I'd passed in the hall and which nightly haunted my dreams.

For days afterwards, I refused to see the colonel and hid away in my room, pretending illness. I felt such guilt. How liberally I had enjoyed myself while my sister lay suffering, her body racked with pain. No wonder Lizzy did not ask for me. She'd come to realize that I was undependable, selfish; at my most panicked, I imagined Mrs. Reynolds had found out somehow that I'd been in the stables with the colonel and had told Lizzy, who now judged me no better than foolish Lydia. When she needed me, I'd been absent from her side; why, then, should she turn to me for comfort now?

On the fifth night, I emerged from my room and, thinking the whole household asleep, crept outside to wander the garden. But I should have known better than to return to the place where the colonel and I had frequently walked, for I found him there, seated on a bench, as though he'd been waiting all this time for me to ap-pear. It was too late to turn back; he had seen me. And, in truth, I did not want to go.

I expected him to ask how I was, but he only leaned forward and, staring impassively at me, said, "Finally come out of hiding, then?"

"What?"

"It was nice of you to read my letters, even if you didn't respond to them."

For the last few days, he had sent several short notes via Bess, asking me to meet him, though I'd honored none of his invitations.

"I'm in no humor this evening to listen to you whine," I replied coldly, making as if to leave.

"It must be very hard to live as you do," the colonel said. "Exhausting, in fact. I would not wish it on anyone."

"How do you mean?"

"To take everything so seriously. Anyone would have thought you, and not your sister, had lost a child."

I nearly choked on my anger. "You have no idea how I've felt these last few days, have you—how I've tortured myself for not being at Lizzy's side. I should have been there. It's the least I could have done—to hold her hand through it, even if it changed nothing." I started to cry. I could not rein back my emotion; too much haunted me: the dead child, the cold damp of my sister's skin as I'd kissed her hand, Jane's arrival, which had quietly signified my own failure as a sibling.

But he continued to look at me, unmoved. "How well you put it, Miss Bennet, when you say you have tortured yourself these last few days. You seem very talented at that—holding on to things, taking them to heart, feeling offended. What good does any of that do, I ask you."

"Better to grieve," I replied, "than to make light of tragedy, as you do."

The colonel's face darkened, and as he stepped towards me, I was fearful that he would be violent. He took one of my wrists and pulled me close to him, though he didn't kiss me. Instead, he spoke softly into my face: "You think, because I am a man, that I don't know anything about how childbirth can turn to tragedy. But you would be wrong. My mother gave birth to me when she was twenty-five years old. By then, she'd already had two children and four miscarriages to show for her troubles. I remember lining up behind my siblings at my mother's bed and saying goodbye to her after she'd had my brother. We all thought she was going to die. I was six years old; I looked into her face and burst into tears, and my father took me aside and knocked me into the wall with his fist. So I take it very hard, Miss Bennet, that you should think I make light of this tragedy, considering I would have been the child's godfather."

I stopped crying and, with my free hand, dried my cheeks.

"Then what would you have me do, if not grieve? Should I ignore the fact that Lizzy won't see me? That she spends all her waking hours with Jane and never asks for me?"

He shook his head. His eyes flickered in the dark like twin flames.

"I would have you live, Miss Bennet," he whispered, as his grip around my wrist grew tighter. Then he took my face in his hands and kissed me.

WHEN I RETURNED to the house, it was nearly midnight, and passing Darcy's study, I noticed the light was still on. I'd seen almost nothing of my host since the *incident*. Like Lizzy, he no longer took his meals downstairs, preferring the seclusion of his private rooms. But now seemed an opportune moment to speak to him, and I knocked on the door.

A voice from within bid me enter, and I found Darcy bent over a large ledger, his pen scratching elegant figures across the page.

"Darcy, shouldn't you be in bed?" I asked. The sight of him, his ink-stained hands and hunched shoulders, strangely moved me. I felt creeping into the corners of my eyes the familiar strain which is a harbinger of tears.

"I could say the same for you," he answered without looking up, though he laid down his pen. I watched him massage his right palm. "What a long day it's been," he sighed, leaning into his chair.

"How is Lizzy?"

"Jane and Mrs. Reynolds are looking after her" was the insufficient reply. "She . . ." He hesitated, unable to finish the thought, and proceeded to rub his face. The ink on his hands added faint streaks of gray to his sickly paleness.

"I think she blames me for what happened," he finally said. The effort of speaking seemed to exhaust him.

"That isn't possible," I replied defensively. "What happened isn't anyone's fault."

"I assure you it is possible. I forget what a way my wife has with words. 'Darcy,' she said to me, when we were alone, 'will you have your heir and a spare at the cost of my life? Which would you choose?'"

"And what did you say?"

"I told her she was tired and to take some rest."

"Oh, Darcy . . ."

"I know, but I was angry with her for asking such a question." He shut the ledger and exhaled.

"She's in the throes of grief—poor Lizzy. I'm sure she doesn't know what she's saying."

"She seemed perfectly lucid to me."

An argument would have been pointless, so I let the subject rest and seated myself in a nearby chair.

"But on to happier subjects . . ." he said at last. "Have you been able to make any progress with our good friend Leonora?"

"Only a single chapter, I'm afraid," I replied, and then added, to whet his appetite, "but a vital one, nonetheless, which will change the whole course of the book."

He smiled. "Then you better tell me what happens."

"Ah, but the hour is late," I said, glancing at the clock.

"It matters little to me, Mary. I have not slept more than three hours these last few days."

At this, I looked down at my hands. "I wish you'd take better care of yourself," I said quietly. "So much of everyone's happiness depends on you. Lizzy's, of course, and Georgiana's, Mrs. Reynolds's, and that of the rest of Pemberley's staff. And all your tenants and their families. They rely on you to stay strong."

I was still tracing the lines of my right palm when he spoke. "And yours?" he asked. I looked up.

"What?" I knew what he meant, but some part of me wished to feign ignorance.

"What about your happiness, Mary?" he asked. "Do I contribute to that, too?"

At the question, my eyes grew heavy. A prickling soreness entered into them. For some moments, it was as though the colonel had never entered the house and my spirit lived in Pemberley's library. I wished I could tell him how much it meant to have someone to talk to about books. My own father, though we read the same novels, would rather keep his opinions to himself than share them with his weak-minded and pedantic middle daughter. And as for Mama and Kitty, they would laugh me out of Longbourn if I regaled them with tales of Denmark's ill-fated queen and her German prince. How could I describe to Darcy the fear which had gripped my soul when he'd first discovered my novel, and the wonder and gratitude which had replaced that fear when I'd realized his interest was in earnest? How could I tell him that in his person I had discovered an unexpected and most treasured friend, possibly the first to treat me as an equal? There wasn't a chapter of *Leonora* which hadn't passed under his scrutiny, no line of this voluminous work which he hadn't read and examined with both care and thought.

My tears preceded my speech.

"What brings this about?" Darcy asked, studying me. He must have thought me a hysterical fool.

"I love Pemberley," I said at last.

This answer, however feeble I considered it, seemed to satisfy him, for he smiled again.

"Tell me what happens in the chapter," he repeated.

"It's pretty horrid," I warned.

"I'm fond of horrid, as you well know," he replied.

So I told him about Leonora and the masked assassin who'd sworn to avenge the grand duke's death—this assassin being, of course, none other than the one person Leonora loved and trusted most in the whole world, her half sister, Agnes. Seconds before the jeweled dagger fell, Wilhelm had burst into the throne room and decapitated with one swift cut of his sword that backstabbing villainess. But he'd come too late—Leonora was mortally wounded, her blood saturating the throne room's stone floor.

"Well?" Darcy cried, as soon as I'd stopped. "Does she live or not? Mary, you can't possibly kill her off! I won't stand for it."

"Haven't decided yet," I said.

"You are cruel."

Laughing, I stood and performed a theatrical bow. It was half past one, and I'd just remembered that I was to meet the colonel in the stables at eight o'clock.

"It's late," I said again, stretching my arms.

"I will let you go for now," Darcy said, affecting a serious attitude, "but you must promise me, Mary, that you won't keep me in suspense for too long as to whether Leonora lives or dies."

"I won't," I assured him before I left. "I promise."

CHAPTER 24

I broke my promise. The colonel, who had pledged to teach me a new way of living, proved too fine an instructor, and a whole week passed in which I immersed myself in his tutelage. First, he taught me to ride, and I left Leonora to recover in her royal bed while I took Marmalade through the scattered wildernesses of the estate. My own mind was a muddled but euphoric version of its former self. One cannot, I think, ever be truly intelligent in the first throes of love. I relished every moment of my newfound ignorance, in which all thoughts revolved like the celestial bodies around a single source of glorious light. Though we talked a great deal, there passed between the colonel and myself no conversations which expanded the breadth of our souls or increased the understanding of our minds. We spoke primarily of ourselves and those we knew. Our language was the wandering speech of lovers who spend whole hours examining a wisp of curly hair or the movement of an earwig across a leaf. He called me his "ugly little thing," and I called him either "Marmalade" or my "womanizing, caper-witted coxcomb."

Pemberley became our playground, and we its reckless and un-ruly children. We fished its waters and caught two trout, which we presented to Darcy's French-German cook, who prepared them very ill. When we grew tired of riding Marmalade, that short-tempered nag, we tumbled and wrestled in beds of soft grass out of sight of the house; and when this, too, lost its appeal, we crept as gingerly as spiders down forgotten corridors where we entered untenanted rooms, giggling like maniacs. The furniture within loomed in dusty corners like phantoms. I could sometimes feel them breathing beneath their white sheets, impatient for the living to leave so that they could resume their conversations—the mahogany sideboard with the walnut armoire, the Grecian couch with the Chinese cabinet.

Jane's condition prevented her from remaining long by Lizzy's side, and Lizzy continued to recover in complete seclusion, with only Mrs. Reynolds to keep her company. Almost as soon as Jane had gone, rumors began to circulate of screams heard in the dead hours of night from the master bedroom. The sounds frequently roused me from my sleep; I found I could not move when I heard them, and so terrifying was the pitch that every hair on my arms would stand on end and I could not close my eyes for hours. Lizzy had nightmares, violent, cruel nightmares that took possession of her body and gave her claws where she had none. Everyone knew it was the remembrance of the child which tormented her, the discovery that nature did not discriminate, even among supposed favorites; one could give birth not only to life but also to death. I'd heard these nightmares had eventually forced Darcy to move out of their room and into his own chambers.

I confess it pained me that, following Jane's departure, Lizzy never once called for me, that the several times I visited her rooms I was gently but firmly rebuffed by Mrs. Reynolds. At Longbourn, Lizzy had never confided in me. I was one of the last to learn of her and Darcy's engagement and the least involved of my siblings in helping with the arrangements for the double wedding. It might have been wishful thinking to hope that anything had changed permanently during my happy months at Pemberley. The theories I entertained as to why I was no longer welcome ranged from the benevolent to the malicious. It was possible that she did not want to worry me (benevolent). It was also possible that she wanted the guilt

I already felt to fester like an untended wound (malicious). I didn't know what to believe.

But I was also too distracted to seriously concern myself. Never in my life had I been happier. And it was on a day of clouds and wind, and in a room memorable for its distinctive wallpaper—a lustrous sky blue dappled with gold butterflies and white pansies—that something was taken from me, for I worried there might never be an opportune moment again. From my youth, I'd listened to sermons expounding the priceless worth of female virtue. I'd borne witness to the aftermath of my youngest sister's disgrace, how her ignominy had nearly ruined us all by association. In the company of other women, I'd listened to tales of daughters who, for a few moments' pleasure, lived the remainder of their lives in penury, disowned by mortified mothers and fathers. Their names carried a bitter taste; they blackened the reputation of womanhood and reminded us of our original sin. Yet that day these cautionary tales with which I guarded my heart crumpled in a hypocritical heap around my bare ankles. The first attempt was too painful for words, but I gritted my teeth through it, and through the quiet tremors of shame that quickly followed in its wake. After the episode was over, I took a bath. When I was clean and had changed into a new dress, I lay down, but the recumbent position brought back fresh strokes of pain between my legs and the impression that I was bleeding. I could not sleep. I had nothing to read, having run out of books in my room, so I went to the library. I knew that the colonel, who might well have considered sex only another form of exercise, had returned to the stables to groom Marmalade.

There were days at Pemberley when the house felt too full of faces. One could never be alone in such a place, not even for the span of a brief walk down Pemberley's shortest corridor, for there was sure to be, waiting at the end of it, a veiled marchioness or a Grecian god seated primly upon his pedestal. There were days when the walls seemed to creak beneath the weight of these faces, when an earl looked ready to finally dismount from his famous thoroughbred and Lady Anne appeared at last to have awoken from her opium-induced trance. Even in an estate as large as Pemberley, one could feel crowded from all this history, especially when the history was not yours to share in. As I passed them—the portraits, the statues, the bronze and obsidian busts—I could sense their eyes boring into the top of my head.

Look, there she goes, Darcy's great-uncle called out. *The deflowered maiden.*

Harlot, Georgiana's likeness hissed from her place of honor. *Just like Lydia.*

The Bennet girls can't seem to keep their hands off the officers, can they?, a beloved family greyhound barked.

The voices ceased once I entered the library, where, fortunately, no life-sized paintings of illustrious ancestors decorated the walls. Yet on this day, I didn't proceed to the shelves, to the leather-bound classics whose spines were a uniform and most soothing woodland green. Instead, hearing the gentle *clop-clop* of hooves outdoors, I went to the window.

The library overlooked one of the side courtyards, from which residents could come and go as they wished without having to pass through the front gates. A phaeton had just arrived, drawn by a large chestnut-colored horse. The driver disembarked from his seat, and three servants came out to meet him and to help him bring several parcels into the house. It was Darcy.

A few days after our last meeting in his study, he'd left Pemberley to go into town. I'd forgotten all about his trip.

Presently, the servants emptied the phaeton of its load, and Darcy exchanged some pleasantries with them before they left his side. When he was alone, he took off his hat and, holding it first in one hand, then passing it to the other, he paced the courtyard's perimeter. His face was grim. He seemed to look at the walls, the shrubbery, the stone beneath his feet without recognition. Then the sound of something—a bird taking flight or the rustle of branches—made him glance up, and he spotted me before I could hide behind the curtains.

It must have been a trick of the light, for I thought his features brightened, that the gloom which I'd discerned as he'd made his rounds of the courtyard vanished. I noted that he smiled, and though I was glad to see him pleased, I admit I despised myself a little. For the whole eventful week, I'd given him no thought, though I'd eaten his food and drunk his wine and traipsed his garden paths. Up until the very moment of his arrival, I hadn't even considered when he would return, so enthralled had I been with everything the colonel said and did. It was the colonel who now occupied all my thoughts and all my time. And, in truth, it was that gentleman I thought of, not Darcy, as I waved back to my neglected friend from the library window, smiling.

CHAPTER 25

꡷

Darcy came down for dinner that evening, the first meal he'd taken outside of his rooms since the *incident*. Over servings of white soup, the colonel sang the praises of his favorite horse.

"Of course, it may have been an accident, but I don't think it's likely," he said, licking the last dregs from his spoon. "I mean, what are the chances that she should bite my sleeve just when I was about to leave? She tore the whole thing off, by the way, and the shirt is ruined. I looked like I'd been attacked by ruffians coming back to the house."

"She's a fine horse," Darcy conceded, still two spoonfuls into his soup.

"She's more than a fine horse, damn it," the colonel said passionately. "I'm convinced our spirits are bonded in some way. I'll never find a horse like her again; I'm quite sure of that."

"I grant you it will be extremely difficult to replace Marmalade when the day comes," Darcy said.

"You should see what a fine figure Mary cuts on Marmalade." The colonel grinned, winking at me from across the table.

Darcy looked up sharply. The third spoonful, which had been halfway to his mouth, promptly returned untouched to his plate.

"The colonel has taught me to ride," I said bashfully.

"Mary's a natural," my lover gushed. "A horsewoman to rival Queen Elizabeth herself, in my opinion."

"Oh," Darcy replied, wiping his mouth, though he'd barely eaten anything.

"It's amazing how Marmalade's taken to Mary," the colonel added, oblivious to Darcy's sudden reticence. "You know from experience, Darcy, that she won't let anyone ride her, not even our saintly Georgiana."

"Yes, all right, Fitzwilliam."

At this, the colonel laughed and, turning to me, said, "One thing you'll learn about our esteemed friend, Mary, is that he won't suffer any person in the world to speak ill of his sister, not even her own guardian. Deficiencies, even those of the vaguest and most useless variety, are strictly forbidden, as I've just demonstrated to you. For that matter, Darcy, I don't think Georgiana is particularly talented at shuttlecock. There, now you may challenge me to a duel. First to draw blood?"

I giggled, which seemed to put Darcy in an even worse humor. I assumed his mind was elsewhere, perhaps occupied with Lizzy's recovery.

"Don't be a fool, Fitzwilliam," he scolded grumpily.

"Have you seen Lizzy since you've come back?" I asked my host.

"I have not," he replied, seeming grateful to change the subject, "but Mrs. Reynolds was kind enough to make a detailed report of my wife's health. She says she still prefers to take all her meals upstairs due to a poor appetite but, in general, appears to be improving."

"When shall we see her, Darcy?" the colonel inquired.

"I don't know" was the terse reply.

"A fine-spirited woman," his friend offered and quickly added, "just like her sister."

Blushing, I quietly thanked him.

For the next several minutes, the colonel was too occupied with consuming the large cut of veal on his plate to speak, and Darcy took advantage of his cousin's silence to mention something of his recent trip.

"Mary, I have brought you the Marquis de Grosse's *Horrid Mysteries,* which I know you've wanted to read," he announced.

"Mary," the colonel piped up, resurfacing from his dish before I could give Darcy my thanks, "I'm thinking of going into Lambton tomorrow to look at a rifle. Will you come with me?"

"Fitzwilliam, that's hardly a proper errand to take a young woman on," Darcy interjected.

"So? You're not her guardian, and she's not, legally speaking, your ward."

"She is, while she's staying under my roof," Darcy said, biting into a slice of veal.

While his cousin chewed, the colonel launched his defense: "Well, we shall let Mary decide. That seems the only thing to do."

Darcy hurriedly gulped down his meat. "Mary," he began, while I considered what to say, "I'm still waiting for you to apprise me of Leonora's fate, as you promised. Have you written anything new while I've been gone?"

"She's been much too busy to write any more of her novel," the colonel answered on my behalf, which, I confess, irritated me. I flashed him a look of annoyance, which he either missed or ignored, for he continued much as before: "And, Darcy, you shouldn't encourage Mary to sit indoors so much. She's been doing that her whole life and doesn't need more of it. Only think how pale she looked when I first arrived and how well she looks now. Marmalade has worked wonders on her."

"A finely written novel may bring pleasure to thousands, while riding gives pleasure only to oneself."

"That is absolute rot, Darcy," the colonel answered, his mouth full.

"Well, we shall leave the decision to Mary," Darcy said. "Mary, what do you think of the matter?"

The dinner table, which had previously been raucous with the two gentlemen's repartee, instantly turned quiet. I looked from Darcy to the colonel, then at the uneaten morsel stuck at the end of my fork. A dizzying warmth proliferated across my neck and face, and I blush to think how I must have resembled, in that moment, a burning lantern.

"I can't think why I shouldn't be able to do both," I said finally, surprised by my own determination. "I will go with the colonel tomorrow morning to Lambton and return in time to write the final chapter of *Leonora*."

This answer seemed to please both men, and the colonel gave a quick hoot of joy. Darcy, allowing himself a small smile, returned to carving another flawless square of meat.

The next morning, I accompanied the colonel to Lambton, and what was meant to be an errand lasting two or, at most, three hours soon turned into an all-day outing. It was eight o'clock when we returned to Pemberley, and the day had already cast its delirious spell. In my happiness, I'd once again forgotten the promise I'd made to Darcy.

CHAPTER 26

✺

The colonel told me it would get better with practice. He said it was something to be mastered, just like riding horses or playing chess.

"Think how frightened you were of Marmalade in the beginning," he urged, "and how comfortable you are with riding her now, even when I'm not there."

"Well, you cannot but be there for what we're talking about, can you?" I replied, snickering.

He told me to trust him. "It will get better. You'll see, I promise you," he said. And he was right. It did get better, explosively better, much to my great surprise and pleasure.

My latest hobby precipitated a rumor, which originated, as rumors often did, belowstairs, among Pemberley's staff, before rising to the surface.

"There's a ghost. Pemberley is haunted," Bess said, in place of a greeting, when we happened upon each other one afternoon. As she spoke, her eyes darted suspiciously over my head from one corner of the hall to another. "Have you heard it?" she asked me.

"Certainly not!" I replied. "What ghost?"

"In the unoccupied wing," she said primly, satisfied by my ignorance. "But I don't suppose you frequent that part of the house, miss."

And she proceeded to tell me the story of how Henderson had entered that wing not two days ago and heard a most unsettling and alien sound emanating from one of the rooms along the corridor. It had turned his hair half-white and sent him running.

"Like the dead sitting up and moaning from their graves, he said," Bess continued. "I haven't heard it myself and am not inclined to, as I'm terrified of all things to do with spirits and apparitions. But Polly, one of the scullery maids, claims to have heard it as well. She said it's not at all like Henderson described but rather like children crying out in pain. Do you think they're child-ghosts, miss? Who got lost in the forgotten wing and couldn't find their way back to their mothers and so starved to death?"

"I wouldn't know, Bess," I said, being unable to conceal my blushing, for I, of course, knew perfectly what the source of the ghosts was.

The rumors of ghosts reached Darcy's ears as well, thanks to the garrulous Mrs. Reynolds. At dinner, while attending to a fillet of salmon, he commented that he'd never taken Henderson for a fanciful individual in all his twenty-three years of service.

"It may have been a wounded animal," the colonel offered helpfully.

"That occurred to me as well," Darcy said between mouthfuls of fish. "A pigeon or something."

And after dinner concluded, I raced my wounded animal to the abandoned wing and made more ghosts with him.

Days later, a carriage arrived, containing Pemberley's first visitors since the *incident*. From behind a bank of shrubbery on the front lawn, I spotted it rattling its way up the drive, like a toy being led on invisible string. When it reached its destination, the coachman jumped down and opened the door, and two dolls and a portly gentleman popped out. The ladies ascended to the house together, the smaller and thicker-waisted of the two dressed in agricultural green, the taller and less nourished one draped in luxuriant folds of burnt orange, her small head fashionably turbaned with an oversized plume that arched threateningly forward. Several steps behind them, the gentleman waddled slowly up the stairs at the edge of their combined shadows.

"Marmalade," I called out. The horse neighed. The man whose head was currently in my lap looked up questioningly, annoyed that I'd interrupted his afternoon nap. "Look, Marmalade," I continued, "we have guests, and I do believe I know who they are, if the color of their frocks is anything to go by. I think it must be Miss Caroline Bingley, her sister, Mrs. Hurst, and Mr. Hurst."

"More ladies?" the colonel said lasciviously, and I rumpled his hair. He cried out in protest: "Now I won't be presentable, thanks to you."

"I forget sometimes that you are no better than a vain peacock," I sighed. This was the sort of aimless conversation we were able to make last for hours between us. "And a womanizing coxcomb," I added cheerfully, rumpling his hair again before he caught my arm and kissed the back of it.

"I have no need for ladies now," he said with a hint of sadness. "I am practically a married man."

"That could not be," I commented gently, pretending to laugh, though the subject made me nervous, "for you have extended no offer of marriage."

From my lap, he reached up to stroke my warm, sunlit face. "You ugly little thing," he said affectionately, "would you be happy married to me, the poorest and most feeble-minded son of an earl? Tell me the truth."

"Have you any money?" I asked.

"No, dearest, only a few measly pounds to rub together. James will get the bulk of everything, being the eldest, though I can get money enough so long as I ask nicely for it and remain my charming self to all the members of my extremely wealthy family."

"Have you any terrible vices?" I questioned in mock judgment.

"Drink," he admitted, "and I do like the odd flutter on horses when I can afford it. Though the worst of it is . . ."

"Yes?"

Sitting up, he kissed me. "The worst of my vices is that I spoil young, respectable women and deprive them of their maidenhoods."

"And how will you repent for this greatest of sins, my lovely, impoverished Marmalade?" I returned his kiss.

"I will marry the maiden, though I warn her that we shall both be penniless and become quite desperate from exceeding our incomes so regularly." He kissed me before I could answer, as though to prevent my forming words.

"Then speaking on behalf of the maidenhood-less maiden," I said, once I had the opportunity, "I accept the womanizing coxcomb's offer of marriage and thank him for his trouble."

"So you really do love me then, my ugly little thing?" he asked.

Gathering his hands to my face, I pressed the wrist he'd once sprained to my mouth. "I do," I replied.

In other parts of the world, one hears tell of miracles that have occurred—the parting of seas, the rising of the dead, the raining of bread from heaven to feed the starving masses. But this day in England, in the county of Derbyshire, on the gently sloping green lawn of Pemberley, an even greater miracle had taken place, though it remained for the time being a secret between two lovers. I, Mary Bennet, had become engaged to be married.

THAT NIGHT WAS a restless one. I could not sleep for all the exuberance I felt, tossing and turning until my bed became too hot and unkempt to lie in. In the third hour of my wakefulness, I put on a dressing gown and went downstairs. My tour took me past the terrace, where I thought I saw someone standing at the end of it, illumined by moonlight, like a sailor poised at the prow of a ghostly ship. I had determined to return to my room, but the figure sud-

denly turned and caught sight of me tiptoeing back in the direction
of the staircase.

"Mary!" Darcy called out, and I begrudgingly retraced my steps.

A few moments later, I stood at his side, midshipman to his lieutenant. The night was so dark, I did not dare lean over the ledge to
peer into the void below.

"So, you could not sleep, either," Darcy said, seeming pleased at
the discovery of a fellow insomniac.

"No, not tonight," I admitted.

"Would you be scandalized, Mary, if I told you that I had my
very first kiss here as a hot-blooded youth?" he asked.

"That would depend entirely upon how old you were and who
the kiss was with," I replied practically.

"Five, and my second cousin, the Honorable Miss Lucy Car-
rington, was eight."

I couldn't help laughing, and Darcy, too, smiled. I asked him
why he was not in bed.

"I was thinking," he answered, looking down at his hands, "of
fatherhood and its difficulties. After all, it cannot be only wealth and
property which a parent imparts to his children. Morality and law
may be studied. But how is goodness attained? How is a noble and
charitable temperament cultivated? Only consider what must go
into the upbringing of an innocent infant; is it not momentous that,
one day, his character, whether honorable or otherwise, should serve
as a reflection of his parents, though he will always be his own person?" He paused, and then bowing his head so that his face was hidden from me, he continued: "Two nights ago, I thought I dreamed
of him. I was riding—I passed a post, which told me how many
miles I still needed to travel before I would reach my destination,
and he was sitting on a large rock at the base of the sign. I assumed
he was a vagrant, a gypsy, so I kept riding; at the next post, he was
there again, calling out to me. 'Stop the horse!' he cried, waving his
arms, but I couldn't. Over and over, I missed him, and as the miles

counted down, he grew more desperate. At the last post, I reached out my hand, but his fingers were too short to catch mine. He said, weeping, 'Father, bring me with you,' and I shook my head. It was impossible; there was nothing I could do. The horse took me past him, and his shape grew smaller and smaller until it disappeared. Then I awoke."

His words had emboldened me sufficiently that I touched his sleeve. "It was only a dream. Please do not think too much of it."

"Do you think fatherhood would have suited me, Mary?" he asked.

"How could it not suit you?" I said with feeling. "You are the embodiment of everything that is good and honorable in the world and the best person I know—superior certainly to anyone of my limited acquaintance."

"Do not tease me."

I pressed my hand harder against his arm, and to my surprise, Darcy caught it in his own and held it. He must have sensed my astonishment, however, because he instantly released it and, in a changed tone, said he'd grown tired. He would finish a letter and go to bed. So we parted on the terrace, and when I returned to my room, I found I still could not sleep.

CHAPTER 27

✧

At last, Lizzy sent for me. Mrs. Reynolds, in her usual prompt manner, asked me to close my book and come upstairs. "You'll go half-blind from so much reading," she chided as I followed her to my sister's room.

When we'd nearly reached our destination, she put her hand on my arm and turned towards me. "A letter's come," Mrs. Reynolds whispered, "in the early hours of the morning."

"From who?" I asked.

"Mrs. Wickham" was the brusque reply before her bony fist rapped the door.

I hadn't seen Lizzy for nearly three weeks, not since the first days following the *incident,* when she still permitted me to sit on her bed and hold her hand.

I expected to find her much improved, and she was. Some color had returned to her face. The swelling of her countenance and the dark circles beneath her eyes had vanished. When I entered, she looked at me thoughtfully, and I could detect in her expression no trace of the weakness or uncertainty which had plagued her in all the days she'd been with child. I was happy to find her so recovered—happy but angry, too, that I'd been intentionally deprived of her company not because she was truly ill and unable to sit up in bed, as I'd been told up till the previous day, but simply because I was unwanted. As soon as Mrs. Reynolds departed, Lizzy gestured to the seat beside her.

"You look much better," I said quietly, though I didn't move.

"Oh, Mary, don't sulk," Lizzy exclaimed. She motioned again to the empty chair. "Sit by me," she instructed.

"You asked for Jane. . . ." I said, remaining where I was. "And when Jane had gone, you asked for Mrs. Reynolds. Why did you never ask for me, Lizzy?"

"Surely it is my prerogative, Mary," she replied, "to choose who should sit by me when I am ill and bedridden. I am very sorry you are hurt. But if we are to throw off politeness and be honest with each other, I'm obliged to tell you the real reason I did not ask for you. You know you have no sympathy for these matters."

"That is both unkind and untrue," I interjected.

"Of course, you are very intelligent," she continued, ignoring me. "I sometimes wonder how your insatiable mind would have benefited from the instruction of a tutor, had Papa been sensible and rich enough to hire one. But you cannot claim to know anything about marriage or about pregnancy, much less motherhood. You are not married. You have never cared for the things that most women attend to in their lives. And except for a passing interest in our ridiculous cousin, you have always shown yourself to be indifferent to subjects of, how shall I put it, a non-academic nature." Lizzy looked away. She frowned, and when she spoke again, her voice involuntarily trembled. "I . . . I was in the throes of grief; to have asked you to sit with me would have been akin to asking a five-year-old girl to tend to her dying mother. It would be a trial to both parties—an impractical arrangement. You can see what I mean, can't you, Mary?"

The force of her words nearly knocked me to my knees. I took a deep breath before venturing to speak again. "In the days after you lost your child and before Jane had come, I sat with you. . . ." I stopped, for all the warmth and color had drained out of her face at the mere utterance of that forbidden word. She shivered. Her hands pulled a richly woven shawl tighter about her thin shoulders.

"But we are talking in circles," she continued. "As I have explained, the problem is one of sympathy. You cannot ask a philosopher to appreciate a poet's torments. We're so different from each other, Mary. There are things you are simply prevented from knowing until you've experienced them, and it is useless to try to make you understand."

"You think I've never loved? That I've never felt pain?"

"That is too extreme. But you must admit that you have always been harder to relate to. Don't you recall Mrs. Hill's cat?"

I made a face. "Mrs. Hill's cat? She never had a cat." Then I remembered. A stray. Female. Black, Mrs. Hill used to joke, for good luck. It was blind in one eye, a dry, dusty socket where an eye should have been. No one knew what had happened, except the air was suddenly filled with screams coming from somewhere outside the house. It was Papa who found Mrs. Hill's cat near the pigpen, sprawled on its side in the mud. And it was Sarah who pointed out that the animal's hind legs were broken. I was sixteen. For three months, I had consumed nothing except heroic literature. I took the shovel, which was normally used to muck out the shed, and put an end to the din, while my sisters stood behind me and wept.

"The animal was in pain. I did the right thing," I said, sitting down.

"But you cannot deny that it takes a certain hardness of character to do such a thing."

"It takes a certain strength of character to do such a thing," I answered. Lizzy stiffened and, turning away, brushed a loose thread from her shawl.

An extended silence settled between us. At last, I said, "Possibly you are right to think I would have been unhelpful had I kept you company. We will not speak of it anymore. It is insensitive of me to press the point when you are the one who has suffered so much."

At this, Lizzy produced a few sheets of paper and held them out to me. "I have a letter from Lydia to share with you," she said. "It arrived a few hours ago."

Taking the papers from her, I began to read.

Dear Lizzy,

I am seriously ill. Could you please come down to London at your earliest convenience? I have written to our parents but still receive no reply from them. Wickham has been missing for ten days, and his creditors grow impatient. I have told them that he is dealing with urgent matters of business in the country, but they know as well as I do that this is improbable, the truth being that I really have no idea where my husband is at all.

I called on our Uncle and Aunt Gardiner at Gracechurch Street three days ago and was informed by their maid that they are currently away from home and en route to Pemberley. If this is true, perhaps you and the Gardiners can come down to London together to visit. And Mary, too, if she is still your guest. We will make such a merry party, even in these rotten rooms, and there is no piano here for Mary to make us all grimace and cover our ears.

I hope you and Baby are doing all right. If due to Baby you cannot travel in person to London, please be so kind as to give Mary or the Gardiners any amount of money you can easily spare. Twenty or thirty pounds would stave off the creditors for a little while longer and enable me to visit an apothecary and attain some medicine.

Yours ever,
Lydia Wickham

P.S. I do not think I shall recover so easily this time from my fever, which is very high indeed. Sometimes I can hardly

stand and faint right back onto my bed again after
rising.

P.S.S. Thank you for the forty pounds, which I have used
to settle a portion of Wickham's debts so that we may
keep these rooms and also the furniture. I would promise
to pay it all back one day, but our prospects seem very
bleak.

"Will you visit her, Mary?" Lizzy asked. "I'd like you to go with
the Gardiners and visit our sister in London."

"Oh . . . I see. Of course I shall go," I said.

"I would make the journey myself, if I were fully recovered,"
Lizzy added by way of explanation. "Also, the city air . . ."

"No, I understand. I will make your apologies to Lydia when I
see her."

I stood and moved to the nearest window. "You know, Caroline
Bingley didn't recognize me at first," I said absently. Looking out, I
spotted the woman in question taking tea with her sister and my
lover in the south garden. "Or she just pretended not to recognize
me. She called me Kitty, and I had to explain that my younger sister
was still at Longbourn. 'My name is Mary,' I told her. And then she
made a strange noise and cried out, 'Oh! How thoughtless of me! Of
course, your name is Molly.' "

"Come away from the window," Lizzy said. "There's something
else I'd like to speak to you about."

"Did you know, Lizzy—there's a little tea party taking place right
now near the rosebushes, which, I'm sorry to say, neither of us has
been invited to."

"Is there? Who's in attendance?"

"Just the colonel, Miss Bingley, and Mrs. Hurst." I turned my
back to the window. The picture of Caroline Bingley eating jam
tartlets while laughing with her mouth open held no appeal for me.

"What is the other matter you wanted to speak to me about?" I asked, returning to Lizzy's side.

She paused and glanced at me before turning away and fiddling with a corner of her shawl. She seemed embarrassed. "It's a sensitive subject," she said, clearing her throat, "but the question must be asked. Do you believe, Mary, that the colonel has taken an interest—a romantic interest—in you? Mrs. Reynolds has remarked that the two of you are rarely out of each other's company these days."

I wish I could have told her the truth, but I'd been sworn to secrecy. "It's to our advantage, our long-term advantage," he had explained, "that Father and Mother find out first before anyone else does, and this is something I must tell them in person. It won't be much longer—I promise." Then he'd patted his pockets, and I'd understood what he meant, though it saddened me, sickened me also, that we were still so dependent on the fortunes of others in order to secure our own.

I replied as generally as I could. "Yes, Lizzy, I think he has. I believe he is extremely fond of me."

Lizzy caught my smile. She bent forward from her seat and took one of my hands, surprising me with the strength of her grip. "I hope I will not offend you by speaking plainly. I know it must be very flattering. . . . I know it is a new experience for you to be able to walk and converse with a man of his estimation, and I will thank him myself when I am fully recovered for being so kind as to divert you from your books and other hobbies. But for your own sake, Mary, I hope you will not take any of this to heart. You see how he turns his attentions to Miss Bingley and Mrs. Hurst just as soon as they arrive. The conclusion we must inevitably draw from his behavior is that your company suited him only when he had no others at Pemberley with whom to socialize. Everyone knows he is a very lively and personable young man who loves to dance, ride horses, and attend parties."

"And I am, of course, unlively and unpersonable," I replied.

"That is a childish remark, Mary. You see, you are angry with me."

When I offered no reply, my sister's expression softened. "I will admit to some fault in allowing this to happen. Darcy and I should have had the foresight to invite a third party to keep the colonel company as soon as he arrived. But, Mary, you must be mature and not make a scene over him. If you were to claim that he loved you or anything of the kind, I'm afraid it would be very embarrassing for you."

I extracted my hand and did not sit down again. "How much money will you give me to take to Lydia in London?" I asked.

"Oh." Lizzy shrugged. It was easy for her to be generous. "Another thirty pounds?"

"Then I shall look forward to seeing the Gardiners tomorrow," I said, preparing to take my leave. "I daresay I like the Gardiners better than they like me, but they are good people."

"Mary, don't be angry with me."

"I'm not so much angry with you, Lizzy, as I am disappointed."

She mistook my meaning. "Well, of course you are," Lizzy replied. "You have, as I said, no experience in these matters, but you mustn't take it too personally. It is natural enough for a woman to misjudge a gentleman's attentions for greater interest, and perfectly acceptable, too, so long as no one is aware of it but herself."

Ignoring this remark, I stepped swiftly towards the door. I had already reached for the handle when Lizzy asked me to wait. Her tone was apologetic.

"Mary, please stay a moment. I didn't intend to be so harsh with you. It's just all those days I spent in bed, I kept thinking of what you had said to me in the library when I was still pregnant. Do you remember?"

Shaking my head, I exerted more weight on the handle, and the door clicked open.

"No, of course you wouldn't remember," Lizzy continued. "You said . . ." She hesitated. "You said you would be governess to my child, and you promised me that everything would be fine." She laughed. The sound of it reached me, hollow and alarming. "I know you meant only to comfort me—what else could you possibly have said when I was so unhappy? But afterwards, I realized, sitting in bed . . . I realized how little you actually know, how naïve you are. I suppose, as unreasonable as it may seem, I resented you for it . . . Mary?"

My hand anchored itself in the solidity of the door, and I stared at a spot of blue in the carpet. I thought I would cry, but I didn't.

"All I wanted was a comfortable life," I heard Lizzy say. "When I married Darcy, I was so happy. It was the attainment of an impossible dream. I felt . . . I felt I'd done something unprecedented. Me, mistress of this place—could you imagine it? But I didn't realize that it came with a price, and that the price would be my life. If I had known what danger awaited me . . . the risk I undertook in marrying him, in marrying at all."

At the mention of risk, I thought of the colonel and myself. From the beginning, he had sworn on pain of death that he would be careful. There had been only the one time when I was forced to push him off me before it was too late, and that incident had never repeated itself. He had been extra cautious since, knowing full well the disgrace which would await us both should I find myself unmarried and with child.

"If I had died but the baby had lived," Lizzy said suddenly, her eyes shining, "I suppose the sacrifice would have been well worth it. I would have fulfilled my purpose, as countless wives have done before me. And once an acceptable interval had passed, Darcy would choose a new wife, and she would begin the process over again and repeat it until he had enough heirs to ensure that Pemberley passed to his children and his children's children. All this"—she glanced around herself—"the spacious rooms, the comforts both great and small— don't let these fool you, Mary. I see them now for what they are:

temptations. I cannot be blamed, for I didn't know. I, too, was naïve and couldn't predict what expectations would be made of my body when I entered this place. Yet here I am. By some miracle, I am still alive and much wiser than I was before. I will no longer be so careless with my life."

"What happened, Lizzy, was a tragedy," I answered angrily, "but Darcy loves you. You know this to be true. He values you more than anything else."

Again, she laughed. Nodding to herself, she said, "This is exactly why I didn't want you by my side. Thank you for proving my point, Mary. Now you may take your soppy platitudes elsewhere and go work on your novel. Have you finished it yet?"

The sting of her words only made me more furious. I imagined how her eyes would pop out of their sockets when she learned of my engagement to the colonel. She would no longer underestimate me then. I, too, could be full of surprises.

But the course of my thoughts was interrupted. Mrs. Reynolds appeared in the doorway with a tray and, looking askance at me, said it was time for Mrs. Darcy to take her medicine. I was only too glad to leave.

CHAPTER 28

A lively party made up dinner that evening, with many exclamations of joy uttered at the sight of Pemberley's mistress. Caroline Bingley professed that she had nearly succumbed to illness herself worrying over my sister's health, and Louisa Hurst, who supported her younger sibling in everything, claimed to have borne witness to Caroline's feverish suffering. Mr. Hurst said nothing, though he ate his soup most heartily.

"What delicate constitutions ladies must have," the colonel said, addressing Miss Bingley. "You have only to hear of a friend's ailment before taking to bed yourself. Well, I am glad that men are not built this way. I would have a hard time on the battlefield if the sight of one wounded soldier made the rest of my troops swoon."

This sent all three women reeling with laughter. I confess my own mouth twitched less in humor than jealousy. Against my will, Lizzy's words had landed. The green-eyed monster had reared its head.

"Women have a hard time of it, though, I grant you," the colonel added in more serious tones, perhaps sensing my displeasure.

"I couldn't agree more," Caroline Bingley jumped in, touching the corners of her lips with her napkin. "And, speaking for myself, I am quite convinced there must be a paucity of good, single men to be found in the world. No sooner do I meet with any well-spoken gentleman at a party than I learn from one or other of my friends that he is also an incurable drunkard and gambler. It makes a dire situation for any woman."

"Yes, we good men of the world know our worth well, being so few in number," the colonel replied, grinning, "which is also why we behave so conceitedly when introduced to fine ladies such as yourself and Mrs. Hurst."

I discreetly rolled my eyes, while the rest of the table erupted in feminine giggles. My silence must have provoked Miss Bingley, however, for after she had recovered herself and dabbed her lips again, she turned to me, her mouth set in a malicious smile.

"And do you, Miss Bennet, agree that it is hard for a woman to find herself a good husband? I'm sure you have many opinions on the matter, being as well-learned as you are." To my left, Mrs. Hurst snickered.

I took a sip of wine before answering. "I believe that, as a general rule, everyone ends up with who they deserve."

Mr. Hurst, who ordinarily contributed only his hunger at gatherings, crooked an eyebrow and surprised everyone by expressing interest in hearing more.

"Mine is the simplistic view that one's faults and virtues will be mirrored in that of a partner," I said. "If one is charitable and kind, then that person, whether man or woman, will almost certainly find someone suited to him or her in character. And the same goes for those whose vices and faults outweigh their goodness."

"And if one never marries for lack of suitors?" Miss Bingley asked sweetly, though her cheeks had turned practically crimson.

"As you say, Miss Bingley, with good men scarcely to be found in society, surely it would be better to never marry than to wed an incurable drunkard or gambler," I answered.

"You are most confident in your opinions, Miss Bennet," Mr. Hurst contributed. He pointed a fork at me. "But your argument is flawed, for I have seen not a few mild-mannered women marry absolute brutes. And while a small fraction of these marriages did fail, the rest were remarkable successes. In fact, one lady of our acquaintance was virtually unrecognizable after the first six months. Do you remember, Louisa," he said, addressing his wife, "young Grace Hall, who always used to dress in demure grays and browns as a young woman? I even remarked one time that I thought she'd enter a nunnery when she came of age. Well, she made a well-matched, if not utterly unexpected, marriage. The man was rich as Croesus but had a reputation for womanizing, and a short temper besides. As there are ladies present, I won't go into too much detail, but suffice it to say that the few times Louisa and I came across her after she married, we never saw her in grays or browns again. I'd never seen a woman so changed."

"I do not think that disproves my argument at all," I said practically. "Surely there are latent qualities in our character which we ourselves are unaware of until we identify these same traits as attractive in another individual. In the case of Grace Hall, I would propose that her husband only brought out those aspects of her personality which were, up until the moment of their acquaintance, subdued."

At this, I happened to meet the colonel's eye, and he winked at me, which, fortunately, no one else around us noticed.

Mr. Hurst only chuckled at my response before draining the contents of his glass. From the head of the table, Darcy suddenly spoke.

"I'm sure we'd all be curious, Mary, to hear what qualities you would find admirable in a prospective husband," he said.

"That is like being asked to explain the components which make a sunset glorious," I replied. "Why should one man triumph over another in winning a woman's heart? The answer could not be that he is, by default, superior. Rather, there must be more than meets the eye—a spiritual connection, a meeting of complementary minds. And there can exist no formula for this. A man may be handsome, of good stock, and rich, yet a woman may still fall in love with one

half his worth. Speaking for myself, I believe that to pursue a prede-
termined set of qualities in a husband would be a mistake. Surely it
is the quality of time spent in each other's company which character-
izes a truly meaningful union."

"I'm afraid we are not all as philosophical as you, Miss Bennet,"
Miss Bingley chimed in eagerly. "I rather believe that the qualities
which make up a good husband are universally acknowledged among
women. Who would not wish to marry a man of fortune and of respectable family, provided he was also of a sociable and even-tempered
disposition?"

"Agreed," Lizzy said, and all eyes turned to her. "But you do not
account for one thing, Caroline, which is that the success of a marriage is not commensurate with the accomplishments and virtues of
the individual man or woman. Every single one of us is subject to
the whims of circumstance. The course of one's feelings can change.
Fortunes can be gained and lost. People may alter in fundamental
ways over time."

"Yet we may also strive to overcome circumstance," Darcy said,
staring directly at Lizzy. "We may, if we permit ourselves, emerge
stronger from the blows that Providence deals us."

Lizzy smiled sweetly enough, though she gave no reply.

"How perceptive of you, Mrs. Darcy, Mr. Darcy," the colonel
said, his face flushing from the amount of wine he'd consumed.
"And speaking of model marriages, we need search no further than
our hosts for a paragon of either sex." He smiled first at Darcy, then
at my sister. "I propose a toast." He raised his glass. "To the finest
couple in England! May we aspire to half their worth, though we
shall never be as rich as Darcy or as beautiful as his wife."

Everyone laughed and raised their glasses. They were too occupied with their merriment to notice, as I did, that Lizzy and Darcy
did not look once at each other. Lizzy uttered a few pleasantries, but
Darcy seemed engrossed in his thoughts, his mind far removed from
the rest of the company.

The remainder of the dinner proved as commonplace and un-eventful as any other. Soon after its conclusion, Darcy and the colo-nel left to play a game of billiards, and Mr. Hurst reluctantly followed. I trailed my female compatriots into a neighboring draw-ing room, and we all seated ourselves on plush settees, sighing con-tentedly into Pemberley's antiquated air.

"What an admirable man that gentleman is," Miss Bingley said after a period of silence.

"Darcy has always been the best of men," I replied, still thinking of how quiet he'd been at dinner.

"Darcy?" Miss Bingley repeated, coloring. "Yes, of course, Darcy, but I didn't mean him. I meant his cousin, the colonel. What a lively man."

It was my turn to redden. "Oh, I see."

"He has a fine sense of humor, don't you think, Louisa?" Miss Bingley asked, ignoring me, and her sister enthusiastically supplied her assent.

Though I was too tired to acknowledge it, I felt another pang of jealousy. I heard Mrs. Hurst yawn and Miss Bingley complain that she had eaten too much at dinner. They made light conversation with Lizzy for another quarter of an hour, and then they, too, re-tired.

At last, Lizzy and I were alone. The night was warm, and I rested my head against a cushion. I might have fallen asleep, except I sud-denly heard my sister's voice. She was sitting across from me, and her right hand absently fingered the long string of pearls which hung, like a rosary, from her neck.

"Cook prepared a fine meal this evening," she said. "I'll have to thank him later for it."

"I thought the fish was a bit overdone."

Lizzy did not answer. I thought we'd settled again into a comfort-able silence when she said, "We never had a chance to finish our conversation."

"No . . ." I stirred, adjusting the cushion at a different angle beneath my head. "No, we didn't."

"I will let you in on a secret, Mary," she began. "When I first came to Pemberley after my marriage, I arrived in the midst of a little drama then taking place among the servants. One of the laundry maids was heavily pregnant. She knew who the father was but wouldn't tell, and Darcy hadn't the heart to dismiss her. A month after I'd settled, she gave birth to an exceptionally large baby, a boy—so large, in fact, that Mrs. Reynolds told me everyone belowstairs called the child Hercules. But there were complications, and a physician was summoned; he recommended that mother and baby should be isolated in a private room with all the windows and doors sealed, and that a fire should be kept burning in the hearth every hour. Additionally, the mother should be wrapped in large blankets in order to sweat out her malady and ward off any colds and fevers. On the third morning, Mrs. Reynolds went herself to deliver breakfast to the mother and child, and found them both dead. She said the air in that room had become unfit to breathe, and I promised myself that day, as I promised myself for every day afterwards, that I would never die the way of the poor laundry maid." Lizzy looked up at me, and the pearls slid out of her hand. "No, Mary, I am determined to live, not only to live but also to live comfortably, as was my intention in entering this marriage with Darcy. I am not the first wife in this nation's fine history to fail her husband in the production of an heir, and I won't be the last. There, I have said it, and it is more real for saying it out loud to another."

For a long time, I did not respond, and when I met my sister's gaze, it was as though I were looking into the face of a stranger.

"But will you be happy?" I asked. "Will fortune and comfort be enough? I do not believe it. You are no Caroline Bingley, Lizzy. You have much more spirit than she does."

"I, too, have changed, Mary." She took from my lap one of my hands and held it in her own. "And I must continue to change, or I shall be a victim again. Next time, I will surely die. I won't let myself go through it again. I won't."

"And what of Darcy?" I asked.

Lizzy shrugged. "Darcy has cousins enough and Georgiana may also have children. Pemberley could very well pass to his own nephew." She squeezed my wrist. "I didn't leave Longbourn so that I could be sacrificed for the honor and the heritage of these stone walls. As my sister, tell me you understand."

"I think I understand," I whispered. I wanted to tell Lizzy I didn't agree with her views of her marriage, of Darcy. But there was no time, and something in my expression must have betrayed my misgivings, for Lizzy released my hand and reminded me that the Gardiners were due to arrive the next morning. I went upstairs to pack, grateful for any excuse to leave her side.

CHAPTER 29

Misery festooned the tight alleyways, the gutter-like courtyards, and the ramshackle buildings of the section of London to which we traveled. No poetic metaphor could dwell in these cloudy windows, no existentialist secret in the movements of bent and broken men whose notions of strength last as long as a bottle of Old Tom. This world demands to be taken literally. The air billows a peculiar fragrance of smoky defecation. The carriage rocks one's insides like the torturous churn of a heavy soup.

At last, Mr. Gardiner, leaning forward in the carriage, tapped the roof with his cane and announced with appropriate morbidity that we had arrived. He was, I think, getting tired of Lydia's antics. Charity is a game of convenience, after all; if our purses do not feel significantly lighter and our meals continue to fill our stomachs to brimming, then we are glad to appear benevolent in the eyes of God. But we refuse to suffer even the faintest pinprick at its hands. If it gives us pain, then it is no longer Charity that begs at our door but Exploitation, and, in her numerous plights, Lydia was fast becoming less pitiable than contemptible.

A dirty maid with yellow skin and yellow eyes led us up the wide-gapped stairs to Lydia's rooms. "Mind where you step," she said sharply. "The floorboards are none too stable," she added, explaining also that there'd been a recent influx of new vermin.

"How do you know they're new?" I asked, clenching my skirts.

She stopped to consider me. "Well! If Miss will ask, I'll gladly tell Miss a' I know. The coats of the old ones are dusty-like, and the coats of the new ones are still shiny, aren't they? And when you live with them all your life, you knows each one of them by sight, don't you, after a while?"

"I suppose so," I replied, more muddled than ever.

When we reached the top of the stairs, the maid kindly battered the door for us.

A fragment of a moving eye appeared in a crack in the door before it opened. But it wasn't Lydia who greeted us, as the maid was quick to point out.

"'Ere! Wot are you doin' 'ere! You're supposed ter be tidyin' the rooms downstairs."

"Lady was sick, wasn't she? And vomitin' for 'alf the day. I had to empty the pots, didn't I? Else you know what she's like: she'll be fussin' until suppertime about how there's none to take care of 'er since 'er 'usband's left."

"Can't blame 'im that 'e did, though I'm sorry for it," the first maid replied superiorly.

"Come, come! Will you keep us on the landing all day?" Mr. Gardiner complained, pushing his way through the two women with the aid of his cane. "I'd like to see my niece now, if you please."

"Ooh-ee!" the first maid cried, putting her hands on her hips. "Is that wot she is to ya? Well! If you'll be so good as ter tell 'er ladyship there ain't no free service to be 'ad 'ere, right? I'm not the bleedin' 'ousemaid at Blenheim, am I? And neither is me friend 'ere, who's supposed ter be tidyin' the rooms downstairs. And she can empty 'er own pots next time she's feeling poorly, thank ya very much indeed, for wot little rent she pays." With that, the maid dragged her gray-faced friend back downstairs with her, and we entered Lydia's rooms.

"Do I have visitors, Sally?" a thin voice called out from the direction of the bedroom.

"You'd better stay here until we call you in," my uncle said to me, squeezing my gloved hand. "It can't be a pleasant sight . . . and if you feel faint, we shall only have more trouble on our hands."

"I'm sure I wouldn't faint, Uncle," I said. "And I have the money from Lizzy to give her as well."

"You'll have time enough to give her Lizzy's charity," my uncle declared firmly. "Just stay put until we call you in, eh? Good girl."

Mrs. Gardiner covered her mouth with her handkerchief. My uncle followed suit, and together, they went in. Not five minutes had passed, however, before they came out again. Lydia had been vomiting blood, and a doctor was to be fetched immediately. Mr. Gardiner left to find one of the maids to help him. And when he'd been some time without returning, Mrs. Gardiner grew worried and went after her husband. In their absence, I entered Lydia's room.

"Mary!" I faced my youngest sister.

Lydia had never been beautiful, not like Jane or even Lizzy. What good looks she may have once enjoyed derived their power from the force of her spirit, youthful and carefree. When she was younger, the coarseness of her personality might have been mistaken by our acquaintances for good humor, but that time had since ended. She possessed no curiosity concerning the workings of the universe. She would never wonder why some apples tasted sweet while others tasted sour or how the tortoise and snail managed to grow their outer shells. Her own reflection and mobility fascinated her more than the rigors of learning a hobby, and when, at the ripe age of sixteen, she finally took ownership of an exceptionally handsome and initially desirable husband, this proved the early fulfillment of every aspiration, every hope, and every dream she'd ever entertained. Take these away—her pilfered bonnets, her pretty skirts, her husband addicted to cards, horses, and women—and what is left when the butterfly's wings are dissected from the butterfly? An ugly, squirming black line in agony. Lydia slumped forward to expel more watery blood into a half-filled chamber pot. When she finished, she fell back against her pillows and smiled at me, haggard and missing, I realized, a front tooth. I remembered that she was only seventeen, and I began to cry.

"Oh, Mary," she pleaded. "Don't bawl so, or I'm sure I shall start, too."

Apologizing, I pulled out my reticule and handed her the thirty pounds, which, I explained, was all Lizzy could spare from her allowance.

"She didn't come herself?" Lydia asked, taking the money quickly.

"No, she couldn't. I'm afraid she didn't feel well enough." I settled into the only chair in the room, which creaked and slanted sideways under my weight. "She lost the baby a few weeks ago."

Lydia's eyes widened. I noticed the flesh under one of them was yellow and speckled with purple, the last remnants of a large bruise. "That is too awful for words," she said. "What was it? Do you know?"

"A boy," I replied.

"What a shame," Lydia murmured. "What a beautiful baby it would have made."

"Yes," I said, not knowing what else to add.

"I also miscarried in the last year."

Seeing how stunned I looked, Lydia shrugged. "Well, there's nothing to be done about it, is there?" she said, biting her lip with her one front tooth. "When it happens, it's just gone. And you can't rescue something that hasn't been born yet, can you? I'll be honest with you, Mary. Sometimes I look around me, and I think, 'Lord! Thank goodness I didn't bring a babe into the world, or it should be as poor and miserable as its mother—with no father to be seen or had, either!'"

"Oh, Lydia . . ." I removed my gloves and touched Lydia's wrist. "Poor Lydia."

"Don't be so easily depressed, Mary. I want to hear what you've been doing and eating during your visit. It must be a dream to stay at Pemberley."

Perhaps it was the intimacy which a small, confined room necessarily inspires in its inhabitants or the smells of regurgitated life wafting upwards from the copper pot. Or it might even have been her missing tooth, the story of which I never got the chance to learn. Whatever the impetus, I told her everything. "I'm actually engaged," I announced shyly and begged that she would keep it a secret. The man was about thirty, tall, and roguishly handsome, which made us both giggle. He was also Darcy's paternal first cousin and the son of an earl, though not the eldest.

"An earl!" Lydia shrieked. "Look at us Bennet girls, eh? First Jane and Bingley, then Lizzy and Darcy. Now you, joining the ranks of the aristocracy with the son of an earl, even if he isn't the eldest." I noticed she had left out any mention of herself, but I said nothing. "Can't you just imagine Charlotte's and Maria's faces when they hear our Mary has found herself a colonel? I'm sure Maria will bite her tongue clean through with envy." Laughing, she began to gag, and we were forced to stop for a few minutes while she retched more bile and blood. "Tell me more about him," she begged, wiping her mouth with her sleeve. "Tell me what you two talk about and how you met and when you knew yourself to be hopelessly in love."

So I told her the whole story, beginning with that sleepless night when he'd mistaken me for a surly and disobedient maid.

"Horrible man!" Lydia interjected in the way that some people are called "awful" or "hateful" when they are actually quite delightful and lovely. "I hope you didn't let him get away with it." I assured her that I hadn't. And then I told her about Marmalade, how she was the most beautiful and wonderful sort of horse there could be and how the colonel had taught me to ride her. I couldn't explain it, nevertheless trying to explain. We could talk about nothing for hours and not realize we'd been talking about nothing until the dwindling light summoned us home, and the next day, we could do it all over again without feeling in the least bored with each other.

"And have you . . ." Lydia coaxed. I blushed and nodded.

"Oh, Mary!" she squealed. "I'm sure I'm so ashamed of you I don't know what to say!" When she'd recovered from her snickering, she asked me if I'd enjoyed *it*.

"Not in the beginning," I replied, shrugging, to which Lydia stuck out her lower lip and wrinkled her nose. "In fact, I didn't ever want to do it again after the first try. The pain was horrible."

"So not that good, eh?" she commiserated.

"Oh no, but it got better," I insisted, clearing my throat. "And is now perfectly clean and fine."

Lydia rolled her eyes at me. " 'Perfectly clean and fine'? It's not elegant penmanship, Mary. It's not supposed to be clean and fine, unless you're Charlotte Lucas and Mr. Collins."

"Can't we talk about something else, Lydia?"

"Why? We're both grown women. Why can't we talk about *it*? I want to talk about *it*. I can't think, as a matter of fact, of anything I want to talk about more right now than *it*. I haven't had *it* in over two weeks, and I'm awfully frustrated by the lack of *it*, as a result."

"Well . . ."

"Yes?" Lydia pressed my hands in encouragement.

"All right, fine, I actually really, *really* enjoy *it*, more than I thought I would. Goodness, I can't believe I've just said that aloud. There! Does that satisfy you?" And I wondered if I should tell her the story about the ghosts in the abandoned wing.

Lydia nudged me playfully, and snuggling back under her filthy covers, she sighed. "Poor Kitty," she said with satisfaction. "Wouldn't it be something if, after everything that's happened, Kitty turned out to be the old maid of the family? If she does attend your wedding, Mary, I'm sure she'll do nothing but bellyache the whole time, and I should like to be there, too, if only to see her sour little face and how she'll never have *it* in her life, except perhaps with someone really dull, like one of Uncle Philips's clerks."

"Of course you must be there, Lydia," I said gently, "even if Wickham cannot."

But before she could answer, we heard footsteps and harried voices outside in the hall. Then the maid, Mr. and Mrs. Gardiner, and a middle-aged, whiskered man tumbled collectively into the tiny bedroom, and my aunt separated me from Lydia, who resumed her vomiting, as though on cue.

In the hours before dinnertime, we felt encouraged by Lydia's progress; she was not only able to get out of bed and dress but even managed a few spoonfuls of soup. It was the night, however, that proved her undoing—the fever, which refused to break, climbed and climbed to such heights that it finally rendered her unconscious. She never woke from it, and the next morning, the whiskered doctor, who had stayed to watch over her, announced in practiced low tones that Lydia was dead and there was nothing he could have done to save her.

Because we were women, Aunt Gardiner and I could not attend Lydia's funeral. And as Wickham failed to return, my uncle was the only one to go and stand over her grave. I stayed with the Gardiners a fortnight in London, and there, at their house in Gracechurch Street, I received replies to the letters I had sent to Mama, Jane, and Lizzy informing them of the unhappy news. Mama's letter was full of rage—she called Wickham a scoundrel and said she'd claw his eyes out, if ever she saw him again. Mentioning nothing of Papa's feelings, she swore to confine herself to her bed, grieved as she was by the loss of her favorite child.

Jane proved equal to our mother in sorrow, if not in anger. "What a tragedy to have occurred only two months before Baby is due," she'd written in a shaky hand, every few words blotted from tears. "Do you suppose," she added in a postscript, "we should name our first child 'Lydia,' if it should turn out to be a girl? But I would not wish the same fate as befell our sister for any daughter of mine," she noted, underlining the word "fate."

Lizzy's reply arrived last. She'd written:

Dearest Mary,

Since I received your letter, I have alternated for hours between shock and heartache. What a wretched end for our sister. How disgraceful, too, that only Uncle Gardiner should be there to attend her funeral—and not even her own husband! It is a sordid business, and as such, I shall not apprise Darcy or any of the guests here of the details of what happened, except to say quite generally that our youngest sister has passed away from fever.

I feel very sorry for Lydia. What cruelties she must have suffered at Wickham's hand in the last year, and still she always called him her "beloved" in her letters. Now that she is gone, all the tender memories return to me—her constant teasing, the way her body seemed always to be moving, flitting from place to place like a bird. I remember when she was seven or eight years old, she made a garland of flowers for my birthday. I wore it for two whole days before it fell apart, and she cried when she no longer saw it on my head. Well, I shall console myself that our sister is in a better place. Wickham's ties to our family are at last severed.

This must be an awful trial for you, poor Mary. And though you are sure to be comfortable residing at our uncle's house in London, can't I convince you to return at your earliest convenience to Pemberley? I regret how we last parted.

Yours ever,

Lizzy

P.S. Also, there is to be a party here. Something *momentous* has happened.

CHAPTER 30

"I was *simply devastated* to hear about your sister." The tall plum-colored feather bobbed as three pristine white fingers alighted sympathetically across my wrist. "Here, allow me." And two white hands worked in fluid synchronicity to refill my cup of punch. I mumbled a few words of thanks, remarked that she was much too kind. My return to Pemberley had been delayed by the poor condition of the roads, and I'd arrived only that afternoon. What with preparations being made for the party, the house was a jumble of activity, and I'd connected only briefly with Lizzy to grieve with her before she was whisked away by Henderson to tend to more arrangements. I'd seen nothing of Darcy. A few hours before the guests were due to arrive, Mrs. Reynolds had looked in on me to inquire if I needed any help with dressing. I'd asked her then what the party was for, and she'd replied with a strange smile that I would find out soon enough.

"My sweet Molly," Caroline Bingley cooed, and I considered it a wonder she did not pinch my cheeks, "we have so much to catch up on. I've hardly seen anything of you since I arrived at Pemberley . . . nearly three weeks ago."

"Yes, well . . ." I searched the crowd for another familiar face, anyone I could drift to, like a foundering vessel looking to moor on the shores of a friendly nation, but I knew no one.

"So how did she—your sister—pass away?" Powerful jaws obliterated a biscuit to powdery dust.

"A fever, but I'd rather not talk about it, if you don't mind. It's all rather recent for me."

Caroline crooked a critical brow. She pouted. Perhaps she had intended an expression of condolence, but hers was an arrogant face, unused to not having its way. Three dark red stones hung from a thick chain around her neck like fresh, shiny organs. She thoughtfully fingered these as she finished the rest of her punch. "Well, I'm certainly glad you're back," she said shortly, brushing off her injured feelings with a brisk shake of her plume, "and, in fact, I congratulate you on the fortuitous date of your return." But before I could ask her why this was, she'd caught her sister's eye between the arch of two enormous decorative fronds, and the temptation of migrating to a more respectable neighborhood within Pemberley's largest and stateliest drawing room proved an irresistible temptation. "Oh, Molly," she lamented. "I'm afraid we'll have to continue our little tête-à-tête later, as Louisa is just desperate to tell me something. But I'm *so* happy you're here tonight and away from that *awful* part of London!" And shuddering at the thought of those persons and buildings she had never seen and likely never would, she swept away, feather eagerly bobbing in the direction of wealthier climes.

Earlier the same day, I had haunted a new room at Pemberley. The occasion of my return seemed to call for a change of scenery, and death, too, proved an unexpected stimulant. Prior to London, we had worked our way down an entire corridor, naming the rooms we conquered as we went along. There was the room we called simply English Breakfast—the colonel's idea—which featured a singularly beautiful table of mahogany mounted on a gilt-wood pedestal with lion's feet. There was also the Cursed Study, so christened because one side of the room was covered with antiquated books, and a few of these had dropped, startling us, during our intercourse. We tried to make the rooms' names funny or, at the very least, curious.

So before long, there were, in addition to the two already mentioned, the Hall of Mirrors (named after the famous gallery at Versailles), Cheapside (my favorite), and the Chapel of the Holy Fountain (for an unfortunate accident I'd had while pressed against a window ledge).

The new room, however, was devoid of any notable features which might assist us in giving it a name. We considered this as the side of my head rose and fell against his chest.

"Wasteland?" he offered.

"That'll have to do, if we can't think of anything better," I murmured, still dissatisfied.

"Mary, I want to tell you something. . . ."

"What is it, Marmalade?"

"I do wish you'd be serious for once, my ugly little thing."

"Only if you'll be serious, too, Marmalade."

"While you were in London," he began, "Darcy and I had a rather upsetting discussion . . . and I'm afraid it turned into an argument. You know we've been friends since childhood; we've never really had any reason to be cross with each other."

His skin had become too warm for my face, and I rolled away from him, onto the cool, hard floor. On my back, my nipples pointed unseeingly upwards at the bare ceiling's one exposed beam. A slight breeze which emanated from nowhere made my legs cold, and my ankles wound together in a belated attempt at chastity. At the ends of my hair, a pair of tangling spiders disappeared through the floorboards, into oblivion.

"What Darcy and I talked about . . ." he said.

"There's a draft in this horrible room," I complained, interrupting him. "I think we shall name it Hell. What do you think?"

"That would make us sinners."

"We are sinners, my dear Marmalade. At least until we are not."

He sat up. "You don't really believe that, do you?" His voice trembled with anger, or perhaps it was fear. "If you're trying to be funny, you can stop right now. It's not funny at all and is in very poor taste."

I saw that he was serious and kissed him. When this didn't work, I stroked the white scar on his chin and kissed the jagged line. "Look!" I teased, playing the nursemaid. "All better now." More kisses.

"Why did you have to go to London?" he continued, and this time, it was despair, not anger, that shook his voice. "Couldn't you have just stayed put at Pemberley?"

"You act as though I've been gone a year, when I've been away only two and a half weeks," I replied more harshly than I'd intended. I didn't want this kind of suffocating attachment after we were married; if we were always in each other's company, it would be impossible to get anything done, and Wilhelm had now been stuck for over a month praying at the same altar for Leonora's recovery. "You're being selfish, Fitzwilliam. My sister is dead, and you're being unforgivably selfish."

To this, he sulked like a boy who had just been told to stand in a corner and think about what he'd done wrong. I began to play with his gold signet ring, which I twisted up to the top of his pinkie before coaxing it back down again.

"Are you not done moping yet?" I asked after a suitable interval and tried the ring on my own finger, where it hung loose and unconvincing. Another mysterious breeze made us both shiver, and we clung to each other, falling back against the strange-smelling wood once more. When we'd finished, we fell asleep, and I dreamed that all the ghosts we'd ever created had come out of the walls and out of the insides of drawers and cabinets and cupboards to stand around us and watch over our bodies, still wet and alive with the fresh imprint of each other's touch.

But that was earlier in the day. Now I was standing with my obligatory cup of punch quite alone on the fringes of a party that had no use for my presence. Every face I met was unknown to me, and I found myself half-hoping that Maria Lucas would materialize out of thin air to rescue me from my isolation. In the center of the room, drifting just beside the decorative fronds, the lush purple feather dipped and nodded, its movement reminding me of a flaccid cock. I smiled and considered, in my boredom, what objects in my surroundings I could count to pass the time, while eagerly restocking my plate with grapes.

A familiar voice interrupted my reverie—it was Darcy's, and he was tapping his glass rapidly with the end of a spoon. "Could I have everyone's attention, please?" he said, and heads obediently turned; they always turned for Darcy. "Could I have everyone's attention, please?" he repeated. Lizzy hovered near his arm, though she did not look at him, and I sensed that very little had changed between them since I'd left.

"I'm so pleased," Darcy continued, "to be able to use this small party of ours to make an announcement, one which I know will bring much happiness to the several friends who are here with us today and who have for many years been closely acquainted with the persons whom this announcement concerns. I've known both Colonel Fitzwilliam and Miss Caroline Bingley separately for a very long time, and you can imagine how genuinely delighted I was when they informed me, no less than a week ago, of their engagement. A couple more in love and more suited to traversing together the long and fruitful road of marriage I'm sure you could not find in the whole of England. As such, please join me, my friends, in raising your glass to *this* man and *this* woman—to Colonel Fitzwilliam and Miss Bingley!"

The room transformed into a floating pond of punch glasses. "To Colonel Fitzwilliam and Miss Bingley!" the guests cheered, and the happy couple mouthed their thanks. I gazed at my lover, who eagerly downed his drink before taking another from a passing server, while the tall feather waved cheerfully at the crowd. Then shoulders, arms, and bodies in glistening finery joined together and barricaded my view of conjugal joy and romantic triumph.

THE MORNING I'D left with the Gardiners for London, I was still awake when the sky had begun to turn bluish black. In one of the abandoned rooms, we'd stood together touching shoulders, peering into the obscurity from which the golden ball of the sun must astoundingly rise, an anchor raised from the depths of a murky lake. It was so dark we couldn't make out the shape of the hedges or the silhouettes of the trees, though we stood in front of a window. When neither of us had said anything for a while, he'd pulled out an apple and fed me a slice on the flat of his pocket knife.

"I wish you wouldn't go," he'd said a little theatrically.

"I think I have to," I replied more sensibly than I perhaps should have, but I wanted to compensate for his overdoing his part.

"I don't know what I'm going to do with myself while you're gone. What am I going to do with myself?"

I smiled mischievously. "Oh, I can think of a lot of things you could do with yourself while I'm gone."

"Do be serious, Mary."

"Just don't terrorize the scullery maids. And don't start bringing them here, into our rooms."

"What do you take me for?"

"My sweet Marmalade, of course!" Even in the total absence of light, I could reach out and cup his chin perfectly in my hand. I gave it a small, tender shake.

"I wish we could live in these rooms!" he cried. "I wish we could spend the whole day just riding Marmalade and sitting under the trees and fishing fat trout in Darcy's lake. Imagine—a whole wing of Pemberley to ourselves!"

"My dear Fitzwilliam, I would give you exactly a week before you started to hate it."

"I say I wouldn't. I'd have you, and that would mean I'd have everything."

I felt his face turn in my direction, burning with earnest desire. I was glad he couldn't see me blush.

"No," I replied with conviction. "I'm quite sure you would hate it. No society. No horses to race. No cards on which to stake more money than you can afford. I know for my sake, you pretend to dislike your relatives and to hate your friends, but it's no good; I can see right through you. You move in a glittering and frivolous world that's all niceties and miniature dramas and beef sirloin."

"Beef sirloin, Mary?"

"Yes!" I said, growing excited. "Beef sirloin! And pheasant shooting! And the London season! And . . . and conversations that culminate in nothing with women who take classes in coquetry and wit." Here, to my own surprise, I began to cry hysterically, for we were the tragic lovers after all—me, penniless and plain; he, dependent and a spendthrift.

"But I love you," he said calmly, and now it was his turn to be sensible. Another slice of apple floated at the end of the knife to the surface of my mouth, and its sweetness mingled with the salt of my tears. "I promise that I love you much more than any amount of beef sirloin money can buy, even if I had a thousand pounds," which was the most he could manage but which perhaps was enough. For a few hours more, we stayed together, not returning to our proper rooms until, like a Grecian myth, the rising of the sun whisked me away in a carriage, and I left him, the poor boy, to face the temptations of this glittering and frivolous world alone.

CHAPTER 31

For days afterwards, I could not leave my room. Most hours I slept, and the trays of food which Bess and Mrs. Reynolds brought up to me were just as heavy for them to carry downstairs again. What little time I was conscious, I spent sitting up in bed, repeating to myself over and over, "Mary Bennet, you are a fool. Mary Bennet, you are an idiot. Mary Bennet, a more superior dupe than you never lived and breathed in this whole world. I hate you, Mary Bennet." Engrossed as I was in passionate self-loathing, I shed astonishingly few tears. My brain was too occupied with rebuilding a precise sequence of events, with sorting through every detail of our numerous exchanges. What had been real, I asked myself, ruminating upon each dog and horse story he had ever told me. What had been deceit? And what had been merely delusion?

Believing I was ill, Lizzy's visits were frequent. She often found me asleep, but on one occasion, I stirred at the sound of someone entering.

"How are you feeling?" I heard her ask from the foot of the bed.

"A headache," I offered.

"I see you haven't touched your food," she said.

"No."

"Be that as it may, I shall stay and keep you company, whether you like it or not. I have just come up from sitting with Caroline Bingley, Mrs. Hurst, and the colonel."

When I made no reply, she continued: "They are both tiresome women, but I am proved right in one thing at least. We'd been talking of which rooms in Pemberley want refurbishing when Miss Bingley suddenly asked, 'Well, why is not Mary here with us? I haven't seen her for days. Where could she have disappeared to?' Mrs. Hurst remarked that she didn't know, but the colonel replied, in a very cavalier way, 'Have you checked the library? And if she is still nowhere to be found, it is entirely possible she has turned into a book.' And this sent Miss Bingley and Mrs. Hurst roaring with laughter."

" 'Turned into a book'?" I repeated.

"Yes, 'turned into a book,' he said. Well, I am glad he is engaged to Caroline Bingley."

I detected no cruelty or triumph in Lizzy's voice, only the nagging good intention pervasive among mothers, aunts, and sisters.

I sat up. " 'Turned into a book,' " I whispered incredulously, weighing the words on my tongue.

"You have to admit, though—it's an amusing notion, even if it is ungallant of him," Lizzy giggled.

That evening, I ate my whole dinner of roasted gammon and potatoes, while Bess bore wide-eyed witness to my hunger.

"Is there dessert tonight?" I asked.

"Yes, miss, but I didn't think you'd want any."

I wiped my mouth. "Nonsense, Bess. What is the dessert?"

"Cook's specialty, miss—caraway cake."

"I'm very fond of seed cake. Will you bring me some?"

We each had one large slice in my room, which we ate with our hands, and I listened as she chattered about the other servants.

"Annie and Emily have raised such a fuss about the cleaning," she said through mouthfuls of cake. "They feel they're being taken advantage of—you know, overworked."

"And are they?"

Bess began to count off the rooms on her fingers: "Yours, Mr. and Mrs. Hurst's, Miss Bingley's, the colonel's, Darcy's, Lizzy's—"

I stopped her. "Darcy's and Lizzy's?" I asked. "Still?"

Bess nodded. "Oh yes, meals have become so awkward now, according to Henderson. 'Stilted,' that was the word he used. And he even said thank goodness for Miss Bingley and the colonel being here, as otherwise there might not be any conversation to be had at all during dinner."

Poor Lizzy, I thought, taking a bite of cake. *Poor Darcy, too,* I considered, finishing the rest of my slice, and we sat in silence for a moment before Bess launched into her next bit of news. When she'd finished her gossip and gone, I went downstairs to the library. There, sitting at my usual desk and chair, I cut a new pen and began to write.

꘎

CHAPTER 32

When Leonora awoke from her month-long coma, she was aware of a change. She could feel it in the air and in the things she touched and in her own movement, and it was an extraordinary sensation. She had lived for so long in fear and in pain, and there hadn't yet existed a chapter in the long and frightfully unhappy course of her adventures whereby at least one part of her body hadn't been made to endure some inconceivable agony that she was at first suspicious of her feelings and checked all the usual places where evil was in the habit of lurking, which was behind the curtains, underneath the bed, and inside her spectacular wardrobe (she was, we should remember, a queen of a moderately desirable kingdom).

Finding nothing in her private chamber, she crept to the window and unlatched it, first just enough to see a sliver of sky and a few shrubs, but then a providential wind blew the shutters to the ends of their hinges, and the entire nation opened up to her like a panoramic landscape. As she gazed over the pastures and the woodlands, the tidy villages with their stone churches, the fluffy white flowers that seemed to dot the hills and that were actually great herds of sheep milling about in the grass, she remembered her father, Albert the Good King, and what he had told her when she was only a young and rather spoiled princess, which was that nothing can ever be so wrong or terrible that someday it will not change for the better and also that nothing can ever stay so wonderful that something will not one day spoil it. She realized, too, that her infancy had been the happiest time of her young life, for the very reason that she remembered nothing about it. What she did remember, and clearly, were the periods of starvation in fetid cells, the procession of kidnappings, the sticky taste of rat's blood trickling down her parched throat, which no amount of water or wine could ever wash away. Every member of her family to whom she had once turned to for affection had betrayed her; the grand duke had admitted to poisoning her father, and her half sister, Agnes, shortly before her death, had confessed to amassing a secret following of several hundred traitors who'd hoped to secure for her, by any means necessary, the Danish throne.

But today something was different. Today, she felt strangely, peculiarly in control of herself, and even the heavens seemed to corroborate this feeling. It was glorious weather in Denmark, and whatever birds they have in that part of the world were singing in the hollows of trees and hedges. A bath was prepared for her, but the water did not scald her skin, and the soap was just that: soap. The dress which fitted snugly around her tiny waist did not poison her; her shoes no longer pinched her feet. A great *something* had been lifted from her person, and she was wary of it.

When she fell asleep that night, after a warm and perfectly ordinary meal of chicken broth and fish, she considered that this day of peace and relative quiet might be to prepare her for something of truly horrific and ghastly proportions in the immediate future. But the next day passed equally quietly. And the following day, when she'd risen late and consumed an adequate breakfast in bed, she even had the urge to complain to one of her handmaids that her toast was dry. It was also on this day that she felt well enough to finally meet Wilhelm, who, for over a month, had remained diligently on his knees in silent prayer. Their union was a most pathetic one, with many "tearful cries" and "loving whispers" and rendered more heart-breaking for the fact that Wilhelm had temporarily lost the use of his legs from prolonged kneeling and so was forced to crawl with only his exceptionally strong arms to Leonora's feet in order to ascertain if she was real or an illusion sent by the Devil to haunt him. At her feet, he begged for her hand in marriage, and she gave it with great joy.

Though she continued to look behind doors and in dark corners for assassins and traitors who wished to ransom her weight in gold, her days of peace pleasantly and surprisingly persisted, and she married Wilhelm as soon as he could walk again, in a lavish but tasteful ceremony which joined their two kingdoms together as eternal and powerful allies. She also had children—three healthy, rosy-cheeked babes—and the royal family lived in comfort and relative harmony until the very end of their prosperous reign.

"This is excellent," Darcy said, laying the final page aside.

"I'm glad you like it. You see, I gave her the happy ending you wanted."

"And which I hope you wanted for her, too," he added gently.

I shrugged. "I must admit to being glad it's over. Sixty-seven chapters! What a monstrous thing. Look at how enormous it is sitting there looking at us, and us looking at it."

"I'm going to be sending that monstrous thing, as you put it, to Egerton's in London," Darcy said.

"Oh, he's not going to publish my work!" I cried, terrified at the thought. "Please don't send it out of mere politeness."

"But I think it deserves to have a chance, and I think people will find Leonora exciting. Can't you picture someone like Mrs. Reynolds or, better yet, one of her maids picking up this book and becoming so riveted, she loses a whole night's sleep just wondering what's going to happen next to our unlucky Danish heroine?"

"Provided the maid can read, yes."

"Then it's settled! This week I'll send the manuscript, and if we don't hear from Egerton in, say, three weeks' time, I'll visit him personally in London and knock down his door! We're friends, you know, so I'm permitted to behave as outrageously as I like."

At the thought of Darcy having to resort to violence, I made a face. "Wait, please," I said, and Darcy, too, made a face, as if to say, *Well, what is it? What more could you ask for?* "I know you're being very kind doing all this for me when you don't have to, but I have just the one stipulation, if you do send my book to your friend."

"And what might that be?"

"My name—I don't want to use my full name, if that's all right."

"You mean you'd prefer to be anonymous?"

"No, not that—just I'd rather no one knew I wrote it. Perhaps an abbreviation of my name instead. Something simple. Something that won't attract attention away from the book and make whoever's reading it say what a bored and unimaginative fool I am, while rolling their eyes and preparing a bad review. I don't want people cursing me when I can't hear them."

"Ah, you mean a pen name. If it's privacy you desire, you can do nothing better than to give up being a woman and pretend to be a man instead," Darcy said, laughing and looking several years younger.

"No, that's silly. You're not taking this very seriously, I'm afraid."

"Well, I once knew a Miss Cassandra Knight who wrote poetry and later a Miss Abigail Breckenridge who sang and played the harp even better than Georgiana," Darcy mused. "Her grandmother was a Lady Susanna Hobbes, and their housekeeper, I remember, was named Mrs. Marianne Price. Perhaps we could take one of their names and switch them around to make something original like Mrs. Cassandra Breckenridge or Lady Marianne Knight. That sounds very elegant. What do you think?"

When I didn't answer, he suggested a few more "elegant" names, which I disregarded. "No, no . . . Oh! I have it—Mary B!" I cried, and the name instantly dispelled all the others. "Yes, it is modest and obscure enough that no one will ever be able to figure it out."

I busied myself with creating a new title page, and when I was finished, we stared for a long time at the mound of paper between us. The silence lengthened with our inner thoughts. I acknowledged I felt proud of the work, even if it should never grace the shelves of bookstores, and was about to begin imagining the lettering and binding which best suited it when I looked up. Darcy's expression had grown somber, and with it, the atmosphere of the room had also shifted.

"These last few days—this week—can't have been easy for you," he said.

For a moment, I considered ascribing the source of my melancholy solely to Lydia's death but decided against it. I touched the manuscript between us and distractedly folded a corner of the page. "I suppose you'd like for me to admit that you were right," I said. "Well, you were. I should have kept my distance. I've been a complete fool."

"Not the first fool to have fallen in love where you shouldn't have, I promise you," he replied.

"I . . . I do not know that it was love." My face grew heavier, as it always did before the onset of tears. I frowned and fought them back. "I think now it was amazement . . . possibly astonishment at the idea of being admired by someone so unlike myself . . . of being admired at all. I felt, 'This is my chance. I must take it. I shall prove everyone wrong.'" My outpouring surprised me, yet I continued: "It is very hard to live one's life perpetually in waiting, and I cannot tell you how many men have passed through Longbourn to court one or other of my sisters, and how all of them never concerned themselves with me, though I sat in the same room and was as equally capable of speech or motion as Lizzy and Jane. My eagerness to be loved made me hasty. I felt encouraged to act boldly when I should have been guarded." I lowered my gaze, unable to meet Darcy's eye. I had perhaps confessed too much.

"Such regret should be tempered in accordance with the worthiness of what has been lost," Darcy said. "It gives me no pleasure to see you in pain."

"While I was in London, is it true you had words with the colonel?" I asked.

Darcy stood and, turning away from me, began to straighten various objects on the desk. "Yes, we argued," he replied. "He came to me one night in a highly agitated state just as I was preparing to go to bed. 'If ever you were my friend, Darcy, you must help me now,' he said, as soon as I opened the door. Then he told me everything—how he'd intended his acquaintance with you to be no more than a passing flirtation but that he'd let his feelings get the better of him and had fallen in love. I rebuked him for behaving so thoughtlessly. He begged me, practically on his knees, to help conceal this incident from his family, for by then he'd already proposed to Caroline Bingley, and she'd accepted him. They'd been acquainted, at that point, only four days."

I swallowed the growing lump in my throat—the bitter taste it left going down. "And what did you say?" I asked, not looking at him.

"I said he'd made the right decision."

"What?"

Seeing my stunned countenance, he continued: "I do not doubt that he was bound to you by honor. But there were, for me, at least three things to consider before I absolved him of his infamous behavior. First, there was the matter of his family. They'd intended, since his infancy, that he should make his fortune by marriage, being a younger-born son. If he'd persisted in marrying you, his parents would very probably have disinherited him, and then you would be poor and miserable for the rest of your life, drowning in his debt and living always beyond your means for the sake of keeping up appearances. I know it is a crude thing to acknowledge, but he needs Caroline Bingley's twenty thousand pounds more than he needs her, God help him, and if he could have gotten the one without the other, I'm sure he'd be a much happier man than he is now."

Through my tears, I agreed that money was likely the prime motivator in the colonel's attachment to Miss Bingley.

Darcy went on: "My second consideration was that I didn't judge him capable of loving you—not, at least, as one should before undertaking as great a responsibility as marriage. The colonel is a highly sociable man, friendly and indeed likable, but he is prone to fits of passion. His performance that evening in my study was unworthy and embarrassing, not at all the conduct of a gentleman. From his behavior, it was evident that you'd become an inconvenient liability for him, an obstacle barring his way to a more comfortable future." Darcy stopped. For a while, there were no sounds but the pleasant crackling of the fire. Then he settled into a damask chair a few feet away from where I sat and, leaning against one arm, cupped his head in his right palm. He seemed to stare at nothing, lost in his own thoughts.

"What was the third consideration?" I found myself asking.

"What?" said the muffled voice from the chair.

"You'd mentioned a third consideration before absolving him of his infamous behavior. What was it?"

"Oh, that . . ." He trailed off, remaining in the chair. "That . . . had everything to do with my own feelings for you."

For what seemed an age, I sat dumbly listening to the continued *pop-hiss* of the fire. Then I became conscious that he was speaking again.

"You're not just a silly young girl who can be fobbed off in marriage," I heard him say. "You're full of ideas and thoughts and stories. When you're sitting in front of me, reading your work, I sometimes wish I could get inside your head, to see what you see, feel what you feel. A man who would pledge his soul to the batting of a pretty eye

or a witty retort is a fool, and these are the same men who have ignored you your whole life. They mistake the transient for eternity
and find out too late their error. But to care for you is not just to care
for a woman by the ordinary purchase of bonnets and trinkets or a
second property in London—it is to care deeply, to understand you
deeply, which is what you deserve."

I couldn't bear to hear any more. A cold sweat had broken out
across my forehead, and my hands shook.

"Stop," I said, and as though it were a blade, the word instantly
divided us. "Stop," I repeated, standing up from my chair, though
he'd said nothing further.

Darcy looked guiltily away.

Even as I spoke, I couldn't cease the shaking of my hands. "My
sister . . ." I stammered, thinking of Lizzy. "You . . . you are married
to her, and you swore an oath before God to honor and love her
until death." Such a confusion of emotions filled my mouth with
unvented words, but there was no time to express them all. "I can't
understand any of this. . . ." I continued weakly.

"I acknowledge that the fault is mine," he said, remaining seated.
"Your sister is a charming and spirited woman. I was drawn to her
for these traits, yet in the few months before we wed, I never seriously examined how suited we were to married life together. In her
bright eyes and flushed cheeks, I imagined I'd met the only woman
who could ever make me happy. But we are neither of us the person
we hoped the other would be, and the illusion, wonderful as it might
have been for the short period of time it lasted, has finally ended."

"Is that all?" I said accusingly, incensed at his resigned attitude. It
seemed inconceivable that one as rational as Darcy could possess
such poor judgment. And was it really possible to fall so easily out of
love? "Will you then do nothing to heal the breach between yourself
and Lizzy?"

At this, Darcy stood. "The loss of our child was the final blow. I
know Lizzy blames me, that she will never forgive me. Though she

is still my wife in name, she will never again be the partner I'd hoped for. She has made that clear in more ways than one, and I am no fool."

"Then you must try harder."

When Darcy made no answer, I continued: "The strife which exists in your marriage has deceived you into believing that you have feelings for me. Though it is, of course, absurd, I will pretend to understand how you could jump to such a far-fetched conclusion."

While I'd been talking, he'd moved closer. Our eyes met, and I whipped my head away so quickly the room spun. I gripped the edge of the desk to steady myself.

"My feelings are real, and odd as it may seem to say so, I believe they are more true and good than whatever claims of affection the colonel might have made to you. Mary, can you honestly tell me that you feel nothing for me? That your happiness here derives only from Pemberley?"

I felt his finger graze my cheek, and I jerked away.

My reaction offended him; he slipped his hand into the pocket of his coat.

At that moment, a new voice entered the room, and I jumped at the sight of Lizzy standing in the doorway.

"Darcy, I have finally found you," she declared, looking quite as she always did. Her face gave nothing away. "Will you come with me downstairs? There is something Mrs. Reynolds and I would ask you about." She waited for him smilingly, glancing only once at the completed novel and ignoring the spot where I stood.

Darcy's eyes met mine a second time as he left. They seemed to search my face, and finding nothing within my features to encourage him, looked unseeingly away.

I heard the door click shut and their footsteps recede in the hall. For several moments, I sat in stunned silence, attempting to make sense of what had happened. Either the world had gone mad or I had, I thought, for it must be one or the other. I tried, too, to make out my own feelings but couldn't. I was both tired and animated, furious and astonished, mortified and flattered. *It isn't possible,* I repeated to myself. *This is the unhappy result of his grief. He doesn't know what he's saying.* And yet . . . when I now reviewed the several instances of our interaction, the signs of his affection seemed so incontrovertible in light of this revelation that I reproved myself for not noticing them earlier. They had existed, in fact, even before the *incident,* and all seemed to fall into place: his resentment over the colonel's attentions, his particular concern for my feelings, the energy he'd committed to *Leonora.* Was it possible that what I'd mistaken for friendship, even for a devoted paternalism, had actually been love?

But what about Lizzy? Much as I still cared for her, the change which Darcy mentioned was certainly irrefutable, and perhaps the sister I had known at Longbourn was lost forever. *Their marriage is over,* a small voice said to me. *Didn't she say as much to you? You know the truth of their relations now. It is all for the sake of appearances that they are still together.*

A sudden exhaustion overtook my senses, and I rested one hand on the completed novel. The other drifted to the place where Darcy had touched my cheek. My fingers hovered there for a few moments before falling like a stone to my side.

CHAPTER 33

The next day boasted such fine weather that Lizzy suggested an outdoor excursion in the form of a picnic lunch. It was the colonel who led us to a spot not too far from the house, midway to the stables, that featured an immaculate view of the lake. In the past, we'd often sat there together, talking of nothing, every inane declaration punctuated with either a soft caress or a kiss. But I'd kept wary distance of that man since his betrayal, and we hadn't exchanged a single word, which, fortunately for us both, required practically no effort, due to the verbosity of his new love. The less attention they paid to me the better, for it permitted me to ignore the sight of their cooing and the constant concern they showed for each other's comfort. At present, the colonel was draping a light shawl around Miss Bingley's bony shoulders and asking if he could pour her a drink.

I felt my eyes would never stop rolling in their sockets.

As to Darcy, he had walked a little behind the rest of us. I'd glanced back at him once, though his gaze had been too occupied by the fine beeches and oaks which lined our path to return my look. In his distraction, I sensed unhappiness, but there was little I could do to console him. I could still make nothing of my own feelings.

We had been sitting for half an hour, filling our bellies with pigeon pie, ham, jam puffs, and ginger-beer when Lizzy announced she had a small entertainment for us.

"Oh!" Mrs. Hurst cried happily. "That sounds delightful."

"Would you really like to know what it is?" Lizzy teased.

"You know we are all dying to find out," Miss Bingley chided.

"Very well," Lizzy replied, and she extracted from her reticule a folded sheet of paper.

"Ah, a letter!" Miss Bingley said, and though she had eaten a good deal already, her face lit up with hunger.

"Or a page from a journal," Mrs. Hurst purred. "How delicious."

"The chambermaid's diary," Miss Bingley suggested, laughing.

"Well, Lizzy," the colonel said. "What is it?"

"It is not a letter, and it is not a page stolen from a journal. It is an excerpt from a book—an as yet unpublished novel," my sister answered calmly, as the blood drained from my face. I turned in panic to Darcy, who sat a little behind his wife. Though he frowned at the announcement, he did nothing to interfere.

"I never read novels," Miss Bingley said. "I find them excessively vulgar."

"Well, I shall read a very short excerpt, so as not to offend your sensibilities too much, Caroline, and then I will reveal all," Lizzy said.

"Lizzy . . ." I had just time to say, but she had already begun to read.

"A shadowy figure emerged from behind the velvet curtains. Leonora, Queen of the Danes, rose from her seat in horror. 'Who are you?' she screamed. 'What do you want?' Then the figure stepped into the light, masked and terrifying to behold, for he wore a laughing demon's face, complete with horns. Beneath a black cloak, gloved hands slowly unsheathed a brilliant dagger, the hilt of which was inlaid with bright rubies and emeralds. Leonora thought she recognized the blade. Then it came back to her—the dagger had been a gift from her own father, Albert the

Good King, to the grand duke, her uncle. But her uncle was dead! She'd witnessed his execution with her own eyes! Was this his ghost come to drag her to hell with him?"

"Well, is it?" Mrs. Hurst shouted in mock horror, as her sister and the colonel snickered.

"Patience, Louisa," Lizzy said, and she continued:

"But it was not her uncle, for the voice that issued from behind the mask, though it was muffled, undoubtedly belonged to a woman. 'I've come to take what's mine—your life and your throne,' the assassin said, coming menacingly towards her. 'And to avenge the grand duke, whom you cruelly and unjustly put to death by the most disgraceful means possible. He is only one, however, of an army of those who stand behind me and who recognize my claim to Denmark.' She had no time to finish her speech, for at that moment, Wilhelm burst into the throne room, having sensed that something had gone terribly wrong. 'Leonora!' he cried, running towards his queen with his sword. But the assassin proved too quick for him. The jeweled dagger plunged into Leonora's stomach. Bleeding profusely, Leonora tore at the devil's horned face with desperate fingers. The strength quickly left her arms, but the mask fell, too. And she came face-to-face with the one person she loved most in the world, her half sister, Agnes. 'Traitor!' she spoke with her dying breath."

Lizzy set the page aside and looked at me, her eyes sparkling with triumph. So, I thought to myself, staring at my hands, she knew. She'd heard enough in the library the previous evening to draw her own conclusions.

"Absolute rubbish," Miss Bingley said, flinging off her shawl. "Now, you mustn't be offended by my reaction, Elizabeth. I warned you I disliked novels—and for how liberally they treat history, too. I'm quite sure Denmark never had such a queen named Leonora. Nor a king called Albert the Good!"

The colonel's face brightened. "Why, Miss Bingley," he exclaimed. "That is exactly what I said the first time I heard of the work. How alike our minds are."

My stomach grumbled. I thought it very likely I would regurgitate all that I'd consumed in the last half hour, and if I did, I sincerely hoped the shower of my wrath would find their intended targets.

"Then, do you mean to say you are familiar with the writing, awful as it is?" Miss Bingley inquired in disbelief.

Darcy, who had up till then been silent, spoke: "Surely the point of fiction is to imagine new histories and characters. I can find nothing wrong with the liberties taken."

"Well, *you* wouldn't, Darcy," the colonel replied callously, "seeing how much you cared about the book's completion."

For the briefest moment, the image of the grand duke's bloody and torturously prolonged execution overlaid the idyllic scene of our picnic, and I grabbed a fistful of grass to keep from lunging at the two-timing villain.

"Come, this is a fine way to treat my surprise!" Lizzy said from the head of the blanket.

"Lizzy—" I repeated, struggling to contain my temper.

"There's more?" interrupted Mr. Hurst, who had hitherto been polishing off a chicken leg.

"I will have you know the author sits among us," Lizzy said mysteriously. Then she pointed at me. "There!"

My face turned scarlet, as everyone stared. No one said anything.

"I own that it is mine," I said in a show of bravado, feeling dangerously close to tears. "It . . . it was a way to pass the time," I added when the silence persisted, and I fixed my gaze on the constellation of crumbs on Mrs. Hurst's plate. "One reads so many of the same books. . . ." The thought vanished before I could complete it. My throat had closed.

"How sweet of you, Elizabeth, to share your sister's work with us," Mrs. Hurst said awkwardly.

"Just like I said, absolute rubbish," I heard Caroline Bingley whisper into the colonel's ear, and the latter laughed.

"You mustn't be too angry with me, Mary," Lizzy said, as though it had all been just a joke, and she tossed the page across the blanket in my direction. I watched, my right temple throbbing, as everyone turned back to their plum pudding and sponge cake, their pigeon pie and bread. The entertainment was over.

An hour later, most of the food had been depleted. Lizzy, Mrs. Hurst, the colonel, and Miss Bingley, their bellies filled to brimming, occupied themselves with playing a game of quadrille. Mr. Hurst had fallen asleep, and Darcy had left with his steward, a giant bearded man named Burns, on some matter of a diseased tree which the latter wished to remove.

"I'm going to take a walk," I said to no one in particular, which was just as well, as no one responded.

Perhaps it was all those trips in the colonel's company, which made the route so familiar, but before long and without meaning to go there at all, I realized that I'd reached the stables. There was then only one stable boy in attendance, a mousy child with stringy arms and legs, and he was napping in a chair with a cap over his face.

I found Marmalade in her usual enclosure. Though all was by then ended between her master and myself, she still stuck her head out to sniff both my hands.

"I haven't got an apple for you today," I said sadly, and she neighed in sympathy as I unlatched the gate.

It was foolish what I did, for I knew I had no more claims to her. But I rode Marmalade out to the paddock, and when we'd completed a few wandering circles within the enclosure, I took her into the surrounding fields. Looking out, I wondered how so much land could come to feel as suffocating as Longbourn's airless drawing room. Was this the extent of the world's offerings? I asked myself. Was this to be my limited scope of the vast universe?

I dug my heel into Marmalade's flanks, and she began to canter.

"Faster," I whispered into her ear, and she obeyed.

The fields soon melted into wind and the sound of my own breathing. From a distance, I saw Pemberley's blue lake.

Marmalade had begun to bluster, and I turned her in the direction of the house. I hesitated only a moment before I made her run as she'd never run before, so fast I could no longer feel the ground beneath me. It was the closest I'd ever known to flight and to freedom.

I saw, several yards away, a low fence which separated the fields from the lawns surrounding the house and also the lake. I remembered that the fence was in view of the picnic. They—the colonel, Miss Bingley, my sister, Mr. and Mrs. Hurst—were sure to be watching, I thought. How glorious it would be to jump it! To make all their mouths drop from the shock of my small feat!

I goaded Marmalade onwards, though I sensed she was growing tired.

My decision proved our undoing. Though she cleared the fence, her legs folded beneath her weight upon landing, and she fell. The air soon filled with screams—both animal and woman. I tumbled off her arched back, and my ribs crashed against hard ground.

For a while, I lay stunned, unable to move. Then I heard my name being called from afar and looked up into the faces of Darcy and his steward.

"Can you stand?" I made out, though I didn't know whether it was Darcy or Burns who spoke.

"I . . . I think so," I stammered, still so shaken, I felt hardly any pain.

"No broken bones as far as I can see," Burns said as he and Darcy helped me to my feet, and looking up, he added, "though I can't say the same about the horse."

I heard Darcy whisper a few words to his steward, and that man nodded before sprinting back to the house.

"Oh, Marmalade . . ." I faltered through my tears, catching sight of the beast, which remained quivering on her side.

"The front legs are shattered," Darcy said quietly to me. I felt his hand steady my arm as I wavered. "Damn it, I hope Burns is quick about it," he muttered.

By then, the rest of the party had also caught up with us. The colonel proved inconsolable. He fell to his knees and beat the ground with his fists. He wept openly, his fingers stroking the mane of his beloved animal. Had I not known the performance to be genuine, I'd never have believed him capable of such grief, suited, as it was, to some Grecian tragedy rather than a scene in the English country-side. When he'd caught his breath, he turned on me.

"You bitch!" he roared. "You damn bitch!" This show of anger shocked the others. Miss Bingley and Mrs. Hurst jumped into each other's arms, cowering, and even Lizzy stepped discreetly behind Mr. Hurst, who looked as terrified as any one of the women.

"That's enough, Fitzwilliam," Darcy cautioned, still holding on to my arm.

"She did it on purpose, that bitch!" the colonel bellowed. "Jealous . . . bitter . . ." he choked out.

My incoherent apologies fell on deaf ears. Burns had returned. He was holding a pistol.

"Shall I do it, sir?"

"No, I will," Darcy replied, releasing my arm. The pistol passed hands. "Can you escort the women back to the house?" But Mr. Hurst had already taken his cue to leave and was then shepherding his wife, Lizzy, and Miss Bingley away.

The colonel's eyes widened when he saw the gun. "No, Darcy," he said, still on his knees. I thought he might try to shield her with his own body. "There are other ways."

"Go back with the others, Fitzwilliam. You know every minute that passes is agony for her."

"No, you don't understand!" the colonel shrieked. "I've read about this. There are slings we can install in her stable for this form of injury."

Darcy shook his head. "Go back to the house," he repeated.

In the end, Burns was forced to drag the colonel from Marmalade's side. It made a wretched picture for any onlooker, and though I despised the man, I could not check my own tears.

When they were far enough away that no intervention could be possible, Darcy knelt beside the horse. He positioned the pistol against a precise spot of her skull, which he measured with his fingers. Then he fired. The body jerked once before going limp. The sound of the shot sent birds into the sky. I gripped my torso, shocks of pain tremoring up and down my spine.

"It's done," he said, standing and weighing the pistol in his hand. His face was damp with perspiration, and he breathed heavily. "You'd better take some brandy when you return." He didn't look at me, though I was unable to take my eyes off him.

"Darcy . . ." I whispered.

"Please say nothing of our exchange from yesterday. We needn't go over it again." He brushed coldly past me. "I'll need Burns and a few other men to dispose of the body."

I pressed my hand against his arm, momentarily forgetting my own pain. The fall had emboldened me, freed me of my former delusions and misgivings. From the terror and the ensuing chaos, a clear voice had emerged, and it would speak.

"You asked me yesterday if I loved only Pemberley," I said quietly. "But I've realized since that it is impossible to love only Pemberley. Pemberley is a house. A grand house but only a house. It would be as any other estate in the country, if there were not something that could make me love it, not as a structure of stone and wood, but as though it were flesh and blood. I realize now it is your spirit which makes Pemberley what it is. Your goodness which lends to the grounds its unaffected beauty and noble character. So, I do not love only Pemberley. You see, I couldn't without also—"

I stopped at the touch of his hand, which had folded itself over my own. The moment necessitated no more words, and we returned to the house in silence.

The next day, Colonel Fitzwilliam quietly set off for his family's estate in a bordering county, accompanied by Miss Bingley, her sister, and Mr. Hurst. His spirits were not long dampened by the loss of his favorite horse, for Darcy gifted him one of his finest geldings. And along with many other things he had won and lost at Pemberley, Marmalade was nearly forgotten by the time of his departure.

CHAPTER 34

Despite being mistress of a great estate, my sister had not entirely given up the industriousness of her youth, and when I met her in the garden a few hours after the colonel had gone, she was expertly felling flowers with a sharp pair of shears.

"The roses are no good this year," she declared when she noticed I'd come. "The whole lot has been eaten away by some pest. Look at them."

She held one out to me, a shriveled, stunted thing. Though the sight was not unique in its sadness, I shivered.

I'd just begun to remark on the loveliness of the day when her hands stopped working. She smiled at an unseen object past my shoulder, and I lost the sequence of my thoughts, for the sun had then illuminated the whole of her smooth forehead. It infused her face with warmth and merriment, and for the most fleeting moment, I imagined we were again in the small garden at Longbourn, cutting flowers side by side with the rest of our sisters.

"Mary," she said, still gazing past me with cheerful benevolence, "do you remember the game we used to play on the bridge to Meryton?"

I assured her I did. The game was not really a game, for there were no winners or losers. It involved five very silly girls throwing stones into a shallow stream and making wishes. We were never permitted to tell each other what we had asked for, as to do so would ensure that the wish never come true for as long as we lived.

I recalled our laughter during those evening walks. Girls' laughter is a thing of power. It can sound cruel unless you are a part of it. If we ever met someone on the lane, which was itself a rare occurrence, whoever we passed would always smile awkwardly at us, as though he had stumbled unwittingly into the feminine exchange of secrets. But when the game was done, when all five wishes had been made, and Lydia had got over her giggling, we'd lean against the parapet and look out quietly at the sunset over Longbourn. We never laughed on the way back; our hearts were too full of wanting to make room for laughter.

I remembered wishing for marriage. And later, when wishing only for marriage became too simple and a bore, I wished for a home and a room to sit in where I could play the piano for as long or as short as I wanted to in peace. Also a garden and a small library. Perhaps one day a child.

Then I realized Lizzy had started talking again. She had picked up the basket and her pair of shears, and she was looking at me in a strange, pitying way, as if I were another one of her roses.

"Things aren't so simple now as they were then, are they, Mary?" she asked sadly. "And every wish," she continued, nearly whispering, "seems to come at a terrible price. I have everything I ever wished for on that bridge, yet I think I shall never be happy again."

"Please don't say such things, Lizzy," I entreated, attempting to comfort her.

"Ah, our dear Mary's platitudes . . ." The ends of her mouth twitched. "Darcy's love, too, comes at a terrible price, and I am, regrettably, unwilling to pay for the attainment of it. I have made the decision to live and enjoy my comforts, though they bring me no real happiness, rather than to die loved by my husband in childbirth. Mary, I have come to believe there is nothing more valuable in the world than one's independence. What I would give to be the Lizzy I once was—the girl who walked miles across muddy fields in her best frock and coat. I had such spirit."

"You still do, Lizzy."

She shook her head. "Marriage changes everything. Here, I am watched, if not by Mrs. Reynolds, then by some other servant. I cannot hum to myself in a corridor without report of the song reaching the ears of Henderson or the cook. I am expected to receive guests, even guests I care nothing about, and spend hours talking with them about the changing fashions of sleeves and where the best table service can be procured for entertaining. I have to know the right sort of people and address them properly when we meet in society, or else be ridiculed behind my back. There is no one I can be my genuine self with—not even Darcy. I am given jewels and furs of unspeakable worth, not to mention enough money every month to feed five or six large families. The meals I enjoy at Pemberley are virtual banquets. Yet I know now it is all to serve one purpose and one purpose alone—so that I may do my duty and bear my husband as many children as I possibly can. What a stupid woman I must have been to think, to believe, that anyone's love could be truly unconditional. It is not only Darcy who possesses such expectations of me; it is also his sister, his aunts and uncles, his cousins, and Pemberley's staff, from the steward to the lowliest kitchen maid. I have decided I am either too weak to go along with it or too intelligent for my own good. I shall admit I'm a poor wife because I am unwilling to give myself to my husband, to lie with him any longer, and this because I choose to live and to exercise whatever autonomy I have left over mindless duty and obedience. If the honor of womanhood demands that I value my existence and my well-being no more than a dumb sow, then I shall be happy to reject its terms."

With the toe of my slipper, I pushed away a decapitated rose.

"I didn't realize how hard it was for you," I said softly. There was much I wished to tell my sister—that I sympathized, that I finally understood. I, too, had flagrantly broken the rules, and I knew well the sensation of being confined in both body and spirit, of having nowhere to go. She was not alone in this; nor did she have to live her life thinking no one of her acquaintance comprehended her feelings.

But before I could speak, my sister had recommenced her execution of the flowers. "What a pity the roses are ruined this year," she said over the snipping of the shears. "I wanted so to have a large bouquet of them on the table in the front hall. That would have made such a lovely sight."

I didn't know how to reply, and perhaps she did not need my answer, for she went on: "Perhaps it is time. . . ." I heard her say, as I stared at the shriveled roses at my feet. "I think, Mary . . . don't you think it is time you went back to Longbourn? That it is time for you to go?"

FOR FOUR MONTHS, I'd been a guest at Pemberley. On my last evening in that great house, I stood with Darcy in our usual spot in the library. With less skill than tenderness his hands had covered the "monstrous thing," my novel, in layers of brown paper and string. The book was now a parcel, and we its grim spectators.

Earlier, I had told him I was leaving, and he'd listened calmly to my every word. An onlooker might have said he appeared detached from the conversation, even indifferent. But they would have missed the change in his face, so subtle it almost went unseen. In that moment, the reflection of the light grew larger in his eyes, until their watery surface filled entirely with the motion of the rippling flames he stared into. I blinked, and when I saw him again, all trace of the emotion I'd witnessed had gone. His expression had been restored to its practiced respectability.

"Well," he'd said, clearing his throat. "You'll just have to come back." Then, he'd smoothed the roll of brown paper, which he had brought to wrap the book, and cut a length of it in one stroke.

But now the packing of the novel was finished, and there remained nothing left with which to busy ourselves. For a while, we lingered in the purgatory of our thoughts. Then, to lighten the mood, I proposed that I should write a sequel titled *Leonora's Adventures: Chronicles of a Tragic and Deeply Unhappy Wife,* detailing the tumultuous domestic adventures of Leonora, Wilhelm, and their several offspring.

"It is, to me, quite logical that neither of them would be able to bear the peace and tranquility for long," I said, "given how thrilling their lives were before."

"You may very well be right," Darcy replied, laughing.

Those unacquainted with Darcy might have found it difficult to imagine that such a gentleman could laugh, so serious and poised was his manner, even when undertaking the most ordinary tasks. He seemed born to sit at the head of a table. His handwriting, each curlicue and dot a picture of excellence, could have emblazoned the signs of London's best stores. But when he laughed, he had a way of tipping his head backwards, as though the angle of the mouth and throat must be positioned precisely for the creation of mirth. It was his laughter I thought of and which moved me—an unpretentious sound, which gave itself, like a hard-won reward, to its listener. I hoped never to forget its music.

The next morning, I left Pemberley. I left its hills and pleasant walks, its blue lake, its abandoned rooms of ghostly furniture. I left this place, where I had lived and loved fully, knowing in my heart I would never return to it again.

PART III

Ｏne might say that tragedy followed me from Pemberley to Longbourn, that it sat, a malevolent and invisible stranger, beside me in the dark carriage and slipped like a wisp of cold wind through the door of my home right before Mrs. Hill was able to shut it out. Once it was inside, it began to work its mischief, diffusing like a toxic fragrance into the air of our rooms and seeping into the grain of our walls, settling as an unseen mist over our furniture and curling into our beds. It gathered strength in undusted corners until it had power enough to seize our home and to uproot it.

Less than two weeks after my return, Papa died. A swift, violent stroke carried him away, though this last blow had been preceded by several episodes of numbness in his limbs. He remained to the very end the stalwart and cheerful intellectual. When he was too weak to sit downstairs in the library, he remained in bed, and Kitty and I took turns bringing him a few offerings on obscure and only modestly important subjects, from which he'd select a volume for us to read. And we'd read to him for as many hours as he liked before he grew tired of our voices or fell asleep.

The day before my father died, he complained of a sharp pain in his right leg. This was already the third day he had been bedridden, and as I read to him, he unexpectedly touched my arm and stopped me.

"Mary," he said. The corners of his mouth involuntarily trembled as he spoke. "Mary, be a good girl, and put aside that awful poetry for a moment. I'd like to speak to you about a letter your mother and I received a few days ago from Lizzy."

"Yes, Papa." I closed the book.

"Being aware of my condition, Lizzy has had the foresight to invite your mother and Kitty to live at Pemberley. And quite right, too—any overlap with the Collinses would prove most awkward and upsetting, certainly more than Mrs. Bennet is capable of enduring."

"That sounds very reasonable, sir," I replied.

"Yes, it is. There are some advantages, I grant you, of being married to money. What I wished to speak to you about, however, is this—Lizzy said, as concerned your situation, that she had already written to Jane, and Jane has agreed that you should stay with her. Would you like that, Mary? To live with Jane and Bingley in their big house?"

This was the first I heard of the arrangement, and though it didn't surprise me, I had no immediate reaction, except to think uselessly again of Darcy and our parting.

"She mentioned that, rather than following your mother and sister, you'd appreciate the change of scenery after spending so much time at Pemberley. I'm sure you'll be well treated at Bingley's, Mary. A kinder, more agreeable man never walked the earth, and Jane will always be exactly as she is."

"And I am to play nursemaid," I mused without smiling.

"Well, it'll be good practice for you," Papa chuckled. "I'll confess, Mary, that I couldn't help laughing when I read Lizzy's letter."

"Laughing, sir?"

"All this talk of 'change of scenery' and writing Jane on your behalf." He tapped me playfully on the wrist. "I don't wholly believe it. Now, tell me, Mary, were you a poor houseguest when you stayed at Pemberley? You may be honest with me, for I am practically at death's door. What did you do? Refuse to stand up for a dance? Stay in bed past breakfast in order to finish a book? My own guess is that you did another of your songs at one of her parties and embarrassed your poor sister in front of her new friends. And if that is the case, then I'm afraid I must side with my Lizzy. You are truly a terrible musician despite your diligence, which, I grant you, is admirable."

"Papa!" I scolded, though I laughed, too. Gibes at my poor playing no longer hurt me.

"It's also very likely Lizzy has turned into a snob," he concluded thoughtfully. "Even a temper as naturally good as hers would not be able to withstand the influence of such a place—with so many servants and carriages and ancestral portraits swarming around her every hour. I suspected, when she was married, that Pemberley would change her. How she will put up with your mother and Kitty, I haven't the faintest idea."

"She has enough finery to distract her," I said, "and Mama and Kitty will be too dazzled by what they see to utter a single word for days."

Papa chuckled. "Very good, Mary," he said. He pointed to the book I still held. "Now keep reading that awful poetry."

I had hoped, in Lizzy's absence, that Papa and I should have become great friends and spent many hours talking about the books we had read and the books we still hoped to read. I'd imagined sitting with him in the library, exchanging quotations or making the occasional joke at Mama and Kitty's expense. I wish that he might have imparted some greater wisdom in his last words to me, but he did not. He passed away the following morning, and having risen late, I had no chance to speak to him again. I was forced to admit I knew as little of my father as he knew of me. Our understanding of each other had been, at the best of times, superficial, and the assumption of affection between us was, of course, not the same as the proof of it.

Mama, for all her diatribes against Papa while he was still alive, mourned his death with surprising calm. Over a cup of spilled tea and a cut of underdone pork, she might have bewailed the undiscerning cruelty of the Fates, but the loss of a lifelong partner, a man whom she must, in some early chapter, have loved with the reckless passion of youth, this she endured with remarkable forbearance and little self-pity. They had, after all, nothing in common, and whereas some wives will only feign annoyance when teased by their better halves, Mama had passed the majority of her days in a condition of continuous vexation. I only ever saw her cry once for him, and even then, the weeping was astonishingly restrained.

I found her one evening soon after at her dressing table, sorting through the contents of a small jewelry box. She had just been trying on a very pretty agate ring that had proved too tight for her own fingers, and giving up the cause as lost, she slipped the ring into my hand.

"Here, Mary," she said. "Why don't you see what luck you have with it?"

I did, and the ring, though it slid onto my finger with ease, dangled so loose that if I tipped my hand even slightly, it came right off again.

"Our poor Mary was never one for trinkets," Mama remarked, picking the ring off the carpet with a sigh.

"True, but only think of how many pounds, shillings, and pence I must have saved Papa in his lifetime because I did not care for such things," I offered.

She tossed the offending bauble back into the box and shut it. "Your father said to me many years ago, 'Our Mary would have made a fine scholar or clergyman, if she could be one.' I didn't like that he could be so flippant about his own children, but he was right, of course. You were always different from your sisters. I think now what a shame we couldn't send you to one of those private seminaries in London or take on a governess. You may have benefited by it, though what can be gained from so much book reading is beyond me."

"I doubt whether a governess or a seminary for young women could have taught me anything the circulating library didn't, Mama," I replied softly, moved by her acknowledgement.

At this, my mother's chest heaved a weary concession. "Mary," she said, and the tone of her voice changed. "I have something I wish to speak to you about. Kitty and I wanted to tell you sooner, but what with all that's happened, there never seemed any suitable moment to impart such news. Also, we were uncertain how you would respond—"

"It is not your own health, Mama?" I asked, alarmed.

"No, no," she said soothingly. "It is, I promise you, good news . . . very good news indeed. You see, shortly before you returned to us, Kitty received an offer of marriage, and she has, after a period of consideration, accepted."

For many moments, the news had no effect on me. Then my blood quickened, and my face felt touched by an intolerable heat. I seemed to feel the reverberation of a pain that did not strike me so much as it flowered from somewhere within my body, the seed something bitter and raw that had been waiting for the right time to unfold itself. After a pause, I heard myself mumble a few meager words of congratulations. "If the man is good and worthy," I said, "then I can be nothing but happy for my sister. Who is he?"

"His name is Christopher Harper. Fairly handsome, though nothing, of course, to either Bingley or Darcy. He and Kitty met at an assembly. They knocked into each other while dancing, and he gave her a sprained ankle. It was love at first sight."

"What good fortune for Kitty."

"Don't lose heart, my dear," Mama said, as her hands warmed my own, which had grown cold. The unexpected tenderness of her voice made my nose twitch in the anticipation of tears. "One day I hope you shall marry as well, and the feat will not be any the less joyous for the fact that it has been delayed."

Sometimes the truth will withhold itself until it is spoken, and until it is spoken, it will not feel real.

"I will never marry," I said and stopped just after I had uttered the words to feel their residue, whether stinging or sweet or tasteless, on my tongue. "I will never marry."

But Mama, who knew no better, insisted I was only discouraged by Kitty's news, and we ended the conversation good-naturedly by talking of a subject which pleased us both: the prospects of my sister's future husband, a gentleman, albeit in trade, who had, at present, no less than four thousand pounds a year, a sum he owed in large part to the munificence of a doting and childless great-aunt.

Afterwards, I went downstairs to find Kitty, and we embraced over her good fortune.

"This is a triumph indeed," I said politely, "and could not come at a more welcome time."

Kitty squeezed my hands. The summer months had browned her skin and given her freckles, which, I confess, suited her. "What good luck," she said, sighing. I noticed then her red-rimmed eyes and asked if she had been grieving our father.

"Mary, you revealed almost nothing in your letter about Lydia, except that she died of a fever. Was it very bad? Did she suffer?"

"I believe she lost consciousness hours before she passed away. I don't think she felt any pain."

Kitty nodded. "Then that is something. I don't think there was anyone more distraught than Mama when we read the news. For two whole days, she would not eat anything. Papa, of course, locked himself away in the library and forbade anyone from disturbing him. And I could not stop crying for hours. Mrs. Hill told me I would go blind from weeping so much, and I told her I didn't care."

"I have faith our sister is in a better place," I said softly. "Wickham treated her poorly, but where she is now, neither he nor anyone else can hurt her."

"People were so cruel to her when she ran off with Wickham," Kitty sobbed. "All they could think about was the shame of what she'd done, the disgrace she'd brought upon the rest of us, and now she is dead. I wish I could have seen her again. I still remember how well she looked when she left Longbourn for the last time with Wickham, the exact dress and bonnet she wore. And afterwards, I wrote her almost every week, but her replies grew shorter and less frequent over time."

"She was quite her usual self when I visited her," I said.

"Did she . . . did she say anything about me?" Kitty stared at me expectantly.

I hesitated, though I smiled at the memory. "She said wouldn't it be rather amusing if, after all, you turned out to be the old maid among us and not me?"

Kitty laughed through her tears. "How like Lydia to speak such nonsense," she murmured.

"But I'm afraid," I said, feigning humor, "that the honor of old maid shall always be mine."

"I do think Lydia would have been happy with my choice of husband, if she were here."

"And unlike the rest of the female population, I'm certain she would ask how tall and handsome he was before inquiring after his income."

"And whether he was an officer," Kitty added.

"Yes, that, too."

For a while, Kitty didn't speak. I watched as she dried her eyes and neatly folded her handkerchief.

"I hope you're not terribly jealous, Mary," she finally said.

"Now, you and Lydia knew a long time ago that I would never marry," I replied, pretending to smile, "and I daresay you were both right."

"Our poor Mary," Kitty said, twining her fingers through mine.

"But you'll be so happy with Jane and Bingley. I know you will. Bingley is as reliable as Papa or Uncle Gardiner."

"He is."

"And there will be no awkwardness, for you'll repay their generosity by looking after Jane's baby when the time comes. So you needn't worry about that."

I said nothing, and she embraced me again. It was then I knew. I would not go to Jane's.

It wasn't courtesy but pride that stopped me. I was the unmarried sister, the woman who could not get herself a husband, let alone a proper one of five or seven thousand pounds a year. For the remainder of my life, I would be shipped like a parcel from one great residence to another, caring for an abundance of nephews and nieces and living, at most, two ranks higher than the housekeeper. No, I told myself, I wouldn't give in so easily. If my destiny was to be a nursemaid, I would not do it for my sisters, where they, their husbands, and my mother should always be on hand to bear witness to my failure in following their fine examples. I would do it for strangers, or for people I did not care about. And I would begin at the place I still considered my home, at Longbourn.

THE NEXT DAY, I informed Mama and Kitty I wished to stay at Longbourn for as long as the Collinses would permit me to remain with them. Time had tempered my dislike of my cousin, and in truth, a part of me professed terrible curiosity as to the state of his marriage to Charlotte. I could never think of Mr. Collins fondly, but to myself, I conceded that there was, in the end, very little to feel resentful about. We were temperamentally unsuited to each other, and I was a much different person now than when I'd claimed to be in love with him. He was neither the hero of my imagination nor a great villain. He was a man, in the plainest terms—small and delicate in stature, doting on the rich and mighty, scornful of the poor; in other words, no better or worse than many of his brethren.

Mama and Kitty were, understandably, incredulous.

"You cannot be serious, Mary," said Kitty, who had attained a great deal more sense since Lydia's departure. "What reason could you possibly have to stay behind?"

"This is my home," I said practically, "as it is yours and Mama's, though we have no claim to it legally. And I am decided. I shall not leave until I feel ready to join Jane and Bingley."

"And when might that be?" Mama cried.

"It could be a week or a month. Maybe a year."

"A year?" Mama and Kitty shouted in unison.

"If it is comfort you are thinking of, I'm sure Bingley's house cannot be unsuitable," Kitty offered. "And he has a residence in London, too, one which does not lack amenities, from what Jane has told me in her letters."

I shook my head. "You misunderstand me, Kitty. I do not doubt that Bingley's estate is ten times as grand as our little home, but I'm convinced I should stay here. Charlotte cannot have turned disagreeable, and being married to our cousin, she is probably most desirous for company."

"You shall be miserable," Mama insisted. "You shall choose to be miserable and make me miserable in turn, as your mother."

"I am very fond of Jane and Bingley," I explained, ignoring Mama. "But I do not think it can be a practical time for me to go. In a matter of days, Jane will have her baby, and I would only be in their way. Also, you forget that I have stayed at Longbourn hardly a month since returning from Pemberley. I should like to say a proper goodbye to our childhood home before leaving."

"Say goodbye to a house?" Mama exclaimed, but she could see my resolve and said no more.

A few days before the Collinses were to arrive and take ownership of Longbourn, I parted from my mother and sister.

"Write often," Mama said, sobbing into her third handkerchief of the morning. "And tell me what you eat at every meal, for I promise the Collinses won't be as generous with their table as I've been, not that you have ever taken notice."

"I have noticed, Mama," I said. Then she kissed my forehead and my hand before entering the carriage, where more lamentations and sobs issued between great heaving sighs.

"It is my sincere wish," Kitty said, while embracing me in a sanguine attitude, "that you should play and sing as long as you like each day when Mrs. Collins moves in."

I laughed. "But you have never liked my singing."

"Exactly!" Kitty replied. "So sing, nightingale! Sing! Please do!" Then she, too, kissed me and, waving goodbye from the carriage window, was gone.

CHAPTER 36

〜つℭℭ〜

Jane and Bingley both expressed regret that I would not come as soon as expected. "Of course you are sorry to leave our dear home," Jane had written in reply to my letter. "But I hope, for reasons entirely selfish, that you will join Bingley, myself, and our healthy, laughing girl the moment you tire of Longbourn's drafty rooms and yellowing wallpaper. We've named her Elizabeth, by the way—do you approve of the choice?"

Though it pained me to admit it, I remained at Longbourn also because of Darcy. If I stayed here, there could be no possibility of our moving in overlapping circles, and I would spare us both the vexation of meeting while being unable to say anything of importance. In order that I might one day forget what I could never have, I refused to succumb to longing. Still, every so often, the fragment of a pleasant conversation or a look would materialize to haunt me, and I would feel desire come to life again, like the first spark of a warming ember. But then I'd remind myself of the futility of such thoughts, and they would vanish for a time.

I will refrain from relating in detail the tedium of the days that followed the Collinses' arrival. Suffice it to say that Charlotte had grown fat and that Mr. Collins remained as small as I remembered in both body and spirit since we'd parted two years ago. Their child, ridiculously named Julius, was a sickly thing, prone to devastating bouts of bad temper. From the first, *he* was permitted to strike and kick me whenever he liked, but I shudder to think what his parents would have done to my person had I repaid his childish violence in kind.

Our reunion began courteously enough. They declared upon their arrival that I shouldn't entertain the slightest idea of going anywhere. I *must* stay at Longbourn; it would always be my home more than theirs, Charlotte generously commented, and Mr. Collins was quick to add that his dear wife was certainly correct in her remark, albeit only from a *sentimental* point of view.

But generosity is a creature of unpredictable temperament, and a few hours later, the following conversation reached my ears from the direction of the drawing room, where Mr. and Mrs. Collins sat alone, drinking hot tea and eating the stale cake and biscuits laid out for them by Mrs. Hill, who'd been asked to stay on:

"That comment was perhaps unwise," Mr. Collins began. Noisy sipping followed.

"What comment, dear?" Charlotte inquired absentmindedly, for I think she had already mastered the delicate art of freely ignoring one's husband without provoking him.

"When you suggested that Mary should stay on indefinitely at Longbourn."

"Well, she should. . . ." Charlotte stumbled over her response. "That is, to an extent. And you as much said the same thing!"

"What? When?"

"When you agreed that she should take as much time as she needed to grieve her poor father."

"What else could I say?" Mr. Collins lamented. "Oh, this has turned into such an awkward business, Charlotte, which is exactly what I feared!"

"I wonder why she did not go to Jane's or Lizzy's with her mother and sister. . . ." Charlotte said slowly, chomping away at a biscuit.

Mr. Collins gave a little gasp. "Do you think it is because of a scandal?"

"Mary?" His wife chortled. "We are talking of Mary Bennet, aren't we? The one who'd sooner put coals in her pockets and swim across a lake than stand up with a man and dance with him? Please, Mr. Collins! Don't speak nonsense."

Mr. Collins said nothing, or at least I heard nothing. I imagined his clever brain turning the matter over, as one inspects a precious stone beneath a magnifying glass, delicately, caressingly handling it before slipping it into an inner pocket. At length, he spoke: "Well, I can't understand why anyone would prefer *these* rooms to the ones at Pemberley, my dear. There must be a reason."

Charlotte removed the jewel from her husband's pocket and inspected it for herself. "Why does it matter what the reason is? The fact remains that she is here, and we cannot turn her out without appearing like monsters to the rest of the neighborhood."

"No, of course not," Mr. Collins agreed. "That might reflect poorly on us."

"But perhaps," Charlotte continued, still fingering the jewel, "perhaps we can come to some agreement with her that would also be beneficial to us."

Another short interval of silence, and then a firm statement of assent from the man I'd once presumed to love and even hoped to marry. "Yes," he said, the jewel dropping discreetly back into his pocket. "Yes, I think that's an excellent idea. Her father is no longer the proprietor of Longbourn. Why should she not make herself useful to us in exchange for our many kindnesses?"

UNDER THE COLLINSES, there was no suffering which I hadn't encountered before. I did not mind the work, and so long as they believed they had not been taken advantage of for their charity, Charlotte and Mr. Collins were both civil enough to me. They always framed their requests as "favors"; to refuse would have been impossible, but I'm grateful that they gave the impression of choice. For instance: "As Sarah is doing the washing, would you mind going to the milliner's and picking up that bit of lace I pointed out to you the other day? I'd be so pleased if you would." And: "I don't think Mrs. Hill will have time to go to the butcher's; her gout is acting up again. Would you terribly mind going in her place? I'll make up a list for you, if that would help you to remember."

When I'd lived with my family, they had generally ignored me, but their indifference had, I think, been the natural consequence of there being four other sisters and a mother who at all times would demand as much attention towards her own person as any one of us. I mention this because I now consider that my years of sitting quietly had prepared me to survive this long interval of stillness. There existed no sense of obligation between Charlotte and me, and friendship, which can subsist only on terms of equality, seemed a dim and unlikely, even undesirable, prospect. So Charlotte and I were no longer friends, and I converted instead into a kind of useful and complaisant companion. I accompanied her wherever she went and stood submissively within her oversized shadow in shops. I sat with her at home, read to her, sewed with her, conversed with her on whatever subject that happened to occupy her thoughts, and offered mild opinions which, in stating the obvious, seemed to satisfy her entirely. Sometimes she asked me to play for her, and she would interrupt me midway through a piece to make a request for a song she desired to hear more. And if I did not know the song in question, then she would call me back to her side and speak to me about something else—preparations for dinner, Maria's recent engagement to a wealthy merchant and what she thought of the man, her brother's letters from overseas, her father's excellent health. She made a point never to be cruel to me, but she visibly enjoyed the new formality with which I was compelled to treat her.

Occasionally my hand would itch to write again. The urge would

come and go like an inconstant flame, ideas transpiring and depart-
ing from my brain as ephemerally as fairies. The notions I'd con-
ceived ranged from the noble (a disfigured prince's tragic love affair
with a shepherdess) to the ridiculous (could it be possible to write, I
wondered, from the perspective of an English sheepdog?). They'd
form in the most inconvenient moments—the second-long lull between Julius's squalls, the undecided pause before Charlotte asked
me my opinion of a new lace cap. But whatever candle of inspiration
burned, I just as soon put it out again. I could not write without also
remembering the wrinkly velvet green sofa. The fragrance of ancient
books. *Him.* I had no editor, no critic, and no audience without
Darcy. *Leonora's Adventures* had finished and come to nothing; a
subpar work born of a conventional mind, I thought. What could
be the point?

Days, weeks, then a whole month passed in this manner. Mornings dissolved inextricably into afternoons, and entire evenings vanished in the space of a single breath. Occasionally I lost count of
what day it was; each hour of consciousness felt like an exact dupli-
cate of what had occurred before. I listened so carefully to Charlotte's stories that I believed myself in danger of forgetting everything
else I'd ever learned or read in my life. For the sake of appearing
useful, I'd begun to spend more time in the garden with Sarah, cutting flowers and weeding. It was after such an occasion that, returning to the house with my basket, I heard Mr. and Mrs. Collins again
conversing about "the state of affairs."

"Are you satisfied with her, Charlotte?" a full mouth asked.

"Mr. Collins, you refer to her as though she were some pet animal," the wife gently rebuked.

"Well . . ."

"Mary keeps me wonderful company, and I don't think I've heard
her complain once about anything, not even when Julius threw up
his dinner on her dress two nights ago."

Mr. Collins said nothing for a lengthy interval. At last, in the tone of a resigned employer who has found no excuse to dismiss a worker he would eagerly get rid of, he added, "Well, my dear, I am glad she is behaving herself."

"I would tell you, William, if she wasn't. Did you notice she's started to help Sarah with her chores? I saw her the other day hanging up the washing and working in the garden."

"Say nothing about it, my dear. She'll look, I'm sure, for any excuse to do less, so give her none."

"I wouldn't dream of it," Charlotte protested. "Just look how nicely this situation has turned out for us, when a month ago you wanted to get rid of her."

"I still wonder why she should want to stay here."

"To keep me company, of course."

"Oh really, my dear! How naïve you are. I mean to say—does she not wish to marry?"

"I shouldn't think so," Charlotte said cheerfully. "She hardly has anything to tempt her here, does she? She doesn't meet anyone. She has no friends in the neighborhood. But Jane, Kitty, and Mrs. Bennet write her often enough, and when you consider how much attention I personally pay her, it is more than ample company to keep any young woman's spirits lively. I wager, Mr. Collins, that in a month she'll have started the ironing, and if she does that, we won't even have to keep Sarah on. I'm sure that miserable girl hates me, and it is so disturbing to have one's servants hate you when you're forced to live with them."

The rest of the conversation became a petty argument over whether the three servants of Longbourn, excluding myself, did in fact dislike their new mistress. I knew for certain that they did and that they felt the same or slightly worse about her self-important, miniature husband, who scuttled around the house like an undergrown cock.

But I gave no more thought to either of them. As I moved away from the door, the basket still dangling from my wrist, I was aware of a change, not in my surroundings, or in the Collinses, or in the air—but in myself.

This change might have been prompted by any number of things: the reminder that Mr. Collins was and always would be an ass, the memory of books, of brave Leonora, of Pemberley. It stirred, like the first worm of life twisting in anger, and awoke me from my diffidence.

CHAPTER 37

The transformation continued that night as I was going down-stairs to retrieve a cup of warm milk for Charlotte. I found Sarah asleep at the kitchen table.

"Sarah," I whispered.

Catlike, she stirred, opened a pair of green eyes, and stretched her freckled arms, curling her sooty fingers as though they were claws flexing.

"What is it, miss?" she yawned. "I've just had such a strange dream."

"Mrs. Collins wants her cup of milk. She can't sleep without it."

"I'm glad you woke me when you did," Sarah continued, stum-bling to the stove. "Can you believe what I dreamed just now? I dreamed I was mistress of this house! Me! Mistress of Longbourn! It's laughable, isn't it? And everyone around me was calling me 'Charlotte' or 'Mrs. Collins,' including you, miss, and I could hardly move for being so fat. Someone had to push me down the hall and up the stairs 'cause I couldn't walk on my own two legs."

"Sarah, you'll want to be careful how you talk about Mrs. Col-lins, even behind her back," I warned, more for her sake than that of the impatient woman upstairs.

"The devil with Mrs. Collins!" Sarah cursed, becoming, for all of five seconds, less greasy-smocked human than auburn-haired goddess. We laughed together, for since Mama and Kitty had left, we'd become good friends, and I returned upstairs with "the mistress's" milk. After this duty had been dispensed with and the cup washed and dried and replaced in the cabinet belowstairs, I was permitted to retire for the rest of the evening. In my room, I slipped out a single sheet of paper. I prepared a pen and a bottle of ink, and I began to write the story of innocent Sarah Ellis, a maid-of-all-work in a small but understaffed household who is regularly thrashed within an inch of her life by her overfed and frugal mistress. The mistress's husband I described as a slender and snobbishly erudite young man two years her junior with a secret proclivity for wearing women's bonnets and shawls. Sarah Ellis wakes up one morning to find herself in the bed of Mrs. Caroline Collingwood, and Mrs. Caroline Collingwood wakes up several hours later in a "small, confined room" belowstairs. I wrote until I had depleted all the candles, paper, and quill pens in my room, and the only survivor of my creative tempest remained a bottle of ink which could perhaps eke out another two sentences or three before outliving its usefulness.

When at last I laid down my pen, I read over what I'd written.

The twenty-first of October held special meaning for Mrs. Caroline Collingwood, mistress of the ancient house of Middlebourne in Bedfordshire County. For one, it was her birthday, and she had arranged several weeks earlier that it should be nothing less than a grand occasion with many people present in order to congratulate her on her accomplishment. This accomplishment, the aging of precisely one year since the previous twenty-first of October, also marked the anniversary of another singular event: her marriage to Mr. Aloysius Collingwood, a religious scholar whose article elucidating the four cardinal virtues of Saint Thomas Aquinas had received praise from sources as high as the bishop. He was a gentleman of truly delicate constitution, slender, with hands as soft as lambskin and veins of faintest blue, as though the blood in his body had been diluted in equal parts with icy water. To their neighbors, they could not have been a more unlikely couple. She was prone to being loud, and he so accustomed to whispering all his "good evening"s and "farewell"s that their closest friends instinctively bent their heads and craned their necks to hear him. Mr. Collingwood had come from a good family, and throughout his life a rumor persisted, never disproved or affirmed, that he had for an ancestor a duke who'd ridden into Agincourt beside the king. The superiority of Mr. Collingwood's relations and the bestowment of a comfortable income from his late father had a very different effect on his wife than it did on his own diminutive person. For Mr. Collingwood, the security of wealth necessitated that he should turn his mind to greater, immaterial things, and thus he passed most of his evenings after supper with the composition of fine religious sonnets by candlelight. For Mrs. Collingwood, the possession of an immodest income meant that she counted among her dearest friends nearly all of the shopkeepers of her industrious little town.

The evening of the twentieth of October boasted no remarkable events for either of them. Mrs. Collingwood enjoyed her dinner of boiled chicken, sweetbreads, tongue, and venison, and Mr. Collingwood washed down the meat of two small prawns with a spoonful of cabbage soup. Waiting on both of them was an emaciated girl of yellow complexion and ginger hair whose name was Sarah Ellis, the only maid employed by the Collingwoods and responsible for a good many things that in any other house would have been divided between two or even three fit young women.

Dinner was nearly over, and all had gone smoothly and well until Sarah Ellis spilled gravy into the lap of her mistress. This was not, as Mrs. Collingwood instantly assumed, a malicious insurrection on the part of her maid. It was only a mistake caused by the many sleepless nights in which Sarah Ellis was obliged to sit belowstairs and polish the silver or finish the washing. But Mrs. Collingwood did not know this, and even if she had, she mightn't have cared. So she called for Mr. Haines, who knew to bring Mrs. Collingwood her riding crop, and Mrs. Collingwood thrashed Sarah within an inch of her life using this monstrous instrument, until her own arms grew too tired and sore from the constant whipping of the poor girl's back.

"That fool has no mind for work," Mrs. Collingwood despaired to her indifferent husband once her victim had been dismissed. "And she despises me. She'd murder me in my sleep if she had the chance. Have you seen the way she looks at me?"

"Tut, tut, my dear," Mr. Collingwood whispered and, taking another spoonful of soup, excused himself from the dinner table.

That night, Mrs. Collingwood retired in high spirits. She fell asleep with the taste of chicken in her mouth, and her thick fingers gripped the sheets of her bed as though they each held a large slice of cake. Sarah Ellis, too, fell asleep for the first time in many days, while in an undusted corner of the house that remained forgotten to all but one, Mr. Collingwood paired a new bonnet with a pretty shawl his wife had given up for lost.

The next morning, the house awoke to screams, no sooner in one quarter of the house than they began with equal fire and liveliness in another.

"Mr. Collingwood!" Mrs.-Collingwood-who-was-really-Sarah-Ellis screamed.

"Mrs. Collingwood?" Mr. Collingwood whispered doubtfully.

"Aloysius!" Sarah-Ellis-who-was-really-Mrs.-Collingwood bellowed, coming up the stairs from the small, confined room she had slept in all night. "What on earth is happening here?"

That was when she set eyes on herself and screamed. To the Cook and the Gamekeeper, to the Butler and the Valet and the Footman, all of whom had run upstairs to see what was the matter, Mrs. Collingwood could be no other person than who she appeared to be. Little surprise then that when she fainted, no one in the whole group of able-bodied men ventured even half-heartedly to catch her.

THE NEXT MORNING, I awoke at my desk with a sore head and a throbbing hand. I heard a rash of hurried footsteps outside; then a fist rapped like an angry woodpecker on my door before the real-life inspiration for Mrs. Caroline Collingwood entered. From the looks of it, she was most upset about something.

And yet she smiled, too.

"Mary, do you not know what time it is? It is nearly a quarter to ten. And you aren't even dressed, by God!"

I began to offer apologies for my remiss behavior, but she batted these skillfully away.

"Never mind all that, Mary," Charlotte scolded. "We have a visitor, and you must come immediately and not keep our guest waiting any longer!"

I smoothed the front of my dress, feeling a flash of excitement. "Has one of my sisters come? Is it Jane? Or perhaps Lizzy and Kitty traveled together from Pemberley to see me?"

"No, no, and no!" Charlotte repeated, flustered. "It's Mr. Darcy!"

CHAPTER 38

Mr. and Mrs. Collins could not account for the honor of Mr. Darcy's visit, but they endeavored to make the most of it all the same. When Julius began to scream in his mother's arms, his warm, fidgeting body was promptly relegated to my lap, where it squirmed painfully against my ribs and bony thighs.

"You'll never get him to be quiet if you hold him like that, Mary!" Mrs. Collins chastised through close-set teeth. Mr. Darcy glanced at the baby, then looked briefly at its bungling caretaker. Our eyes met. He had on his best blue coat, the one which made him appear invincible, like a hero in a painting. Though only two months had passed since we'd last parted, I wondered if he found me changed.

"I hope you are in good health, Mr. Darcy," Mr. Collins suggested in a childish voice.

"Thank you, I'm perfectly well," the gentleman replied.

"We're so pleased to hear it," Mr. Collins declared, and Charlotte, too, nodded her assent over her teacup.

"I had some business to take care of in this area on behalf of a friend," our honored guest explained, "and recalled when I'd finished that Longbourn was not far away."

A good many people had lost interest in Charlotte after her marriage to Mr. Collins, and not least of these was Lizzy, who sought to keep up as short and infrequent a communication with her former friend as politeness would permit. Charlotte's reply to Lizzy's most recent letter had already gone for over four months unanswered, so she inquired now how her visitor's charming spouse fared.

"She's perfectly well," Mr. Darcy said, swirling the dregs of his teacup. "And my sister is also perfectly well," he added, anticipating any query which might eventually have been made on that front.

After everyone's health had been fully established, and by this I mean that Mr. Darcy, Lizzy, and Georgiana were all "perfectly well" and Sir William, Lady Lucas, Maria, and the Collinses all "well enough," Mr. Darcy, gazing absently out the sitting room window, expressed an interest in taking a tour of the grounds. Mr. Collins at once offered his services, but his guest declined.

"No, please don't put yourself to any more trouble," Mr. Darcy said, standing. "I've already taken up enough of your time as it is and, I fear, interrupted your morning schedule."

"Not at all! Not at all!" Mr. Collins protested. "Please permit me to dispel your concern by assuring you that I had nothing planned this whole day which would prevent my giving you a thorough tour of the house and the surrounding land."

"I'm sure I wouldn't dream of disturbing your plans," Mr. Darcy remarked, plainly ignoring his host. "I wonder, however, if Miss Bennet could be prevailed upon to accompany me, provided she can be spared from her other duties." And he looked with open disdain into the sour, disapproving face of the tiny Roman emperor still enthroned on the edge of my knees. I held on to Julius, warm blood flooding my cheeks.

The Collinses had no choice but to give in to his wishes. Julius was promptly removed, and Darcy waited for me at the door while I put on my coat. My fingers fumbled uselessly with the buttons. Of course, in passing through the area, he wished to pay his respects, I thought to myself. Nothing less. Nothing more.

When we were alone and a reasonable distance from Longbourn, Darcy inquired again after my health.

"I am well," I repeated. We kept our gazes fixed on the view in front of us and did not look at each other. Speech, which had once flowed liberally from our mouths, was now a stilted, agonizing thing to undertake. I knew he must leave; whether that would be an hour from now or after dinner mattered little. He would leave, and once he was gone, I would feel his absence like a wound which I couldn't locate on my body, though I must suffer its pain.

"And you?" I asked more coldly than was my intent.

"Well enough," he replied and offered nothing further. "Do the Collinses treat you well?"

"I've no reason to complain," I said, which was the truth. "The Collinses treat me as civilly as they can, and Charlotte has grown used to my company. They are very happy to keep me busy with small tasks, and I am willing enough to oblige them, so long as I can remain at Longbourn."

We'd been walking for some time away from the house and into the surrounding fields, and I confess the morning did not feel any more extraordinary for the fact that Darcy had come. The air still smelled, as it always did, of animals and earth, and the sun, which had never been educated in the art of moderation, shone too hot and bright on everything. There was no soothing wind to be felt, no birdsong to be heard. Then he said, "Mary, I have come with a purpose—to deliver some news."

We stopped. The light, at that moment, was just behind his head, and I could not look at him without also blinding myself. I waited for him to speak.

"Egerton has agreed to publish your book," he said, as my eyes adjusted to the sun, "and he will pay you two hundred pounds for it."

Two hundred pounds.

"*Leonora?*" I asked, incredulous. I was aware that my mouth remained open, yet I had no sense to close it.

"Yes."

For a whole minute, I seemed to lose all faculty of speech. *My* writing would be printed. *My* novel, which had been ridiculed by my detractors at Pemberley, would be sold to complete strangers in bookstores. People would pay money in order to read *my* work. In the precious hours before bedtime, a duchess might very well seat herself in her favorite armchair and read the opening lines of *Leonora,* while downstairs, the housekeeper and cook argued over which princely suitor would win the Danish queen's heart. No longer was *Leonora* merely a jumble of paper, of handwritten passages and blotched ink. It would be reborn into that most sacred of man-made conceptions: a book.

"There are some papers you'll need to sign," Darcy continued. "The terms are quite simple, and I'm fairly confident you'll find the language agreeable, as I helped to negotiate several of the provisions myself."

"I've never earned any money before," I said, my mouth twitching into a smile. "What would I do with two hundred pounds?" At the mention of money, I remembered the measly allowance which Papa would distribute among us at the beginning of every month, and which Lydia and Kitty would oftentimes deplete in the space of a single afternoon upon visiting the milliner's shop in Meryton. My sisters and I had learned, practically from our infancy, that a lady's fortune was always inherited, never earned. It was an act of Providence that Caroline Bingley should have twenty thousand pounds to her name and Georgiana Darcy thirty thousand pounds. How different the concept of wealth becomes, I thought, when it is actually of one's own making. How frighteningly glorious.

"I hope you didn't have to bribe Egerton into publishing my novel," I said. My feet felt so light I was in danger of skipping.

"A preposterous notion," Darcy replied. "Egerton is a businessman before he is my friend. He would never lose money for the sake of sparing my feelings."

"I would like the cover to be a dark red," I spouted, knowing I was getting ahead of myself. "And the title to be printed in a pretty script, preferably in silver or gold."

"There will be time enough to make such decisions later," Darcy said, seeming pleased by my enthusiasm.

We continued to walk. After we'd covered another short distance, I asked him when he planned to return to Pemberley.

"This evening" was the reply, and instantly, I felt a small pang of grief. The wings which my feet had sprouted vanished, and like a lead weight, my spirit returned to earth.

When I'd recovered from the moment of pain, I inquired after Lizzy.

"She has gone to Bath to take the waters with your mother. I have rented a house for them there. It's possible they may stay the whole season."

"And was Kitty well when you left her?"

"Very well. I believe the wedding will take place in a few months' time."

"Yes, she wrote me in her letters about it," I said. "I am very happy for her." For a while, we stood and observed everything in our surroundings except each other—the hedges and dirt paths, the woolly strands of clouds, and the black lines of geese that threaded through them.

"I have started writing again," I said, as there seemed little else remaining which was innocuous enough to discuss. "It is to be a satire of masters and their servants."

"Anyone we know in it?"

I grinned. "I won't reveal too much, except to say the main character is a Mrs. Caroline Collingwood, tyrannical wife of the scholarly but very dull Mr. Aloysius Collingwood."

The air was so quiet I could hear the sound of our breathing. In that moment, we exhaled together.

"I have missed our talks," he finally said, his eye caught in the branches of a nearby tree.

"Yes, poor Queen Leonora always gave us much to discuss."

"No, not just *Leonora,* Mary." His gaze still unmoving, he added, "If I could choose for you, Mary, if it were in my power to craft a perfect life without blemish, I would have you live at Pemberley. For the rest of my life, I'd be content to sit with you for a few hours every day in the library, as you wrote your stories and read your books. You'd be the first person I saw each morning, and your voice would be the last thing I heard before retiring."

I stole a glance at him, and a curl of hair loosed itself, tickling the bottom of my chin. I imagined having Pemberley's library to myself and falling asleep and waking up at whatever hour of my choosing on the wrinkly velvet green sofa. For the briefest moment, I luxuriated in this fantasy of independence. In my mind's eye, I saw the shelves, which reached like Ionic columns from the floor to the ornate ceiling, the thick forest of books they contained, the dusty pages that had not been opened for decades. I envisioned afternoons of rigorous study, and in the evenings, solitary walks in the fragrant gardens. Yet Pemberley still had walls and gates. It belonged to another, and I knew one day I would outgrow its dignified beauty. I could never call it home.

"Leave this place, Mary," he said, turning towards me at last. "Even if I can't have you by my side, I would have you leave these awful people and never set foot in Longbourn again."

There was a pause, long enough that I looked curiously into Darcy's face. I waited for him to continue.

"There is a cottage not five miles from Pemberley which has been vacant these several years, since its previous occupants left Derbyshire. If you consent, I will draw up an agreement with my solicitor to permit you to live there free of rent for as long as you wish. Even if anything were to happen to me, I would ensure that the agreement could not be broken."

I shook my head, though my heart quickened at the prospect. "I fear it's not a practical arrangement. How could I live alone? It would be unheard of."

"You will have a companion—and servants. Two, three, if you wish."

"I still couldn't. . . ." I heard myself utter mechanically, even as I envisaged sitting down to a dinner for one, a silver platter of roast beef to my left, an entire stewed partridge to my right. I would be a kind mistress, I thought, and treat my servants well.

"Why?"

"It's not simply what I want to do," I said, though I could feel my resolve weakening. "I have Lizzy to consider, to say nothing of my mother and sisters. What would they think?"

"Does it matter?"

"Of course it matters," I said, turning away and attempting to dismiss the temptation of what he was offering.

"When have they ever considered your happiness? Or gone out of their way to ensure it? Kitty will be married soon. Jane has had her first child with Bingley. And Lizzy has made her decision; she has everything she wants from our marriage in the form of society parties and a generous monthly allowance." Seeing me shake my head again, he persisted, growing excited. "Why are you so willing to live the rest of your life in obscurity, catering to the likes of Mr. and Mrs. Collins and their infant? Why can't you pursue your happiness as your sisters did? This is no way to live, Mary. This is not you. I am giving you the chance to start again, to leave all this behind. I beg you to accept it."

The sky blurred behind a film of tears. At Pemberley, I had come the closest I'd ever known to freedom. I'd regulated my days as I wished and behaved improperly, even recklessly. Everything had been the product of my own choice: the liberality with which I gave my body and love, the heartache that followed, the mornings and nights spent in solitude at a desk, alone but far from lonely, a single pen scratching far-fetched tales across a blank page. "It is true," I said softly. "I was happy at Pemberley."

Once again, I saw before myself the unattainable line of the horizon. It did not feel so very distant anymore. Somehow, what had been denied to Jane and Lizzy, Lydia and Kitty, my mother, my aunts, and all my female acquaintances was now being offered to me. If I held out my hand, it would be mine—a life of my own. And like my book, it would be of my own authoring. I would compose its pages, whatever shape and course they took. The creation would belong wholly to me, to Mary Bennet, to the writer known only as Mary B.

"You could be happy again," Darcy whispered.

Was it his hand or the sun that then touched my cheek and warmed it? Was it love or the brightness of light that dazzled my eyes and muddled my brain? I hardly knew.

"A third path has opened to you, Mary, where you'll never be a governess or a nursemaid or a companion," I heard him say. "Take it, Mary. Accept this chance of happiness. Say that you will."

I'd entered this field many times before, and it had always seemed to me a stark and unattractive landscape. It remained so now, nondescript and inscrutable, yet a calming breeze had begun to blow. It combed the flat plains of grass like soft hair, stroking waves of verdant gold to an iridescent shine beneath the sun. The trees, too, shook awake, and a solitary bird emerged from its green nest to ride the wind until it soared to impossible heights. Myth overtook my senses, and I saw the sun embrace this bird, though it was common, small, and gray. I imagined that from the flames, a new bird of fire would fraternize with dancing stars, headstrong comets, and tempestuous meteors. As I stood in the center of this familiar field, my spirit ascended higher and higher, until fire touched and transformed it, and what emerged was as lustrous and freeborn as the phoenix.

"I will," I said through my tears. "I will take it."

EPILOGUE

✜

This last scene is one of springtime. A lonely cottage with an over-grown garden and a drooping wych elm sits between two hills, and a green-eyed, catlike girl emerges from the newly painted front door to sweep the path. If anyone wonders why this pretty housemaid should smile, it is because, at that moment, her mistress has company, which is always, I suppose, a good enough reason for a woman to smile, but especially so if the visitor is pleasant, tall, and gentle-manlike, which this guest certainly is.

At present, this gentleman sits elegantly poised on a large blanket spread across the only clearing the overgrown garden has to offer. His friend, the proprietor of this humble country cottage, is a young woman of middling height, plain dress, and even plainer exterior. They are talking between themselves of the "monstrous thing" at her feet, which is wrapped in brown paper and string and bound for Egerton's in London, her third in as many years and a behemoth of pretty words and decadent sentences, full of "lovers' sighs" and "tear-ful adieus." Behind them, a few feet away, the promised lady's companion, Mrs. Helena Crosbie, of excellent and unsullied reputation, sits slumped in her chair, snoring and emitting sleepy grunts. A thunderstorm wouldn't wake her, which suits the others just fine. In fact, a forgetful memory and an insatiable appetite for sleep played an instrumental role in her securing the position in the first place.

"Tell me what you shall write next," Darcy said, helping himself to another slice of cake.

"I think I have run out of ideas," I replied.

"Never!" my guest cried out.

"Oh yes, I'm afraid so. Try as I might, I can't think of a single worthwhile subject to write about. I am done composing novels about servants and beautiful ladies and great houses. I require a challenge—a new story to tackle."

"Well, I shall help you think of something. . . ." Darcy furrowed his brow.

Three years had come and gone since I moved into Darcy's cottage. Within a week of my arrival, I forgot all about the Collinses and their tyrannical infant. In my own sitting room, I unwrapped the first bound copies of *Leonora's Adventures: Chronicles of a Tragic and Deeply Unhappy Queen*. A year later, I added *The Strange and Peculiar Tale of Mrs. Caroline Collingwood and Her Most Unlucky Housemaid* to my modest bookshelf. As for my sisters: Kitty, engaged when I left her at Longbourn, had since settled in a great mansion in Norfolk, and Jane, who proved equally successful as wife and mother, gave birth to her second child, a healthy, laughing boy whom she and Bingley named Fitzwilliam. Having grown fond of Bath, Lizzy convinced Darcy to purchase a house for her in one of the fashionable seaside neighborhoods. To the rest of the world, even to Jane, all was exactly as it should be between Mr. and Mrs. Darcy. Every year, they attended enough balls that the appearance of conjugal joy seemed undiminished; in front of their acquaintances, they laughed and gibed and bartered terms of endearment with convincing authenticity. But at Pemberley, they continued to live and to sleep, even to dine, separately, and Lizzy, who had become a staple of the most glamorous parties in both the city and the country, was frequently away from home. At least half the year she spent in England's most famous spa town, under the pretense of needing to take the waters for her health; another three months she passed in Lon-

don, which left only three to spend in Derbyshire. Mama, finding
an aloof companion in her second daughter, moved to live with Jane
and Bingley permanently, much to the chagrin of the happy couple.

As our lives took shape and deviated from what we had known
of each other in our youth, letters grew fewer in number, though I
continued to write my sisters and Mama. Jane and Kitty proved as-
siduous in keeping me apprised of dinners hosted, new introduc-
tions, and the vicissitudes of married life. Mama could always be
counted on to complain about her nerves, but my letters to Lizzy
asking after her health and happiness went unreturned.

Aside from my writing and books, my friendship with Darcy
remained the single most important part of my life. In his person, I
discovered the intellectual outlet I'd craved since childhood, and the
many evenings spent in his company eventually dissolved all memory of the unhappiness which had been caused by others, keeping at
a distance the distress caused by Lizzy's silence. Not a day passed
during his visits that wasn't also spent in laughter, and I became as
easy in his company as when I was alone. To love him was to love the
better part of myself, and this was as natural as breathing.

But returning to this scene in springtime, the plain young woman
suddenly says, "As it is a few years ago, you will have probably forgotten. But do you remember what you said to me after you'd read
the first chapter of *Leonora*?"

Darcy shook his head.

"You asked me if I'd ever been to Denmark or lived in a castle or
worn a 'dazzling gown encrusted with precious stones of a hundred
brilliant facets each' when you knew full well that I hadn't done any
of those things. I was thinking the other day how you were absolutely right. I should go away. After all these books and with all this
money, I should see and experience what I've been writing about for
years."

"That's impossible," Darcy grumbled.

"Why?" I pressed.

"It just is . . . you can't possibly go on your own."

"I don't intend to go on my own. Sarah and Mrs. Crosbie will accompany me. Traveling with a companion and a servant is not unheard of."

Darcy tossed three lumps of sugar into an empty teacup with annoyance. "Your new fortune has gone to your head," he chided. "Money has that effect on people, unfortunately. Well, there's only one thing for it. I shall go with you."

"But you're needed here!"

"Georgiana is perfectly capable of running the estate with Mrs. Reynolds's and Henderson's help."

I did not speak for a long time. Then, glancing over my shoulder to ensure that Mrs. Crosbie was still asleep, I slid my hand tenderly through the crook of Darcy's arm. "But this is an adventure I want for myself . . . with Sarah and Mrs. Crosbie to accompany me, of course, but not . . . not with you. Tell me you understand."

He stayed silent for a while, brooding. Then he poured all the sugar out of his teacup, into the saucer beneath it. "I can see you're determined to leave me," he finally said.

"I am."

"You might even forget me while you're away."

I sighed. "As unlikely as such an event would be, I must acknowledge the possibility of my bringing back a French or Spanish husband to live with me in this cottage, whereupon I would, I'm afraid, be forced to forget you. His jealous foreign temperament would also have the unhappy consequence of preventing you from visiting me nearly every day, as you do now."

At this, the gentleman flushed. He muttered something I didn't catch, for I was then looking beyond his head, over the hills, to the horizon from which the sunburned roofs of Italian villas, the bowl-shaped domes of cathedrals, the mellifluous waves of the Tiber would soon rise. I thought briefly of a foolish young girl who had once, a long time ago, made a foolish wish. In a dream, she had asked the Holy Virgin to make her beautiful and had wept to find herself unchanged the next morning. She couldn't know then the strength of her own wings: how high she'd soar, how marvelous her many flights and how diminished in size and importance the people and places she left behind would eventually become to her as she dared the brilliance of the sun.

AUTHOR'S NOTE

I'd like to acknowledge these sources for the quoted material that appears on the following pages:

Page 93: "Age cannot wither her, nor custom stale her infinite variety." From act II, scene II, lines 271–72 of *Antony and Cleopatra* by William Shakespeare.

Page 119: "That will do extremely well, child. You have delighted us long enough. Let the other young ladies have time to exhibit." From volume I, chapter XVIII of *Pride and Prejudice* by Jane Austen.

Page 125: "My reasons for marrying are, first, that I think it a right thing for every clergyman in easy circumstances—like myself—to set the example of matrimony in his parish." From volume I, chapter XIX of *Pride and Prejudice* by Jane Austen.

Page 131: ". . . a small income go a good way." From volume I, chapter XIX of *Pride and Prejudice* by Jane Austen.

Page 147: "The mistress of the mansion came, mature of age, a graceful dame, whose easy step and stately port had well become a princely court." From canto I, lines 576–79 of *The Lady of the Lake* by Walter Scott.

ACKNOWLEDGMENTS

Christina Clifford. A good friend, a trusted agent, the fairy god-mother of my life in more ways than one. Her contributions to this novel (the title, a happy-versus-tragic ending, Mary's occupation as a writer) have been as vital to its creation as my own pen, to say nothing of the impassioned guidance and mentorship she has freely offered over the years, dearer to me than gold.

Caitlin McKenna. Editor extraordinaire, whose vision for the book surpassed even my own. Deepest thanks for the tireless edits, which vitally reshaped the work, and for being devastatingly sharp and brilliant in every suggestion both big and seemingly small. The honor of collaborating with such young and remarkable talent as yours has never been lost on me, nor the contagious love you've possessed in all the years of our acquaintance for the written word.

The team at Random House: Andy Ward, Benjamin Dreyer, Bonnie Thompson, Caroline Johnson, Christine Mykityshyn, Denise Cronin, Donna Duverglas, Elizabeth Gaffin, Erin Valerio, Jess Bonet, Jessica Cashman, Joelle Dieu, Kathy Jones, Melissa Sanford, Rachel Kind, Victoria Wong, and Vincent La Scala.

.   .   .

Many thanks to my father for having faith in my writing and for having had supported it.

And last, but not least—Mom. Thackeray wrote in *Vanity Fair,* "Mother is the name for God in the lips and hearts of little children." Though I am twenty-seven years old, the principle still holds. My mother will always be the holiest and greatest of persons to me.

ABOUT THE AUTHOR

KATHERINE J. CHEN is a graduate of Princeton University. This is her first novel.